A NICHE IN TIME

And Other Stories

The Best of William F. Temple
Volume #1

John Pelan Presents:
Classics of Science Fiction & Fantasy
Volume #4

A NICHE IN TIME

And Other Stories

William F. Temple

Edited and Introduced by
Mike Ashley

Afterword by John Pelan

RAMBLE HOUSE

Four-Sided Triangle, *Amazing Stories,* November 1939
The Green Car, *Science Fantasy,* June 1957
The Legend of Ernie Deacon, *Analog,* March 1965
Brief Encounter, *Nebula,* #25
The Smile of the Sphinx, *Worlds Beyond,* December 1950
Uncle Buno, *Science Fantasy,* #16 November 1955
A Niche in Time, *Analog,* May 1964
The Whispering Gallery, *Fantastic Universe* October/November 1953
Double Trouble, *Science Fantasy,* Winter 1951/1952
The Two Shadows, *Startling Stories*, March 1951
Pawn in Revolt, *Nebula* #4 1953
The Undiscovered Country, *Nebula*, October 1958
Forget Me Not, *Other Worlds*, September 1950
Conditioned Reflex, *Other Worlds*
Testimony, *Interzone,* November 1992

ISBN 13: 978-1-60543-615-9
ISBN 10: 1-60543-615-1

Cover Art: Gavin L. O"Keefe
Preparation: Fender Tucker
Preparation: Kathy Pelan

JOHN PELAN PRESENTS

R H

Dancing Tuatara Press SF Series #4

TABLE OF CONTENTS

INTRODUCTION:
THE TEMPLE TREASURES

Mike Ashley

It is a sad fact that writers all too rapidly become forgotten if their work falls out of print. For every H.P. Lovecraft or Robert A. Heinlein, whose works are never out of print, there are hundreds of writers who, for the lack of exposure, have drifted into the shadows awaiting, hopefully, rediscovery.

It would be wonderful if the moment has arrived for the rediscovery of William F. Temple. His close friend, Arthur C. Clarke, reflecting on the early days of British science-fiction fandom, said of Temple:

> I can recall that in the 1937-8 period most of us aspiring young writers looked up at him and his advanced years ... with something like awe. And when he sold his novel *The Four-Sided Triangle* to the movies, our admiration (and envy) knew no bounds.

Temple's first published story, "The Kosso", appeared in 1935 and so was just a few years ahead of that young generation of hopefuls that included not only Arthur C. Clarke but Sam Youd (the future "John Christopher"), David McIlwain (the future "Charles Eric Maine"), John F. Burke, Eric C. Williams, E.C. Tubb and others. Most of these had to wait until after the Second World War to begin their careers. Temple established himself before the War.

Of the British writers contributing to the new science-fiction magazines that were flourishing in the United States, only really John Beynon Harris (the future "John Wyndham") had preceded Temple, and Harris kept himself somewhat removed from the heart of British fandom. Temple was right in the thick of it. He was one of the early members of the Science Fiction Association, founded in 1937, and the British Interplanetary Society.

Temple lived in London at that time and rented a flat in Gray's Inn Road that he later shared with Arthur C. Clarke and Maurice K. Hanson. It became the hub of London fandom and it was from there, for a while, that the leading British fan magazine, *Novae Terrae* (the forerunner of *New Worlds*) was produced as well as the *Journal* of the British Interplanetary Society.

Whilst immersed in fan activities, and working full time as a clerk in the London Stock Exchange, Temple continued to sell stories to the magazines. An early classic, and one which has remained his best known story, was "The Four-Sided Triangle" first published in *Amazing Stories* in November 1939. It's a science-fiction romance that turns to tragedy and back to romance. The girl in the story, Joan, was based on Temple's own girlfriend, Joan Streeton, who became his wife on 16 September 1939, almost the same day that that issue of *Amazing Stories* was released. That original story, which was later expanded into a novel and subsequently filmed, leads off this collection.

Another of Temple's early stories, also included in this volume, is "The Smile of the Sphinx", which considers the extraterrestrial origins of cats. The story is set in and around Woolwich, where Temple had been born (in 1914), though he grew up in nearby Eltham. Eltham was also the home of the writer Edith Nesbit, author of *The Railway Children*, *Five Children and It*, and much else. Temple could remember buying apples from her when he was very young.

Temple's early writing career was cut short by the outbreak of the Second World War. His wife Joan and new baby Anne were evacuated to Cornwall during the Blitz, which was fortunate as the London Flat was bombed a few months later. Temple was called up for military service and became a signaller in the Royal Artillery. He saw action throughout North Africa and Italy, including at the Anzio beachhead. He continued to write, producing the novel version of *The Four-Sided Triangle* whilst he was in service in North Africa. He lost the first half of the manuscript during the Battle of Takrouna in Tunisia in April 1943 and had to start all over again.

After the War, Temple became the one of the reliable cornerstones of the growing edifice of British sf. He resigned from the Stock Exchange in 1950 in order to write full time but it was still a difficult period to survive solely from a writing income and he returned to work, though he had another attempt at freelance writing in 1961. During his career he produced eleven novels and over a hundred short stories, plus a range of other works including a copious amount of fan journalism. Almost up to his last days he continued to send in long, usually humorous but sometimes caustic letters to amateur magazines, notably Richard E. Geis's *The Alien Critic* (also titled *Science Fiction Review*).

His novels include a trilogy for young adults featuring Martin Magnus, a special investigator for the Scientific Bureau, whose adventures take him to Venus and Mars. Temple enjoyed crime and spy fiction. The very first novel he had completed, but which never sold, *Master of the Doors*, featured a Raffles-like hero who was a respected citizen by day but a master criminal at night. He later revised it as *The Dangerous Edge* and it became his second published novel in 1951. *Shoot at the Moon* (1966), which many—including me—consider his best novel, is a murder mystery in which, one at a time, members of a lunar expedition meet a violent death. His last published novel, *The Fleshpots of Sansato* (1968), involves the investigations of a spy trying to track down a scientist who has vanished in the sin-city of an alien world. This novel was brutally edited by the publisher and this soured Temple on the world of writing and for years he barely wrote a word.

Thanks to the support of his lovely wife, Joan, and his two children Anne and Cliff, Temple did gradually return to writing and began a new novel, *The Healer*, about a faith-healer, but hopes were dashed when his agent told him it would never sell. Temple gave up, but his prologue to the novel, "Testimony", survived and is included in the collection.

In between "The Four-Sided Triangle" and "Testimony" is included a wide selection of some of Temple's best work. "Forget Me Not", which I regard as his most powerful short story, inspired by the horrors of War and the Nazi concentration camps; the humorous "Conditioned Reflex" which considers the origins of human life; the ghostly "The Whispering Gallery", which shows that Temple could turn out a good supernatural story when he had a mind to; "The Legend of Ernie Deacon" which almost presages virtual reality; "Uncle Buno" which reveals Temple's attitude towards colonialism and racism, and "The Green Car", an ingenious investigation into something that is investigating us.

William F. Temple died in 1989, aged 75, after a writing career that spanned fifty years. This selection is just a sample of what Temple produced during those fifty years, one that shows what a creative, polished and ingenious writer he was. It casts a light into the shadows into which his work has retreated and hopefully will encourage a search for more.

THE 4-SIDED TRIANGLE

THREE PEOPLE PEERED through a quartz window.

The girl was squashed uncomfortably between the two men, but at the moment neither she nor they cared. The object they were watching was too interesting.

The girl was Joan Leeton. Her hair was an indeterminate brown, and owed its curls to tongs, not to nature. Her eyes were certainly brown, and bright with unquenchable good humour. In repose her face was undistinguished, though far from plain; when she smiled, it was beautiful.

Her greatest attraction (and it was part of her attraction that she did not realize it) lay in her character. She was soothingly sympathetic without becoming mushy, she was very level-headed (a rare thing in a woman) and completely unselfish. She refused to lose her temper over anything, or take offence, or enlarge upon the truth in her favour, and yet she was tolerant of such lapses in others. She possessed a brain that was unusually able in its dealing with science, and yet her tastes and pleasures were simple.

William Fredericks (called "Will") had much in common with Joan, but his sympathy was a little more disinterested, his humour less spontaneous, and he had certain prejudices. His tastes were reserved for what he considered the more worthy things. But he was calm and good-tempered, and his steadiness of purpose was reassuring. He was black-haired, with an expression of quiet content.

William Josephs (called "Bill") was different. He was completely unstable. Fiery of hair, he was alternately fiery and depressed of spirit. Impulsive, generous, highly emotional about art and music, he was given to periods of gaiety and moods of black melancholia. He reached, at his best, heights of mental brilliance far beyond the other two, but long bouts of lethargy prevented him from making the best of them.

Nevertheless, his sense of humour was keen, and he was often amused at his own absurdly over-sensitive character; but he could not change it.

Both these men were deeply in love with Joan, and both tried hard to conceal it. If Joan had any preference, she concealed it just as ably, although they were aware that she was fond of both of them.

The quartz window, through which the three were looking, was set in a tall metal container, and just a few feet away was another container, identical even to the thickness of the window-glass.

Overhead was a complex assemblage of apparatus: bulbous, silvered tubes, small electric motors that hummed in various unexpected places, makeshift screens of zinc, roughly soldered, coils upon coils of wire, and a network of slung cables that made the place look like a creeper-tangled tropical jungle. A large dynamo churned out a steady roar in the corner, and a pair of wide spark-gaps crackled continuously, filling the laboratory with a weird, jumping blue light as the day waned outside the windows and the dusk crept in.

An intruder in the laboratory might have looked through the window of the other container and seen, standing on a steel frame in a cubical chamber, an oil painting of "Madame Croignette" by Boucher, delicately illuminated by concealed lights. He would not have known it, but the painting was standing in a vacuum.

If he had squeezed behind the trio at the other container and gazed through their window he would have seen an apparently identical sight: an oil painting of "Madame Croignette" by Boucher, standing on a steel frame in a vacuum, delicately illuminated by concealed lights.

From which he would probably not gather much.

The catch was that the painting at which the three were gazing so intently was not quite the same as the one in the first container—not yet. There were minute differences in colour and proportion.

But gradually these differences were righting themselves, for the whole of the second canvas was being built up atom by atom, molecule by molecule, into an exactly identical twin of the one which had felt the brush of Francis Boucher.

The marvellously intricate apparatus, using an adaptation of a newly-discovered magnetic principle, consumed only a moderate amount of power in arranging the lines of sympathetic fields of force which brought every proton into position and every electron into its respective balancing orbit. It was a machine which could divert the flow of great forces without the ability to tap their energy.

"Any minute now!" breathed Will.

Bill rubbed his breath off the glass impatiently.

"Don't do that!" he said, and promptly fogged the glass over again. Not ungently, he attempted to rub a clear patch with Joan's own pretty nose. She exploded into laughter, fogging the glass hopelessly, and in the temporary confusion of this they missed seeing the event they had been waiting days for—the completion of the duplicate painting to the ultimate atom.

The spark gaps died with a final snap, a lamp sprang into being on the indicator panel, and the dynamo began to run whirringly down to a stop.

They cleaned the window, and there stood "Madame Croignette" looking rather blankly out at them with wide brown eyes that exactly matched the sepia from Boucher's palette, and both beauty spots and every hair of her powdered wig in place to a millionth of a millimetre.

Will turned a valve, and there was the hiss of air rushing into the chamber. He opened the window, and lifted the painting out gingerly, as if he half-expected it to crumble in his hands.

"Perfect—a beauty!" he murmured. He looked up at Joan with shining eyes. Bill caught that look, and unaccountably checked the impulsive whoop of joy he was on the point of letting loose. He coughed instead, and leaned over Joan's shoulder to inspect "Madame Croignette" more closely.

"The gamble's come off," went on Will. "We've sunk every cent into this, but it won't be long before we have enough money to do anything we want to do—anything."

"Anything—except to get Bill out of bed on Sunday mornings," smiled Joan, and they laughed.

"No sensible millionaire would get out of bed any morning," said Bill.

The steel and glass factory of Art Replicas, Limited, shone like a diamond up in the green hills of Surrey. In a financial sense, it had actually sprung from a diamond—the sale of a replica of the Koh-i-noor. That had been the one and only product of Precious Stones, Limited, an earlier company which was closed down by the government when they saw that it would destroy the world's diamond market.

A sister company, Radium Products, was going strong up in the north because its scientific necessity was recognised. But the heart of the three company directors lay in Art Replicas, and there they spent their time.

Famous works of art from all over the world passed through the factory's portals, and gave birth to innumerable replicas of themselves for distribution and sale at quite reasonable prices.

Families of only moderate means found it pleasing to have a Constable or Turner in the dining room and a Rodin statuette in the hall. And this widely-flung ownership of *objets d'art*, which were to all intents and purposes the genuine articles, strengthened interest in art enormously. When people had lived with these things for a little while, they began to perceive the beauty in them—for real beauty is not always obvious at a glance—and to become greedy for more knowledge of them and the men who originally conceived and shaped them.

So the three directors—Will, Bill, and Joan—put all their energy into satisfying the demands of the world for art, and conscious of their part in furthering civilisation, were deeply content.

For a time.

Then Bill, the impatient and easily-bored, broke out one day in the middle of a Directors' Meeting.

"Oh, to hell with the Ming estimates!" he cried, sweeping a pile of orders from the table.

Joan and Will, recognizing the symptoms, exchanged wry glances of amusement.

"Look here," went on Bill, "I don't know what you two think, but I'm fed up! We've become nothing but dull business people now. It isn't our sort of life. Repetition, repetition, repetition! I'm going crazy! We're *research* workers, not darned pieceworkers. For heaven's sake, let's start out in some new line."

This little storm relieved him, and almost immediately he smiled too.

"But, really, aren't we?" he appealed.

"Yes," responded Joan and Will in duet.

"Well, what about it?"

Will coughed, and prepared himself.

"Joan and I were talking about that this morning, as a matter of fact," he said. "We were going to suggest that we sell the factory, and retire to our old laboratory and re-equip it."

Bill picked up the ink-pot and emptied it solemnly over the Ming estimates. The ink made a shining lake in the centre of the antique and valuable table.

"At last we're sane again," he said. "Now you know the line of investigation I want to open up. I'm perfectly convinced that the reason for our failure to create a living duplicate of any living creature was because the quotiety we assumed for the *xy* action—"

"Just a moment, Bill," interrupted Will. "Before we get on with that work, I—I mean, one of the reasons Joan and me wanted to retire was because—well—"

"What he's trying to say," said Joan quietly, "is that we plan to get married and settle down for a bit before we resume research work."

Bill stared at them. He was aware that his cheeks were slowly reddening. He felt numb.

"Well!" he said. "Well!" (He could think of nothing else. This was unbelievable! He must postpone consideration of it until he was alone, else his utter mortification would show.)

He put out his hand automatically, and they both clasped it.

"You know I wish you every possible happiness," he said, rather huskily. His mind seemed empty. He tried to form some comment, but somehow he could not compose one sentence that made sense.

"I think we'll get on all right," said Will, smiling at Joan. She smiled back at him, and unknowingly cut Bill to the heart.

With an effort, Bill pulled himself together and rang for wine to celebrate. He ordered some of the modern reconstruction of an exceedingly rare "94."

The night was moonless and cloudless, and the myriad of glittering pale blue points of the Milky Way sprawled across the sky as if someone had cast a handful of brilliants upon a black velvet cloth. But they twinkled steadily, for strong air currents were in motion in the upper atmosphere.

The Surrey lane was dark and silent. The only signs of life were the occasional distant glares of automobile headlights passing on the main highway nearly a mile away, and the red dot of a burning cigarette in a gap between the hedgerows.

The cigarette was Bill's. He sat there on a gate staring up at the array in the heavens and wondering what to do with his life.

He felt completely at sea, purposeless, and unutterably depressed. He had thought the word "heartache" just a vague descriptive term. Now he knew what it meant. It was a solid physical feeling, an ache that tore him inside, unceasingly. He yearned to see Joan, to be with Joan, with his whole being. This longing would not let him rest. He could have cried out for a respite.

He tried to argue himself to a more rational viewpoint.

"I am a man of science," he told himself. "Why should I allow old Mother Nature to torture and badger me like this? I can see through all the tricks of that old twister. These feelings are purely chemical reactions, the secretions of the glands mixing with the blood-stream. My mind is surely strong enough to conquer that? Else I have a third-rate brain, not the scientific instrument I've prided myself on."

He stared up at the stars glittering in their seeming calm stability, age-old and unchanging. But were they? They may look just the same when all mankind and its loves and hates had departed from this planet, and left it frozen and dark. But he knew that even as he watched, they were changing position at a frightful speed, receding from him at thousands of miles a second.

"Nature is a twister, full of illusions," he repeated . . .

There started a train of thought, a merciful anaesthetic in which he lost himself for some minutes.

Somewhere down in the deeps of his subconscious an idea which had, unknown to him, been evolving itself for weeks, was stirred, and emerged suddenly into the light. He started, dropped his cigarette, and left it on the ground.

He sat there stiffly on the gate and, considered the idea.

It was wild—incredibly wild. But if he worked hard and long at it, there was a chance that it might come off. It would provide a reason for living, anyway, so long as there was any hope at all of success.

He jumped down from the gate and started walking quickly and excitedly along the lane back to the factory. His mind was already turning over possibilities, planning eagerly. In the promise of this new adventure, the heartache was temporarily submerged.

Six months passed.

Bill had retired to the old laboratory, and spent much of that time enlarging and re-equipping it. He added a rabbit pen, and turned an adjacent patch of ground into a burial-ground to dispose of those who died under his knife. This cemetery was like no cemetery in the world, for it was also full of dead things that had never died—because they had never lived.

His research got nowhere. He could build up, atom by atom, the exact physical counterpart of any living animal, but all such duplicates remained obstinately inanimate. They assumed an extraordinary life-like appearance, but it was frozen life. They were no more alive than waxwork images, even though they were as soft and pliable as the original animals in sleep.

Bill thought he had hit upon the trouble in a certain equation, but re-checking confirmed that the equation had been right in the first place. There was no flaw in either theory or practice as far as he could see.

Yet somehow he could not duplicate the force of life in action. Must he apply that force himself? How?

He applied various degrees of electrical impulses to the nerve centers of the rabbits, tried rapid alternations of temperatures, miniature. "iron lungs", vigorous massage—both external and internal—intra-venous and spinal injections of everything from adrenalin to even more powerful stimulants which his agile mind concocted. And still the artificial rabbits remained limp bundles of fur.

Joan and Will returned from their honeymoon and settled down in a roomy, comfortable old house a few miles away. They sometimes dropped in to see how the research was going. Bill always seemed bright and cheerful enough when they came, and joked about his setbacks.

"I think I'll scour the world for the hottest thing in female bunnies and teach her to do a hula-hula on the lab bench," he said. "That ought to make some of these stiffs sit up!"

Joan said she was seriously thinking of starting an eating-house specializing in rabbit pie, if Bill could keep up the supply of dead rabbits. He replied that he'd already buried enough to feed an army.

Their conversation was generally pitched in this bantering key, save when they really got down to technicalities. But when they had gone, Bill would sit and brood, thinking constantly of Joan. And he could concentrate on nothing else for the rest of that day.

Finally, more or less by accident, he found the press-button which awoke life in the rabbits. He was experimenting with a blood solution he had prepared, thinking that it might remain more constant than the natural rabbit's blood, which became thin and useless too quickly. He had constructed a little pump to force the natural blood from a rabbit's veins and fill them instead with his artificial solution.

The pump had not been going for more than a few seconds before the rabbit stirred weakly and opened its eyes. It twitched its nose, and lay quite still for a moment, save for one foot which continued to quiver.

Then suddenly it roused up and made a prodigious bound from the bench. The thin rubber tubes which tethered it by the neck parted in midair, and it fell awkwardly with a heavy thump on the floor. The blood continued to run from one of the broken tubes, but the pump which forced it out was the rabbit's own heart—beating at last.

The animal seemed to have used all its energy in that one powerful jump, and lay still on the floor and quietly expired.

Bill stood regarding it, his fingers still on the wheel of the pump.

Then, when he realized what it meant, he recaptured some of his old exuberance, and danced around the laboratory carrying a carboy of acid as though it were a Grecian urn.

Further experiments convinced him that he had set foot within the portals of Nature's most carefully guarded citadel. Admittedly he could not himself create anything original or unique in Life. But he could create a living image of any living creature under the sun.

A hot summer afternoon, a cool green lawn shaded by elms and on it two white-clad figures, Joan and Will, putting through their miniature nine-hole course. A bright-striped awning by the hedge, and below it, two comfortable canvas chairs and a little Moorish table with soft drinks. An ivy-covered wall of an old redbrick mansion showing between the trees. The indefinable smell of new-cut grass in the air. The gentle but triumphant laughter of Joan as Will foozled his shot.

That was the atmosphere Bill entered at the end of his duty tramp along the lane from the laboratory—it was his first outdoor excursion for weeks—and he could not help comparing it with the sort of world he had been living in: the benches and bottles and sinks, the eye-tiring field of the microscope, the sheets of calculations under the glare of electric light in the dark hours of the night, the smell of blood and chemicals and rabbits.

And he realized completely that science itself wasn't the greatest thing in life. Personal happiness was. That was the goal of all men, whatever way they strove to reach it.

Joan caught sight of him standing on the edge of the lawn, and came hurrying across to greet him.

"Where have you been all this time?" she asked. "We've been dying to hear how you've been getting on."

"I've done it," said Bill.

"Done it? Have you really?" Her voice mounted excitedly almost to a squeak. She grabbed him by the wrist and hauled him across to Will. "He's done it!" she announced, and stood between them, watching both their faces eagerly.

Will took the news with his usual calmness, and smilingly gripped Bill's hand.

"Congratulations, old lad," he said. "Come and have a drink and tell us all about it."

They squatted on the grass and helped themselves from the table. Will could see that Bill had been overworking himself badly. His face was drawn and tired, his eyelids red, and he was in the grip of a nervous tension which for the time held him dumb and uncertain of himself.

Joan noticed this, too, and checked the questions she was going to bombard upon him. Instead, she quietly withdrew to the house to prepare a pot of the China tea which she knew always soothed Bill's migraine.

When she had gone, Bill, with an effort, shook some of the stupor from him, and looked across at Will. His gaze dropped, and he began to pluck idly at the grass.

"Will," he began, presently, "I—" He cleared his throat nervously, and started again in a none too steady voice. "Listen, Will, I have something a bit difficult to say, and I'm not so good at expressing myself. In the first place, I have always been crazily in love with Joan."

Will sat up, and looked at him curiously. But he let Bill go on.

"I never said anything because—well, because I was afraid I wouldn't make a success of marriage. Too unstable to settle down quietly with a decent girl like Joan. But I found I couldn't go on without her, and was going to propose—when you beat me to it. I've felt pretty miserable since, though this work has taken something of the edge off."

Will regarded the other's pale face—and wondered.

"This work held out a real hope to me. And now I've accomplished the major part of it. I can make a living copy of any living thing. Now—do you see *why* I threw myself into this research? I *want to create a living, breathing twin of Joan, and marry her!"*

Will started slightly. Bill got up and paced restlessly up and down.

"I know I'm asking a hell of a lot. This affair reaches deeper than scientific curiosity. No feeling man can contemplate such a proposal without misgivings, for his wife and for himself. But honestly, Will, I cannot see any possible harm arising from it. Though, admittedly, the only good would be to make a selfish man happy. For heaven's sake, let me know what you think."

Will sat contemplating, while the distracted Bill continued to pace.

Presently, he said: "You are sure no physical harm could come to Joan in the course of the experiment?"

"Certain—completely certain," said Bill.

"Then I personally have no objection. Anything but objection. I had no idea you felt that way, Bill, and it would make me, as well as Joan, very unhappy to know you had to go on like that."

He caught sight of his wife approaching with a laden tray.

"Naturally, the decision rests with her," he said. "If she'd rather not, there's no more to it."

"No, of course not," agreed Bill.

But they both knew what her answer would be.

"Stop the car for a minute, Will," said Joan suddenly, and her husband stepped on the foot-brake.

The car halted in the lane on the brow of the hill. Through a gap in the hedge the two occupants had a view of Bill's laboratory as it lay below in the cradle of the valley.

Joan pointed down. In the field behind the "cemetery" two figures were strolling. Even at this distance, Bill's flaming hair marked his identity. His companion was a woman in a white summer frock. And it was on her that Joan's attention was fixed.

"She's alive now!" she whispered, and her voice trembled slightly.

Will nodded. He noticed her apprehension, and gripped her hand encouragingly. She managed a wry smile.

"It's not every day one goes to pay a visit to oneself," she said. "It was unnerving enough last week to see her lying on the other couch in the lab., dressed in my red frock—which *I* was wearing—so pale, and—Oh, it was like seeing myself dead!"

"She's not dead now, and Bill's bought her some different clothes, so cheer up," said Will. "I know it's a most queer situation, but the only possible way to look at it is from the scientific viewpoint. It's a unique scientific event. And it's made Bill happy into the bargain."

He ruminated a minute.

"Wish he'd given us a hint as to how he works his resuscitation process, though," he went on. "Still, I suppose he's right to keep it a secret. It's a discovery which could be appallingly abused. Think of dictators manufacturing loyal, stupid armies from one loyal, stupid soldier! Or industrialists manufacturing cheap labour! We should soon have a world of robots, all traces of individuality wiped out. No variety, nothing unique—life would not be worth living."

"No," replied Joan, mechanically, her thoughts still on that white-clad figure down there.

Will released the brake, and the car rolled down the hill toward the laboratory. The two in the field saw it coming, and walked back through the cemetery to meet it. They reached the road as the car drew up.

"Hello, there!" greeted Bill. "You're late—we've had the kettle on the boil for half an hour. Doll and I were getting anxious."

He advanced into the road, and the woman in the white frock lingered hesitantly behind him. Joan tightened her lips and braced herself to face this unusual ordeal. She got out of the car, and while Will and Bill were grasping hands, she walked to meet her now living twin.

Apparently Doll had decided to face it in the same way, and they met with oddly identical expressions of smiling surface ease, with an undercurrent of curiosity and doubt. They both saw and understood each other's expression simultaneously, and burst out laughing. That helped a lot.

"It's not so bad, after all," said Doll, and Joan checked herself from making the same instinctive remark.

"No, not nearly," she agreed.

And it wasn't. For although Doll looked familiar to her, she could not seem to identify her with herself to any unusual extent. It was not that her apparel and hair-style were different, but that somehow her face, figure, and voice seemed like those of another person.

She did not realize that hitherto she had only seen parts of herself in certain mirrors from certain angles, and the complete effect was something she had simply never witnessed. Nor that she had not heard her own voice outside her own head, so to speak—never from a distance of some feet.

Nevertheless, throughout the meal she felt vaguely uneasy, though she tried to hide it, and kept up a fire of witty remarks. And her other self, too, smiled at her across the table and talked easily.

They compared themselves in detail, and found they were completely identical in every way, even to the tiny mole on their left forearm. Their tastes, too, agreed. They took the same amount of sugar in their tea, and liked and disliked the same foodstuffs.

"I've got my eye on that pink iced cake," laughed Doll. "Have you?"

Joan admitted it. So they shared it.

"You'll never have any trouble over buying each other birthday or Christmas presents," commented Will. "How nice to know exactly what the other wants!"

Bill had a permanent grin on his face, and beamed all over the table all the time. For once he did not have a great deal to say. He seemed too happy for words, and kept losing the thread of the conversation to gaze upon Doll fondly.

"We're going to be married tomorrow!" he announced unexpectedly, and they protested their surprise at the lack of warning. But they promised to be there.

There followed an evening of various sorts of games, and the similar thought-processes of Joan and Doll led to much amusement, especially in the guessing games. And twice they played checkers and twice they drew.

It was a merry evening, and Bill was merriest of all. Yet when they came to say goodnight, Joan felt the return of the old uneasiness. As they left in the car, Joan caught a glimpse of Doll's face as she stood beside Bill at the gate. And she divined that under that air of gaiety, Doll suffered the same uneasiness as she.

Doll and Bill were married in a distant registry office next day, using a fictitious name and birthplace for Doll to avoid any publicity—after all, no one would question her identity.

Winter came and went.

Doll and Bill seemed to have settled down quite happily, and the quartet remained as close friends as ever. Both Doll and Joan were smitten with the urge to take up flying as a hobby, and joined the local flying club. They each bought a single-seater, and went for long flights, cruising side by side.

Almost in self-protection from this neglect (they had no interest in flying) Bill and Will began to work again together, delving further into the mysteries of the atom. This time they were searching for the yet-to-be-discovered secret of tapping the potential energy which the atom held.

And almost at once they stumbled on a new lead.

Formerly they had been able to divert atomic energy without being able to transform it into useful power. It was as if they had constructed a number of artificial dams at various points in a turbulent river, which altered the course of the river without tapping any of its force—though that is a poor and misleading analogy.

But now they had conceived, and were building, an amazingly complex machine which, in the same unsatisfactory analogy, could be likened to a turbine-generator, tapping some of the power of that turbulent river.

The "river," however, was very turbulent indeed, and needed skill and courage to harness. And there was a danger of the harness suddenly slipping.

Presently, the others became aware that Doll's health was gradually failing. She tried hard to keep up her usual air of brightness and cheerfulness, but she could not sleep, and became restless and nervous.

And Joan, who was her almost constant companion, suddenly realized what was worrying that mind which was so similar to hers. The realization was a genuine shock, which left her trembling, but she faced it.

"I think it would be a good thing for Doll and Bill to come and live here for a while, until Doll's better," she said rather diffidently to Will one day.

"Yes, okay, if you think you can persuade them," replied Will. He looked a little puzzled.

"We have far too many empty rooms here," she said defensively. "Anyway, I can help Doll if I'm with her more."

Doll seemed quite eager to come, though a little dubious, but Bill thought it a great idea. They moved within the week.

At first, things did improve. Doll began to recover, and became more like her natural self. She was much less highly strung, and joined in the evening games with the other three with gusto.

She studied Will's favorite game, backgammon, and began to enjoy beating him thoroughly and regularly.

And then Joan began to fail.

She became nerveless, melancholy, and even morose. It seemed as though through helping Doll back to health, she had been infected with the same complaint.

Will was worried, and insisted on her being examined by a doctor.

The doctor told Will in private: "There's nothing physically wrong. She's nursing some secret worry, and she'll get worse until this worry is eased. Persuade her to tell you what it is—she refuses to tell me."

She also refused to tell Will, despite his pleadings.

And now Doll, who knew what the secret was, began to worry about Joan, and presently she relapsed into her previous nervous condition.

So it continued for a week, a miserable week for the two harassed and perplexed husbands, who did not know which way to turn. The following week, however, both women seemed to make an effort, and brightened up somewhat, and could even laugh at times.

The recovery continued, and Bill and Will deemed it safe to return to their daily work in the lab, completing the atom harnessing machine.

One day Will happened to return to the house unexpectedly, and found the two women in each other's arms on a couch, crying their eyes out. He stood staring for a moment. They suddenly became aware of him, and parted, drying their eyes.

"What's up, Will? Why, have you come back?" asked Joan, unsteadily, sniffing.

"Er—to get my slide-rule: I'd forgotten it," he said. "Bill wanted to trust his memory, but I think there's something wrong with his figures. I want to check up before we test the machine further. But—what's the matter with you two?"

"Oh, we're all right," said Doll, strainedly and not very convincingly. She blew her nose, and endeavoured to pull herself together. But almost immediately she was overtaken by another burst of weeping, and Joan put her arms around her comfortingly.

"Look here," said Will, in sudden and unusual exasperation, "I've had about enough of this. You know that Bill and I are only too willing to deal with whatever you're worrying about. Yet the pair of you won't say a word—only cry and fret. How can we help if you won't tell us? Do you think we like to see you going on like this?"

"I'll tell you, Will," said Joan, quietly.

Doll emitted a muffled "No!" but Joan ignored her, and went on: "Don't you see that Bill has created another me in *every* detail? Every memory and every feeling? And because Doll thinks and feels exactly as I do, she's in love with you! She has been that way from the very beginning. All this time she's been trying to conquer it, to suppress it, and make Bill happy instead."

Doll's shoulders shook with the intensity of her sobbing. Will laid his hands gently on them, consolingly. He could think of nothing whatever to say. He had not even dreamt of such a situation, obvious as it appeared now.

"Do you wonder the conflict got her down?" said Joan. "Poor girl! I brought her here to be nearer to you, and that eased things for her."

"But it didn't for you," said Will, quietly, looking straight at her. "I see now why you began to worry. Why didn't you tell me then, Joan?"

"How could I?"

He bit his lip, paced nervously over to the window, and stood with his back to the pair on the couch.

"What a position!" he thought. "What can we do? Poor Bill!"

He wondered how he could break the sorry news to his best friend, and even as he wondered, the problem was solved for him.

From the window there was a view down the length of the wide, shallow valley, and a couple of miles away the white concrete laboratory could just be seen nestling at the foot of one of the farther slopes. There were fields all around it, and a long row of great sturdy oak trees started from its northern corner.

From this height and distance the whole place looked like a table-top model. Will stared moodily at that little white box where Bill was, and tried to clarify his chaotic thoughts.

And suddenly, incredibly, before his eyes the distant white box spurted up in a dusty cloud of chalk-powder, and ere a particle of it had neared its topmost height, the whole of that part of the valley was split across by a curtain of searing, glaring flame. The whole string of oak trees, tough and amazingly deep-rooted though they were, floated up though the air like feathers of windblown thistledown before the blast of that mighty eruption.

The glaring flame vanished suddenly, like a light that had been turned out, and left a thick, brown, heaving fog in its place, a cloud of earth that had been pulverised. Will caught a glimpse of the torn oak trees falling back into this brown, rolling cloud, and then the blast wave, which had travelled up the valley, smote the house.

The window was instantly shattered and blown in, and he went flying backwards in a shower of glass fragments. He hit the floor awkwardly, and sprawled there, and only then did his laggard brain realize what had happened.

Bill's habitual impatience had at last been his undoing. He had refused to wait any longer for Will's return, and gone on with the test, trusting to his memory. And he had been wrong.

The harness had slipped.

A man sat on a hill with a wide and lovely view of the country, bright in summer sunshine, spread before him. The rich green squares of the fields, the white ribbons of the lanes, the yellow blocks of haystacks and grey spires of village churches, made up a pattern infinitely pleasing to the eye.

And the bees hummed drowsily, nearby sheep and cattle made the noises of their kind, and a neighbouring thicket fairly rang with the unending chorus of a hundred birds.

But all this might as well have been set on another planet, for the man could neither see nor hear the happy environment. He was in hell.

It was a fortnight now since Bill had gone. When that grief had begun to wear off, it was succeeded by the most perplexing problem that had ever beset a member of the human race.

Will had been left to live with two women who loved him equally violently. Neither could ever conquer or suppress that love, whatever they did. They knew that.

On the other hand, Will was a person who was only capable of loving one of the women. Monogamy is deep-rooted in most normal people, and particularly so with Will. He had looked forward to travelling through life with one constant companion, and only one—Joan.

But now there were two Joans, identical in appearance, feeling, thought. Nevertheless, they were two separate people. And between them he was a torn and anguished man, with his domestic life in shapeless ruins.

He could not ease his mental torture with work, for since Bill died so tragically, he could not settle down to anything in a laboratory.

It was no easier for Joan and Doll. Probably harder. To have one's own self as a rival—even a friendly, understanding rival—for a man's companionship and affection was almost unbearable.

This afternoon they had both gone to a flying club, to attempt to escape for a while the burden of worry, apparently. Though neither was in a fit condition to fly, for they were tottering on the brink of a nervous breakdown.

The club was near the hill where Will was sitting and striving to find some working solution to a unique human problem which seemed quite insoluble. So it was no coincidence that presently a humming in the sky caused him to lift dull eyes to see both the familiar monoplanes circling and curving across the blue spaces between the creamy, cumulus clouds.

He lay back on the grass watching them. He wondered which plane was which, but there was no means of telling, for they were similar models. And anyway, that would not tell him which was Joan and which was Doll, for they quite often used each other's planes, to keep the "feel" of both. He wondered what they were thinking up there . . .

One of the planes straightened and flew away to the west, climbing as it went. Its rising drone became fainter. The other plane continued to bank and curve above.

Presently, Will closed his eyes and tried to doze in the warm sunlight. It was no use. In the darkness of his mind revolved the same old maddening images, doubts, and questions. It was as if he had become entangled in a nightmare from which he could not awake.

The engine of the plane overhead suddenly stopped. Reopened his eyes, but could not locate it for a moment.

Then he saw it against the sun, and it was falling swiftly in a tailspin. It fell out of the direct glare of the sun, and he saw it in detail, revolving as it plunged so that the wings glinted like a flashing heliograph. He realized with a shock that it was but a few hundred feet from the ground.

He scrambled to his feet, in an awful agitation.

"Joan!" he cried, hoarsely. "Joan!"

The machine continued its fall steadily and inevitably, spun down past his eye-level, and fell into the centre of one of the green squares of the fields below.

He started running down the hill even as it landed. As the sound of the crash reached him, he saw a rose of fire blossom like magic in that green square, and from it a wavering growth of black, oily smoke mounted into the heavens. The tears started from his eyes, and ran freely.

When he reached the scene, the inferno was past its worst, and as the flames died he saw that nothing was left, only black, shapeless, scattered things, unrecognisable as once human or once machine.

There was a squeal of brakes from the road. An ambulance had arrived from the flying club. Two men jumped out, burst through the hedge. It did not take them more than a few seconds to realize that there was no hope.

"Quick, Mr. Fredericks, jump in," cried one of them, recognizing Will. "We must go straight to the other one."

The other one!

Before he could question them, Will was hustled between them into the driving cabin of the ambulance. The vehicle was quickly reversed, and sped off in the opposite direction.

"Did—did the other plane—" began Will, and the words stuck in his throat.

The driver, with his eye on the road which was scudding under their wheels at sixty miles an hour, nodded grimly.

"Didn't you see, sir? They both crashed at exactly the same time, in the same way—tailspin. A shocking accident—terrible. I can't think how to express my sympathy, sir. I only pray that this one won't turn out so bad."

It was as if the ability to feel had left Will. His thoughts slowed up almost to a standstill. He sat there numbed. He dare not try to think.

But, sluggishly, his thoughts went on. Joan and Doll had crashed at exactly the same time in exactly the same way. That was above coincidence. They must have both been thinking along the same lines again, and that meant they had crashed *deliberately!*

He saw now the whole irony of it, and groaned.

Joan and Doll had each tried to solve the problem in their own way, and each had reached the same conclusion without being aware what the other was thinking. They saw that one of them would have to step out of the picture if Will was ever to be happy. They knew that that one would have to step completely out, for life could no longer be tolerated by her if she had to lose Will.

And, characteristically, they had each made up their minds to be the self-sacrificing one.

Doll felt that she was an intruder, wrecking the lives of a happily married pair. It was no fault of hers: she had not asked to be created full of love for a man she could never have.

But she felt that she was leading an unnecessary existence, and every moment of it was hurting the man she loved. So she decided to relinquish the gift of life.

Joan's reasoning was that she had been partly responsible for bringing Doll into this world, unasked, and with exactly similar feelings and longings as herself. Ever since she had expected, those feelings had been ungratified, cruelly crushed and thwarted. It wasn't fair. Doll had as much right to happiness as she. Joan had enjoyed her period of happiness with Will. Now let Doll enjoy hers.

So it was that two planes, a mile apart, went spinning into crashes that were meant to appear accidental—and did, except to one man, the one who most of all was intended never to know the truth.

The driver was speaking again.

"It was a ghastly dilemma for us at the club. We saw 'em come down on opposite sides and both catch fire. We have only one fire engine, one ambulance. Had to send the engine to one, and rush this ambulance to the other. The engine couldn't have done any good at this end, as it happens. Hope it was in time where we're going!"

Will's dulled mind seemed to take this in quite detachedly. Who had been killed in the crash he saw? Joan or Doll? Joan or Doll?

Then suddenly it burst upon him that it was only the original Joan that he loved. That was the person whom he had known so long, around whom his affection had centred. The hair he had caressed, the lips he had pressed, the gay brown eyes which had smiled into his. He had never touched Doll in that way.

Doll seemed but a shadow of all that. She may have had memories of those happenings, but she had never actually experienced them. They were only artificial memories. Yet they must have seemed real enough to her.

The ambulance arrived at the scene of the second crash.

The plane had flattened out a few feet from the ground, and not landed so disastrously as the other. It lay crumpled athwart a burned and blackened hedge. The fire engine had quenched the flames within a few minutes. And the pilot had been dragged clear, unconscious, badly knocked about and burned.

They got her into the ambulance, and rushed her to a hospital.

Will had been sitting by the bedside for three hours before the girl in the bed had opened her eyes.

Blank, brown eyes they were, which looked at him, then at the hospital ward, without the faintest change of expression.

"Joan!" he whispered, clasping her free arm—the other was in a splint. There was no response of any sort. She lay back gazing unseeingly at the ceiling. He licked his dry lips. It couldn't be Joan after all.

"Doll!" he tried. "Do you feel all right?"

Still no response.

"I know that expression," said the doctor, who was standing by. "She's lost her memory."

"For good, do you think?" asked Will, perturbed.

The doctor pursed his lips to indicate he didn't know.

"Good Lord! Is there no way of finding out whether she is my wife or my sister-in-law?"

"If you don't know, no one does, Mr. Fredericks," replied the doctor, "We can't tell which plane who was in. We can't tell anything from her clothes, for they were burned in the crash, and destroyed before we realized their importance. We've often remarked their uncanny resemblance. Certainly you can tell them apart."

"I can't!" answered Will, in anguish. "There is no way."

The next day, the patient had largely recovered her senses, and was able to sit up and talk. But a whole tract of her memory had been obliterated. She remembered nothing of her twin, and in fact nothing at all of the events after the duplication experiment.

Lying on the couch in the laboratory, preparing herself under the direction of Bill, was the last scene she remembered.

The hospital psychologist said that the shock of the crash had caused her to unconsciously repress a part of her life which she did not want to remember. She could not remember now if she wanted to. He said he might discover the truth from her eventually, but if he did, it would take months—maybe even years.

But naturally her memories of Will, and their marriage, were intact, and she loved him as strongly as ever.

Was she Joan or Doll?

Will spent a sleepless night, turning the matter over. Did it really matter? There was only one left now—why not assume she was Joan, and carry on? But he knew that as long as doubt and uncertainly existed, he would never be able to recover the old free life he had had with Joan.

It seemed that he would have to surrender her to the psychologist, and that would bring to light all sorts of details which neither he, Joan, nor Bill had ever wished to be revealed.

But the next day something turned up which changed the face of things.

While he was sitting at the bedside, conversing with the girl who might or might not be Joan, a nurse told him a man was waiting outside to see him. He went, and found a police officer standing there.

Ever since the catastrophe which had wrecked Bill's laboratory, the police had been looking around that locality, searching for any possible clues.

Buried in the ground they had found a safe, burst and broken. Inside were the charred remains of books, papers, and letters. They had examined them, without gleaning much, and now the officer wished to know if Will could gather anything from them.

Will took the bundle and went through it. There was a packet of purely personal letters, and some old tradesmen's accounts, paid and receipted. These, with the officer's consent, he destroyed. But also there were the burnt remains of three of Bill's experimental notebooks.

They were written in Bill's system of shorthand, which Will understood. The first two were old, and of no particular interest. The last, however—unfortunately the most badly charred of the three—was an account of Bill's attempts to infuse life into his replicas of living creatures.

The last pages were about the experiment of creating another Joan, and the last recognizable entry read:

"This clumsy business of pumping through pipes, in the manner of a blood transfusion, left a small scar at the base of Doll's neck the only flaw in an otherwise perfect copy of Joan. I resented . . ."

The rest was burned away.

To the astonishment of the police inspector, Will turned without saying a word and hurried back into the ward.

"Let me examine your neck, dear, I want to see if you've been biting yourself," he said, with a false lightness.

Wonderingly, the girl allowed herself to be examined.

There was not the slightest sign of a scar anywhere on her neck.

"You are Joan," he said, and embraced her as satisfactorily as her injuries would permit.

"I am Joan," she repeated, kissing and hugging him back.

And at last they knew again the blessedness of peace of mind.

For once, Fate, which had used them so hardly, showed mercy, and they never knew that in the packet of Bill's receipted accounts, which Will had destroyed, was one from a plastic surgeon, which began:

"To removing operation scar from neck, and two days' nursing and attention."

THE GREEN CAR

THIS WAS ONE TIME I really saw an accident happen.

Other times, I'd just miss such things. There's the shriek of locked wheels. I look round and someone's lying in the road. There's a stationary, car nearby, slewed half round.

After, I'd tell people: "I saw a nasty accident today . . ."

One embroiders to make the story vivid.

But this time I saw it happen. I wish to heaven, I never had. Accident? It was more like plain murder.

The lane through Trescawo was serpentine in the extreme. It looped back on itself as though it were reluctant to reach the village at all, as though it were afraid it would run into something horrible.

The white-faced man in the green car had no such qualms. He came fast and unbelievably silently. Franky Lockett never even saw him. But I did.

I was leaning on my front gate when Franky erupted into his garden. He was eight and lived in the bungalow opposite. He was a sandy-haired kid, snub-nosed, blue-eyed, bright as a button, supercharged with energy. He seldom walked: he galloped.

He saw me and came charging across the lane. "Mr. Murdoch will you let me—"

Without a sound, the green car rushed into Trescawo from the dusk and hit him. He was thrown into the hedge of his front garden. I glimpsed the white, set face of the driver, and then the car was past. Shocked and horrified though I was, I noted the rear number-plate before the gloom swallowed it.

Then: "Franky!" I ran across to him. He was a muddied little bundle at the foot of the hedge, twitching pointlessly. I lifted his head and blood ran from the back of it. His eyes were closed. His mouth hung open, showing the gaps in his milk teeth. Then all at once he gave a great sigh and died in my arms.

Something moved beside me.

Blurrily, I looked up. Franky's father was standing over us, shaking like a man with fever. His hands fluttered uselessly. His eyes were round, staring. He said thickly: "I was always afraid it would happen. He *will* rush—"

He choked over the broken sentence, knowing the tense was wrong and afraid to face the right one. He dropped on his knees beside us, clutched his son and wept like a woman.

I yielded Franky to him and stood up. I felt numb all over.

Trescawo sprang alive. Doors opened up and down the lane, garden gates banged, people came hurrying. It was a small village. People had lived close together here from infancy. Trescawo was like a single organism, aware immediately when some part of it was hurt.

Crooning wordlessly, they helped bear Franky into his bungalow. Some brave soul went ahead to meet the mother. Somebody ran for Dr. Trevose.

Still numbed, I reached my own bungalow and raised the local exchange. "Minnie, put me through to the police at Merthavin—hurry, for God's sake."

Minnie was an efficient operator before all else. For the moment, she forgot to be a woman and put me through without question. But doubtless, then, she listened.

Merthavin was a small coast resort five miles along the lane. In all that distance there was no single turning from the lane, and for a three-mile stretch if you turned left you went straight into the sea. Unless it stopped at either of a couple of farmhouses, or unless it turned around and came back, the green car must go by way of Merthavin.

The station sergeant there answered me. I told him what had happened and described the car. "Big, dark green saloon. Maybe twenty years old but runs smoothly. The number is WME 2195. A man driving—seemed to be wearing a bowler hat. White-faced fellow with a thick black moustache."

"We'll stop him, Mr. Murdoch," said the sergeant.

"Then arrest him for murder," I said, bitterly.

I went across to the Lockett's bungalow. Dr. Trevose was there, but there was nothing he could do, or I could do, or anyone could do.

"Mr. Murdoch, will you let me—" The excited little voice kept calling through my memory. I should never learn what Franky was going to ask of me. When the ache got too bad I went back to my own place, alone, looking for the whisky.

The 'phone rang. It was the police sergeant again.

"He hasn't shown up yet, sir. You say he was travelling fast?"

"Too damn fast," I said, grimly.

"And he's not gone back your way?"

"No—half the village is out waiting for him. They'll lynch him if they catch him—I'll do it myself."

"I understand your feelings, sir. But try to keep him for us if he comes that way. I reckon he must have stopped at one of the farms. Else he should have been here long ago."

"I suppose so."

The sergeant made undecided noises. Then, suddenly: "I'd better stay on watch here. I'll ring George Peters and get him to start from your end and check up at the farms."

"All right, sergeant. If there's anything I can do—"

"Not at the moment, sir. I'll let you know when we locate the man." He hung up.

I poured my whisky, neat, and brooded over it. George Peters was a country police-constable. He lived alone in a cottage a couple of miles north of Trescawo and was the "local" policeman for four villages. He was pure Cornish and from the district and yet, somehow, never seemed of it.

This wasn't just my own impression. I'd lived in Cornwall for only three years and was still the complete "foreigner." But Peters was a "queer 'un" even to those who'd attended the same school.

"Deep," they said. "Knows a lot more than he lets on."

I'd bumped into him a few times but got no further than exchanging formal greetings. Politely, he kept me at arm's length. He didn't want to talk. This piqued me a bit, for he had a scholar's face with quiet eyes and I imagined we might have interests in common. I was an artist but I'd read a few books.

Still, maybe I was wrong about him. People who don't talk much usually don't because they haven't much to talk about.

He drifted from my attention. Franky Lockett came back and the whisky failed to make anything seem better. I was in for a bad night. I was pacing up and down the room, glass in hand, when the door-bell rang.

It was Constable Peters. Gaunt and looking seven feet tall with his helmet on, he regarded me from the step and said in his soft voice with only the echo of a Cornish accent: "Sorry to trouble you, Mr. Murdoch. I had to pass this way, and I'd just like to check the details about the green car."

"Certainly, constable. Come in."

He refused, gently but firmly. He just didn't want to mix. So I told him what I'd told the sergeant. This, clearly, he already knew. He listened impassively, making no notes. Then he asked: "Was it a Morris Sixteen?"

"I wouldn't know. I'm afraid I don't know much about cars."

"I see, sir. Thank you. Good night."

He seemed to reach the front gate with but a couple of strides of his long legs, mounted the bicycle he'd leant against it, and rode off towards Merthavin. The uncertain smear of light cast by his oil lamp weakened with distance and died away altogether.

I duly had my bad night, dozing on and off. Between dozes I thought too much. One of the least worrying questions I kept asking myself was the one Peters had asked me. Was the green car a Morris Sixteen?

And why on earth had Peters asked me that? Did he really "know more than he let on?" If he didn't, the question seemed pointless.

By morning I'd come to hate the wallpaper. I just had to get out in the open. I was cleaning my brushes to escape for a day's painting then the 'phone rang. It was Constable Peters.

"Could you spare the time to come up to my place for a few minutes, Mr. Murdoch?"

I didn't think my heart could sink any lower but it managed it. He'd be wanting my evidence as the sole witness, of course, and I hated the idea of living through the tragedy yet again. I'd been doing it most of the night.

Anyhow, it was his duty to call on me, not the other, way round.

I said, rather irritably: "All right . . . Did you trace that driver last night?"

There was a moment of silence. Then Peters said quietly: "He hadn't been to either of the farms. He never reached Merthavin. He never came back to Trescawo."

There was another moment of silence while I absorbed that. "Damn it," I said, "he can't have been snatched up into the sky. Did you find the car abandoned? Or what?"

"That's what I want to talk to you about, Mr. Murdoch."

Obviously he didn't want to say more on the telephone in case Minnie was listening. I was interested now, my irritation gone. "Right, I'll be there in ten minutes."

But I was there in less on my motor-bike. P.-c. Peters was waiting at his cottage door, uniformed but hatless. He showed me into a sizeable room: it took up more than half the cottage. It was very neat but unusual. There were bookshelves all around it, ceiling-high, and they were packed tight with books, folders, filing boxes, and a row of hefty albums.

The floorboards were highly polished. There was a plain oak desk and a couple of wooden office chairs. That was the full inventory.

"My reference library and, you might say, my home," murmured Peters.

He selected one of the large albums and carried it to the desk. "This is what I want you to see, sir. I'd have brought it down to you but it's too bulky to strap on the carrier of my bike."

Our relationship was changing. Peters was becoming quite loquacious and I could find no answer but a grunt. His thin fingers turned the wide pages which were covered with pasted cuttings. He found the one he sought and indicated it. I bent over the desk to look.

It was a two-column story clipped from the local paper, the colour of weak tea. The headlines said: CAR GOES OVER CLIFF and TRAGIC DEATH OF MERTHAVIN MAN. There was a smudgy photograph of a middle-aged man with a heavy black moustache.

"Does he look at all like the driver you saw, sir?"

I looked more closely. The photo disintegrated into a crowd of meaningless black dots.

"Afraid the detail isn't very clear," said Peters, apologetically.

"Even if it were, I still wouldn't be sure," I said. "I had the merest glimpse of the man. But certainly it *could* have been this man. Or his twin brother, for obviously this chap's dead."

"Yes, he's dead—been dead some seventeen years. Albert Wolfe, plumber, of Merthavin. I knew him pretty well. He had no brothers."

"So? Then I wouldn't know him—until three years ago I'd never been anywhere west of Plymouth."

"No, you wouldn't know him, sir. But I'd be glad if you would read the story."

I read it with some effort—the tiny type was eye-straining. It told how Wolfe, driving alone along the coast road between Trescawo and Merthavin in October 1940, swerved to avoid a car· coming the other way. His car, a green Morris Sixteen plunged over the 100-foot cliff at that point into the sea.

At the time of going to press his body had not yet been recovered.

"Was it ever?" I asked Peters.

He shook his head. "There's a strong undertow around there. The body must have been washed out to sea. There was a war on at the time, you know, and it was a week before we could get hold of a diver to go down. The car was there, all right, upside down with a door open. No body, though."

"Well, it was a nasty affair but it was a long time ago and I still don't get why you've brought it up here—or me either."

Peters reached down a small ledger. "I'm a hoarder of data," he said. "In this book I've kept a note of the license number of every car or vehicle owned by anyone living within a fifteen miles radius of here during my time in the force. Cross-indexed between numbers and names, you see."

He thumbed open the "W" section and showed me an entry:
Wolfe, Albert Geoffrey. Morris 16 (Green) No. WME2195

"Th-that's the number of the green car!" I stuttered.

"So you said, sir. And so far as I can ascertain, that number hasn't been re-issued to anyone since Bert Wolfe died."

I stared first at him, then out of the window at the little hedge - enclosed lawn, perhaps to be reassured that the world was still real out there. It was, anyway. I bit my thumbnail and that was real too.

"Are you implying that I saw Wolfe's ghost?"

"I don't know what you saw, Mr. Murdoch. I'm trying to find out."

I took another look at the indistinct photo and paced up and down trying to compare it with the even more indistinct face in my memory. I found myself surveying book titles, at first unconsciously, then consciously. Most of one corner of the room was occupied by works on psychic research and a few odd men out like the books of Charles Fort.

"Ghosts seem to be a particular interest of yours, Peters," I said. "Personally, I don't believe in them. What are you trying to sell me?"

Peter's rather ascetic face showed no reproach. "I'm a hoarder of data," he repeated. "Facts are what interest me, Mr. Murdoch. If you'll examine the rest of the shelves you'll find more encyclopedias, atlasses, year-books, and scientific works than anything appertaining to psychic research."

"Nevertheless, you include ghosts among your 'facts'?"

"Apparitions would seem to be a genuine phenomenon according to the annals of the Society of Psychical Research," said Peters, carefully. "Probably they're mostly, if not wholly, subjective, though some might conceivably be explained by past and present time getting temporarily out of phase, as it were, and overlapping. Whether you can call them 'facts' depends on what you mean by a fact. Is imagination itself a fact? Anyhow, what's indisputable fact about ghosts is that people report seeing them."

"As you think I've done?"

"I don't know what to think you saw, sir. Except that it was no subjective phantom. The car was solid enough to kill that poor boy. I'm just surveying the facts. I spend a lot of my life in this room merely comparing facts. It fascinates me. Sometimes the oddest facts fit together, and sometimes the most commonly accepted facts just won't correlate at all. Either way you can't avoid seeing one big fact: this world is a much stranger place than most people think it is."

I looked at him. "If you were an artist, Peters, and saw like an artist, you'd know there was no need to tell me that."

"It's because you're an artist and observant, Mr. Murdoch, that I accept as facts what you say you saw. The bowler hat, for instance."

"What of it?"

"Bert Wolfe always wore a bowler. It wasn't all that common in these parts even back in the forties. He was wearing it the day he died."

I frowned. "Look, are you so sure it's a fact he's really dead? I mean, the car was found empty. Supposing he was thrown clear, fell into some crevice, lay there unconscious unseen then later climbed out and wandered away heaven knows where, having lost his memory from concussion?"

Peters shook his head. "Practically impossible. The cliff is sheer at that point and unbroken. I interviewed the other motorist, who saw him go over. The thing happened in broad daylight. He told me he'd never forget the expression on Bert's face behind the windscreen. It was white with the fear of death. And he watched the car fall the whole way, turning half over as it went. Wolfe didn't fall out. Nothing did. The door must have opened when the car hit the sea-bed."

"Still, if he were thrown out even as late as that, he yet might have escaped somehow."

"I don't see how," said Peters. "The motorist never took his eyes off the spot for twenty minutes. He had to sit that long by the roadside, getting his nerve back to drive on—he was an old man. Nothing came up after the bubbles died away."

In the microscopic hall, the telephone rang.

"Excuse me," said Peters. He went. I heard him replying: "Yes, he's here, sarge . . . Yes, I already knew that. I've checked with Mr. Murdoch. He insists he got the number right and I'm sure he did, too . . . Of course I know what I'm saying . . . Yes, I'll come right away. 'Bye."

Peters came back. "That was Horrocks, the police sergeant at Merthavin," he said, unnecessarily. "He's been ringing your place. He found who the license number belonged to and assumed you were mistaken. When I said you weren't, I heard his blood vessels bursting. Now I've got to go and explain myself. Horrocks thinks I'm mad, but then he always did."

"I'll come with you, if you like, though I'm not certain who's side I'm on. But I'll swear in person I got that number right."

Peters smiled—the first time I'd ever seen him smile.

"I'd be glad if you would, Mr. Murdoch, for on the way there's another fact I should like to bring to your attention."

I raised my eyebrows, but the only question I asked was:

"Would you care for a lift on my pillion? It would save you pedalling all that way."

He accepted, and off we went, down to Trescawo and through it and along the lane the green car had followed yesterday evening. The sea came into view on our left. It was dun-coloured like the dismal clouds that hung over it. Rain looked imminent again and we'd had too much of it lately.

You saw plenty of the sea whether you wanted to or not, for the lane—serpentine as ever—kept wandering dangerously near to the edge of the cliffs. Sometimes there wasn't six feet of grass verge between it and the empty air.

We climbed in low gear towards the worst spot of all, where the cliffs reached their topmost height. The lane went over the brow and you couldn't see if anything was coming the other way. Ninety-nine times out of a hundred, on this lonely road, nothing was. But I guessed this was the place where the hundredth chance had gone against Albert Wolfe.

I was right. "Stop here, please," said Peters in my ear.

I stopped on the crest and could see the lane running down into Merthavin. I preferred to look at it rather than seawards, for I've always been nervous of heights. Peters wasn't bothered, though. He slid off the pillion and paced to the very brink of the cliff, examining the grassy verge.

"Look at this, Mr. Murdoch."

So I had to. The verge was wet and muddy from the rain. I slid about on it with my heart in my mouth. What Peters pointed out did nothing for my heart, either.

In the sticky soil were the shallow ruts made by a car's wheels. The pattern of the tread was plain. They swerved across the verge the whole way to the brink. Clearly a car had gone over that brink, and probably within the last twenty-four hours—since yesterday's rain.

"I found them by torch-light last night," said Peters, soberly. "When it was apparent the car had disappeared, I had a hunch this was the place where it had left the road. Just where poor Bert Wolfe bought it."

My spine crawled. "And where he bought it again—yesterday?"

Peters shrugged. "Those tracks are another fact—that's all," he said, shortly.

I was scared but morbid interest made me peer over the brink, down at the sea a hundred feet below.

"There's never less than twenty feet of water there," commented Peters.

I drew back. I looked again at the tracks. "The car ran past me weirdly silently," I said. "As silently as a ghost. But if it were immaterial, like a ghost, it couldn't have killed—nor left tracks like that."

"Then obviously it was material," said Peters.

"Transposed from the past to the present by some inexplicable freak of time, d'you think?"

Peters shrugged again. "That's a theory which one fact doesn't fit. Bert Wolfe's car was old when he bought it. He got through a hell of a lot more mileage in it. The engine knocked like fury. You could hear that car coming from a mile off. But yesterday, you say, you didn't hear it coming. Or going. Now, if the car were here materially, then surely its material parts—the cylinders, tappets, and so on—must have caused just as many soundwaves as they always did."

"But just now you said it obviously *was* material!" I cried.

"So I did," said Peters, bestriding the pillion lankily. "We need another theory. To get it we need more facts. Let's go on and see Horrocks. Maybe he'll have some."

But Horrocks had no more facts. However, he accepted ours, though refusing to believe there was anything unnatural about them. He was a solidly built man who assumed the world was equally solidly built. He laughed us to scorn and then assured us that it was no laughing matter.

"Manslaughter has been done," he said, "and I suspect maybe other crimes. Still, it seems the criminal has paid for them with his life."

"What criminal?" frowned Peters.

"The man in the bowler hat who was driving the car, of course," said Horrocks, impatiently. "Mr. Murdoch is quite sure the car number was WME 2195. Right, I'll accept that. There's no such registered number. Therefore, the car had false number-plates."

"But why?" I asked.

Horrocks, still impatient, said: "There can be only one reason, sir—it was a stolen car. Changing the number-plates is a routine dodge."

"It was such an old car, pre-war type, that it could scarcely be worth stealing," I said.

"Perhaps not for its own sake," said Horrocks. "I'd say it was stolen to be used for a job. Pay-roll snatching, perhaps. There was a snatch in Exeter on Friday. Two more in Plymouth—big money every time. The culprit—or one of 'em—was on the run out this way. Obviously, a stranger in the district. He didn't know that tricky coast road very well, if at all, probably missed the turn in the dusk—or skidded on the wet road—and went over the cliff."

He turned to Peters. "Straightforward enough, isn't it, George? No call for spooks."

It was so glib I'd all but accepted it, until Peters said: "That's really *some* coincidence, sarge. I'd hate to have to work out the mathematical chances against two green cars, of the same vintage, driven by a man with a black moustache and wearing a bowler hat, going over the same cliff—and carrying the identical number-plate!"

Horrocks wasn't even shaken. "Coincidence? *Everything's* co-incidence. It's merely a coincidence that you're you, Peters, and not somebody else. The chances are well over two thousand million against it, you know."

Peters sighed. "Sometimes I think you'd be happier if I *were* somebody else, sarge."

Horrocks laughed. "Not at all, George. You're the queerest flatfoot I've ever run across, but I never met a more conscientious one. You do your job. But if you'd only stick to facts and not let your imagination run away with you, I think you'd do it even better."

Peters lifted his eyes to heaven. His lips moved wordlessly. For the first time since Franky's death, I laughed.

Horrocks regarded us with surprise, then said abruptly: "We'll have the truth within a few hours. I've contacted the Aqualung Club and some of their chaps are going down for a look-see any time now."

I'd forgotten about the Aqualung Club, Merthavin's own group of skin-diving enthusiasts.

"Why, of course," I said. "That'll settle who the man was."

"I'm hoping they'll recover his body," said Horrocks. "But it'll be a dicey do with that undertow. Still, they think they can handle it. They're certain to locate the car, anyhow, and perhaps the pay-roll too. Care to come along and see the operations? I've got a launch laid on."

I accepted the invitation. Peters got over his chagrin and came with us, though he remained silent and thoughtful. When we got there, the Club's motor cruiser was already anchored beneath the cliff which stood above it like the wall of a great warehouse.

We tied up alongside the cruiser. We didn't want to risk bobbing against that rock wall, even though the dirty-looking sea was still smooth under the overcast sky. The rain was still holding off.

A couple of Club members were standing on the cruiser's deck making final tests of their equipment. Each had a safety line around his waist to guard against being swept away by the undertow. Three others stood by ready to join the hunt if it became difficult.

The pair slipped on their goggles and dropped over the· side. There was a brief flurry of flippered feet, and then the sea was smooth again.

Twenty minutes later they came up empty-handed.

"Pretty murky down there but we've covered the area fairly thoroughly," one of them reported. "Not a sign of the damn car."

Horrocks bit his lip. "But you could have missed it?"

They agreed, and went down again, and presently the others joined them. There were five of them at it, on and off. An hour went by. Then the organiser bobbed up by our launch. He said, rather breathlessly: "Sorry—drawn another blank. Can't even see anything of the car that was supposed to have been down here for years. But probably that's silted over by now. The bottom's very sandy."

Horrocks was disappointed. So was I. Peters remained expressionless.

"All right, old man—thanks for taking the trouble," said Horrocks. "You'd better call your hunting pack off now."

They came up one by one. The last carrying something. He thrust it over the side into our launch. It was corroded, barnacle - encrusted, and enmeshed in seaweed, but was fairly obviously a car's number-plate.

Horrocks and Peters chipped and scraped at it with spanners from the tool-box. Bit by bit, the number became dimly apparent: WME 2195.

"From Bert Wolfe's car," said Peters. "It must have come adrift."

That encouraged the skin-divers to forage about for another half an hour, but without any luck. Then they gave it up. They were unanimous in believing that no car had fallen into the sea in this area lately, else they would certainly have found it.

We returned gloomily to Merthavin. Horrocks got the station car and came part way back with Peters and me. He wanted to see those wheel-marks for himself. He did so. Then he peeped over the cliff. Yes, we'd been searching the right spot: it was directly below.

"It beats me," said Horrocks. He turned his car and went back. I ran Peters up to his cottage. He'd become the reticent type again, and went in muttering something about mulling over the facts again. He obviously didn't want me to mull with him.

I returned home, had some tea, then looked out and found a breeze had sprung up, the heavy clouds were moving off, and the sun was breaking through as it sank towards the sea. It would be a fine evening, after all.

I stared across at the Lockett's bungalow. The window with the blind down made my throat feel dry. The funeral was tomorrow. I was just too close to it all here. I escaped again, riding in the evening sunlight along the lane as it wound out of Trescawo in the opposite direction to Merthavin.

There were no cliffs this way. The lane led gently down to the beach. There was over a mile of level sands here. I parked my bike at the edge of them and began trudging along at the sea's constantly moving rim. There were no living things in sight save seagulls.

The sunset was a splendid show of coloured and gleaming clouds, and the sea made a rippling carpet of its reflection. It took my mind off things, as I'd hoped. I began to wonder what Turner would have made of it.

The glory had died and the sea had claimed the sun when I turned back. The beach looked desolate in the grey light now and the wind had become chill. I tramped back a deal faster than I'd come.

I was almost within arm's reach of my bike when I saw the wheel-tracks grooving the sand not five yards beyond it. They ran from the lane clear across the beach and straight into the sea. My heart missed a beat. I went on a bit shakily to examine them.

The tide was on the ebb, and on the mud-smooth wet sand it left behind it the tracks were clear enough for me to recognize the pattern of the tread.

The tracks weren't there when I'd come—I couldn't have missed seeing them. While I'd been traipsing away from this spot, entranced by the sunset, behind me the green car must have rolled silently into the sea.

Or have emerged from it.

It was impossible to tell which from the tracks.

I looked at the blank sea under the dulling sky. The wavelets advanced, slopped, and retreated, and. the wind was beginning a thin, high keening. I shivered, and it wasn't just because of the cold wind.

I stumbled back to my bike, started her up, and began hitting it back along the lane. But I turned off before Trescawo, and headed uphill. I was making for Peters' cottage. I wanted him to see those tracks before the tide turned.

Up the gloomy, deserted lane I tore, rounded a curve, then pulled to one side, braking like mad. For plunging noiselessly down between the hedges towards me was the green car. I had a full head on view of it. But only for a few seconds. It missed me by inches and I felt the wind of its passing.

During those heart-stopping seconds the white face of Albert Wolfe regarded me stonily from behind the windscreen. I was certain it was he—or a zombie using his body. Things had become so nightmarish now that I could almost believe it *was* a zombie.

But I didn't stop to think about it. I wrenched the bike round and rode like fury downhill after the car. I caught it up on the outskirts of Trescawo, but couldn't get past it: the lane was too narrow.

So I began hooting continuously. We shot between the Lockett's bungalow and mine at over fifty, despite the snaking bends. The blare of my horn had preceded us. The villagers were peering from their windows and doorways. But nobody had time to do a thing. We were out into the open country again before they'd reached their garden gates.

And there the green car began to move away from me with contemptuous ease, though I tried hard to hang on to its tail. I must have been doing close on eighty, which was lunacy in that lane and in the gathering dark.

But at least I had my headlamp on. The car showed no lights at all.

A minute or two later we were continuing the fantastic chase along the margin of the sea, and then climbing the rise to the high cliff. I was a hundred yards behind. As we emerged from the dead ground, the pale light of the moon, rising over the inland hills, reached us.

So I saw what happened. The green car reached the crown of the rise, then spun abruptly to the left and went flying out into space. It curved down towards the cliff-shadowed sea. The moonlight couldn't reach there, so I never saw the splash.

I pulled up, sweating, my nerves jumping.

Albert Wolfe had plunged to his death for the third time—at least. And there was no cause at all to assume that he would stay dead.

I switched off my engine and went gingerly to peer into the shadow beneath the cliff. But I could see nothing and there was no sound but the wash of the sea and the shrill note of the wind.

I took it easy on the way back to Trescawo. I had to. My nerves kept twitching like the leg of Galvani's frog. The village was in ferment. Somehow, Peters was already there taking notes. I beckoned him into my bungalow and poured us both stiff whiskies. Then I told him all about it.

"It *was* Wolfe—I saw him distinctly," I repeated. "I noticed other things, too. The front number-plate was missing."

"That's interesting," said Peters. "No one else noticed that. But Claude Farmer and Bill Jones glimpsed the back number plate. WME 2195, sure enough."

He scratched his chin. "Wolfe's car—minus the number—plate we found today. What are we to make of that?"

"I don't know," I said, pouring another double. "But it was some car. I touched eighty and it was leaving me standing."

"Now, that doesn't sound like Wolfe's car at all," said Peters, thoughtfully. "It was in such bad shape I'm certain it would have seized up at anything over fifty."

"It was Wolfe's car," I said, and gulped a mouthful. "It had masks over the head-lamps—war-time pattern for driving in the blackout. Circa 1940. The lamps weren't switched on, though. That zombie could see in the dark."

"There are no facts to support the existence of zombies," said Peters. "I've been mulling over the facts we have, and a few more I've dug up, and I don't believe there's anything supernatural about this whole thing. You say you felt the draught as the car passed you. Right: it's solid. It displaces air. Let's see if it can displace a road barrier."

"That's fine—if you know when and where to plan the barrier."

"I'd say tomorrow at dusk, on the road between here and Merthavin—the best place would be Crowley Farm," said Peters, calmly.

"Good heavens, Peters, just because the car went through here two evenings running at roughly the same time, there's no reason to suppose it'll do so again tomorrow. What d'you imagine it is—a local bus keeping to a time-table?"

Peters remained calm. "When a phenomenon repeats itself, there's always a chance it'll go on doing so. We can but try. Anyhow, we've got more facts for Horrocks. Also, this time, a whole crowd of eye-witnesses. He'll have to do something."

Sergeant Horrocks did plenty. From somewhere or other he rustled up no less than three police patrol cars with two-way radio.

The following evening one of the cars lay concealed behind a hedge in the lane skirting the bare beach where I'd seen the wheel-tracks. Another blocked the turning leading up to Peters' cottage. The third was parked in the gateway to Crowley Farm, a mile out of Trescawo on the Merthavin road, and as well as its constable-driver and his observer, Horrocks, Peters, and I waited with it.

Across the road was drawn the biggest of the farm-carts, still loaded heavily with sacks of potatoes.

It had drizzled all morning, and the funeral had been a damp and depressing affair. During it, I'd found myself becoming angry at I knew not what. Anger at fate generally, I suppose, for killing a child so pointlessly. Somehow it was difficult to get angry with the occupant of the green car. How can one be angry with a man already dead? Or the shade of that man? Or—?

Something that was out of this world, anyway.

Perversely, the sun came out brilliantly after lunch. Now the fine afternoon was passing into another fine evening. In the darkening blue of the sky the pinpoint of Venus was just visible.

We were grouped around the car parked just inside the farm gate, listening to the faint etheric wash of the radio net.

Monotonously at intervals came from the other two waiting cars: "Able—nothing to report. Over." And "Baker—nothing to report. Over."

"Light the lanterns, George," said Horrocks, presently.

Constable Peters lit the four red-glassed hurricane lamps, carried them out into the lane and set them down in pairs on either side of the farm-cart barrier. A policeman was stationed at Merthavin to stop any traffic using the lane from that direction, but there was always a chance some motorist might slip past him. We didn't want any accidents.

Time ticked on. Venus became ever brighter as its setting became darker. The faint points of a handful of stars began to appear.

Every now and then, one or other of us would give way to impatience and peer round the gate and up the lane with the dusk thickening between its bordering hedges.

None of us seemed in the mood for talking.

Then the carrier wave rustled on the car radio and a voice, a little indistinct with excitement, said: "Able—there's a dark object rising from the sea, moving slowly landwards. Over."

We all tensed up.

Horrocks grabbed the microphone. "Dog—okay. Watch it. Over."

Soon: "Able—it's the green car all right. Coming slowly up the beach. Water streaming down its sides. No lights—but seems to be a man inside, driving. Over."

Horrocks: "Dog—okay. Baker—are you getting this? Over."

"Baker—yes. We're standing by. Over."

In a moment: "Able—it's turning into the lane ahead of us. Heading for Trescawo. We're about to start. Over."

Horrocks snapped back: "Dog—right, off you go. Just follow. Don't try to overtake. Over."

"Able—wilco. Over."

"Baker—standing by. Over."

The tempo was speeding up. I felt Peters grip my wrist. It was too dark to see his expression clearly, but his whole attitude said: "This is it. We'll soon know."

He let go and began to loosen his truncheon. I had no weapon beyond a heavy torch. We hadn't a gun between us. Horrocks had vetoed it. "When we corner him, we'll be nine against one—he'll have no chance," he said.

I reflected, yes, but nine men against one—*what?*

I licked dry lips, and my cursed nerves began jumping again.

The radio crackled, and a voice unsteadied by the bumpy journey reported: "Able—he's approaching Trescawo at speed. Fifty, maybe. We're keeping pace behind. Over."

"Baker—we're ready. Over."

Horrocks answered neither. His bulky figure was motionless as he waited.

"Baker—he tried to turn up here, saw us, swerved back, stayed on the road. We pulled out after him. Passing through Trescawo now. He's piling on speed. Look out there, Dog—he's got no lights and you can't hear his engine. Over."

But now through the fading twilight, from the direction of Trescawo, we could hear the distant engines of the two police cars heading this way—with the silent phantom car fleeing before them.

"Dog—okay. Out." snapped Horrocks. He dropped the microphone and ran out into the lane, waving an electric torch. Peters and I and the observer constable weren't two paces behind him. We formed a human barrier across the narrow lane, in front of the cart, adding our flashing torches to the red warning of the lanterns.

And then it carne at us without a sound along the lane, a dark blur on the dim ribbon, travelling at a terrific speed. It could not swerve off the lane. High hedges, as well as deep ditches, on both sides prevented it—that was why this spot had been chosen.

We shouted and waved our torches wildly. The oncoming car seemed only to accelerate.

"Scatter!" yelled Horrocks when it was clear that the green car wasn't going to stop.

We jumped aside, I stumbling into a ditch and dropping my torch.

Crash! The green car smacked straight into the cumbersome cart and overturned it with a great cracking and splintering of wood. Potatoes went rolling all ways. The car, still upright and apparently undamaged, went on trying to climb over the wreck. Its wheels spun rapidly, seeking a purchase.

The white-faced driver remained at the wheel. The buzzing wheels got a grip, and the car, lurching from side to side, began to work its way over the shattered cart.

The two pursuing police cars came, with screeching brakes, to a halt a few yards back. Their crews scrambled out.

I climbed out of the ditch with clumsy haste but Peters was faster. Truncheon in hand, he leaped up on the running board of the escaping green car.

"Stop!" I heard him yell. "Come out of there—whoever you are."

And he yanked open the door of the car.

It was like a flood-gate being opened. A mass of water came pouring out of the car, washing the driver out with it—a legless, struggling, oddly-shaped figure. He—or it—flopped into the ditch where I'd just been. The water gushed briefly over the creature and drained away along the ditch. The being continued to struggle helplessly and in silence down there. It threshed about like a landed fish.

A strong smell of the sea was filling the air.

Then, horribly, the figure expanded slowly like a toy balloon being blown up. And all the while it moved convulsively. And then there was a sickening sound, and it collapsed in a still, limp heap at the bottom of the ditch. There came a stench which drowned out the sea-smell.

We had to back away from it, and I, for one, was glad to.

The green car had ceased to move, too, and save for the water still trickling from it, all was silent.

The nine of us stood awkwardly in the lane. I don't know how the others felt about it but I had more than a twinge of guilt about the dreadful death of the thing. We hadn't meant to kill it any more than—probably—it had meant to kill little Franky Lockett.

The foul smell dissolved into the evening air. The sea-smell returned faintly—obviously, the water in the car had been sea-water. We braced ourselves to go and inspect the thing by torch-light. It was a grisly and bewildering business, and while we were occupied with it the stars were corning out overhead in strength.

What we learnt that night merely confused me more than ever. The creature belonged to no species known to marine biology. It was cold-blooded, dark-skinned, and had gills and a tail. It had two main tentacles which branched into whole deltas of thinner tentacles—as Peters pointed out, much more useful for precision work than man's stubby fingers.

It also had a face. A grotesque, noseless, stalk-eyed face, which it had concealed behind a plastic death-mask of Albert Wolfe. About the upper part of its body was wrapped Wolfe's coat—the genuine article, as we found from the tailor's label.

The incongruous bowler hat, which we found farther along the ditch, was also genuine.

When the Maritime Biological Station at Plymouth dissected the creature, they found it had a brain of a size to command respect.

The green car had its mysteries, too. In the first place, it wasn't Wolfe's old car at all, but a careful replica even to the headlamp masks, although the front number-plate was missing. Yet it was only a replica so far as outward appearance went. There was a front seat, a steering wheel, and a few odd controls. Beyond that, it was little more than a travelling sea-water aquarium, very stoutly built and heavy.

Small wonder we'd not heard its engine: there wasn't one. The theory grew that it picked up and used power radiated from some distant source.

"Beamed in this direction from some point out to sea," Peters guessed. "They are well ahead of us."

"They" were still the staple talking point between Peters and me even a month later. We never tired of discussing "Them," usually in Peters' library. If the affair had lost me one friend, it had gained me another.

Peters hunted through the charts and showed me the long, deep crack in the continental shelf which reached almost to the headland from which Wolfe's car had plunged.

"They came up here," he said, tracing it with a forefinger. "First they took Wolfe's body from the car. Some time later they came back for the car itself. They overlooked the front number-plate, which had been torn off—and which remained there until it was found by the Aqualung Club."

Mentally, I pictured "Them" dragging the battered green car down towards the dark depths where they dwelt. It was obvious on several counts that they were creatures of the oceanic abyss. Firstly, because they could see in the dark, and ventured on land only when darkness was falling. Secondly, because the fake car had been constructed of tremendously strong material to contain the pressure of the sea-water with which it had been filled.

Peters—the facts at his fingertips, as usual—told me that water *is* compressible, though only by one per cent for every 3000 pounds per square inch of pressure.

It was a pity we'd had no chance to measure the pressure of the water in the car and therefore deduce the depth from which it had come.

Thirdly, of course, was the manner of death of the creature when that balancing pressure had been drastically lowered.

"We have to allow them that it was a bold piece of camouflage, and opportunism," I said.

Peters agreed. "If it weren't for that unlucky accident at the outset, the creature might still be carrying out its nocturnal exploration, venturing ever farther inland. As it was, it had little chance to learn much about the world-above-the-water."

"But they must have known of our existence for hundreds of years—from sunken ships," I commented. "Why start only now to investigate our species?"

"I'm not so sure they didn't start long ago," said Peters. "Think of the missing crew of the *Marie Celeste*." He tapped the spine of one of Charles Fort's books. "And in here you'll find plenty of other reports from last century of whole missing crews, as well as ships themselves mysteriously disappearing in fair weather. What of the two ships and 129 men of the Franklin expedition, which vanished over a hundred years ago, and were never seen again despite prolonged searches? Specimens for *their* research, like as not."

"But why do they have to be furtive about it?" I complained. "They must know we're intelligent and would welcome contact with another intelligent race."

Peters smiled cynically. "You imagine they think us intelligent because we invented magnetic mines and sent them more free specimens of men and ships in 1939 and 1940 than they'd ever had before? It's my guess that's why they came up to investigate things a bit in 1940 and found that car."

I thought about it, then said: "Perhaps you're right. They had reason to be cautious about us. In fact, we really began to invade their territory during World War Two. All those sinking ships, all those submarines and U-boats. And now atomic submarines and underwater H-bombs—"

"And all the Aqualung Clubs of the world," smiled Peters. I smiled, too, then said: "But it's no joke, really. They've intelligence, resource, boldness, and obviously a technology in some respects more advanced than ours. If it ever came to war—"

"If it ever came to war, I think we'd be far outnumbered," cut in Peters, grimly. "Remember this: there's more than twice as much land beneath the sea as there is above it. And presuming it's as thickly populated . . ." He trailed off speculatively.

Presently, he said, looking out at the tiny lawn: "Two races with a common nursery—the sea. We came out of it. They stayed in. Would a war decide who was the wiser?" His gaze wandered round the room and all its books. "Knowledge is a great thing, but wisdom is a greater," he said. "Let's hope that between us we can muster enough wisdom not to have a war at all."

THE LEGEND OF ERNIE DEACON

MY SWORD DARTED SWIFT as one of my own famous arrows. Via my wrist, I felt its point glance off a rib. A flash of agony lit Sir Roderick's eyes. Then all life left them. My blade was through his heart.

His weight as he fell wrenched the hilt from my fingers. He lay, whiteface up, on the dark green grass in the shade of an oak tree. Thick blood spread slowly on his tunic.

My fighting fury ebbed, gave place to serene triumph. Justice had been done. They that live by the sword shall perish by the sword. Truisms were true, and everyone knew who and where they were and what they stood for.

Or did they?

The dead Sir Roderick said: "I love you, Robin."

Moreover, he said it in Maid Marian's voice.

I said, listening to myself incredulously: "Draw thy sword, Sir Roderick, for but one of us shall leave this glade alive."

The said glade immediately quivered like a mirage. A huge, ghostly drawbridge crashed down in the middle of it, silently raising dust clouds. A troop of mounted Norman knights galloped across the bridge and through the trees. Not between the trees: *through* them.

Suspension of disbelief collapsed. I removed the headset and switched off the Teo.

"Yes, the Asps were right to throw this lot back at us. Every last spool's a dud. Sound and vision completely out of phase, for one thing. You think you're going crazy."

Ernie pointed out: "Every spool is stamped 'Tested and Passed'."

"Doesn't mean a thing, Ernie. You know how those inspectors go about it. They test one Teo spool at random out of a batch, then pass the whole batch. Thirty-seven spools returned this time. Thirty-seven kilos of *varos* lost to Earth—enough to treat maybe five thousand people. It's a wicked shame. I'm filing a complaint at top-level directly when we get back."

"Sure, you do that," said Ernie, absently.

I studied him. "I've a notion you couldn't care less."

"I wouldn't say that, Art. But I wish I could care more. It's a worthwhile job, I suppose. I thought it was for me, but it isn't. Whoever made the stars set them too far apart for humans. Life's too short."

"Maybe it's just that you're too young, Ernie. You know, I was against your appointment. I told the Board you were too young. You've really got to be through with women on this job."

"Darn it, Art, it's not woman trouble. It's . . . being pent up in this ship. Restlessness, boredom, frustration. I want to be *doing* something."

"About what?"

"About my career. I want to *be* someone, Art."

I knew then I'd lost him. This would be his first and last trip. Well, I could go it alone, if necessary. I'd done it before. In fact, at heart I was a loner, like most dreamers.

Still, I'd miss Ernie. He was an idealist and an enthusiast for life. "real" life, he termed it, as opposed to dream life. I was older and—I kidded myself—wiser. I suspected that "real" life itself was just a dream, as Prospero had said.

"What kind of someone?" I asked.

"Well, for instance, I'd like to be the guy who finds the secret of growing *varos* on Earth. Someone's going to pull it off, sooner or later. I wish it could be me."

"And throw me out of a job?"

Ernie smiled. "That could be the best thing that ever happened to you, Art. Then you might begin to get somewhere instead of being batted to and fro like a ping-pong ball."

I smiled, too. I was older and—remember—wiser.

"I'm where I always wanted to be, son: sitting on a cloud, watching the world go by."

"There'd be no parade to watch unless some folk got up off their seats and started going somewhere."

"True enough," I said. And then Tigot waddled in from his cabin, where he spent most of the time recumbent, running through his favorite Teo spools, of which he never tired. The bulk of them featured Sherlock Holmes.

Asps always waddle. They're all fat from inaction: the long-term result of automation plus. Spidery robots tended them from the cradle to the urn. Also, sowed, reaped, treated, and packaged *varos:* the plants which refused to take root in any soil or compost on Earth. Which made it tough for Earth. For the treated *varos* was the only known cure for the otherwise fatal blood condition which many Terrestrials had contracted, and passed to their offspring, from the excess of radioactive waste.

Earth bartered Teo dream spools for *varos.*

In a sense, it was exchange of life for life. Until the Earthman came, the Asps were being stifled by their own boredom. This Terrestrial invention offered them new life.

"Only a dream life," Ernie would sniff. But dreams can be very real, and the Teo-induced kind were exceptionally so. Everything was on the tape: vision, sound, color, smell, tactile sensations. They were projected directly into the relevant brain centers.

Earthmen used them, too, but generally only for relaxation. They weren't enslaved addicts, as the Asps had become. Earthmen still had to work for their living.

Tigot greeted me with a grin and: "There was the curious incident of the dog in the nighttime.' "

I returned, smartly: "The dog did nothing in the nighttime."

"That was the curious incident," he laughed, and patted my shoulder. "You're coming along nicely, Arthur. You'll be one of us yet."

"One of us" meant a member of the Sherlock Society, of which he was President. This was the Asparian equivalent of the Baker Street Irregulars, still flourishing on Earth. Devotees of the Holmes cult. I was one myself in an uncommitted way. I was temperamentally unable to join the conspiracy to pretend Holmes had really lived. I preferred to read the stories, see him as a Paget illustration, rather than dream I was he—or, alternative role, Dr. Watson gasping at his brilliance—through the Teo.

Asps didn't often visit Earth. They're not incurious, just lazy. Also, the round trip absorbed eighteen months. Tigot was a special case. He was on a pilgrimage to London, representing his Society, to visit the haunts of Holmes. A labor of love: his idolatry was extreme.

Inactive nonproducers, the Asps had few colorful characters among their own race. The Teo opened up a whole new heroic world for them. Each had his particular favorite, and they were childlike in their self-identification.

Tigot's great ambition was to walk on Baker Street. It was worth traveling more than four light-years to do simply that.

I pointed out that Conan Doyle hadn't even seen Baker Street when he conceived Sherlock Holmes. Tigot just smiled and shrugged. Even more than humans, Asps believed what they wished to believe.

Ernie was amusedly contemptuous of the Asparian way of life. He liked Tigot but couldn't resist ribbing him.

"Coming out for air after breathing all that fog?"

Tigot replied, evenly: "The fog stimulates me. All the wonderful mysteries emerge from it."

"You won't find any fog along Baker Street nowadays," said Ernie. "Nor a lump of the coal which caused it. Nor yet a single hansom cab. Queen Victoria is dead."

"Possibly. But Holmes is immortal."

"You're right," I said. "Doyle killed him once, but he came back from the grave."

"Holmes," said Tigot, "was no ordinary man, but a spirit. You can't kill a spirit."

I didn't pursue the matter. You can't have a logical discussion with folk who use entirely different terms of reference. Even so, I understood the Asp outlook far better than Ernie. As a commuter I had a foot in both worlds.

I could be hard and practical. Also, I could abandon myself to dreaming. I knew the function of every instrument in my ship and could explain it in technical terms. At the same time, I knew that such terms explained nothing really. That they merely described methods of using forces of whose basic nature we were ignorant. That the ship itself, its immensely tough hull, its mass of machinery, was once no more tangible than a dream in a designer's mind. For the material world is just the dream world frozen hard.

In a sense, everybody and everything is mind-stuff.

Including Sherlock Holmes.

Then my instruments warned me that the ship was nearing the frontier of the solar system, and I must switch to my practical role and make planet-fall.

I had a parting drink with Ernie in a Spaceport bar. He reaffirmed that he would resign next day. I didn't try to dissuade him.

He said: "Aspar is just one big opium den. And you're playing drug-peddler to the junkies, Art. Pardon my bluntness."

I did, because he was semidrunk.

"You're wasting your life," he said.

"It's my life, Ernie. For me, the only life. Manwatching is my fad: observing mankind in the making. The normal growth-rate is too gradual to register. But time dilation gives you an accelerated motion picture: twelve-year hops for the price of only eighteen months. It's like walking through history in seven-league boots."

He regarded me hazily over the rim of his glass.

"A thousand ages in your sight is but as an evening gone . . . You get a kick out of feeling like some minor god, then?"

"I don't think of it that way. Here's how I'll spend my furlough. I'll look around and see what's actually happened about the new ideas and projects that were in the air here a dozen years back. What ideas took root, how they've shaped. What ideas died, and why. I'm plumb eager to learn what kind of a harvest we're getting. Then I'll take a look at what's new in seedlings. I'll mull 'em over in my mind during the next trip out and see what I can make of them myself. Then come back here and see what man's really done with them—or what they've done with him. The onlooker sees most of the game, you know."

"That's O.K., Art, if you're a born onlooker. But I want to *play*. Remember Jake Herren?"

"Sure. Your pal. A mechanic here."

"He was . . . twelve years ago. Now he's Chief Engineer. He's been climbing the promotion ladder three rungs at a time. What have I been doing all these years? Riding guard over a cargo of pickled plants."

"Which plants, incidentally, will save thousands of lives. Isn't that something?"

"Oh, sure. But what about *my* life?"

"You took the job with your eyes open, Ernie. Quit whining. Jake's aged better than ten years on you—don't forget that."

"Oh, I know. I'm Peter Pan. I never grow up. Hell, I feel awful."

He pushed his glass aside. I stared at him. His face was sweat-damp and pale. He looked bad. I called a taxi, took him home, left in the care of his sister. His morale was dragging along the ground. He seemed bewildered, like a man who had missed his way in the dark and become dis-orientated.

Next morning his sister phoned. Ernie's doctor had advised he be taken to the hospital for observation. The ambulance had just left. I told her I'd keep in touch. I did, for some days. No news. No change. Then, behind schedule, I jetted off on my global roundup of developments in the realm of ideas.

In London, in the Space Club, I ran into Tigot again. He insisted I share his ecstasy: a walk on Baker Street. So I did.

Lower Baker Street was a long way from Victoria's age: almost entirely rebuilt. Monolithic blocks of offices and flats towered above the nose-to-tail traffic. But the upper length of the Street, close to Regents Park, remained much as it had been a century ago. Here Holmes was supposed to have lived, at No. 221·B. No such number, of course.

But Tigot held that the only fictitious thing was the number. The house was still there. He pointed it out. Both the Irregulars and the Sherlock Society had tracked it down. He even showed me Camden House—and that was still the name over the door—which was described as "the Empty House" in the story which brought Holmes back to life and introduced the formidable Professor Moriarty.

Tigot's fat cheeks were flushed with excitement. I marveled again at the way the Asps could live in a world of fantasy and juggle the facts to make it seem real. I said as much.

Tigot said, seriously: "My race is much older than yours. We've learned what you find it hard to understand: facts are the children of imagination. It's only through the eye of the imagination that you see the true picture of this strange universe. If imagination is strong and pure, unsullied by doubt, its truth is the only truth. Facts are simply what they're imagined to be."

"True facts can be verified," I said. "Imagined ones can't."

Tigot promptly launched a complex argument purporting to show that verification was also imagination. It confused me and I waved him to silence after a while.

"All right, I go some of the way with you. But nothing can persuade me to believe that Holmes was anything more than a creation by Conan Doyle."

"Are you anything more than a creation by your parents?"

I laughed. "Of all the obvious false analogies! Look, Tigot, Doyle didn't even know what to call his detective. He fumbled over names—it was 'sherrinford Holmes" at one time."

"But didn't your parents hesitate over what names to give you?"

I was silently thoughtful. He'd scored there. Instead of "Arthur" I was very nearly "Arnold," my mother once told me. But was it any more than a debating point, mere verbal cleverness?

I found myself recalling a visit to Dorset, the Hardy County, in this country long ago. The guide took us to the farm where Tess of the d"Urbervilles had labored as a milkmaid and the church where she'd married Angel Clare. My fellow tourists became alert with interest. Those places meant something. The church at Stinton, where Thomas Hardy's heart was interred, scarce got a glance. The creator was relatively unimportant, his creations everything.

A famous fictional inhabitant of Hong Kong was Suzie Wong. The hotel called the "Nam Kok" was still visited by her admirers. Somehow, she'd acquired flesh and bones. When I visited Hong Kong, people would tell me how their grandfathers often saw her in the dives after she'd taken to the opium pipe.

The World of Suzie Wong actually existed for those who believed in it.

In Berlin they'll show you the haunts of Harry Lime, born of a fiction, "the Third Man."

The Cornish folk love to show you the ruins of King Arthur's Castle at Tintagel. The ruins are real enough. But was King Arthur? Maybe, in a queer kind of way.

And Robin Hood? Ask the Asps. They believe he was as real as Sherwood Forest undoubtedly is.

Even human kids know he was real, just as they know Santa Claus exists—for from whom else do the presents come? The parents chuckle quietly. They know better. They know where the presents came from. But do they—really? The real origin was the legend, and spirit, of Santa Claus.

Long-running TV soap operas persuade millions that their characters are real people. A scriptwriter dictates—he thinks—that one should fall ill. Flowers, fruit, letters by the truckload pour into the studios. Not for the scriptwriter for few of the donors even know his name. He is a shadow. His creation is three-dimensional.

And when such a character is written out in the brutal way, killed off, the grief is nation-wide. No new thing. The whole world cried over the death of Little Nell, though none was more heartbroken than Charles Dickens. Yet he was in the position to know better than any of the other mourners that she never really existed at all.

Or did she?

If these creatures are so real to skeptical Terrestrials, there was small chance of my convincing an Asp that he was a victim of his own delusions.

As if he were reading my thoughts, Tigot broke in: "Every day, for more than a century now, letters arrive in London addressed to Holmes at No. 221-B imploring his help. Did you know that?"

I didn't, but I could believe it. I'd reached a state of mind where I could believe almost anything.

On the way back we glimpsed, down river, the gray dome of St. Paul's.

Tigot commented: "Every cathedral in this world of yours was built from belief and not from ascertainable knowledge. Belief, Arthur, is everything."

Chasing ideas, I found myself back-tracking to New York. Bad news about Ernie awaited me. He had polio and was paralyzed from the waist down. Even *varos* was no answer to polio.

I felt terrible about it. How much worse he must feel. He couldn't endure confinement, and now he was to be confined to a wheelchair for life.

I shrank from going to see him, but went.

We had quite a talk. During it he said: "Don't feel too bad about me, Art. Everything has its compensations. I always wanted to be someone but I was never sure who I wanted to be. That made me pretty miserable. I had this blind drive conflicting with the realization that I had no special talent of any kind. Medical research attracted me most, I suppose, but I don't have the kind of brain it takes."

"Maybe not, but you were doing a good job for medicine ferrying *varos* to Earth."

"Nothing personal, Art, but any slob could do that. I imagined it was a man's job: braving the perils of space to get the *varos* through. Ta-ra-ra! Hell, there weren't any perils. There's more danger on the freeways. It was like serving a term in some kind of windowless prison cell. You're surrounded by a billion stars but you can't see even one of them. I couldn't take the tedium or the claustrophobia. Now I don't have to. I don't have to make any decisions. That's a relief, man, that's my compensation. I've got me an alibi. I'm a cripple. Now no one can expect me to become someone."

He laughed, but I could see the despair behind it. Idealists have a tough time. The superego nags them to death if they fall short of their ideals. That's the way they're made and you can't change them.

Yes, it was quite a talk. But it didn't solve anything.

I knew Tigot was due in New York as a guest of the Irregulars. Soon, I looked him up. He was being banquetted like royalty and his girth was ridiculous. His eyes were just slits between folds of fat and gleamed with good humor.

I described Ernie's predicament and Tigot considered it. He'd often been Ernie's butt but never resented it. He knew youth was a rebellious phase and was tolerant of it.

"You can tell a boy's aspirations by his heroes," he observed, presently.

"Ernie's were Pasteur, Lister, Fleming, Ehrlich . . . oh, almost every pioneer in medical research."

Tigot nodded. "Also Irving, Kean, Booth, Olivier, the Barrymores . . . almost every great actor. Perceive any pattern in that duality?"

"Pattern?"

"Psychological pattern."

I rubbed my chin. "Are you hinting at schizophrenia?"

"Don't sound condemnatory, Arthur. All art is a form of controlled schizophrenia."

"But Ernie's no artist."

"How do you know? He's still fumbling for self-expression. My guess is he can't get onto his true path because it's barred—by a chunky mental/emotional block. But he knows where his goal lies. It lies in the center of a pool."

"Pool?" I was becoming just an echo.

"A pool of bright, ego-warming limelight. The Mecca of every actor."

"Act—" I strangled the echo. "You think Ernie's just hunting glory? His motive's simple attention-getting, like a child's?"

"The need for signficance is a basic one for both Terrestrials and Asps. If you fail to win it by achievement, you tend to assume it in imagination. As we Asps do continually. As an actor assumes a role. Ernie admits he lacks the analytical mind of a top research man. So he would like to dream he was one. But he admires men of action and despises dreamers. So he begins to despise himself. The conflict is painful. To ease it, he needs an excuse for his inaction. Naturally, he wouldn't consciously infect himself with polio. But sub-consciously a man can lower his guard against disease."

"Be that as it may, Tigot, the tests have shown his case to be incurable. Nothing can be done now."

"I disagree. Something can be done. Ernie should be made to see that he's choking his own special talent by despising it. That young man is a natural actor."

More thoughtful chin massage for me. "Tigot, you could be right. But how many parts are there for a semi-paralyzed . . . Oh, I get you: the Teo."

"I was talking to a producer only yesterday, Arthur. "There're plenty of actors who can walk and talk convincingly—on the surface. But the spools go *below* the surface. The calculated, puppet-type acting just doesn't get across—the strings show. Only the Stanislavsky approach works with the Teo. Don't just pretend you're a character: *be* that character. Wholeheartedly, sincerely. There's a shortage of actors who can do that. Ernie could do it, because Ernie was meant to do it."

"I'd have a tough time convincing him of it, I'm afraid."

"Yes, you would. You said it yourself. You're afraid—afraid you might be wrong. You can't convince anyone of anything unless you're convinced yourself. Well, I'm convinced. And I'll convince Ernie, too."

Tigot did just that. How, I don't know, for I wasn't there. I was at a marine station in the South Pacific where conditioned dolphins were responding to the sight of simple words. One day, I told myself, I'll be in business with the dolphins—with Teo spools.

When I made New York again, I was still behind schedule. Only a day remained before blast-off. I spent it trying to contact Ernie, and failed. Teo Spools Inc. were his bosses now. They were tough. They kept him incommunicado at the studio where he was working all hours to complete his first feature. It was a pilot effort they wanted to ship to Aspar right away—on my ship.

It meant recording far into the night. I hoped Ernie was standing up to the strain.

Tigot made the return passage with me. He was free as air, but I was, as usual, madly busy the first day out, setting and checking the course. I recalled Ernie's quip about this chore: "Simple enough. Second to the right, and straight on till morning." Those were Peter Pan's directions for reaching the Neverland—and Ernie derisively called Aspar the Neverland.

Yes, I'd miss him this trip.

Well, I did and I didn't. For he was there with us—on a spool. Tigot ran it through thrice that first day, and told me: "Arthur, we're justified. Ernest Deacon will become a name, all right. He's great. You'll enjoy the experience."

One "experiences" spools. When I got around to experiencing Ernie's, I agreed with Tigot's verdict. "The Healer" was written by Ernie himself, with some help from a pro-spool author. It was the story of a man who, by chance, discovered he was a faith healer. At first, by the touch of his hands. Later, merely to touch his robe was enough. Ironically, he was a paraplegic who could cure other paraplegics but not—somehow—himself.

He became besieged by multitudes. They devoured his life. His wife scarcely ever saw him. Finally, she delivered an ultimatum. He must ration the attention he gave the sick, and give more to her. Else she would leave him.

This tore him apart. He loved and needed her. Yet he couldn't bring himself to turn away the sufferers and prolong their pain even for a day.

Basically, the old "love versus duty" plot. But Ernie's performance lifted it out of the rut and gave it blazing life. As the spool spun, it was *you* who was being torn asunder. *You* who saw the pain leave a woman's eyes, and relief, then devotion, fill them because you touched her. *You* who saw devotion leave another woman's eyes and pain fill them, because you had no time to touch her: she was your wife and she was not ill.

Later, she *would* become ill, from losing you. And then pride would forbid her coming to you to be cured, because you had already rejected her.

And then, in the end . . . But everyone knows that story, literally by heart: for it comes from the heart to the heart.

Corn? Maybe. But when you're experiencing it, the critical sense is drugged. You become hypnotized.

I told Tigot: "This is going to hit Terrestrials right where they live—I don't know about your folk. It'll sell the series on sight, and be the making of Ernie. Though I don't see how he can ever better this performance."

Tigot said: "My people will love it, too. I agree it's a hard one to follow up. When I last saw Ernie, he was planning to play his heroes—Pasteur and the rest—in the next batch. Well, he's a born actor. Maybe he'll get away with it. But the Healer is Ernie dramatizing himself, not thinking himself into another man's skin. He's projecting a cherished private fantasy from deep inside. He gives it all he's got. The big question now is: does he have enough left to give to the other roles?"

The big question was never answered. Ernie died suddenly a few days after completing "The Healer."

The radio waves bearing this news took eighty days to overhaul my ship, which was traveling almost as fast as they were. I was shocked by the stupidity of it as much as anything. Just as he'd found his true metier, Ernie's youth, talent, and ambition had been trampled into the ground.

This news would reach Aspar well ahead of me, of course. When I got there, the Asps would already know that Ernie's series could never materialize, that the pilot spool joined onto nothing. They might well refuse it, and another kilo of *varos* would be lost.

Tigot said not to worry: "The Healer" was a unique gem, and he would bang the big drum for it.

But, happily, he had no need to. The radio waves trickling past us were heavy with praise of it. As I'd predicted, it was a smash hit on Earth, arid was pre-sold when we reached Aspar. The Asps were standing in line to bid for reproduction rights. I got seven kilos for it. Ernie would have been pleased.

When I set foot on Earth again a dozen years—Terrestrial standard—later, the Ernie Deacon legend was deep-rooted. Already fact and fantasy were inseparable. It was believed that Ernie's story contained a high percentage of autobiography. (All authors find this a common assumption by laymen.) That he'd certainly possessed some healing power himself. When I queried this with his sister, she said the only possible basis for it could be the fact that sometimes he'd eased her headaches by massaging the back of her neck.

But the character of The Healer went on metamorphosizing into reality as though some law of nature.

The chalet near the studio where Ernie had lived during the making of the spool became a kind of temple. Here were kept his holy relics: his wheelchair, his rack of pipes, and—most potent— the robe he'd worn on the set. Touch the robe, believing, and you would be healed—or, at the least, lifted onto the road to recovery.

It became a rival to Lourdes. Be as skeptical as you like, but if you were honest with it as you judged the recorded cases you had to admit that inexplicable—even medically impossible—cures had happened there.

So they began to happen in that little chalet.

Yet Ernie Deacon was no saint. Just a likable, ordinary guy, who'd gotten a bit mixed up and ended as an actor. No—not "ended." That was the beginning. He ended as a legend.

I watched the legend grow like a magic beanstalk over the decades as I batted to and fro. It was a seed watered by hope, nourished by belief, until it bore the fruits of fact. The facts were indisputable. Pilgrims *were* cured. Even radiation sickness, in its early stages, was often completely checked. I could see Ernie throwing me out of a job yet . . .

The Healer was an archetype even to the Asps, who were almost disease-free. Their rare serious illnesses were usually the consequence of overweight and lack of exercise.

All the same, I was surprised at the increasing numbers pilgrimaging to Ernie's little house. Usually it takes more than just a hope to persuade an Asp to walk a block, let alone travel several light-years.

My really big surprise came the day Tigot boarded my ship again. He confided he had fatty degeneration of the heart and had decided to join the pilgrims. Talking with him, I found he had more than just a hope. He had faith.

And this struck me as ridiculous. I didn't tell him so, though. You can't attempt to destroy a sick man's faith in his eventual cure.

But—Tigot, of all people! He who knew better than anyone what made Ernie tick. Who talked him into becoming an actor. Who knew "The Healer" was pure fiction.

How could such an intelligent person so deceive himself?

But then I realized that time had been at work on Tigot's memories of Ernie far longer than on mine. About eight times as long. And time gradually but constantly refashions events in the minds of Asps and Terrestrials alike.

I recalled the case of Dillinger, the gangster, in the 1920s. The legend, started by a newspaper reporter, was that he'd made his famous jailbreak bluffing with a wooden gun. In fact, it had been a real gun, smuggled in. But the legend was more colorful and so it overcame the truth. In the end, Dillinger himself believed the legend, although he was the man who'd actually handled the gun.

Again, there were the sourdoughs of the Yukon Gold Rush of 1898 who believed in their declining years that they'd witnessed the actual shooting of Dan McGrew. No use telling them that Dan

McGrew never existed, except in the mind of poet Service, who'd never even set foot in the Yukon when he wrote that saga.

Time had worked on their memories.

I suspect this kind of transmutation can happen to all of us who knew the real truth. Or thought we knew.

I hope so. For when I brought Tigot to Earth that second time it was my last voyage. Soon afterwards, I was compulsorily retired as medically unfit. Arthritis. Painful and disabling.

Yet I'm still comparatively young. And I hate living at this slow-motion pace. It isn't really living to me. I feel like a genie corked in a bottle. I yearn for the old, free, swinging strides through history.

There remains one ray of hope that I might yet be healed and return to the wide ranges of space-time. And that is the legend of Ernie Deacon. I'm not ready to accept it completely yet but I'm aware of the steady pressure of its persuasiveness.

Give it time.

BRIEF ENCOUNTER

THE CITY WORE ITS SILENCE LIKE A ROBE. And silence became it: it gave it a dignity it had largely lacked in life. The skeletons were decorous too. They didn't, sprawl or lapse into mere heaps of bones. They reclined serenely, as though each body had been laid out religiously and the last rites given. Segmitis was an easy death and began with a doze.

The rats had done their job cleanly and without haste: there was plenty of food for all and no one to disturb them. There was nothing to fight for or to run from. They fed quietly reflected awhile, dozed, and died. And were eaten in their turn.

Patricia remembered the city as once it was: when thousands of pedestrians clashed on the sidewalks like opposing armies and in the streets the cars jockeyed for position like racing chariots. Penning them in these overcrowded ways were walls of plate-glass. Behind the glass, magically withheld by the invisible laws of economics and sociology, were the prizes they were hurrying for: the shiny big cars the mink coats, the console TV sets . . .

She first saw the city on such a day when she was sixteen.

She was fat and homely even in those days, and aware of her lack of attraction for boys. She was also aware of her lack of money. She frowned through the transparent barrier, resenting its presence. She regarded the minks, the sable stoles, the flimsy primrose evening dresses, the tiaras and necklaces that scorned the label "Genuine" because everyone knew that behind those particular windows they *were.*

And she vowed: "One day I shall walk into these shops and have anything I like."

She meant that. Fat she might be, but not flabby: her mind was as tough as gristle. It might take time, it would take ruthlessness, but she would get what she wanted in the end.

And now, any and every day, she could walk into those shops and have anything she liked. The invisible laws were broken. Civilization couldn't stop her: there was no civilization.

Civilization had been over-cautious. It had refused to use the hydrogen bomb because it wanted in some form to survive the war. Instead, it experimented carefully with bacteriological warfare. The virus of segmitis was nothing like so careful. It went bustling rudely about the world in and out of the fleshy sanctums, indifferent to stations, nationalities, ideologies, souls, or even antibodies.

But a chosen few of the violated were equally indifferent to it. Patricia was one of them. It had made her feel sleepy for a while, and that was all.

She knew she wasn't alone in the world, nor even in Britain. But there weren't many people left. So far she'd seen only two, both women: one at Southampton, one at Salisbury. They were very old and she didn't worry about them.

She hadn't seen a man but she believed there must be one somewhere. There had to be. In all the stories she'd read about the end of the world by decimation, there was always the Adam and Eve gimmick. There was often only one sample of each, but never less.

What had happened recently had kept faithfully to the conventional grooves of those stories. Therefore it followed almost axiomatically that somewhere there survived a man for her, a man whom the Lonely Hearts Club had never succeeded in providing for her, a man in no position to discriminate about his mate. But to get him she might have to fall back on smoke signals, it seemed.

Either her instinct or her memories had guided her to make the long trek from the West Country to London. There had been eight million people in London. Surely there were some left?

But she'd now been here for two months without seeing a soul. She had established herself in a flamboyantly luxurious apartment overlooking an area once claimed by the citizens (as Times Square and the Place de la Opera had also been claimed) as the centre of the world. Maybe the proximity of Eros had subconsciously influenced her, but the choice also had logic behind it. Anyone exploring London would inevitably visit the Circus, if only for the sake of sentiment.

After a time she became tired of looking out of the window and finding, day after day, that the only other inhabitant of the Circus was the God of Love. He was a nice-looking boy but one could scarcely expect much response from a well-shaped chunk of aluminum. However, she'd make him carry a torch for her, in a sense. With some difficulty she managed to hang a poster from his free arm. It said:

I AM LIVING IN LONDON, NOT FAR
FROM HERE. PLEASE CONTACT ME BY
FIRING THE GUN IN THE CASE BELOW.
P. STANLEY.

The gun which she left in its case on the steps had come from a famous sports store in Piccadilly. The cartridges she'd put in with it were blanks. She had a considerably better gun in her apartment, together with cartridges that were not blanks.

She had hesitated over the "P. Stanley" but finally decided to be non-committal. One secret of being the master of any situation was not to lay all one's cards on the table, and she intended always to be the master—even if the man turned out to be the film star of her dreams.

Again, the first reader of the notice might be another woman. Patricia didn't object too strongly to a man hunting her, knowing that she was a woman. But she didn't want a woman on her trail knowing that she was a woman. She allowed that there might be saints, but she never visualized any of them as female. Men might be brutal or they might be kind. But women . . . she was a woman and therefore she knew what they were like: predatory, intolerant, jealous, ruthless.

Mainly because of that, she carried a small but lethal automatic in her handbag.

The days passed slowly in the silent city. Patricia inspected the poster and the gun daily and neither appeared to have been touched.

Spring came, a time of sun and showers and something in the blood. Patricia became restless.

Was she really alone in the city? Should she not forage further afield?

One warm bright day she stood on the top floor of London University staring at the fresh green woods on the distant hills of Hampstead. Daffodils were growing wild up there and no doubt afresh cool breeze was stirring the leafy branches. Down here in the city nothing stirred except her blood. And that seemed to be racing. She was alive, more alive than she ever remembered being before.

She looked at the far woods again. She recalled Sunday evening walks up there, herself always alone, while all about her young lovers sauntered hand in hand between the trees.

She gave a great sigh of bitter longing.

The woods called, but she was afraid to answer that call. The Circus remained the best bet—surely? Perhaps the very day she turned her back on it a man would come—and go. Even at this moment he might be approaching, coming from the south over Westminster Bridge . . .

She turned from the window and went down the stairs.

Back in the Circus Eros remained poised untiringly upon the ball of one foot. His stringless bow and invisible arrows of love were a mockery. So was the poster he bore: she felt like yanking the stupid thing down.

To calm herself she dressed in her best summer frock, gaily flowered, made up her face and took out with her a pale lemon parasol to keep the early afternoon sun from dazzling her eyes. She carried her handbag slung from her shoulder.

She walked below the turrets and cupolas of Whitehall to the Victoria Embankment, and along beside the river. The air was fresher here, and the sight of the quietly flowing water soothed her. She recalled, from school, the Tennysonian jingle:

"Men may come, and men may go, But I go on for ever."

It ran through her head, over and over, and became wishfully abbreviated: "Men may come, men may come, men may come . . ."

Presently, she found herself on Westminster Bridge, waiting. Someone was coming. She sensed it. The man from the south? She leaned on the parapet looking steadily along the bridge between the blocks of the County Hall and the big hospital. And as she waited the serenity of the afternoon settled on her. The sun was benignly warm, the brown river ran gently. On such a spring day as this there must be other life about besides her own. Strong male life too.

"Waitin' for someone?" asked a voice behind her.

The shock of hearing another voice, suddenly, was great. With it came a wave of disappointment. It was a female voice and coarse at that.

Patricia composed herself and turned.

The girl surveying her was perhaps twenty. She had a fine tan and was showing plenty of it. She was wearing merely one piece of a two-piece swim-suit, and sandals. It seemed that she was accustomed to going around that way for her breasts were as brown as her legs. Her eyes were pale blue and showed well against the bronze. Her hair was Celtic black and reached to her slim waist. She wore no make-up, but her lips were very red.

The two looked each other over from top to toe and back, in the calculating way peculiar to women. Patricia sought a flaw in the other, and apart from the unmusical voice, could not find one.

What the young girl found became evident. She smiled sneeringly, crushingly—and in the act gave back to Patricia her self-possession. For the smile was ugly, and the tan apparently extended to the teeth, which, additionally, were spotted with caries.

Patricia said nothing, which slightly disconcerted the other.

"Dressed to kill, ain't yer?" ventured the girl, presently. "Ain't much use, is it, when anybody can 'elp themselves to the best clothes goin'? Lord, I've thrown away better rags than you've got on."

"It so happens that I didn't dress to impress you," said Patricia, levelly.

"Who did you want to impress, then—men? You got some funny ideas about men, lovey. They're not interested in 'ow women dress; only 'ow they undress. But maybe you knew that all the time. Maybe that's really why you're all dressed up."

"And presumably why you're undressed."

"Of course. A girl's got to make the most of 'erself."

"Then you'd better go and see a dentist."

The girl flushed.

"Now, see 'ere, Fatty—"

"Oh, shut up!" snapped Patricia. "What the hell difference does it make whether we dress or undress or jump in the river? There aren't any men left."

The girl looked at her narrowly. "Who says not?" she said, quietly.

Patricia caught per breath. "You—You mean you've seen one?"

"More than *seen* one," hinted the girl, her, unpleasant smile returning.

"Where?"

"Wouldn't you like to know!"

Patricia closed her parasol deliberately and leaned it against the parapet. She clicked open her handbag, dug in it, and suddenly the little pistol flashed in the sun. She held it a foot from the girl's bosom, which began to display signs of agitation.

"Where did you meet this man?" Patricia persisted.

"Put that thing away, madam—miss—please. You wouldn't—"

"I would. Don't run, or I'll shoot you in the back. Answer me."

"Up on 'Ampstead 'Eath. 'E's not very bright, really. Nice-looking chap, mind you, and young too, but kinda dopey. Always spoutin' poetry. Not my kind. Put that gun away, lady, go on."

"What are you doing in my area?"

"Your area? You don't own all London, y'know. I gatta right to 'unt 'ere, same as you. What d'you call your area?"

"Anywhere within five miles of Piccadilly Circus."

"Picc—Did you 'ang up that notice at the Circus?"

"You read it?"

"No, I can't read. But I thought it looked funny. You live near the Circus?"

"Never mind," said Patricia, and then, as the girl began to giggle, "What's funny?"

The girl stopped giggling. "Nothing."

Patricia searched her face. "You're hiding something. What's amusing you? Tell me, or by heaven—"

The girl blurted: "It's only that a man lives right near the Circus. I seen 'im. A big tall man. Looks a proper gent."

"What? What?" Stammered Patricia.

"I seen 'im twice. Both times I called out to 'im, and 'e ran away. The first time I lost 'im down an alley. The second time I chased 'im across the Green Park. He runs like a bloomin' champion. Left me standin'. Ain't you ever seen 'im?"

Patricia didn't answer. She was thinking.

The girl looked around her uneasily, as if seeking an excuse to go. The tall tower of the Houses of Parliament stood silently over streets as empty as the eyeholes of the skeletons, and the hands of Big Ben were clasped together to register that it was five past one. Big Ben had been claiming that it was five past one for almost a year now.

"Look," said the girl, suddenly. "You can 'ave my feller up at 'Ampstead. 'E won't run away. 'E'll be glad to see you. You leave me this pigeon in Piccadilly. I'll catch up with 'im one day."

"I'm afraid you won't," said Patricia. "I'm sorry, but I can't risk having any rivals around."

She raised the gun a trifle and pulled the trigger. The girl whose name she did not know fell backwards under the impact of the bullet, her arms flung wide. Her young body lay draped over the grey old parapet like a virgin laid on a sacrificial altar stone. Her breasts pointed to the bright blue sky of spring and her long jet hair hung down towards the scummy water. Patricia replaced her gun, seized both the slim ankles and heaved. There was a dirty white splash near the foot of one of the piers, and then the brown river had absorbed the brown body.

Patricia picked up her parasol, hesitated, then tossed it over the parapet too. She was impatient to get to the Circus and set off in quick strides.

When she got there she noticed at once that the gun-case on the steps had been moved a couple of yards from where she'd left it. But probably the girl had done that. Nevertheless, Patricia opened it. There was a note on fine vellum, paper stuffed into the trigger-guard of the gun. It was terse almost to the point of discourtesy.

"I'm not far from here, too. Tell me more about yourself.
F. Harrison."

It was he! Or was it? J for John—or Jean, or James, or Josephine . . .? She was annoyed with the writer for playing her own game.

She examined the gun. It hadn't been fired. That annoyed her too.

After a moment of reflection she scribbled across the note "PTO," and on the back she wrote: *"Let's meet here. Fire the gun and wait.—Pat."*

Then she went up to her apartment and settled herself comfortably at the window with a pair of field-glasses at one elbow and a box of chocolates at the other.

The afternoon was very long. No one came. The sun sank and slowly the shadows filled the unlit Circus, submerging Eros. Then it was night. Patricia dozed off, still by the window.

Late in the night she was dreaming. It was a pleasant dream. She was walking along Oxford Street and all the shop windows were ablaze with strip lighting, and from behind her, from all the shop doorways, came soft wolf whistles. One of her admirers began to follow her, a long way behind, whistling melodiously. It was a sad little tune. Gradually she awakened to it.

She was in her room and the plaintive whistling was dying away somewhere down there in the quiet streets.

She fought herself properly awake and peered hard through the window. There was nothing to see but darkness. She found a torch and stumbled down the stairs and out into the cool air of the Circus.

Six streets converged on the Circus. Which of them had the whistler taken? She looked a little way down each of them in turn, waving her torch, but saw no other light nor heard any further sound.

Then she looked in the gun-case. There was a fresh sheet of vellum notepaper there. Written on it was: *"Dear Pat, I'll meet you here tomorrow at sunset. No, I reuse to fire the gun—I abominate noise. Jeffrey."*

It *was* a man! Her heart started to pound. She returned to her apartment in a happy daze, made herself some tea on the oil stove, lit a cigarette and settled down to wait for the dawn. She was too excited to sleep further, and the fire within her could not be damped down until sunset.

She chain-smoked through the rest of the night, trying to visualize what sort of man Jeffrey was. The girl had said he was big and tall and a gentleman. Presumably he was moderately young and physically fit, for he'd outrun the girl. But why had he run from her? Patricia told herself that it was because he was sensitive to vulgarity—his last note indicated that—and although the girl had been pretty, her utter lack of good taste and modesty was obvious at a glance.

Occasionally Patricia found herself humming that sad little tune of his, which she'd now identified: Tchaikovsky's *Chanson Triste*. Jeffrey, it seemed, was a music-lover.

In the pale dawn she dressed very carefully in quiet colours, modestly, tastefully, and was at pains to get her stocking seams straight.

Then she set off hunting, quartering the immediate neighbourhood. She could write off most buildings after a brief examination of their halls, where the dust-coated floors showed no signs of footprints. But some were doubtful and she wasted much time plodding around in them, opening doors and climbing stairs.

By noon she was hot, dusty, rather tired and irritable. She came out into Piccadilly, wondering which way to turn.

Then she heard it—distant music. An orchestra or rather, a recording of one. Her tiredness and irritation vanished. Her heart melted at the music. It was Tchaikovsky's *Romeo and Juliet* Overture, and it was building up towards the introduction of the love theme. There could have been no more appropriate music for her. Jeffrey must be feeling as she felt.

She traced the strains to the Albany, that ancient and exclusive private way, a nest of luxurious and strictly bachelor apartments. She pushed at the gate and it opened. She wandered along the narrow way. The music was much louder and the Montagues and Capulets were clashing with a great ringing of swords.

She found the right stairway, and paused at the bottom of it to mop and then powder her face. She was trembling, and her finicking amounted to small improvement. As she smoothed her dress down, the music stopped suddenly in the middle of the battle. Presumably the noise had become a little overpowering for Jeffrey.

She braced herself, and went, upstairs. There were three doors. She heard a slight movement behind one, and pushed it gently open.

A tall, broad man in a silk dressing-gown was in the act of putting another record on the old-fashioned acoustic gramophone. He looked up, raising his eyebrows. She saw at once that he was strikingly handsome. His eyes were big and dark, his nose thin and aristocratic, his lips rather full but quite firm. His black hair was brushed immaculately. His short sideboards were cleanly shaven and just beginning to grey. She put his age at thirty-five.

And then his brows came down in a frown. There was antipathy in his aspect.

"Who are you, and what are you doing here?" His voice was cultivated, almost exquisitely so.

"I'm—I'm Pat."

The antipathy changed to utter disappointment and frustration. His eyes held pain. He sighed.

"Pat? I thought you were a—"

"Yes?"

"Never mind. I'm sorry, Pat, I shan't be along at sunset after all."

Patricia gave a little hurt cry. "Am I really so repulsive? I'm not very old really, and I'm sure I could slim—"

"It isn't that. I just want to be left alone. You're probably quite a sweet wom—girl. But I'm a natural recluse. I prefer to live in solitude here. My books and records and paintings and memories are sufficient solace."

"Solace for what? Was there another woman?"

"No, Pat. You wouldn't understand."

"Oh," Patricia turned away. Her eyes were moist with her own disappointment. "You *are* Jeffrey?" she muttered, clutching at the flimsiest of straws.

"I'm afraid so."

Patricia wandered around the room picking up this and that aimlessly, trying to pull herself together. She looked dully along the bookshelves, seeing familiar titles: *Leaves of Grass, Moby Dick, the Picture of Dorian Grey, Apostate, Bevis, A la Recherche du Temps Perdu . . .*

She looked at the fine glassware, the etchings, the oil-paintings which seemed to be mostly of young men, the sculptures and the thick rugs, and realised that elegance of a kind alien to her unified the room.

Jeffrey watched her with growing impatience.

"Tut-tut." He reached out and adjusted the position of the statuette copy of Michelangelo's "David," which she had replaced all of an inch from where it had stood.

Often before she had been made to feel that she wasn't wanted, but never so forcibly and unmistakably as now.

"I'll be going, then," she said, listlessly.

"Goodbye—and good luck," he said, quickly and relievedly.

She closed the door behind her. Halfway down the stairs she broke down into tears. As she sobbed, the gramophone started again. This time it was a heart-breaking wail of despair and loneliness, again fitting her mood. It was the last movement of Tchaikovsky's last symphony. Jeffrey seemed to have a strong penchant for the melancholy Russian. Even in her grief, part of her mind wondered why.

And then a suspicion sprang to life and spread like a fast-growing evil weed. She might be quite wrong, she told herself. But the weed gathered strength from small selected evidences and grew all over her mind, darkening it, strangling reservations for the side of innocence, killing merciful judgment.

She dried her eyes, set her lips in a prim line, and marched back up the stairs. She flung open the door. Jeffrey was sitting dejectedly in the chair by the gramophone. He raised a startled, tear-stained face. The tears did not touch her heart: they were not for her, and so they only strengthened her purpose.

She shot him twice as he sat there, and then made quite sure that he was dead.

The heart-cry of the *Pathetique* suddenly changed into a silly scratching noise. She lifted the tone-arm from the record and slammed the lid shut. Then she slammed the door behind her just as noisily. But all the noise in the world could not disturb him now.

Back in her own apartment she packed essentials for her move to Hampstead.

In the early afternoon she set out, carrying them.

As she reached Eros, she paused and looked up at him. He seemed almost like an old friend now, so she told him confidentially: "I had to do it, you know. I never had much on the ball at any time and I'm past my best now. A girl's got to watch out for herself. Especially me. I just can't afford to risk having any rivals around."

Then she went on past him, beginning the long walk to the promise in the north.

THE SMILE OF THE SPHINX

The Sphinx

I gaze across the Nile; flamelike and red
The sun goes down, and all the western sky
Is drowned in sombre crimson; wearily
A great bird flaps along with wings of lead,
Black on the rose-red river. Over my head
The sky is hard green bronze, beneath me lie
The sleeping ships; there is no sound, or sigh
Of the wind's breath,—a stillness of the dead.
Over a palm tree's top I see the peaks
Of the tall pyramids; and though my eyes
Are barred from it, I know that on the sand
Crouches a thing of stone that in some wise
Broods on my heart; and from the darkening land
Creeps Fear and to my soul in whispers speaks.
—Lord Alfred Douglas.

I

IT WAS PAST MIDNIGHT when I went tearing along the Dover Road in my two-seater, at fifty miles an hour, to meet the strangest adventure of my life on the summit of Shooter's Hill. But that lay twenty minutes ahead in the future, and I was as unsuspecting of it as a traveler in the Dover Coach, a century and a half ago, was unaware of the highwayman lying in ambush somewhere on this same road.

Personally, I had no business to be on that road that night, for it is hardly the direct route to Salisbury. I was returning from an East Coast holiday, and had gone a good deal out of my way to cover Shooter's Hill. But I had been reading *A Tale of Two Cities* on my vacation, and the opening scene was so vivid in my memory that my confounded romanticism—I write historical novels for a living—had to be satisfied.

The road, no longer mire, but hard and darkly shining under the eerie blue mercury-vapor lamps (I wondered: what would Dickens have thought of those lamps?), led me up past the massive water-tower that looks like a tall Norman castle, up to the very summit of the hill. I braked then, and pulled the car into the curb a few yards down.

An hour's driving had brought on stiffness, and here was the time and place to stretch my legs. There was not a soul in sight, and the road ran emptily away into a string of blue lights, towards the horizon and London. I extricated myself, and lit a cigarette, meditatively eyeing the dark woods that fringed this side of the road.

Although the moon was high in a cloudless sky, the woods looked too thick and gloomy for a pleasant stroll. So I sauntered across the road, and came to the head of a narrow lane that sloped down towards Woolwich. Constitution Hill it was called.

There was an old mansion on the right; the windows behind its portico were shattered. Farther down was a railed-in, grassy space, containing a few trees. It had once been part of the mansion's grounds, and was now the only part not built upon. The rest of the grounds was covered with a vast housing estate that stretched all down the hill. I stood on a corner and surveyed the view.

Two miles away, and below, an arm of the Thames lay across the middle distance like a strip of dull metal. Street lamps pricked the darkness in Woolwich, but the familiar neon signs were out— the cinemas and public-houses had long shut their doors for the night. The low buildings of the great Arsenal, which ran for miles along the river bank, were indistinguishable from the rest of the shadowy blur of Woolwich. Across the river, an immense derrick showed its head above the dockyards and the grey vagueness of Essex, and from this distance it looked like a very small toy.

Of all the houses of the estate before me, I could not see one with a lighted window. All the town was asleep and dreaming, and I stood there on the corner like the last living inhabitant of this world. It occurred to me how awful a fate that would be, were it true—the loneliness, the intimidating silence, the absence of any response or hope of it. And then, to spoil the illusion, came a distant shout from somewhere down the hill.

I looked down the steep road, but could see nobody. The faint shout came again. "Woe!" it sounded like. "Woe!"

I looked more narrowly, and then it seemed that the inky shadow of one of the houses down there had detached itself, and was advancing up the moonlit street towards me. Yes, it was moving! A strange black shadow on the ground, steadily approaching . . .

It gave me something of a qualm. I turned to retreat to my car, then hesitated out of sheer curiosity. On sudden impulse, I clambered up the base of the nearest lamp-standard, and waited, hanging there uneasily. Now I could discern some little human figures far down the hill, behind the long, black shadow. They were shouting and laughing. I felt relieved. It could not be so bad.

The dark mass on the ground approached swiftly and silently, and resolved itself into a herd of little bodies. Green eyes began to glint amongst them. A plague of large rats? I leaned over, peering intently, as the leaders of the herd came into the light cast by the lamp above my head.

They were *cats!* Hundreds of them, of all shapes and sizes. Led by three big, black toms—one had white paws—they swept past me in a slinky, undulating wave, covering every inch of the road and footpath, parting to pass my lamp-standard, and joining again into a compact mass.

Tabbies there were, Siamese and tailless Manx, fat, bushy Persians and hosts of the common breed, some with kittens in their mouths. They ignored me completely, and casting never a glance aside, pressed forward with an apparently common and urgent purpose, up the hill, past the decrepit mansion, towards the Dover Road. Their small, padded feet made no sound on the tarmac, and not a kitten so much as mewed.

" 'S'truth!" I murmured, rather inelegantly for a literary man, while the feline multitude thronged past like a Chinese army. At last the rear came in sight, together with a dozen or so human beings, who had happened upon this strange phenomenon and were following it with eager curiosity.

There were some lively town lads amongst them, who kept trying to grab the tails of the last few cats—there were no actual stragglers—and pull them back. "Whoa!" they shouted boisterously. "Whoa!" But I noticed that the cats always eluded their clutches, and hastened on.

The end of the procession swept rapidly past, and had vanished over the brow of the hill before I had lowered myself from my perch. I almost trod on the toes of an old man in a slouch cap who had dropped out of the chase. He leaned against the standard, panting.

"In a 'ell of a 'urry, ain't they?" he gasped, jerking his thumb up the hill. "Cor'!"

"Yes," I said. "What's it all about?"

"Damdifino. All the ruddy cats in Woolwich seem to 'ave taken it into their 'eads to leave 'ome. My Lizzie's there—somewhere. Jumped aht the bedroom winder."

"Have you any idea as to where they're going?"

"To the woods, I bet. Yus; to the woods, o' course." He chuckled, and winked at me.

"Beats me," I said, shaking my head and turning away. "I think I'll go and see what's left of my car."

"Hi!"

I turned again. It was not the cockney but a uniformed constable, mounting the hill in lengthy strides. He came up to us. "Seen anything out of the ordinary along here?" he questioned abruptly.

"Not 'arf we ain't," chuckled the cockney. " 'Bout fifty fousand cats gorn up there, mate."

The constable looked sharply at me. I nodded. "He's right, strange as it sounds. They're probably all over in the woods by now."

"I was told something like that by a man down the road," said the policeman. "Well, I suppose I'll have to go and dig out whatever's at the bottom of it all." He walked quickly on.

"Promises to be interesting," I remarked. "I think—"

I stopped, as a tremendous flash of white light leapt into the sky over Woolwich. For a split second, the landscape for miles around stood out clearly, weirdly lit by a pale, quivering glare. And then the night plunged down again, darker than before.

For a moment, my confused mind struggled with this new phenomenon. Then a fierce, orange plume of flame suddenly spurted up from somewhere in the same direction, cleaving the night sky in twain. Silently it jumped and flickered over the Arsenal buildings, while thick, black smoke boiled up from its base, and a reflection of it danced redly in the waters of the Thames. It seemed tall from this distance: down there in Woolwich it must have looked a fearful height.

"Gor' blimey, the Arsenal's on fire!" croaked the cockney excitedly. And at that moment the noise of the first explosion reached us; a battering crash of sound that smashed half the windows in the estate, shook the ground so that I bit my tongue with the concussion, and knocked me deaf, sick, and dizzy.

I remember that I reeled about for a space, with my hands over my ears, in a state of blind confusion, and recovered to see that the flame over the Arsenal now had eight companions, twisted towers of fire spanning its entire length. Some high cloud-mist in the heavens glared in sympathy with the flames, and reflected them, so that the whole northern hemisphere was an awesome sight, like a tremendous bowl-fire glowing down on Earth. And reaching vertically up into the heart of it was a mighty column of dense black smoke, a pillar of hell.

The heavy rumble of explosions was continuous, and periodic, sharper detonations almost split our eardrums. They had been heaping up the shells down there, and now the fireworks had started in earnest. Electric-blue flashes played like lightning around the bases of the great flames, and the debris which they threw up rose in showers of black dots against the throbbing, furnace light.

Some of these flying fragments began to hum about us, and slash their way through the leafy branches of the few trees. I became aware that the constable had returned, and was standing beside the cockney; and both their faces were florid with the glare. Suddenly there was an almighty crash up the road: a hurtling mass of machinery had caught the water-tower squarely and piled it into rubble across the ancient highway.

The constable shouted something that I could not catch above the din. He pointed down the hill, and I saw a wall of smoke billowing up towards us. It came swiftly, and there was no escape. In a second it was over us, and we were in a dense, sulphurous fog that made us cough and choke and run at the eyes.

Our surroundings were now veiled in a murky obscurity, and even the eruption in Woolwich was but a diffused glow in the mist ahead. I think I would have made my way back to my car then, had it not been for the action of the constable. He obviously entertained no thought of retiring, but clasped his handkerchief over his mouth and nose, and set off through the smoke-wreaths down Constitution Hill. His duty lay in Woolwich, and he would get there somehow.

The cockney, stifling a paroxysm of coughing, jerked his thumb after the policeman and looked at me inquiringly. Feeling suddenly ashamed of my lack of spirit, I nodded vigorously, and caught his arm.

We started off through the whirling smoke-screen after the dim figure ahead, and came up with him in a clear patch of air. If it hadn't been for those occasional rifts in the smoke, we should have suffocated. The three of us gulped fresh air for a few moments, then plunged on again, until at last we descended into the stricken town.

II

THE NEXT ACT OF THIS STRANGE and swift drama came on the following evening. From where I reclined in a deck-chair beside my lonely cottage—it was three miles to the nearest dwelling—the tremendous expanse of Salisbury Plain rolled out to meet a red-gold sunset. The sky was a darkening blue above, and smeared in the east with salmon-pink cloud-wisps.

I lay and stared at the slowly changing shapes and colors of the clouds tumbled around the departing sun, and gently stroked the grey, furry body of my cat, Peter, who was curled up and dozing on my lap. He had spent the last fortnight in a home in Salisbury, and hadn't left my side since I picked him up on the way back from Woolwich.

I looked down at him, and noticed my hands again. Scratched and bruised they were, with skinned knuckles and torn fingernails, and now and then they trembled uncontrollably.

Visions of last night kept floating between me and the sunset, and I could not put them out of my mind. Things had happened so much in a rush that I'd had little time to ponder on them; but now, spoiling my attempt to rest, it was all coming back.

The streets of houses shattered and burning, looking far worse than many bombing raids I had seen, and the moans of the poor souls imprisoned in and under them. The frantic tearing with bare hands to extricate the tortured victims before the arrival of the eager, untamable flames, and the sickening horror of failure, when one rushed madly away from a scene too appalling to witness. The clanging fire-engines and ambulances, and, the tear-stained faces of lost children and bereaved mothers.

All this in a choking, dust-laden atmosphere, every particle of which jumped and quivered with the detonations of the unceasing barrage in the Arsenal, and seen only in the blood red light of flames. For the whole town had lain under the shadow of a pall of black smoke, which blotted out the sky like an immense raven's wing, so that none could tell when morning came. Ever and again, shapeless things of steel and concrete dropped like thunderbolts out of the jet heavens, and sometimes molten metal, and sometimes parts of once living creatures . . .

A faint breeze came rippling over the grass of the plain, and stirred the newspapers at my feet. They were late morning editions, black with headlines describing the scenes in Woolwich. There was a brief interview in one of them with myself—a few sentences I had jerked out to a reporter while bandaging the broken shoulder of a little boy:

"Mr. Eric Williams, the well-known novelist, who saw the whole thing from Shooter's Hill and immediately rushed down to help in the rescue work, mentions a queer sight which he witnessed just before the first explosion in the Arsenal. A procession of hundreds of cats . . ."

In the stop press columns were hints of perhaps even stranger news. Munition factories had been, and still were, blowing up all over the world. Springfield, Illinois, was a smoldering wreck. Ammunition dumps left over from the war were going off like jumping crackers all over Europe. There were rumors of such things happening in Russia—the Soviet government would release no definite information, but it seemed that there was consternation beyond the Urals.

The most significant item was one smudged sentence, stamped in crookedly and hastily at the foot of the column: "The U.S. atomic research center at Oak Ridge, Tennessee, has been almost totally destroyed by fire."

Sabotage, I reflected. But sabotage on such a large and indiscriminate scale that it must be the work of a tremendously powerful and marvelously organized international secret society of militant pacifists, seeking to save man from himself.

Deep in speculation, I raised my eyes from the paper and gazed again at the glorious painting of the sunset. And there, black against it, far out on the plain, was the little figure of someone cycling steadily in my direction. The person was approaching along a hardly discernible track over the grass, and presently I saw that it was a middle-aged man in a sports jacket.

He dismounted at the rough palings of my fence, regarded me for a moment, then called: "Excuse me, but does your name happen to be Williams—Mr. Eric Williams?" I nodded, and he said he wished to speak to me for a few minutes.

"Certainly, but it's no use trying to sell me anything," I replied, eyeing with suspicion a brown attaché case strapped to the carrier of his cycle.

"Oh, I'm not a salesman," he said, propping his cycle against the gatepost and advancing up the short path. "I would just—" He broke off as he noticed Peter on my lap. He had brown, very tired looking eyes, and there was an odd, irresolute expression in them at the moment. "I would just like some information," he went on, recovering, and seating himself rather gingerly on the lawn beside me.

"Go ahead," I said, curiously.

He removed his old hat, revealing a large, bald head, fringed with greying hair. He jerked a couple of newspapers from his pocket, and indicating one, said:

"This interview with you. About what you saw on Shooter's Hill . . ." He breathed deeply and paused.

"Yes?" I asked.

He rounded on me suddenly. His brown eyes were agonized. "For God's sake!" he blurted. "Please take that cat away! I—I can't bear them near me. I know it's silly; but, really, the sight of them upsets my nerves."

I arose quietly and carried Peter to the front door of the cottage, dropped him inside and shut the door. The stranger apologized incoherently as I sat down again.

"It's quite all right," I said. "I know several people who share your phobia. Why, the old Duke of Wellington, although he conquered Napoleon, was scared stiff of cats—wouldn't go into a room where there was one."

"Yes, subconsciously, he was aware of the incredible truth," muttered the stranger. "How fortunate for him he didn't realize it more fully."

I didn't get the drift of this, and he saw that I didn't, and went on in a more matter-of-fact tone, gaining confidence now that Peter had gone.

"I should introduce myself. My name is Clarke, and I live in Salisbury. I'm a retired schoolmaster. Lately, I have evolved an unusual theory, and those cats you saw leaving Woolwich last night form a real, corroborative link in my chain of evidence. So I should be glad if you would be good enough to describe the scene in a little more detail than this newspaper paragraph gives."

I obliged, to the best of my ability, describing the silent and purposeful way in which the cats had passed, and mentioning the leaders.

He pondered over this, and remarked: "Doesn't it seem odd to you that they should all leave the town just before the calamity struck it? And that they put the protecting bulwark of a high hill between Woolwich and themselves?"

"You mean that they somehow sensed what was going to happen?" I asked. "I admit that cats, like dogs, are sometimes credited with a sixth sense, but I can't imagine how they could possibly foresee something so—well, so unprecedented as that."

"I am going to say something rather startling, so please don't think I'm out of my wits," he said, slowly. "I say those animals knew the catastrophe in the Arsenal was coming, *because they planned it!*"

I gaped. Then, perceiving that I had a psychological case to deal with after all, passed it off with a mild remark: "Really, do you think so?"

He grasped my reaction immediately, and flushed.

"I see you do think I'm a crank. Perhaps you imagine my dislike of cats is some sort of warped hatred, finding expression in blaming every conceivable mishap onto them. Believe me, it is not so. I was very fond of cats—once."

With an unsteady hand, he picked up his other newspaper.

"Have you seen this evening edition? No? Listen to this bit about the Springfield disaster: 'Inhabitants of neighboring towns report that large numbers of cats have taken up residence there. They apparently fled from Springfield last night. The police stations are crowded with the mewing fugitives.' "

I took the paper from him, and read the item through carefully.

"It certainly is odd," I agreed. "Well, what is your theory?"

"This: that all cats are not so innocent as they appear. That they are an ancient and alien race, with intellects far greater than ours. That they are parasites of the human race, and move amongst us as unsuspected spies, hearing, seeing everything we do, yet never betraying themselves in any way. Believe me, they're the world's best actors! They know their role by heart—they've practiced it for thousands of years, and never yet made a slip."

"What could possibly be their motive?" I inquired.

"I do not think there is any evil intent: they are above evil. It just suits their convenience that we should make pets of them and keep their physical bodies alive for them, for their bodies really are only husks—they live their true lives in their minds. But these husks are necessary, for mind must have a living body to keep it supplied with energy.

"The idea of reincarnation actually works for them, too. When a cat's body dies, the mind that inhabited it transfers itself to some newly-born kitten."

"Whoever originated the saying about cats having nine lives must have felt the truth unconsciously," I murmured sarcastically.

"Yes," agreed Clarke. "This process has been going on for many ages. In fact, the race of minds existing in the bodies of cats today is almost identically the same that landed upon this planet thousands of years ago."

"Landed upon this planet?" I repeated weakly.

Clarke mopped his shining head again.

"Let me give you a brief history of these creatures," he said. "I don't expect you to believe it, but it's true. Firstly, the moon was inhabited much more recently than some astronomers think. It was shared by two races, the feline and the canine. They were incompatible from the start, and finally a terrific war broke out between them.

"Now, the feline mind could detach itself at will from any body—though it could not remain apart from that body long without its store of energy becoming exhausted—and these minds were practically indestructible, even if they happened to be inhabiting a body at the time it was destroyed. But there was an Achilles heel, and the canine race knew of it. One thing alone could harm a feline mind, and that was a violent explosion adjacent to it. By 'adjacent' I mean within a foot, or two at most, for the feline mind is a tenacious and almost unshakable structure. But a really concentrated effect of disruption slapped up against it will somehow upset the balance of forces which holds that incorporeal mind together. It disintegrates, and to all intents and purposes it is finished as an entity forever.

"So the canine race made their first attacks with immense bombs, shells, and land-mines in an effort to blast the cat intelligences out of existence. It was a hit-and-miss business, and it didn't fare very well. Only near-enough direct hits affected the cats, and even with the size of the explosives used these were few and practically negligible in number.

"And then the canines discovered the secret of the atomic bomb. This was a different proposition altogether. You didn't need direct hits with these. I believe the nature of the bomb, as distinct from the mere blast of the cruder explosives, had an added effect, too. Anyway, this meant death from a distance for the cats, and they were nearly wiped out. You can see yourself how thoroughly the canines pounded them—those great craters which pit and scar the face of the moon give some idea of the number and size of the bombs used.

"But the ruling mind of the cats, which was the most powerful intellect in this universe, produced a triumph, just in time. It was a long-distance ray which, when turned on the canine creatures, caused a corruption in their thyroid glands, so that they rapidly degenerated into a race of dullards.

"Thus the cat race triumphed, and ruled the moon. But the war had made such havoc of that world—almost all vegetation was destroyed by radioactivity—that food of any sort was scarce. They had to give more and more time to searching for nourishment as the moon grew more barren. This was not to their liking, for, as I've said, they live a life of the mind, and they resented having to waste time and energy in mere food-hunting.

"At last the resourceful ruling mind invented a form of space-ship, and in large numbers of these vessels the entire race migrated to Earth. Here they still are—and we are their unconscious servants . . ."

I have always believed that anything is possible, no matter how improbable, and so I did not immediately scoff at this seemingly wild theory. In fact, I was curious to hear more.

"What became of the mentally weakened canine race?" I asked.

"The larger part of it was left on the moon to perish of starvation. But the cat-people brought some specimens with them, and these flourished and multiplied enormously on this planet, and they still do."

"Do you mean—*dogs* are the descendants of that defeated race?" I asked incredulously.

"Yes. But they have never recovered their original mind-power; beside the cold and vast intellects of the cats, they are just amicable dolts. A remnant of their sixth sense—telepathy—remains, but it is not developed to anything like the intense degree that it has in cats today."

"Perhaps other old habits also linger in the muddled canine minds," I suggested, suddenly carried away on the wings of this fantasy. "For instance, the hitherto inexplicable enmity between dogs and cats. Dogs chase cats because they have a dim memory that they are old enemies. And I suppose cats allow themselves to be chased to keep up the appearance of innocence?"

"Yes; they're devilish subtle actors. Another old problem is explainable, too. Why do dogs bay the moon? Simply because the sight of it arouses a vague memory of their old home—they howl with homesickness, though they may not realize it."

Followed a short silence, in which I weighed up possibilities.

"About the cats blowing up all these munition works," I ventured. You think—?"

"I know why. It is obvious. As I have said, atomic bombs spell death to the feline minds. Now, very little of the explosives tossed about in the mud of France in the first world war came anywhere near cats, and they ignored that war. But towards the end of the second World War they were preparing to intervene.

"Too many of their number were being killed in the heavy air raids. I mean, their *minds* were being killed—not their bodies, because they don't care a damn about that: there are always plenty of fresh ones to move into. But once a mind is disintegrated by explosive, it is finished and not replaceable. Also, food supplies were being totally disorganized, and men—their servants—were everywhere leaving them to fend for themselves: a great distraction from the work they were giving their minds to. But, like the canines, man stumbled upon the atomic bomb, and that finished the war, which satisfied the cats in one way but disturbed them in another.

"Suppose these stupid servants of theirs started another war, but this time rocketing atomic bombs about? Then that would mean destruction for everyone, feline minds included.

"They bided their time to see whether man would have the plain common sense to see that war was a practice that had become mass lunacy, and that the only way to end war between nations was to end nations by uniting under one world government. Well, we don't, to our eternal shame, as you know.

"So they are effectively nipping the third world war in the bud, by destroying the tools necessary for it. Men look upon themselves as minds above animals. I'm afraid the truth is that the cats are the minds, and men are just animals."

"H'm." It was certainly an explanation of the strange thing I had seen on Shooter's Hill. But—

"Look here, this theory is taking a hell of a lot of things for granted," I objected. "It cannot be anything but supposition. You have no proof?"

He bit his lip, and began nervously to pluck blades of grass from the lawn.

"No," he admitted. "Nothing tangible, beyond the strange behavior of the cats which you yourself saw. But I tell you I *know* all I've said is true. I have an odd feeling of certainty. Call it intuition, call it faith—I just *know*, that's all."

"It's hard to accept such a theory just because one man feels that it's true!"

He flushed a little.

"I know; it's absurd. But haven't you ever had a flash of that insight yourself? I remember when I used to play darts . . . Sometimes, when I was aiming, I just knew that the dart in my hand was going to hit the bull's-eye, and it invariably did. I have that feeling of certainty now, about my story."

He shivered slightly again, and so did I, for a chill breeze swept in from the plain, and I looked up to find with a mild shock that it was nearly dark. The sun had long since gone, and bright Venus was glittering above the somber night rack.

Clarke scrambled to his feet, and apologized for keeping me so long. I said it had been intensely interesting, and would he drop in again sometime to resume our discussion? He promised he would.

I watched him cycling off into the western dusk, and folding my chair, I turned to take it indoors. And immediately I saw Peter, a shadowy outline against the darkening sky, squatting on the roof of the cottage. He gave me quite a qualm, with such weird thoughts still roaming my mind.

It was obvious how he had escaped. I had converted the one upstairs room of my cottage into an amateur observatory, enlarging the skylight all round to give the four-inch telescope latitude. When I shut Peter in, he had simply gone upstairs and out through this wide window onto the tiles. He had done that trick before.

I called to him, and he glanced idly down at me. His eyes were shining greenly in the dark.

"Jump, Peter-boy," I called, extending my arms. I had to repeat it several times before he arose, yawned hugely and stretched lazily, then condescendingly jumped from the gutter into my arms. He commenced to purr softly as I carried him indoors.

All the time I was preparing my supper, I kept shooting surreptitious glances at him as he crouched, half asleep, in the big armchair. What Clarke had said about subtle acting recurred to me. Was Peter really watching me? Peter, whom I had reared from a kitten, and who I flattered myself had some affection for me? Had he come out on that roof behind and above us to eavesdrop—literally?

I rolled him over on his back, and he stretched lazy paws up at me. "Brrr-ow," he said.

"It's no use, Peter, old man," I said deliberately, poking his tummy. "You needn't keep on acting. I can see through you all the time. You're a spy—that's what you are!"

He took not the slightest notice, but lay dreamily accepting my caresses. I gave it up, switched on my battery radio, and sat down to supper. With a mouth full of bread and cheese, I heard the late news coming through as the tubes warmed up.

". . . great damage and martial law has been declared in the city. The President has issued an appeal to the nation to remain calm. The Federal authorities have the matter well in hand, he said, and precautions now taken make it impossible for any further such outrages to occur. From Sweden, Denmark, and Northern Italy come reports of widespread fires in government-controlled laboratories of physical research. Nearer home, three ammunition dumps in the Welsh hills blew up simultaneously this morning . . ."

There was a good deal more of it, and a late flash that the rocket testing buildings at Peenemunde had been wiped out in a series of explosions apparently begun by a mishap in an experimental petrol and oxygen mixing chamber.

Although sabotage was suspected in many cases, so far no arrests had been made, because in each instance the eruptions had been so sudden and violent that no human beings in the vicinity had survived to be suspected. It was assumed that either the saboteurs were using time bombs or else they were suicidal fanatics.

For my own part, the fact that no evidence of human activity had been found in anyone of all those catastrophes was itself evidence that no human agency was at work here. But whether it was cats or . . . Oh, it was all too fantastic!

I switched the radio off, and decided I would refuse to think any more about the whole business this day.

I sought refuge in a book of short stories from my shelves. It was an admirably written collection by C.E. Montague, called *Action*. In its vivid pages I lost myself until, in a story called "Wodjabet," I happened upon a character who "only blinked the way a cat does, letting on that it's sleepy when really its eyes are aglow with some grand private excitement or other . . ."

Which caused me to peep from under my brows across at Peter again.

He was curled up, really asleep. Or was he?. . .

III

THE NEXT MORNING was bright and fresh, and as I pushed the lawnmower up and down in the sunshine I wondered how I could have been so foolish, on the previous evening, as to consider seriously, even for a moment, the quaint Mr. Clarke's cock-and-bull story. Thus does the normal round reassure us, and melt away the dark underside of our imagination.

Peter was dashing about the lawn like a mad kitten, chasing errant leaves and several times coming near to being churned up by my mower. I paused to watch him, just as a butterfly made its erratic flight into the garden and settled. Peter eyed it eagerly, and approached with stealth. A couple of yards away he stopped, nose down and rear up, quivering all over with the intensity of his purpose.

Suddenly he leapt, and missed the butterfly by an inch. It fluttered drunkenly away, and Peter bounded after it, clawing the air wildly and ineffectively. He wasn't looking where he was going, and smack he went against a water-butt.

I had to laugh. How absurd it was to suspect Peter! Peter, the good-natured—I'm sure that cat had a sense of humor—but Peter, the stupid, who could never learn the simplest of tricks. An amoeba would have beaten him in an intelligence test. All he had ever done was eat, sleep, and play.

I leaned on my mower and ruminated on Peter, who had settled down on a heap of cut grass. Why were cats ever born? What useless lives they led! How the devil did they pass the time, when they could do nothing constructive, physically or mentally? They never even had to hunt for their food, which is the chief occupation and reason for existence of the wild animals. Mostly they just sat about—brooding.

Were they really thinking in those long spells of passivity, or were they just bored stiff? I found myself considering, after all, the arguments that Clarke had raised . . .

And suddenly the man's voice broke into my thoughts: "Er—Good morning, Mr. Williams."

I turned, and beheld him standing rather awkwardly outside the gate, holding his bicycle.

"Ah, good morning," I said, with a heartiness that was not wholly genuine. "I was just thinking about you."

"Er—I was wondering," he began again, with a nervous eye on Peter, "wondering whether you would care to accompany me on a cycle ride this morning, over the plain? There are some new points I'd like to discuss with you. I noticed you had a cycle, and thought perhaps—"

"Yes, by all means," I said. "It's a lovely morning for it. Just come inside for a moment, will you, and have a drink while I clean up?"

He came hesitantly into the cottage parlor, making an arc to avoid Peter. It occurred to me that I never saw a man who looked less in need of a cycle ride and more in need of a drink. He looked haggard and careworn, and his eyes were more tired than ever. I poured him a whisky and soda, and left him to it while I had a wash and brush up.

When I returned from the kitchen, there he was slumped in a chair, staring white-faced at the opposite wall. There were wet spots on his coat where he had spilled some of his drink. I followed his gaze, and saw that the center of his interest was a framed photograph of the Sphinx at Gizeh. It was a souvenir brought back from Cairo, through which city I'd passed on my way to join the war in the desert—only then the Sphinx had had its chin propped up with sandbags, and didn't look nearly so romantic as it did in the commercial photograph.

"Hello—whatever's the matter?" I asked.

"N-nothing," he answered, dropping his gaze. "Coincidences can be unsettling sometimes, that's all."

He gulped the rest of his drink, and got up. But he vouchsafed nothing further until we were miles out on the plain, riding slowly side by side towards the monoliths of Stonehenge on the skyline. Then, suddenly, he said: "Do you know why that picture affected me like that?"

I shook my head.

"Because the Sphinx is an image of the Ruling Mind of the feline race. The body is not that of a lion, *but of a great cat!*"

He lapsed into reverie again.

Stonehenge was deserted. The modern road ran over the plain to a bare horizon, and the remains of far more ancient roads and the faint tracks made by the Bronze Age peoples might never have been trodden since the days of those long-departed civilizations. It was not the tourist season, and if there had been any watchers for the dawn, they had gone.

We wheeled our cycles between the massive obelisks and laid them beside the Altar Stone. I noticed that Clarke's brown bag was still strapped to his carrier. Clarke sat himself on the flat slab, and brooded there like "The Thinker," as silent as the stones around us.

I decided not to press for information, but to let it come in its own way. So, irreverently, I struck a match on the Altar Stone, the death-bed (so the stories go) of countless souls who had been sacrificed by the Druids, and squatted down beside him, striving patiently to get my pipe going.

The tobacco caught just as Clarke broke his silence. "I brought you out here so that we could not possibly be overheard," he said. "That cat of yours—I don't trust it."

He paused again in that irritating way of his, then went on: "You remember what I told you about the Ruling Mind of the feline race? Well, it is still alive, still directing their activities, and it is the power behind all these recent happenings. More than that, *it is somewhere very close to me!*"

His voice shook a little. He took out his handkerchief and mopped his almost hairless head.

"I *know* it is very close to me, as surely as I know those other things I told you. And as certainly as I know other things which have become plain to me since. All the time, I am aware of it watching me. In my rooms, in the crowded street, in empty lanes and fields, in the cinema—everywhere I go, I can feel that the Mind is somewhere very near. Even now—"

He looked almost apprehensively around at the order and disorder of the big stones, and the sweep of the plain. But apart from some bird in flight away to the east, there was no indication of any living thing.

"I cannot understand," he said, huskily. "It must be occupying a body of some sort. Even that Mind can't exist for long without physical nourishment. But what—or who? I regard every animal I see with suspicious fear. Sometimes I even think it may have taken command of some *human* body. That milkman who spoke to me this morning may have been only a masquerader, and behind his smile—"

"You shouldn't pay any attention to thoughts of that kind," I said. "It will develop into a phobia; you will be afraid of everybody. And this infallible knowledge of yours— What are the other things you mentioned had since been revealed to you?"

"I know some more of the history of the feline race. It is pictured as clearly in my mind as if I had witnessed it all. If you look in the *Encyclopedia Britannica*—and, in fact, if you study all that is known of the origin of the cats—you will find that they suddenly appear in one country, and one alone—Egypt. That is where *felis domestica* first enters into our knowledge. Why? Because that is where the feline spaceships from the moon landed thousands of years ago."

"I know the ancient Egyptians regarded cats as supernatural beings," I mused. "They worshiped them, made statues of them. It was a crime to kill a cat, wasn't it?"

"Yes," said Clarke, absently. "The penalty was very severe. In fact, when the King of Persia invaded Egypt, the spearhead of his army was a group of soldiers carrying cats in their arms. The Egyptians were so terrified of harming the animals that they submitted tamely to defeat."

"Usen't they to embalm the bodies of cats and bury them in the holy city of Bubastes?" I asked. "They're still finding them, hundreds of their mummified bodies. Why, only the other day—"

But Clarke was not listening. "The remains of those spaceships are still there in Egypt, covered by the sands of the desert," he, muttered. "I could lead you to them."

"That would be tangible proof at last," I said.

"The feline and Egyptian races more or less adopted each other," went on Clarke. "The Egyptians worshiped the strange invaders as near-gods, and appreciated their high intelligence, even though they understood little of it. They offered up food to the cats, and kept them in their houses and temples. Naturally, after the hardships of the moon, the cats took kindly to this life. At last they could relax from the pressing preoccupation of searching for food, and devote their time to thought."

"Regarding this life of thought—" I began; but Clarke had got under way now, and he went ahead like a gramophone, perhaps fearful that if he stopped he might not be able to start again.

"One reason immensely increased the reverence of the Egyptians for the cats: the discovery that they were, in reality, deathless spirit-minds inhabiting transient bodies. The Egyptians soon based their whole religion on this—that's where they got their famous belief in the immortality of the spirit, its life after death, and possible reincarnation.

"The rite of mummifying the worn-out husks of the cats symbolized the eternal life of the feline minds, and the Egyptians extended this to embalming their own dead—and hoping. They took the emblem of the feline race, the *crux ansata*, and regarded it as the symbol of life.

"For a long time the two races lived in this fashion of mutual convenience. The Egyptians knew there was a Ruling Mind of the cats, though its location and appearance was a mystery to them. But they built the Sphinx in its honor, and to represent the harmony of the two races, gave its cat's body the head of their reigning Pharoah.

"The Egyptians derived a few ideas from the cats and their old lunar civilization, particularly methods of building, metalwork, and decoration, some of which even our modern scientists have failed to rediscover. Malleable glass, imperishable enamels, the ever-burning lamps so often mentioned in the literary fragments of the time, and some miraculous way of reducing precious stones to fluid state and remolding them.

"But actually there was little intellectual intercourse. The Egyptians were not equal to grasping even the simplest conceptions of the feline mind, and the cat had no intention of trying to educate a race which they regarded as being hardly above the lower animals.

"The cats, you must remember, have none of the warmth and generosity of humanity: they are, and always have been, coldly logical, and their main interest is self-preservation, whatever guise or ruse they adopt to that end.

"For instance, when Egypt became entangled in wars, a great proportion of the cats migrated to other countries, and left the Egyptian civilization to decay. They thought it wise, too, to let the knowledge of their existence fade from the mind of man with the decline of the Egyptians. For they foresaw that man's intelligence would grow again, and become a keen, questioning probe and a constant interruption in their work. Only in his ignorance would they have peace.

"At first, they suppressed all reference to themselves. The cat is not mentioned once in the Bible, though the dog is many times, and this might be considered strange, for Egypt was next door to the Holy Land. But that is the reason.

"However, they got the idea later that it was better to suppress only the knowledge of their being super-minds, and then they could mix with mankind again and be looked after without being bothered by investigations into their work.

"Britain was one country they came to where their real identity was unknown, but even so they managed to influence men and women to protect them. In A.D. 900—you may look it up—there was a law passed forbidding the wilful murder of any cat. And in the *Ancren Riwle*, the book of rules for nuns written in the 13th century, was the injunction: 'Ye shall not possess any beast, my dear sisters, *except only a cat.*' "

He fell silent again.

"You mention their work," I ventured. "Can you describe this mysterious 'life of the mind'?"

"Well," he answered, "The cats' minds are like a multitude of cells—"

His face, all of a sudden, went ghastly pale. His brown eyes were horror-struck; his mouth opened and shut in silent gasps.

"What's up?" I cried.

"I—I—If I thought—" he gulped, then whispered tremulously: "No, I must not believe that!"

I regarded this enigma of a man with detached curiosity for a moment. I had never come across such a bundle of nerves. It occurred to me that if I had to put up with this proneness to sudden nervous attacks much longer I should become jumpy myself.

He produced a hip-flask, and promptly choked over a mouthful of undiluted spirit. But it took effect, and presently he mopped his head again and resumed, in a slightly thicker voice:

"A multitude of cells all working independently, but in telepathic communication with each other. The Ruling Mind, though, is in constant contact with all of them at once, and sorts and correlates their thoughts and reasoning's, fitting them together too get the whole aspect. They have no need of books or pens: their infallible memories are their only records. No need to travel: they can cast their minds over great distances. No need of materials: they balance and control the forces of nature with the unsupported force of their own minds.

"But one force has so far beaten them—they cannot master the activity behind the chemical change of metabolism. It is the major problem they have in hand. You see, they don't like being dependent on energy from food to sustain their bodies, which in turn sustain the brain cells they must use to keep up their life of thought. So they are seeking other ways of getting that energy—so far, without success.

"You know," he went on, "There is much to envy in their mode of living. Many of our own philosophers have come to the conclusion that research workers, engrossed in their work, probably live the happiest and most satisfying life of all. The cats believe that, too. Their life is an infinite adventure into the unknown, solving intriguing problems and puzzles, their interest sustained by the promise of unbounded novelties to come.

"It is a pleasurable and absorbing hunt for fundamental truth. What are our vanities and posings, our squabbles and outsmarting, beside that great search? We are as worthless as a cloud of gnats."

"Do you know any of the other problems receiving their attention?"

"Mostly they are beyond my comprehension," he said. "Especially their stupendously advanced mathematics. But I could mention investigations into the strange fibre life on the second, planet of the companion of Sirius, into the minute organisms which infest and corrupt typhoid bacteria, into the structure of individual suns in island universes thousands of light-years beyond the reach of our most powerful telescope, into the newly-discovered Law of the Three Probabilities of the Future, and into the cause—"

BOOM! BOOM! BOOM!

We jerked our heads round, to see three mushrooms of white smoke standing on a low hill across the plain. Slowly their heads uncoiled and expanded, and they merged into one shapeless cloud.

Then again: BOOM! A whole row of fresh mushrooms sprang out of the earth almost simultaneously, running in a line towards us.

We jumped up in alarm, and as if our action had caused it, another row of explosions went streaking across the plain, and this time we glimpsed the red flashes in the heart of them.

"The cats again!" I yelled to Clarke above the uproar. He nodded dazedly, staring at the jumping clouds of smoke and dust. He made an answer which I could not catch.

The thunderous noise grew worse; it was like an intense shell barrage. Were they shells, coming from some unseen guns on the artillery ranges beyond Larkhill? I caught Clarke's eye again.

"Where the hell are they coming from?" I shrieked. He, pointed down at the trembling ground, and mouthed: "Below!"

A series of thuds like hammer-blows, from somewhere quite near, jarred us almost physically. It was difficult to locate the explosions that had caused them, for the pallid, whirling wall of a smoke-screen lay across that way, and the thick pillars of the ancient temple stood between it and us like a stockade. I pointed at the open, untouched expanse behind us, and indicated that we must retreat across it.

"We'll have—" I began, and instantaneously a whole acre of the stretch at which my finger pointed squirted itself up like a huge, white oil-gusher—it was almost pure chalk—which balanced there for a split second, then exploded in midair. It was as if someone had burst a great bag of flour. The air was full of white particles flying before the sound-waves of a concussion which equaled that first mighty explosion in Woolwich Arsenal.

The ground seemed to rise in a wave beneath our feet, and I remember that as I went sprawling backwards I caught a glimpse of one of the pillars of Stonehenge lurching out of the vertical, and the slab that had rested upon it falling corner-wise to the earth. The thump of that block landing was the last shock of the mad tattoo.

Silence descended abruptly, and I became conscious that my ears were tingling almost unbearably. I picked myself up shakily. Clarke was in the act of doing likewise.

"Gosh, look at that!" I said, and my voice sounded faint and far away because of my deafness. "That" was the immense dust-cloud which hung over and veiled half the plain, drifting and changing and mounting tenuously towards the zenith.

"I'll never be able to get through that," I said. "I think I'd better come back with you to Salisbury and wait until it's settled a bit."

Clarke nodded. He had fallen into one of his periods of taciturnity again, and remained so throughout the ride back. But I managed to get one piece of information from him.

"What did you mean by saying those explosions came from below?" I asked.

"There are subterranean caves running for miles underneath the plain," he said shortly. "Few people know of them. The government did. They used them during the war for storing explosives, for safety in air raids."

"And, of course, the Ruling Mind touched them off?"

He nodded sharply again, and shut up like a clam. By his furrowed brow I could see that he was cogitating deeply, and from his expression I saw that the thoughts were not pleasant.

We had a solemn tea in Salisbury, while the street outside was alive with yelling newsboys and excited, arguing people. "Long range rockets, that's what they were . . ." I caught, and ". . . knocked Stonehenge down like a row of ninepins."

We had a short walk, pushing our cycles and talking, and we parted by the cathedral. That scene remains in my mind in every detail. The spire tapering to a fine point four hundred feet above our heads, and Clarke's last words before I went my way, enunciated almost pedantically:

"As long as the cats keep up their acting with such infallible assurance, there will always remain an element of doubt in even the most credulous human mind. That little crumb of self-distrust is what will save them. And, believe me, the cats know it!"

It was late evening when I reached my cottage by a circuitous route. The craters were pretty numerous around my way, and the settling chalk-dust covered the torn earth like a thin layer of snow.

A scared-looking Peter was waiting for me on the doorstep. He was jumpy and nervous, and it looked as though the upheaval had nearly frightened him out of his wits. I let him in with peculiarly mixed feelings.

IV

I FOUND IT HARD to get to sleep that night. A queer unease possessed me. I felt that something strange and terrible was going to happen soon, and I had no idea what the nature of the thing could be. I lay fidgeting and constantly turning, finding neither bodily nor mental peace.

And then there came a wail, like a sick baby's, outside the window. I sat up, startled.

Silence.

Came another wail, sobbing up the scale to an extremely high pitch. It descended rapidly to a throaty growl, and then a familiar "Mee-ow."

It was only Peter. He had wandered out again after supper. I'd never heard him giving tongue in the night before like this, because other cats rarely strayed out this way. But there was another cat there tonight, for presently she answered. She had a remarkable range: thin shrieks, mournful howls, mid an individual, staccato series of noises like an outboard motor.

A most painful duet presently began. I lay and listened to with interest rather than annoyance. How would Clarke have explained it? No doubt he would have said it was a cunning psychological ruse, to impress the notion in the subconscious mind of man that cats were indeed only animals, having the customary sexual and courting instincts.

If that were true, and it was all acting, then it was indeed finesse! I could not imagine the feline race carrying things so far, but perhaps, as Clarke had said, this acting had become an almost unconscious habit with them, requiring no effort.

My mind played with other explanations. Suppose these outbursts were the more artistic souls of the felines giving expression to their love of music! Were those weird sounds, so discordant to our ears, feline songs of great beauty?

Certainly I had heard Chinese songs that sounded somewhat similar. But I could not accept this explanation, for I could not imagine the cat race having any sort of emotions. All art springs from the emotions, and if Clarke's story were true, those intellects were too cold and logical to waste time on music or any other of the art forms.

In the midst of such speculations, I fell into a doze.

The next day was pure idleness. I could not concentrate on anything, though a half-finished story lay in my drawer. I pottered about, reading snatches of books and papers, listening to the radio, and for the most part just reclining in my deck-chair on the lawn, meditating.

Sunset came—an unusually glorious one. The fine dust thrown up by the explosions of yesterday was still drifting in the upper atmosphere, and producing an effect similar to those after the famous Krakatoa eruption. The western sky abounded in color, in streaks, flames, wedges, and mists. I wished I had a camera that could catch and preserve the beauty of the scene.

I watched it greedily, half-fearful of the dulling that would presently overcome and dissolve it. And then, just as he had first entered into my life, the tiny black silhouette of Clarke on his cycle appeared out there on the plain. He was winding his way slowly between the dark ovals of the craters which had obliterated parts of the old grass track, and it was some time before he reached my gate.

He dismounted clumsily, and almost fell over. I got up and went to help him, smiling. But I stopped smiling when I saw his face. It was grey, and moist with sweat, and the dark circles under his eyes had grown more pronounced during the night.

I took the bicycle from his trembling hands, and leaned it against the fence. The strap around the brown case on the carrier was loose. I tightened it automatically, and took Clarke's arm. He leaned on me, drawing little shuddering gasps I now and then as I helped him along to the house.

"Take it easy," I said.

"My God!" he muttered. "My God!"

He seemed on the verge of hysteria. The fellow was a constant puzzle to me; he seemed to have so many personalities. The nervous inquirer, the almost rudely terse man, the didactic schoolmaster—and now this shaking wreck. I wondered whether he could possibly be a drug addict.He lowered himself uncertainly into my armchair and rested his head on his hand. I poured a neat whisky, and had to help him get it down his throat. He lay back.

"Be all right—in a minute," he breathed.

Peter was curled up on the hearthrug. For a few moments he had watched the visitor with faint curiosity, but now his interest had waned and his eyes were closed in sleep again. Apparently . . . I grabbed him up in two handfuls, intending to put him outside, but Clarke stopped me with a weak gesture.

"Doesn't matter now," he murmured. "He knows all about it, anyway."

I sank into the opposite chair, and waited. Until, at length, Clarke began his strangest narrative yet, in broken sentences punctuated with sighs and sometimes uncontrolled invocations to the Almighty.

At first, there was a lot of physiological stuff about the structure of brain-cells, which he rushed through too rapidly for me to grasp properly. But I remember he said that the average person uses only a small percentage of his brain-cells in his lifetime, the larger proportion remaining undeveloped and unused. He made fleeting references to schizophrenia, 'split minds," and enlarged upon the question of multiple personalities.

This last was due, he said, to the brain-cells forming in two or three separate groups, instead of the one whole. Thus, one man's brain could contain two or three totally different minds, each with its own independent memories and reactions, yet each drawing its energy from the same bloodstream.

And something of the sort, only far worse, had happened to him. When he had mentioned the word "cells" yesterday, at Stonehenge, some idea of the terrible truth had dawned upon him. Now, after a sleepless night and day, he was sure that he had found the answer.

No wonder he had felt the strange presence of the Ruling Mind so constantly. *It was occupying the larger part of his own brain!*

At this amazing assertion, I just sat gaping at him. In looking back at the whole affair, I don't think I had taken Mr. Clark very seriously up to this point. Admittedly, at times his story had carried me away, but only as one is carried away by a good film. When I had parted from him, the impression had faded each time, as the characters in a film cease to be real after one has emerged from the cinema into the solid life of the street.

As an author myself, whose work it was to spend half my life in a fictitious world, I knew how easy it was sometimes to confuse that world with fact. I'm afraid I must have looked upon Clarke as an expert weaver of fantasies all this time. I had taken him for one of those involved psychological cases, full of repressions, complexes, escapism, and all that jargon. In short, a queer fish who had swum into my life to entertain me for awhile, and provide an interesting passage in my autobiography, when that amusing volume came to be written.

But now it came to me with quite a shock of realization that the man sitting huddled in the opposite chair was not dramatizing himself, but genuinely believed in the astounding things he had said, and was overcome by the horror of them.

I gazed at the top of his bald and shining head, and tried to imagine a complex and utterly foreign brain working beside his in that cranium. My imagination boggled.

Clarke slowly raised his head again, and looked up at me. His eyes were red and bleared from lack of sleep. He spoke in a strained, but steadier voice.

"Maybe that's how I knew the things I did. There must have been a leakage of knowledge, filtering through from the pirated brain-cells into my own. Perhaps through the bloodstream; perhaps because such a powerful radiating instrument, in close proximity to my own, stimulated my telepathic powers, made my mind more receptive. I was sure the information in my mind was correct, though I couldn't understand where it came from."

"Yes—yes," I stammered. "I suppose that's it."

He went on bitterly: "And the reason for my chronic fatigue—this damned parasite is draining my energy. To think that the thing has always been with me! Why, when we went out to Stonehenge to escape it, it was there all the time with us, overhearing everything. Not that I expect it paid us much heed . . . And it was simple for it, with its complete control of electrical forces, to create a spark in just the right place in those caves under the plain. Just as all the other places were blown up or set on fire."

A gust of rage seized him. "If I could get my hands on it! If only I could get my hands on it!"

The spasm passed. "It must be overhearing me now," he said, wearily.

I felt it was up to me to say something.

"Well, there it is," I said hesitantly. "What on earth are we to do about it?"

He jumped up so suddenly that I started, His unstable emotions boiled over in another flood of rage. His face was convulsed.

"I'm going to do something," he gritted. "I won't be used like this. What's my life become? Another week—another day—of this, and I'll be insane!"

He snatched up his dingy hat ferociously, and made for the door. He was not too steady on his feet, but the intensity of his passion upheld him.

"Good-by, Williams," he flung at me. "I can't tell you anything more. I mustn't even think about it." And he was out and down the path before I could comprehend his swift words.

I followed hurriedly. "Wait," I called. "What—?" But he had mounted his cycle and was already riding away, the bag on his carrier at the rear bumping up and down in derisive farewell.

I stopped at the gate, looking after him. He was shouting as he rode, and the words came back more and more faintly as he dwindled into the distance. They were mostly blasphemy . . .

I hesitated, and cursed my hesitation. But I could never catch him now: I had been cleaning my bike, and it lay in hopeless dismemberment in the toolshed. The fellow was very ill. He shouldn't be allowed about like that. He should be under observation.

Observation! An idea suddenly occurred to me. I rushed back into the cottage, almost tripping over Peter, who was coming out of the door, and went clattering up the stairs to my cramped observatory. Sliding the skylight window aside, I swung the telescope window down, and directed it out into the dusk after Clarke.

I looked through it. Everything was a blur, and I fiddled impatiently with the focusing screws. The scene would not come clear. Then: "Fool!" I swore at myself, and delved on the floor for the terrestrial eyepiece.

It was under a heap of star maps. I snatched it out, and with hasty fingers screwed it in place of the astronomical lens. I peered through, and the dark little mote out there between the obscure land and the pale green sky fairly leapt at me, and became the figure of Clarke, dismounted now and crouching on the lip of one of the recent craters.

He was unstrapping the brown bag. I could not see his face, for the brim of his hat shadowed it. He produced a bunch of keys, and used one of them to unlock the case.

I watched with interest, waiting to see what was in that mysterious case. Wads of newspapers—evidently packing—came out first, and then Clarke extracted some sticks—yellow sticks, each about ten inches long.

He put them down and stood up. He gazed around at the darkling plain. He seemed to be undergoing some sort of mental struggle. Then, as if in sudden resolution, he bent swiftly, gathered the sticks in his arms and seemed literally to hurl himself over the rim of the crater.

I gasped as he disappeared from view, for those craters were pretty deep—some went right underground. I waited a minute or two hardly daring to breathe, my eye glued to the spot, where he had vanished. His bicycle and the abandoned case were still there on the rim.

Then, without warning, a fountain of dirt, smoke, and flame spurted up from the interior of the crater, catching up and tossing the bicycle fifty yards away and spraying out in a tall, grey plume. Quite slowly, the dust and smaller debris rained down from this erection, and seemed to rebound gently as it landed. A lower layer of white smoke appeared, and rolled along the edge of the crater as if it were a steaming cauldron.

I found that I had bitten my lip, and there was the taste of blood on my tongue . . .

When I reached the scene twenty minutes later, after a breathless run in the gloom, the cloud had settled, and the crater was nearly half-full of loose debris. It was quite obvious that there was nothing I could do.

Those yellow sticks had been dynamite.

That was a fortnight ago. And now here I sit in my parlor, penning this account of the adventure from beginning to end. I suppose it *is* ended.

Yet could an intelligence of the quality of the Ruling Mind of Clarke's story be trapped by such a trick, even though Clarke did his best to conceal his intention to destroy it through its Achilles' heel—an explosive "slap up against it"? I find that hard to accept.

Certainly, there have been no more explosions since, but that is probably because there is nothing left to explode. Funnily enough, poor Clarke's few sticks of dynamite must have been about the last left upon this planet. As a New York paper said the next day: "There just isn't enough gunpowder left in the world to make a two-cent Fourth of July squib."

Nor was a single plant for manufacturing atom bombs anything but completely gutted walls. Nobody could have taught the cats anything about incendiarism.

Throughout this narrative, I have endeavored to confine it to personal experience only, hardly touching upon the broader events of this globular annihilation of the stuff of war. For that is history.

We know now the all-round sense of relief that has come to the peoples of the world. The pact that has been signed to keep the world in its weaponless condition, and to outlaw arms races, may well be the foundation stone of that common world government, after all. Perhaps now the vicious circle has been broken for is, we shall maintain the good sense not to get caught in another.

In any case, if Clarke's story was true, an atomic war will never be able to get started. The feline race will see to that. *If Clarke's story was true . . .*

I always come back to that "if." When I try to sum it all up, doubt defeats me. It is so fantastically far-fetched. I cannot make up my mind whether Clarke was a martyr, or an obsessed lunatic who committed suicide in a remarkably complicated way.

And yet, you know, there are Clarke's own words . . . *"As long as the cats keep up their acting with such infallible assurance, there will always remain an element of doubt in even the most credulous human mind. That little crumb of self-distrust is what will save them. And, believe me, the cats know it!"*

It is sunset again, that seemingly fateful time of day in this story. The mellowing rays steal in through the diamond panes of the windows, and there is a golden patch of light moving gently on the opposite wall. There are spots of shadow in it, giving it the effect of a mask. It seems to grin.

I look across at Peter squatting on the arm of the chair in which Clarke sat on his last visit. He is in a semi-doze; his eyes are almost, but not quite, shut, and he is purring very softly. There is a look of complacent felicity about him. Is that really a smile on his face? I am sure it is—as much as a cat can smile.

He is crouching like a little sphinx, and my gaze lifts to the framed photograph hanging on the wall above him. The Sphinx of Gizeh—maybe a stone image of the Ruling Mind.

The dread thought occurs to me again. If the strange being left Clarke's body in time before he blew himself to smithereens, it must by now be occupying some other body. It could not remain disembodied long. *Where has it gone?*

I look across at a mirror, and study my head uneasily. For the Lord's sake, not that! My gaze returns to the Sphinx. I scrutinize its battered features.

What an enigmatic expression! Is it a smile?

UNCLE BUNO

HE WAS ALWAYS "UNCLE" BUNO TO ME, though of course he wasn't my uncle—he was a Martian. I had no true uncles. As if they blamed themselves for the lack, my parents always introduced their male guests to me as "Uncle" this or "Uncle" that. A common enough custom, but they kept at it when I was past the kid stuff.

I must have been around twelve when Uncle Buno came. I guess that's the age when a lot of the glory starts to pass from the earth. A year or two later comes puberty and then imagination becomes channeled for a time largely in one direction. "Romance" ceases to mean besieged castles or mysterious space wrecks off Jupiter or heroics in Normandy, and comes very much down to earth. Sex is *the* fascinating mystery.

It still is something of a mystery to me, for I've never married nor pursued any sexual adventure to its natural climax. Polio in infancy withered my limbs and didn't do much for my self-confidence. I hated being a burden to anyone. It was pain enough to have been a burden to my parents.

My father was vital and impatient, with frank eyes. Too frank, maybe, for they said what he thought even when he was silent. They said: "Too bad about you, Paul. We've both had a raw deal. I wanted you out in the spaceways with me. Maybe sometime you'd have your own ship too, and we'd stage a clipper race. Or fire rocket salutes at each other just for the gag. Or rendezvous in Syrtis Major City and . . . But no. It's too bad."

You have to be physically one hundred per cent to be a spaceship skipper.

What opinions my mother had of me she kept to herself. When I was very small, needing the assurance of constant love, like any kid, I used to ask her: "Do you love me, Ma?"

Sometimes she replied "Don't ask silly questions, Paul," and sometimes she just didn't seem to hear me. And presently I ceased to ask, because I knew.

When I was ten she wasn't even there to ask.

Pop had been on the Earth-Mars run for a long spell at that time. Too long for Ma, who could never be called patient either. She went off one day with the man I'd been taught to call "Uncle Barry," and I never saw either of them again. Of course, there was a divorce, but I wasn't told anything about that.

I was sent to live with "Uncle Vie," while Pop went back on the Earth-Mars run. Then one hot Sunday his little green car appeared from the August dust-clouds, and when he stepped out he patted me on the head and walked past me as though it were a casual encounter. And I hadn't seen him in eight months. He talked with Uncle Vie, and my things were packed, and he told me to get in the car with him. We drove off.

"Where are we going, Pop?"

"Home, Paul."

"Is . . . Is Ma back?"

He frowned over the wheel.

"She won't ever be back, son. Forget her. Your Uncle Buno will take care of you for the next couple of years. Then you'll be a big boy, and pretty soon go to college and get a degree. Mathematics, huh—how about that?"

My heart sank. "I'll never get a degree in maths, Pop. I was never any good at it. I've tried, but figures . . . I just can't seem to *see* figures in my head."

"Don't worry. Uncle Buno is going to coach you. One way and another he knows the score. If he weren't Martian, he'd amount to something."

"A Martian?"

"That's what I said."

At that time there was far more racial prejudice against Martians than there is now. They were looked upon as an inferior species. Yet they were much like us in appearance, except that they were albinos. But Mars was a poor, spent planet, and they were a spiritless, lack lustre people for the most part, and their standard of living was low. Like poor people everywhere, they were not respected, especially as sometimes they were forced to beg. Mars became known as "the beggar Earth."

Most of them were too listless to desire change, but a few wished to emigrate to Earth—and straightway ran into a "Keep the Martians Out" barrier. Only a handful negotiated it, through string-pulling by really important Terrestrials, like senators, diplomats, big business tycoons—or spaceship captains.

I understood that Martians made good house servants. They never answered back.

I had never seen one in the flesh. Uncle Buno was striking. He wasn't in the house when we got there, and we found him sitting on a canvas-topped stool at the end of the garden, painting in oils.

The picture on the easel was of the farm below, in the valley. I'd seen the farm countless times, played there until I knew the appearance of every knot in the timber of and about it. But I'd never seen it like it was on the canvas. It transcended two dimensions, even three. It was Valley Farm set imperishably in its place in the space-time continuum, glowingly alive. Its very particles seemed to be moving to the rhythms of this wave-shot universe.

Even my father said: "That's pretty good, Buno."

Uncle Buno regarded us mildly, tolerantly. I could see our appreciation meant little to him. He was tall and spare with a noticeably erect back. It's not easy to judge a Martian's age in Earth-years, but I should have guessed he was thirty. One had to ignore the thick white hair—Martian babies are born with white hair. His eyes were light lashed, pink-lidded, and the irises were as pale as his skin.

Because of this lack of pigmentation, his general effect might reasonably have been bleak. It wasn't.

Because he shrugged off our praise for his work, his attitude might reasonably have been condescending. It wasn't.

He knew that his real critic was not the layman, not the connoisseur, not even time. It was himself. Or rather, the artist in him who told him: "This feels right. This *is* right. It says everything."

And there was no need for anyone else to say anything.

"This is Paul," said my father, introducing me. The tall Martian looked down at me, seated though he was, and I felt the warmth of friendliness flow from him to me. It was a magic moment. I'd never experienced anything quite like it before. I'd received little but coldness from my mother and indifference from my father.

"If I can serve as your mentor, I'm sure we shall both learn, Paul," said Uncle Buno. His English was perfect, his voice pleasantly deep.

I didn't know the meaning of "Mentor." My father did, in his usual limited way. He said: "Uncle Buno will give you at least a grounding in three-dimensional geometry."

Then I saw my father's new hope plainly. I couldn't become a space-skipper like him, but I might become the next-best thing: a space-navigator. Most captains leaned heavily on their navigators, whose prestige therefore was high. You could become a navigator even if you had only one arm. The brain was the important thing. The only necessary function of the body was its ability to push a pencil.

There was a time when prophets said digital computers would oust navigators. Sometimes they still said it, but spacemen didn't believe them any more. Computers were still too heavy for the smaller ships. And on the bigger ships someone had to know the questions to ask them.

I hoped Uncle Buno was a magician. It would take a magician to make me understand mathematics.

Well, he tried. He was patient and kind. I tried, too. At first because I wanted to please Pop and become a navigator. Later because I wanted to please Uncle Buno.

He taught me to appreciate art in many forms, but painting chiefly. Until then, sunsets were to me but the end of a day, presaging bed. He made me see them. He never missed one if he could help it. We sat watching together in the garden, and he would name all the shades of colour that smeared the tumbled clouds, amending the list as they faded, brightened, changed. He taught me how to sketch and label them, so that their glory could be resurrected and fixed on canvas, the next day.

With new eyes I saw the marvellously intermingled colours of flowers, the structure of trees, the form of the land, the delicacy of living creatures. Yet I knew that, compared with his perception, I was seeing them through smoked glasses.

He even got me interested in mathematics. Interested, but not very able.

Time and again he told me: "If only you could see it, Paul, mathematics has all the delight of painting. The rightness of equations as they work out, each part falling into place so inevitably, gives supreme aesthetic satisfaction. It's fate itself—in figures."

"Figures!" I echoed gloomily.

"Figures, yes. Think of figure-skating, Paul—sweeping, interlacing curves. The curves of graphs are no less beautiful. And they're only two-dimensional. With the extra dimension, in three-dimensional, geometry, they come alive. They dance in your brain to fine music! Oh, if only I could make you see!"

But he couldn't.

The long summer faded, the wind began to moan, and the winter snows came delicately but inexorably to block the valley.

I remember one night I went out to the woodshed and on the way was enraptured, uplifted, by the spectacle of the Milky Way. It was a procession of thousands of infinitely distant torchbearers marching across a sable sky arched over a glimmering floor of snow.

The planets shone more steadily, like signal lamps. Somewhere up there, awfully remote, my father was guiding his ship through the immensities. And yet, as I was realizing now, his was not the guiding brain. A keen, clever-faced man, Norridge—I had met him—sat in a smaller cabin, among his charts, dividers, and electronic instruments, and was the power behind the throne. Father respected Norridge. If I could become like Norridge he would respect me also and forget my physical weakness.

Then I saw Uncle Buno leaning against the side of the shed. He was staring up at the sky too, but only at its lower rim. The snow seemed to shine with its own light and his pale face, paler yet, was visible. I followed his gaze and saw an unwinking red dot of light, low on the horizon. Mars.

I could see his expression only dimly, but unmistakably it was sad.

He became aware of me, turned, smiled . . .

"Hello, Paul. I was thinking of getting something of this" —he swept his arm vaguely before him— "on canvas. Call it 'Winter Nocturne,' eh?"

But I felt he'd been thinking about something else.

He helped me carry wood back. We made up a roaring fire and sat by it. I watched the red-lit shadows playing over his face and wondered. Through the summer and fall we had walked far and talked much of general things. But he had always been reticent about his background, his way of life on Mars. I had learnt that he was married, his wife's name was Jona, and they had no children. It pleased me that he had no children of his own, for I was lonely enough and greedy enough of his affection to have been really jealous.

It was childish jealousy which made me ask: "Do you miss Aunt Jona, Uncle?"

He looked into the fire and said quietly: "Of course, Paul."

"Can't she come and stay with us, then? Father's away most of the time. We've plenty of room."

"The immigration laws don't allow it. Your father had trouble in getting permission for me to stay only two years."

"Oh, aren't they silly! I think people should be able to come and go as they please."

Uncle Buno smiled. "Politicians don't think like we artists."

"Do you think Aunt Jona would like it here?"

"Yes, I do."

"One day," I said, shrilly, "I'll get to be President and change these stupid old laws! Then Aunt Jona can come."

"But I thought you wanted to be a space-navigator?"

"Oh—*that!* I'll never be that. I can't figure well enough."

For the first time since I'd known him I saw anxiety touch him. He frowned. "We'll do a little revision, Paul," he said, decisively, and reached for a book. It was *Elementary Orbits* and my spirits fell, for there was nothing elementary about the contents of thet book to me. Besides, I'd hoped we were in for a nice cosy chat by the fire, and that at last I should learn something of Aunt Jona's and Uncle Buno's home life.

But it was astrogation for the rest of that evening. I didn't do so well, and went to bed unhappy, knowing that Uncle Buno was unhappy also.

I progressed slowly with maths through the winter, but much faster with learning Martian, written and spoken. Maybe it was because I had a flair for languages, as Uncle Buno surmised. More probably it was because it was my own idea and I was under no compulsion.

My painting was coming on, too, but I knew I could never hope to be more than a second-rate artist. The example of the first-rate was before my eyes all the time. Whenever he was through coaching for the day, Uncle Buno began to mix his colours, prepare his brushes and canvases, and, amazingly quickly, produce a masterpiece before the daylight quite faded. The weather hampered him little. If it rained, he'd keep at it till he'd wrought a rainswept landscape that glistened even after it was dry. In gales he would stand like a rock, the long white hair streaming, until he captured in paint the row of tortured elms.

He did still-life too, seeing beneath the surface of commonplace things like a super-Cézanne.

He did only one portrait. That was of my father. I could hardly recognize it. There were the frank eyes, all right, but there was kindness in them. I had never seen that look myself in my father's eyes. I doubted very much that Uncle Buno had, for Pop was becoming increasingly curt and impatient with him. It was dawning on father that his dream for me was no more than a dream.

I applied myself until my mind reeled and my skull felt it would crack open trying to discover the sense in mathematics. My advance was snail-slow.

During my summer vacation my father put me on trial. He'd asked Norridge to get out a reasonably simple test paper on astrogation. After some high pressure preparatory coaching by Uncle Buno, who again showed signs of anxiety, I faced the paper.

I doodle, chewed the end of my pen, held my head, and finally all but burst into tears through frustration.

I answered one question out of nine and then got it only half right. My father made no verbal comment. His eyes showed disappointment so deep it was grief.

Uncle Buno was sad, too, though also saying nothing. As I was going to bed that evening, he said goodnight by the stairs and, surprisingly, held my hand for a moment. "Don't worry, Paul," he said, quietly. "I still think you can do it."

He pressed my hand and relinquished it. "Write me sometimes, won't you?" he said, and turned back into the lounge.

"What was that, Uncle?" I called after him, but the door closed on him.

In the morning, I overslept and came down just in time to see father's green car pulling into the drive. I wondered where Pop had been.

I sought Uncle Buno. I wanted him to explain his parting remark. He was nowhere around. Dad came in.

"Have you seen Uncle Buno?" I asked.

"I have. I've just taken him to the station. He's catching the next ship back to Mars. You were sound asleep, so I didn't waken you."

I stood there like an idiot, my mouth open. I'd gone numb in mind and body. At last, I stammered: "He wanted to go back to Aunt Jona?"

"I expect that was it."

"How—how long will he be away?"

Pop compressed his lips. "He's not coming back, Paul."

"Oh!" The exclamation was more anguish than surprise. A terrible feeling of loss and desolating loneliness came over me. Uncle Buno had become more than a part of my life. He *was* my life—I lived through him, seeing the world with his eyes and with something of his understanding, He had made it seem a very wonderful place.

I went back to my room to fight my misery in solitude.

I don't know how much later it was when I wandered into what had been Uncle Buno's room and found the neat stack of his canvases still there, and his palette, paint tubes, and brushes on the rack under the easel. They sent another stab of pain through me, and then I began to feel glad. At worst, he'd left something of himself behind. At best, surely it meant he intended to return eventually? He wouldn't just abandon the tools of his craft—I knew what painting meant to him.

I mentioned it to Pop.

He said: "I paid him in advance for two years' tuition for you. He spent the credits on Mars before he came—mostly on household thing for his wife. So he still owes me a year's work. Or owed, rather."

"Owed?"

"He offered his paintings and materials in lieu of returning the credits. I accepted. They're no use to me, of course, but maybe you can use 'em."

"Oh, father—couldn't you have let him off for that one year?"

My father looked at me strangely, and then looked away. "Uncle Buno was not like the general run of Martians. He had pride. He didn't want to take something for nothing."

Yes, that was like Uncle Buno. But somehow I felt something was being kept from me.

"Pop," I said, "Did you *send* Uncle Buno home?"

He still wouldn't look at me. "Yes, Paul, I did."

I tried not to hate him. "But it wasn't his fault I'm so slow at learning. I was getting better at maths, really I was."

He made no answer. That meant he didn't believe me. I wasn't sure that I believed myself. And that made me angrier.

I blurted out: "You never did care about me, and he did. That's what you didn't like about him. You don't want anybody to like me. You were jealous of him—that's why you sent him away."

He was surprisingly patient. Without raising his voice, he answered:

"You're contradicting yourself there, son. You'll never learn maths until you learn to think logically. Better go out and get some air and cool off."

I ran out of the house, down into the valley, among the trees where it was quiet and I could be alone. I wandered there for hours, mentally composing letters to Uncle Buno. Sometimes I urged him to return, saying he could stay at the farm, because they were my friends there, and I would see him every day. Sometimes I hinted at my stowing away on a ship to Mars—maybe even Pop's ship—and coming to live with him and Aunt Jona. The plans were all childish, impracticable, and—illogical.

Nevertheless, I wrote actual letters very like them during the following weeks. I received but one answer. I came across it the other day, among my once cherished collection of interplanetary stamps. It said:

> *Dear Paul,*
>
> *Thank you for your letters. I should like to return to Earth, but it isn't possible. Your Aunt Jona is well and sends you her love.*
>
> *Uncle Buno.*

That was all, in return for my pouring out my heart in my boyish, uninhibited letters. Aunt Jona sent her love but Uncle Buno didn't.

I responded indignantly, asking why he had requested me to write him at all, if my letters were to be largely ignored. He ignored that one completely—at least, no answer came.

I was miserable for a long time. I tried to paint, but without Uncle Buno's encouragement there seemed little point in it. When I compared my daubs with the work he'd left, there seemed even less point to it.

Sometimes I imagined him sitting before his easel, beside one of the stagnant canals, capturing the quiet mood of a Martian evening—the blue, star-pricked sky, the green scum on the canal contrasting with the orange desert all blending somehow into significant life on his canvas.

Then I would bite my lip and vow that, if Uncle Buno couldn't come to me, then I should go to him. Somehow I would get to Mars.

Every time Pop returned from Mars, I'd pounce to ask whether he'd seen Uncle Buno. Often he had not been near Buno's village. And when he had visited him, the report was always brief and unsatisfying. "Uncle Buno? Sure, he's rubbing along okay."

At such times I often noticed my father looked hurt, as though he were pained by my being more interested in Uncle Buno's affairs than his. I put it down to nothing more admirable than wounded vanity.

Eventually I went to college and found companionship. I even found what I thought was my vocation. It wasn't painting or art in any form or farming or any of the professions I thought I might adopt. It was the last thing I'd imagined I was fitted for—mathematics.

All the divisions of maths I'd struggled with and despaired of merged into one meaningful whole in my eighteenth year. Uncle Buno had been right all along. I had the gift. It had taken long to mature.

All the groundwork Uncle Buno had put in for me hadn't been wasted. It had taken root down there in my subconscious. Now suddenly it had flowered and borne fruit.

I spent most of a vacation studying for a degree in pure maths. Near the end of it I felt safe and sure enough to quit, put away my books, and loaf around.

Pop—who these days was a changed person, manifestly proud of my progress—was out in space, and I had the house to myself. I went into what had been Uncle Buno's room, dug out all of his paintings and arranged them as a one-man exhibition. I hadn't looked at them closely in years. As I sat scrutinizing them now, it seemed to me more than ever that they were works of genius.

I'd never lost my interest in art, and college had given me the opportunities to study the works of the masters, old and new. So I looked at Buno's work with some understanding of the way he'd handled the technical side of it, besides feeling the direct impact of the pictures.

I didn't think he had a thing to learn from any painter before or after Michelangelo.

A college buddy happened to be the son of an art dealer who combined the aesthetic and business senses. I got him to persuade his old man to come and take a look at a Martian's views of Earth. The novelty was the bait and it drew the dealer.

He came on a day which is a date in art history. Buno was officially "Discovered." The dealer saw to it that it didn't remain just a personal discovery. He pushed Buno. It seemed odd to me that he had to do any pushing at all. I said to him one day: "Surely the pictures sell themselves? Why, you've only got to take one look at them—they hit you like a sunburst."

"There's an awful lot of people who don't know whether the sun's shining or not, Paul," he said. "The ones who do rarely have the money. It's the other kind we've got to sell the pictures to. If it weren't for the money, this game would have broken my heart long ago. Believe me, I'd like to have all the Bunos on *my* walls. But if I don't sell 'em, I soon shouldn't have any walls to hang them on."

It was years before Bunos became safe canvas currency among the rich and the big money came rolling in. At that time I was neck-deep in a course at the School of Astrogation and my respect for space-navigators rivalled that for artists. I'd imagined I had mastered maths. Now I realized I was still down in the foot-hills.

No wonder any space-skipper who knew anything at all was always polite to his navigator.

Father insisted the Buno paintings were mine and therefore the proceeds were also. I had other views about that, and just salted the cash away. I'd written Buno a couple of times about his growing fame on Earth, repeating that I'd be glad to see him. I should have, too, though I had plenty on my plate and my days were full. I wasn't a lonely kid any more. I had many friends now, and some close ones who shared my work. So when Uncle Buno failed to reply, I was disappointed but not heartbroken.

One day the dealer came right out to the School to see me. As we strolled under the elms in the sharp spring sunlight he said: "You have seven Bunos left, haven't you?"

"That's right. My favourites. I'm keeping them."

"Wouldn't you rather keep twenty-five thousand pounds? That's what I'll give you for them."

"My, my. Where have you been lately—slumming?"

"All right, Paul—thirty thousand."

"But I have a sentimental regard for this batch."

"How much is your sentiment worth—thirty-five thousand?"

I considered. "You can have six for that. One I must keep." I was thinking of the Valley Farm painting, the one Buno had been doing when I first met him.

The dealer sighed. "You're wasting your time on the wrong kind of figures here, Paul. You should have gone on the Stock Exchange. Hang onto that last one long enough and it'll be worth thirty-five thousand by itself—if the fashion doesn't change. That's what you've got to watch."

"To hell with fashion! 'Valley Farm' is worth precisely what I think it's worth and—believe it or not—I don't think in terms of money. If you want more Bunos why don't you go to Mars and buy them direct from the producer? I should have thought that by this time half your profession would be standing in line at his door."

The dealer coughed. "They all think Buno's signed up exclusively to me. I just let 'em think. Why haven't I gone? Space travel makes me sick."

"Send a representative, then."

"No, you don't understand, Paul. To make this game pay, you've got to balance one thing against another. You can have too much of a good thing. Rarity value counts more in this racket than in any other. To squeeze the last penny from this Buno panic we'll want him to produce no more than one painting a year. Genius or not, overproduction will kill the market. Besides, the public is still sold on the Martian view of Earth angle. They don't give a darn about the Martian view of Mars. Tell you what you do. Get your pal to come back here and paint another twenty, say, and they'll keep him in luxury for the rest of his life. We'll peddle them out, one by one."

I thought that over, and said I'd write Buno. Then I thought it over some more. I wasn't bothered about squeezing out the last penny for Buno. I had plenty stashed away for him already. I'd planned to take it to him personally in the shape of Martian credits on my very first trip as a space-navigator. I felt I had a big debt to repay him.

Often I pictured the scene: my bursting in on them, in my new uniform, making Buno happy because his faith in my mathematical ability had been vindicated, making Jona happy because she would be able to buy all the household gadgets she'd ever fancied.

How we'd talk! In Martian too, for I was really glib in that tongue now.

But the more I thought about it, the more remote that happy picture seemed. I was moving on very slippery ground at the School of Astrogation and not always forward. Maybe I'd been over-ambitious. I had a talent for maths certainly, but was it good enough to carry me into the ranks of the select band of navigators?

When I learned that nineteen out of twenty students, on the average, were plowed, I sweated.

Yes, I wanted Uncle Buno to come back. Not just for his kindness or his company. Not even for his own sake, that he might reap his reward in fame and money on Earth. But for my sake, because I needed to be helped like a lame dog over a stile. I knew he was my last chance. None other could make the enormously advanced mathematics intelligible to me. Without further guidance from him I knew in my heart I should never become a space-navigator.

So I wrote him at once, telling him all this, imploring him to come back. I pointed out that there would be no difficulty about a permit to stay, for he was a world celebrity now and everyone would welcome him with open arms. The Ministry of Culture would make his path easy, ankle-deep in rose petals.

Not long after I'd mailed the letter, Pop dropped over to the School to see how I was making out. I was frank about it, and told him I'd written to Buno, and why I had.

He said: "Paul, I wish you hadn't done that."

"But you *do* still want me to become a navigator?"

"Sure. But not at the cost of Buno's life."

"What?"

"You haven't met any other Martians but Buno, Paul?"

"No, I haven't."

"There are a couple working at the Washington Spaceport. Take a look at them if you're ever that way. Then you may learn why the Immigration Board aren't so hard-hearted as you'd supposed, and why the two-year limit obtains. Those two Martians look like bent old men and move like tortoises, yet neither is as old as Buno. If they hadn't been near the starvation level, it would have been no charity to give them terrestrial jobs."

"But why, Pop?"

"Gravity drag, of course. It's nearly three times what they're used to, you know. I suppose you never thought of that because Buno never showed us any sign of it. He wouldn't. I told you—he has pride."

I thought of Buno's stiff, upright back and the effort it must have cost him.

"It gets their hearts," said Pop. "A Martian heart isn't meant to pump all that extra weight of blood."

"Was there anything wrong with Buno's heart?"

"He wouldn't admit it, but I had him examined. The doctor said he wouldn't last another six months on Earth. So I sent Buno back home at once. He didn't want to go right away. He thought he could get you to understand maths pretty soon. Maybe he was right, but I couldn't take the risk.

I tried to look into his eyes but he stared up at the school facade, pretending an interest in architecture. Was it a tradition of space-skippers, I wondered, to regard kindness as softness and try to conceal it? It was clear now from Buno's portrait that the Martian had understood my father better than I ever had.

I remembered my childish attack on Pop for sending Buno home, my accusing him of jealousy. Yet Pop had given up his life's chief hope to avoid risking the life of one of a supposedly lesser breed. How could I do less? Figuratively, I waved goodbye to a career in space, and said: "I'll write him express, Pop, and tell him not to come."

"Good," said Pop, quietly. He lowered his gaze and I saw that he looked very like his portrait.

I wrote Buno urgently, trying to counter all my arguments in my last letter. If he had any regard for me, I said, then stay put. I would soon come and see him—as a passenger. The express letter I reckoned, would get there a trifle before the one in the slow ordinary mail.

Therefore as I approached the house on the first day of my next vacation I was shocked when I saw him standing at the bottom of the garden and gazing out over the valley.

I dropped my baggage and hurried over to him. He heard me coming, turned, smiled—the same old warm, friendly smile.

"Buno!" I cried. "Didn't you get my letter?"

He continued to smile. "I got them both, Paul. You're in trouble. I had to come."

"But—"

He waved a deprecating hand. "I feel fine. I've seen the doctor. He says a month on Earth shouldn't hurt. That'll be time enough to get you well on to the home stretch."

"You shouldn't have come," I said, lamely. Gratitude and fear conflicted within me and sapped my spontaneity. I fumbled for his hand, clasped it, said "Thanks," and could think of nothing else to say except a perfunctory inquiry about Jona.

Pop would be out in space for all of two months yet and wouldn't even learn of Buno's visit until it was over.

Later, after a drink in the house, I loosened up and we really got talking, first about old times, then about painting. And then Buno made me unpack my maths books and notes, and out came the log tables, the slide rule, and a mass of graph paper, and he said seriously: "Time's short, Paul, so let's get started."

We got started. That was all. The 'phone began ringing and cars came rolling up the drive as regularly as though the house were a filling station. Buno had travelled incognito, so there had been no press reception at the space-port. But somehow his arrival had got around and the interviewers had tracked him here.

After all, he was probably the world's most famous artist now and had never been interviewed before. The reporters made up for lost time. He bore them patiently. I was glad for him because of this recognition, yet I kept wishing he'd raise a hand, say "That's enough, now," throw them all out—and attend to me.

But I had to write the rest of that day off and all of the next—when TV cameras came peering round the house like inquisitive robots.

It died away at last. Buno began to coach me in earnest. This time it was different. This time I wanted to learn. So I did—and fast.

On the eve of the first day of the examination session I said goodbye to Buno, adding: "I'll be back in a week with my navigator's ticket in my wallet."

"I'll be waiting," Buno smiled.

After the session the candidates had to stick around the School for another two days, awaiting the results. We passed the time mostly in one bar or another till at last the typewritten sheet was tacked upon the green baize. Then we returned to the bars, some of us to celebrate, some of us to drown our sorrows.

I was celebrating. I had cleared the first, and higher, of the two hurdles. I'd passed Space Navigation, Theory. Space Navigation, Practical, would be easy. I'd always been able to use my fingers pretty well—except for counting on.

Then I stopped hitting the bottle and drove home all the afternoon and half the evening and, surprisingly, didn't hit anything else either, except ninety.

A good percentage of alcohol in the blend always makes me feel fonder of people than I am normally. The house seemed full of rosy mist and I swam through it, from room to room, seeking Buno and calling blurrily: "Uncle Buno, I love you!"

He was in his own room sitting beside his easel. A part-done canvas rested there. The sunset glowed beyond the window and he seemed to be studying it. One hand held a brush. His palette lay on the floor before him.

I was full of tipsy *camaraderie* and affection. I slapped him on the back.

"Buno, old man, we've done it."

He tilted stiffly forward. He held the brush tightly and did not put out a hand to save himself. His face hit the floor, hard, half on the palette. He rolled sideways, one leg raised in the air a little, the colours of the rainbow smeared across his face, his white hair standing up fuzzily.

It was dreadfully reminiscent of the climax of a circus clown act.

But the sight of the blob of crimson lake on the cornea of an eye that was wide open wasn't at all funny.

Such a shock is supposed to sober one at once. But it only made me more confused.

Strangely, it took a tumbler of near-neat Scotch to steady me enough to take another look at Uncle Buno.

At least two previous sunsets must have flamed and died before his sightless eyes while he'd been sitting there. Now this one died too while I sat sobbing over him.

The doctor came sometime around midnight. I suppose I must have 'phoned him. I don't remember.

"It was his heart, I guess," he said.

I nodded heavily, still maudlin. "It was his heart," I said. "It was too big."

In due course I became a space-navigator. My ship was the *Flagstaff,* almost as new as my uniform. Pop came to see me off on my maiden flight—to Mars. He was as pleased and as excited as I was, but there was something on his mind.

He asked: "You're still calling on Jona?"

"Of course, Pop. How could I dodge it?"

"She won't be glad to see you, son. Best skip it."

"I'd never feel right about it if I did."

"She's okay, Paul. Thanks to your sending her those credits, she's the richest woman on Mars now."

"And the bitterest."

"Yes. And the bitterest. So stay away from her."

I shrugged. We'd had the argument before, and we each had our own answer, and no talk could change it now.

I didn't think much about it on the trip. The skipper was newly promoted too, and a worrying type. He was dubious about the new ship, dubious about the new navigator, and dubious about the new skipper. The latter he wouldn't admit, the ship couldn't hear him, and so I got the brunt of it all. He had me re-checking our position so often that I found myself nail-biting as much as he.

The landing came as a distinct relief.

But then Mars began to play its part in getting me down. It wasn't unattractive at first sight—the orange sandstone houses in the orange sandy desert, the still-surfaced canals, the cloudless blue sky.

But there was a pervading darkness about it. After a bit, you felt you were wearing smoked spectacles. At the time the planet was fifty million miles further away than Earth from the sun, which despite the thin clear air, gave noticeably less light.

The dark blue of the sky was too dark: it looked as though it had been painted with a brush previously used for black and not properly cleaned. The same shadow seemed to lay behind the other colours, of which there were few, for there were no flowers on Mars and the inhabitants dressed and lived drably.

You always felt it was the moment of dawn and subconsciously waited for the sun to rise. But, of course, it never became any lighter. The disappointment nagged, irrationally, breeding irritation. The tenuous atmosphere didn't help. You could breathe it, but only if you stood still and gulped. If you walked half a dozen paces you began to flounder like a landed fish. So most of the time you wore an oxygen mask, spoke muffledly, and had trouble with saliva.

Buno's village was like all the other Martian villages I'd seen, and his house was like all the other houses in the village. I had expected something better. Buno had been one of the few Martians to bring Earth credits back. And it was months now since I had sent Jona a fortune. Yet there were three cracked and patched window-panes.

In this village Buno was born. I doubted if the scene had changed since that day. Buno had grown up here with little to see but the harsh ochre plain and the slate-coloured canal. Yet he had become one of the greatest painters of all time.

Geniuses, I reflected, truly have an inner eye which sees a world beyond the material one.

Often in imagination I'd pictured myself approaching this house, smart in my new navigator's uniform. Now the reality was here—but the circumstances were miserably different.

I shrank from the encounter to come. But I knew I had to go through with it.

The door stood ajar, thick with its insulation against the freezing Martian night. I hesitated before it, feeling suddenly doubtful about the almost comically outsize bunch of flowers I carried. The problem of just the right present had worried me. All I'd learned that Jona prized were terrestrial household gadgets. But these were obtainable in any of the bigger Martian stores. I could only presume that now she was rich she already possessed all she needed in that line.

I badly wanted to say and do the right things. It would be all wrong to say: "Jona, I'm sorry. It's my fault you're a widow. Please accept this as a token of my regret" —and then hand her a vacuum cleaner.

Hence the flowers, beautiful and rare. Probably there were no flowers on Mars at the moment except these, brought from Earth, the life in them carefully and expensively preserved.

I had made no sound, but the door was pulled slowly open from within. And there Jona stood watching me. I had noticed that sometimes Buno had sensed my approach without actually seeing or hearing me. Apparently his wife shared the faculty.

Like he, she was tall, thin, white-haired, with pink-rimmed but steady eyes—unnervingly steady now.

"I'm Paul," I blurted, indistinctly through my mask. "I—I brought you these."

I held out the flowers. She took them solemnly and silently. Now that my hands were empty I didn't know what to do with them. I stuck them in my pockets but felt that was impolite and withdrew them. Then they felt like a pair of silly, dangling appendages.

She watched me unblinkingly. Somehow I felt like a kid dressed up in his father's uniform.

"I came to say how sorry I am about Uncle Buno," I said, in my best Martian but still muffled by that damned oxygen mask. "I feel, you know, it was all my fault."

She nodded gravely, which didn't help at all. Pa had said she was bitter. I knew that many of the Martians were bitter towards our race, because they'd reached their apex of material civilization with the canal system, and then fallen away from it without ever having mastered space travel.

They'd failed to escape from their dying world and were dying with it. Whereas we, a younger race, were possessed of a rich, living world and yet could leave it whenever we chose. They resented our vigour, our youth, our wealth, our power, and they chose to pretend we liked to flaunt them in their faces. They had one hell of an inferiority complex, together with its concomitant pride.

But Jona had a personal reason to be bitter. I'd rather she showed it, screamed and clawed, than gravely agree with my self-accusations. It made me feel so completely condemned, that atonement or forgiveness were not to be considered.

She made no move to invite me in.

I clasped and unclasped my useless hands, then said all in a rush: "Uncle Buno was the greatest man I ever knew. And the kindest. I could never repay what I owe him. But I should like to be the first to write his biography. Of course, I can't presume to judge his works. That must be left to someone better qualified. I just want to describe what sort of person he was, what he thought of life and art and so forth. I was wondering if he left any personal papers that I might borrow for the purpose. I promise you I'll be most discreet and publish nothing without your approval."

My voice died away because Jona was regarding me with such intensity that I wondered whether I was exciting her enthusiasm or her hatred.

She nodded sharply, and said in a strangled sort of voice: "Wait."

She closed the door to. A couple of minutes later she reappeared, thrust a small cloth-bound book into my hands and then shut the door between us with finality.

I sighed, half with relief, half with regret. I looked at the book. The neatly formed Martian writing was recognizably Buno's. It appeared to be a volume of a private journal. It began, I noted, on the day Buno returned to Earth from Mars.

I leafed through it and it was as though the book became a living viper in my hands. Phrase after phrase darted out at me like a forked, venomous tongue.

> *"That pampered little fool, Paul ... No wonder the mother abandoned her idiot child ... The humiliation of having to be civil to him ... Trying to get simple self-evident facts through his thick skull was like trying to push your finger through a wall ... His father is a typical specimen of that culturally backward race, arrogant because they were handed paradise on a plate ... Another infuriating letter today from the moronic Paul ..."*

I snapped the book shut, crushing those hurtful fangs back in there. The blind-windowed house, itself tightly shut, seemed to sway before me. But it was I who was rocking. The poison had entered my bloodstream and the shock was beginning.

Somehow I blundered away in an erratic curve, which, as it lengthened, revealed to me the area back of the house. And there was a pit half full of smashed terrestrial gadgets: a refrigerator, a washing machine, a cooker, cleaners, things large and small. As I looked at them as dully and uncomprehendingly as the moron *he'd* said I was, a backdoor opened and my offering of flowers was tossed out, into the pit.

I never even glimpsed Jona's hand. Perhaps because of the silly, childish tears filling my eyes. I turned away again, seeking blindly for the haven of the ship, and the tears wouldn't stop but ran over the oxygen mask and besprinkled my stiff new uniform.

In my pain I lost my precarious grip on the art of walking under the Martian gravity. My feet became almost beyond control and lifted me in high-floating steps. Altogether, bouncing, zigzagging, and blubbering, I must have looked ridiculous. All-conquering Earthman! No doubt I was a joke to the Martian villagers, behind their closed windows, and balm to their bruised egos.

The Captain was as fretful as ever on the voyage back, but this time I was glad of it. The constant neurotic double-checkings helped to save me from too much brooding about Buno and Jona and their contemptuous rejection of me.

When I got home I wasn't at first going to tell Pop about it. But the mystery nagged at me like an aching nerve. Why? I'd thought Buno had, in his way, loved me, risked his life to help me—and lost it. Then *why* . . .? Why in his recorded private thoughts did he seldom mention me without a dislike at times amounting to hatred? Only Pop might know. So I told him about it, after all.

He read the Journal slowly, because he wasn't all that good at Martian.

When he laid it aside at last, I asked: "Well? Can you explain why he was such a great man and yet so two-faced?"

Pop smiled faintly. "That combination isn't peculiar to Martians. Think of Richard Wagner. No—don't. It would be a false comparison. Buno was never two-faced. He was just two persons."

"What do you mean?"

"Paul, I once mentioned that pair of Martians working at Washington Spaceport. Have you ever conversed with them? I have. The gravity drag cripples them. In time it will kill them. But they are calm and amiable. Yet the average Martian—*on Mars*—is suspicious, envious, spiteful, always beefing. We're so largely the creatures of our environment, you see."

I reflected, then said: "Buno, in the Journal, kept referring to Earth as paradise. As Paradise Lost, in fact. It was almost as though he blamed us for dispossessing him."

"Yes, Paul, it was sheer jealousy, and you became the focal point of that jealousy. Buno was a born artist. But he never became an inspired one until he saw Earth, with its beautifully coloured flora and fauna, its landscapes and—above all—its cloudscapes and sunsets. He'd never seen such marvellous play of light before. What a contrast to Mars, with its weak sunlight, its cloudless sky of one monotonous hue, its feeble range of colour . . . In the Journal there are two whole pages of ecstasy about a remembered rainbow."

"I know, Pop. But why did he pick on me?"

"You're the lad he would have given everything to be, with all Earth to paint and all a lifetime to do it. He could never hope to live here for more than a few months, *in toto*. He envied your opportunities, despised you because you couldn't make use of them the way he would have done."

I sighed. "And all that was fermenting in him while I thought he was helping me only from kindness."

"It didn't ferment in him *here*," said Pop. "Only on Mars. Here he *was* kind and helpful. He was two different people in two different places. To some extent we all are. On Mars I always feel depressed and take things hard. I expect you did too. And it's a lot tougher for the Martians—it was toughest of all for Buno, with his artistic temperament. I think the thin Martian air is mostly to blame: the Martians are oxygen-starved. It devitalizes them, makes them morose and irritable. It would do the same for us, if it weren't for the oxygen masks."

"Then we should supply all Martians with oxygen masks."

Pop shrugged. "There's more to it than oxygen. There's some other element missing from their atmosphere which we have. Maybe one of the inert gases. Maybe some other infinitesimal but important constituent that gives our air sparkle. Buno breathed freely and saw clearly in his short time on Earth. On Mars he was sick physically and in his soul, like the others. Think of him always as you knew him, when he was healthy."

"I shall," I said, picking up the Journal. "I'm going to burn this." I hesitated. "Let's face it, Pop, he didn't return to Earth just to help me."

"That's right, son. And so you can't be blamed. Your letter was the excuse he needed. He wanted to see Earth again before he died, and paint again, because Mars was making him impotent as an artist. Painting was his life. He came back to Earth to live—and die."

"It was hard on Jona."

"Yes. She loved him, and I think he loved her—but not so much as he loved art. Now she curses everything terrestrial. Earth stole away her husband."

"I'd hate her to go on feeling that way for the rest of her life. Do you think, Pop, we can ever persuade her to come and stay with us for a short holiday, just so that we can meet the real Jona? And she can meet the real us?"

Pop shook his head. "Never. But there's one hope. There's a plan already under way to re-oxygenate the whole Martian atmosphere. Oxygen can be recovered from the deserts there. We must make our scientists understand that's still not enough. They've got to track down the other vital element in our atmosphere, and introduce that. That's the one way we can help Jona."

"You're right, Pop." I thought a little while, and became conscious of the kindling of a purpose. I added, quietly: "It's the only way we can repay Uncle Buno, too."

A NICHE IN TIME

IT HAD TO BE A PAINTER THIS TIME. My kind of painter.

I've catholic taste, but a natural bias. Music, literature, poetry, the theater, sculpture, architecture: all stairways for my spirit. All tracks up the slopes of Parnassus.

Yet to me the crest meant just one thing: a certain masterly arrangement of colors and of light and shade, bringing blazing exaltation.

It had to be van Gogh.

Concerning others there was usually doubt about the right Moment to choose. Vincent's Moment for me, personally, was the painting of his masterpiece, "The Yellow House." For my employer, the University, Department of History, sub-Department A.E. (Active Encouragement), the Moment was in the Borinage, during van Gogh's period of greatest early discouragement. The Church Council had declared he was a most unsatisfactory preacher, and flung him out.

He didn't know which way to turn. So I visited him.

Shortly afterwards, he wrote to his brother, Theo: "I decided to take up my pencil and start drawing again, and from that moment everything looked different."

He was twenty-seven then.

I had been the man of that "Moment," which it's my job to be: I am a Visitor.

It's a responsible job, and the strain of saying the right thing at the right time can be wearing on the nerves. So the University, which is sometimes understanding—but often not—allows me the odd trip now and then purely for relaxation. A little holiday.

This holiday I wanted to see a painter. My kind of painter. I chose to revisit Vincent eight years after the Borinage—eight years of *his* time, of course. On a day when the paint on the canvas of "The Yellow House" was still wet. . .

In my excitement I miscalculated, and instead of the tree-sheltered park set the chronocab plumb in the center of the lawn in Place Lamartine. But no one was around to witness me stepping out of nothingness. I was in costume, as always. This time masquerading as a French agricultural laborer, with walnut juice brown-staining my face and arms.

One must never excite the attention of the populace.

There it stood, on the corner. The yellow house itself, with its green door. The sun drenched it, but the yellow was hard, lacking the honeyed warmth from Vincent's brush. The sky above it was pure cobalt, lacking the magic ingredient of black Vincent had worked into *his* sky. It takes a master painter to gild Nature.

Beyond, on the right, the glamorous Café de Nuit—dusty, crumbling, prosaic in plain daylight.

Also, the two railroad bridges, and just crossing the nearer—a timely gift from Time!—a slow, slug-black, smoky train.

Wide open to every precious nuance of awareness, I lounged across the brown grass.

This time it wasn't necessary to explain that I was a Visitor. It's never easy to do, and it was nice to be able to relax. Vincent van Gogh still had two more years—the terrible years—to live, and there was nothing I could do about that. His disease was already deep-rooted in his brain.

My French was far better than his, and he accepted me as a Frenchman. An odd type, admittedly: a laborer who knew something about the technique of painting. But Vincent was already dwelling in a fantasy world, and I became merely part of it to him.

On my first visit it had been more difficult. He had been let down badly. He was suspicious: thought I was an agent of the Evangelist Committee. I was a pretty good linguist, even then, but Dutch wasn't my strong suit. He'd been teaching—and preaching—in England, so we got by in English that time.

And that time I took him hack to England—in the chronocab.

London in midwinter, 1948. A dark gray day by the dark gray Thames. There was an endless drizzle from a sky of mud. We arrived behind a telephone booth—its red was the only visible splash of color—on a side street.

I led him around the corner, and there on the sidewalk, patient in the rain, was a line of more than a thousand people. Slowly, they were shuffling into the Tate Gallery. And as the big building swallowed the head of the line, so others joined the tail, keeping the line at a constant length.

"That," I told him, "has been going on all day. It went on all yesterday. So it will go on, day after day. A thousand people an hour, every hour. All records for attendance at an art exhibition have already been smashed. These people, weary after a long war, are starved of sunshine and color. They flock here to feast their souls on the work of one great artist."

"Rembrandt?" he guessed, innocently, watching the traffic on the street with a wondering but wary eye. It was thin today, but I had warned him of it.

"No. You—Vincent van Gogh."

He was stunned, and had no words. Those wild pale-blue eyes rolled more wildly. I feared he would have one of his fits, but his shaking was only excitement at this evidence of his unbelievable success.

We stood in line, so that presently he could see for himself the blazing sunflowers and orchards of the future in his style of the future . . .

And now, in that future of his, in Arles, on my second visit, I stood with him again, looking at some of those very same paintings: un-hung, unwanted, unbought.

The thick paint of "The Yellow House" was damp as tooth-paste on the canvas: he'd just brought it in from the square. I could have left my thumb print on it for posterity—theoretically.

I savored this historical Moment.

I pictured this little house when the mistral howled around it, setting the windows rattling, the doors banging, and Vincent's su-per-sensitive nerves on edge.

I looked at the mess of dropped paint on the floor and the splashes on the walls. Soon Vincent would clean that up and whitewash the walls. For his hero, Gauguin, was coming to stay.

And one day, during Gauguin's stay, the red-tiled floor would become redder yet, with Vincent's blood, and all the splashes on the walls would be crimson.

I glanced at his right ear, and felt again the old awe of Neme-sis. Effectively, the chronocab was like a fly buzzing across the path of a runaway truck.

Maybe the universe is mad. If so, the most you can do is try to give people courage to face it.

If ever a man needed encouragement, Vincent did. Pick a moment at random in his life and you could reasonably call it the Moment. Here and now in Arles, for instance. He still hadn't sold a single painting. He was to sell only one in his life, and that for under four hundred francs.

Would it help if I told him that in Paris, in 1957, just one of his paintings would be sold for the equivalent of two hundred fifty thousand of those same francs? And at that period his total output was to be valued at thirty million francs? He needed money and food *now*. More likely it would embitter him to learn that art dealers, of the same ignorant breed that had spurned him all his life, would make fortunes from him when he was dead.

So I didn't tell him.

In any case, this time I had no authority to back such a statement. The first time, I revealed my identity and proved it by demonstration. Then, my mission completed, electronically erased the traces of it, which was standard procedure. This time I was just François, an appreciative peasant, who wanted to learn about technique from an obvious master.

As I hoped, lonely Vincent, deprived of communication on the subject, except in letters to Theo, was eager to expound.

Finally, he settled on the bed, smoking and talking nonstop. While I sat on the rush-seated chair he was to make so famous, drinking his words in. My hero, the genius who it had been my privilege to help, explaining himself and his work to me personally, on a warm evening in Arles, far away in time and space . . .

It was unforgettable. Nevertheless, I dutifully transcribed it from the tape directly I returned. It was practically a two-hour monologue.

Would you like to know what Vincent van Gogh said? You can. Just read on.

My mind is purely that of an artist. It feels its way through a kind of colored fog. It reasons poorly, sees nothing sharp and clear in black and white. Mathematics has always baffled it. It can't grasp scientific technicalities. It merely apprehends form, tone, shades . . .

How was such a vague person as myself appointed a Visitor? Well, of course, I'm restricted to the Arts, just as my colleague, Blum, is confined to the Sciences. Sometimes I envy him his keen, precise mind. His task is to encourage the scientific geniuses at times when superstition, incredulity, or prejudice are stifling their creativity.

At least, he can offer a logical explanation of how past, present, and future are not merely interdependent but an immutable whole. And how an as yet unborn man can put his oar into some current human situation and add his pennyweight of influence to the scale-pan when a despairing creator is wavering between renewing the struggle or giving it up altogether.

When my particular nurslings of immortality ask me to explain the apparent time paradox, I begin to stammer. I fall back on insisting: "Well, it *is* so. For here I am. For further proof, I'll take you through time to my world, which is your world also: for you have conquered it."

Once, of course, they've tasted future—and often posthumous—fame, they never revive the argument. It might spoil the dream. When they've seen their paintings or sculptures in the Louvre, heard audiences cheering their operas or plays, handled many editions of their books in libraries, they're reborn.

The surly Beethoven, for instance, bitter through neglect, anxious about his growing deafness. Following that visit to Carnegie Hall he was as benign and joyous as his own Pastoral Symphony. It was the joy of faith vindicated.

Another paradox. Man is never without faith. He always believes. If a man says he has lost his faith, he yet has faith—in his belief that he has lost his faith. All the same, this seeming loss of faith can cause spiritual stasis. It's a whirlpool trap for a man's soul, which could circle pointlessly until he dies.

I explained to Ludwig von Beethoven that it was a Visitor's job to throw a line to such trapped souls.

He said, typically: "I am not the only one. I know of friends—"

"I cannot help your friends," I said. "Even if I tried to, I couldn't give them what fate has denied them. They have talent, not genius. Experience has shown that genius responds, talent does not. I can do nothing for them."

This led to a discussion on the nature of genius.

Beethoven's view was . . .

You can learn Beethoven's view on genius. And it will cost you nothing. Read on.

Analyze the most magical lines in poetry and you'll find they're evocative of the inexorable passage of Time.

But at my back I always hear
Time's winged chariot hurrying near.

Or:

Brightness falls from the air,
Queens have died young and fair,

Dust hath closed Helen's eye.
Or.
Nymphs and shepherds, dance no more. (A line which always moved Housman to tears.)

Shakespeare, of course, was the most Time conscious of them all. He refers variously to Time as: "The clock-setter, that bald sexton . . . That old common arbitrator . . . A whirligig . . . A fashionable host . . . The king of men . . . Eater of youth . . . A great-sized monster of ingratitudes . . . Envious and calumniating Time."

And bids us: *See the minutes, how they run.*
And asks:
What strong hand can hold his swift foot back?
Or who his spoil of beauty can forbid?
And:
But wherefore do not you a mightier way
Make war upon this bloody tyrant, Time?
And declares:
Time, that takes survey of all the world,
Must have a stop.

His Sonnets are one long defiance of "Devouring Time." Constantly he repeats that, although Time will devour him, his lines will defeat Time.

Not marble nor the gilded monuments
Of princes shall outlive this powerful rhyme.

Which led to a mystery. After his retirement to Stratford he made no attempt to publish any of his plays. After his death, they would have been lost forever had not a couple of his friends collated some old prompt copies.

Was Shakespeare finally resigned to the inevitable victory of Time? Or was he just thumbing his nose at it?

I wanted to visit him in his retirement and solve this mystery. Some day I shall.

I must hear that beautiful, gentle voice again, speaking his lines with that fascinating Warwickshire accent he never lost. Men have wondered that, reputedly, in his manuscripts, "he never blotted a line." Of course not. He was an actor. It was his practice to speak his lines aloud many times until they *sounded* right. Then it was merely a clerical job to write them down. So naturally, as Heminge and Condell remarked: "His mind and hand went together."

I would have thought that his Moment for A.E. treatment was fairly late in life. Say, when in bitter despair at human ingratitude, he wrote the searing "Timon of Athens." But the departmental heads held that it lay somewhere in the Sonnet period, when he was in distress over his capricious rejection by the Dark Lady.

Maybe they were right. Anyhow, I visited him officially then.

The mysterious Dark Lady was certainly a *femme* fatale. There was poor Fortesque who, because of her, jumped from Old London Bridge . . .

She was . . .

Perhaps you know who she was. Again, perhaps, like those who strove for four centuries to uncover her identity, you are still in the dark. You need be no longer. On the last page of this brochure you will find the key enabling you to unlock not only her mystery, but also many other mysteries of history.

It was the night of March 3, 1875, the premiere of "Carmen" at the Opéra Comique in Paris.

The audience was ice-cold. It didn't understand the opera, so it was bored. The curtain came down to a snake-pit chorus of hissing.

There was a well-known report, repeated by Bruneau, that Bizet walked the streets of Paris till dawn next day, hysterical with shame and despair. Later, Halévy testified that such was not the case. That after the show Bizet returned with him to their lodgings. That was so. I know. I walked behind them.

In some ways, this was the strangest of all my missions. Doomed to failure, yet it was written that I had to try.

The whole point of life is that we all have to try.

What I shall never quite understand is how encouragement given *after* a work is created can assist its creation. Blum tells me I must cease to think of time one-dimensionally, as a continuous line. I should picture it three dimensionally. Say, as a cube.

A man's conscious mind moves from point to point over the surfaces of the cube. But his subconscious mind moves below those surfaces, darting around like a firefly within the cube. It can touch points of time anywhere on the cube long before conscious attention does.

Not that this is any new discovery. In the late Nineteenth and early Twentieth centuries experimenters confirmed the phenomenon of pre-cognition clearly enough.

Anyhow, the fact remains that the subconscious is aware of the Moment of Active Encouragement, and it's immaterial whether that Moment lies in the conscious future or past. For it is from the subconscious that all creation proceeds.

Bizet was alone in his room when I called in the small hours. He was still fully dressed, sitting at a table with a bottle of champagne and a half-full glass before him. He'd drunk only a little and was quite sober.

His face was impassive—and haunts me still. He had just received a mortal blow, but his self-control was almost superhuman. I respect him as a man perhaps more than any other man I've met, past or present. I've painted his portrait from memory. It depicts merely a fair-haired, fair-bearded man who looks thoughtful and—nice. (That unsatisfactory, and yet the only satisfactory, word.)

I've failed to capture, in paint, the essence of Georges Bizet. I shall try again.

I introduced myself and explained my presence. He seemed to believe me without proof, almost as though he were expecting me.

I told him: "In 1880 Tchaikovsky will publicly predict that within a decade 'Carmen' will become the most popular opera in the world. I'm glad to assure you that he will he perfectly right."

He smiled and poured me a glass of champagne.

"Let's drink to Tchaikovsky, then."

"No," I said, raising my glass, "To Bizet."

"Thank you. You are the only man to toast me tonight. At this moment, all the critics are busily ripping 'Carmen' to shreds with their pen-nibs."

"Critics! On the rare occasions when their verdicts are unanimous, their reasons for giving them are totally different. Ignore them. You didn't write 'Carmen' for them. You wrote it for the people."

He sipped at his glass.

"That is true. And the people have rejected it."

"Come," I said, rising, "we'll go to the opera. I'll take you into 1905, and the night of the thousandth performance of 'Carmen.' "

He remained seated. "No, Monsieur Everard. The next generation is not my concern. I shall not live to know those people. I wrote for *this* generation, my fellow human beings. I have failed them."

"Nonsense! *They* have failed you."

"We've both failed—to communicate. And now something has broken in here."

He tapped his chest.

In three months—at only thirty-seven—he was dead. Of heart disease, the doctor said—though Bizet had shown no symptom of it before. Bizet's friends said yes, it was heart trouble: a broken heart.

It is true that when a man's spiritual mainspring breaks, it's beyond repair. The best that one can do is face the situation with calmness and courage. Bizet did just that. I shall always envy him his maturity.

There were other composers, too, of course, who died even younger, neglected "failures." The poverty-stricken Mozart, for one: he was buried in a pauper's grave. And the equally poor Schubert, for another, deeply frustrated in his love life also. Jon Everard met them both. His descriptions of those meetings will move you profoundly.

Vincent van Gogh and I are totally dissimilar in style, although I owe so much to him. If there is a distinct Everard style, then I have achieved it in my "Calvary." The version on my studio wall is actually my third attempt: I destroyed the others.

Strange how people who have admired it all assumed it to have come solely from my imagination. In fact, all three were painted in the neighborhood of Golgotha, and depicted the actual scene at the actual time.

Three crosses on a distant hill against a stormy sky . . .

Why didn't I approach nearer? I tried to, but something barred me each time. Possibly my own awe. Possibly some influence I don't understand.

Earlier, with the innocent daring of youth, I sometimes wondered whether I could possibly be intended to serve as a humble instrument in the Second Coming . . .

Naturally, we hope that these brief extracts from the famous JOURNAL OF JON EVERARD *will whet your appetite for the whole wonderful story. You can have copies sent to you in two handsome cloth-bound volumes. Simply fill in the form below and mail it to us. SEND NO MONEY until you have inspected this bargain of a lifetime at your leisure in your own home.*

Escape from the long winter evenings on golden journeys through time with Jon Everard to meet face to face many of the greatest men who ever lived.

When he had finished reading the shiny brochure, Jon Everard pursed his lips and laid it on his desk.

He looked at the Visitor, who eagerly and a little nervously awaited his comment.

"An ill-judged selection, I'm afraid, Mr. Bernstein. Certainly not the best of my passages, and the balance is poor. And that cheapjack get-the-customer-hooked gimmick is deplorable."

Bernstein looked crestfallen.

"Of course, some of the advertising copywriters do tend to lack taste, Mr. Everard. But their job is to sell the book to the widest possible public. They have to set their sights low . . . But that wasn't very tactful, was it? I'm making a mess of this. I thought bringing that brochure was a good idea. It would show you at a glance that you would become the most famous and popular diarist since Pepys. Maybe I should have brought one of the tooled leather editions—"

"No, it's all right," cut in Everard. "You did well. Forgive my carping. My nerves have been in poor shape lately."

"Yes, I know. I must be your greatest fan, Mr. Everard. I know your Journal almost by heart. I can tell from the tone that around this period you had a bout of nervous depression, although you didn't record it in so many words."

"It showed, huh?"

"It seemed to me you'd gotten in the way of measuring yourself against these great men you were meeting, to your own detriment. You were losing the sense of your own worth. That's why I picked on this period to come back and show you that, probably quite unconsciously, you were writing a masterpiece. None of your successors has accomplished anything like it. I know I'll never he able to touch it, though I do keep a Journal. I'm still green at the job. Frankly, I hoped to pick up a few personal tips from you, as you did from van Gogh."

"This visit is one of your holiday choices?"

"Yes. The very first. The University doubted you needed encouragement, and refused to sanction an official journey. You know what these things cost. There's always trouble over expense."

Jon Everard nodded. "Then I shan't make the account any heavier for you by insisting on going for a peek-a-boo at your world. Sounds like the same old world, anyhow. Thanks for calling, Mr. Bernstein."

Bernstein unhappily felt he was being dismissed. He hesitated. Everard read his thoughts, and smiled kindly at him.

"I'd like to be able to help you, son, but nothing I could say would be of any practical use to you. It's such a personal kind of job that everyone's approach is bound to be different, according to their nature. Experience is the only teacher. So concentrate on developing into the first Bernstein rather than a second Everard. If it'll increase your confidence, I'll tell you this: in all my travels I never had a cold welcome . . . What's the reading on your chronometer?"

Bernstein started, then inspected a dial on his tape recorder.

"Twenty-one minutes, thirty-five seconds."

"Play safe and set a round twenty-five on your Eraser," Everard advised.

Bernstein fumbled in his jacket pocket. Then he flushed.

"I really am a fool. I've forgotten to bring it. I was so eager to meet you, came away in a rush . . . Now I'll have to go back and get it."

"And add another fifteen thousand to the account?"

"Closer to forty thousand these days—that is, in *my* days," said Bernstein, gloomily. "The Governors will be mad at me for making a costly boob like this, especially on a privilege trip. Nevertheless, even if they fire me, I shall never regret making this trip."

"They need never know about it," smiled Everard. "You can use my Eraser."

He went across to his chronocabinet. It looked like a telephone booth in the corner. It was meant to look as ordinary as that, to avoid arousing curiosity. For Jon Everard was the first official Visitor, and at this time his reports were on the Restricted List.

He pulled the door open and patted a leather holster fixed to its inner side.

"Here's one tip, anyhow. Keep your Eraser stowed in the chronocab itself. Then you can't very well leave it behind."

"Thanks, I'll do that, Mr. Everard."

Everard pulled the pistol-shaped Eraser from the holster. The dial in its butt gleamed as it caught the light. He turned a knurled knob to set the pointer.

"Twenty-five minutes." He handed the instrument to Bernstein.

Bernstein checked. "Right."

Everard returned to his desk, settled back comfortably in his chair.

"It must be a relief for you to skip the explanation this one time," he said. "I always find that a tough chore. Sometimes they're a little afraid in case I'm going to kill them. Make sure you replace that Eraser in my chronocab—don't stick it in your pocket and take it with you. O.K., I'm relaxed now. Fire when ready."

He closed his eyes with a kind of deliberate finality.

Bernstein thought: he doesn't want to see me any more. Maybe *he* never had a cold welcome, but I've had warmer ones than this. Not even a good-by handshake. I tell him he's my idol—and it doesn't mean a thing. He's decent enough, sure—but I thought we'd have such a lot to talk about. Thought I'd be here all day. Twenty-five minutes!"

He walked behind Everard's chair, pressed the point of the Eraser against the nape of Everard's neck, thumbed the button.

The force-field of an Eraser sets up a block in the prefrontal area of the brain, eliminating the neuron paths consciously recorded within any set period. The subconscious retains the relevant memories but they can never re-emerge into consciousness: the bridges are down.

There was no visible reaction from Everard, but that was normal. Mental numbness usually persisted for three or four minutes after the shock. An artist, say, would awaken on his studio couch and imagine he'd merely fallen asleep. Whether he had been robbed of a few hours of his working life by sleep or by an Eraser made no odds. His dream life, at any rate, had been enriched, and his work is an embodied dream.

Bernstein pocketed the brochure, then glanced out of the window at the sea in sunlight. He had visualized himself strolling along its margin with his old hero, discussing life and what makes a man great, until those western waters were blood-tinged by the sunset. But sundown was way off, and he must leave Everard and his world, to meet him again only on familiar printed pages.

He sighed, taking a farewell look at the calm, still face. Then he went into the corner by the tall bookcase—and disappeared. It was as though he had stepped through an invisible door into another dimension. And, indeed, this was what had happened. For an invisible projection of his own chrono-cabinet was located there.

Five seconds later, he re-appeared, flushed and chagrined. He blundered across to Everard's solidly visible chronocabinet, and thrust the Eraser back in its holster. Sentimental mooning, destroying my concentration, will lose me this job yet, he chided himself.

A faint, unobserved smile touched Everard's lips, and was gone.

And then Bernstein, back in his own chronocabinet, was gone also. Everard, waiting for it, had heard the faint rising hum end abruptly with a snap, like a breaking violin string.

He opened his eyes, but no amusement lingered in them. They were sad. He ran his fingers through his hair, then rested his elbows on his desk and brooded.

He had boobed over the Eraser, too. Its battery was flat, and he had intended to replace it before his next trip. But, until Bernstein had attempted to use it on him, he'd forgotten that.

Why, then, had he shammed unconsciousness?

Why hadn't he simply apologized, and replaced the battery?

Pride, covering up that the great Jon Everard, famed as a perfectionist, could make elementary mistakes like a tyro—like Bernstein?

Consideration—to spare the young man further embarrassment?

Opportunism—to make use of foreknowledge?

Egotism—to be able to gloat over his coming election to the Hall of Fame?

No, none of those reasons. They were absurd. For he would be happier minus the memories of the past twenty-five minutes. Fame he desired, and fame would be his—but for the wrong reason. His life-long ambition had been to become a great painter. He had poured his soul into his painting.

But Bernstein had made no mention of Everard, the painter. Neither had the brochure. Therefore, his work could have left no great impression. He had failed and was doomed to fail.

And he hadn't the guts of a Georges Bizet.

As he brooded, he gradually began to understand why he had chosen to stay conscious. Bernstein's visit had succeeded only in imbuing him with a sense of failure and inadequacy. If the Eraser had functioned, it would have left his subconscious mind filled with discouragement, the reverse of what Bernstein had intended. And he would never know why he felt that way.

The instinct for self-preservation had induced him to play possum.

Self-awareness meant that he wasn't chained in bondage to his subconscious. He still had the power of choice. He must try for Bizet's kind of courage, and accept the situation as philosophically as the Frenchman did.

And that same self-awareness told him that there was one great difference: *nothing had broken inside him.*

He must simply learn to adjust. He must learn to exchange the brush for the pen, and become another kind of artist.

He picked up his pen and opened his Journal. He had not yet finished the account of his meeting with Georges Bizet.

He wrote: *The whole point of life is that we all have to try.*

He paused, remembering the words. That brochure was helping him, after all. Yet . . . it was fated, too. The future supported the past just as much as the past supported the future. Cause and effect were like two balancing sides of a Gothic arch. It was nonsense to pretend one came "first."

Yet he still had the power of choice. It made it no less a choice because his future self made that choice.

Time was an edifice, all of a piece, like some vast cathedral, architecturally perfect. Arch beyond arch, myriads of interlocking arches . . .

Soon, he told himself, I must visit an architect. Say, Christopher Wren, when the Commissioners for rebuilding London after the Great Fire were doing all they could to thwart his plans for completing St. Paul's Cathedral . . .

THE WHISPERING GALLERY

"NOW, IF YOU WILL JUST COME THIS WAY . . ."

The voice was sibilant and insinuating. It hinted at wonders which would make all you had seen so far become thin and flat and forgotten. Marvels unmatched lay just around the corner and the voice knew the way.

But Frederic was five years old and therefore he knew what voices really said and it wasn't always what the words would have you believe. This voice said, really, "I hate you all, especially the boy, and this is the way out and I shall be glad to see the last of you."

The voice had no intention after all of leading the way up the secret staircase to the golden ball.

This guide was a tall lean fellow, with yellow sunken cheeks and eye-sockets so deep and shadowed you could not be sure whether there were eyes in their recesses or not. Not unless you looked hard into them, that was, and so far Frederic had not found the courage to do so and make sure.

He peeped up at the guide's face only now and again from the corners of his own eyes and the sight of the strangely small nose—(as if the original had been pared down to the bone)—and the almost lipless mouth, with the big white teeth that seemed set in a sort of sardonic grin that would always be there whatever the outward facial mask expressed, had frightened his timid glance away every time.

If only this man had been like the jolly Beefeater in the fancy dress who had shown him the room in the Tower of London where the little Princes had been murdered. The Beefeater would have taken him up to the golden ball and perhaps given it to him. Especially if he had known that Frederic had wanted it for years. Since yesterday morning.

Yesterday was the magic morning when Jim was driving him around London in the open tourer. Just him and Jim. They were caught for a few minutes in a traffic jam in Fleet Street and their car was facing east.

"Gosh," said Frederic, pointing over the bonnet, "That must be the biggest building in the world!"

The chauffeur looked tolerantly up at the Cathedral.

He said, "It looks big from here because it's standing on top of a hill—Ludgate Hill. But it's not so big really. It's hardly knee-high to the Empire State and you've been up that."

Frederic craned his neck. The great gray dome swelled up like an enormous bubble above the twin flanking towers and on top of the dome stood another high tower with a golden gallery around its base. And right at the top of this tower was a golden ball with a golden cross planted on it like a tree. All the golden things glittered in the sunlight but the ball gleamed brightest of all. It seemed to give a light of its own rather than reflect.

"Don't be stupid, Jim," said Frederic, scornfully. "Anybody can see it's higher than the Empire State. It's the biggest thing I've ever seen. What a lovely golden ball that is! I wish I had it to play with. I wonder if it—comes off?"

"Would you like me to climb up there and unscrew it for you?" Jim asked quizzically.

"Would you?" said Frederic eagerly. "*Would* you?"

Jim laughed. There was a time when he would have sighed and muttered under his breath, "These rich folk are all alike—big kids and little kids. But all kids. Get me this, get me that—look, the moon shines pretty—get me that."

But he had served them for a long time now and he had grown philosophical. They weren't happy, these people—they were poor. They were always wanting something—not only to have something but to go somewhere, see something new, have someone praise them, reassure them, do things for them. When they were little kids the world was too big for them and they tore around it in deadly fear of missing any of it before they died.

And when they were big kids, with dulled eyes and desensitized palates, the world was too small. It was a pile of cinders which they prodded wearily, hoping against hope that one day they might uncover something that gleamed bright and new and fascinated the attention. Like the dimly-remembered silver ring hanging from the hood of the baby carriage. Like the golden ball atop St. Paul's Cathedral on a sunny day in your fifth year.

"*Jim!* You're not listening."

"Yes I am, Freddy. See here, son, when you're small you get all balled up over sizes and heights and distances. I remember when I was a kid telling my Ma that telegraph posts were just the tallest things in the world, higher than any old church steeple. But when I grew up I saw I hadn't been talking sense."

"Get me the ball, Jim," said Frederic gravely.

"I'm trying to tell you, son—it's too big. Why, half a dozen grown-up men could get inside it."

"Why, it's no bigger than an apple! Perhaps it *is* an apple—a golden apple. The golden apple in the story."

"What story?"

"Oh,"—impatiently—"the one Mr. George told me about Paris giving Aphro—Aphrodotty"— he hadn't got the name right but it didn't matter—Jim wouldn't know—"a golden apple for a prize. I've always wanted a golden apple. I wonder if it *is*, Jim? Do you think it is?"

Jim Bates opened his mouth, then closed it again. He had often done that in the service of the Staggs. Mrs. Stagg frequently found the truth unpleasant. Her son also obstinately believed what he wanted to believe. There wasn't much use fighting against it. The rich were always right—if you wanted to keep your job.

"I don't know, Freddy. I don't suppose I shall ever know."

"Why not climb . . .?"

"Chauffeurs aren't allowed in churches," said Jim hastily but firmly, as though it were a thing everybody knew.

And Frederic, who knew that there were many holy sanctums in his native Boston where chauffeurs weren't allowed entry, said "Oh," disappointedly as the jam broke and the car rolled forward.

"Jim, perhaps *I*—"

More haste and firmness. "We must go back to the hotel now. Your mother said you're to be back at one for lunch."

And the tourer swung sharply left at Ludgate Circus and angled back through side-streets to Holborn and the straight run to the hotel at Marble Arch, and though he kept looking back Frederic could not see St. Paul's again for the shops and office buildings. He couldn't understand how such little buildings could block out such a towering magnificence as St. Paul's.

Perhaps they're jealous, he thought. *They're getting together and trying to stop anyone from seeing St. Paul's because it makes them look so unimportant beside it.*

"But I *can't*, Frederic—not this afternoon. We're having tea with Lady Cornford."

"Can we go tomorrow then, Mom?"

"No. We're going home tomorrow."

The corners of Frederic's mouth turned down. His eyes began to water.

"Oh, my!" said Mrs. Stagg and her self-harassed mind darted about seeking to forestall the shrieks which would have drowned the orchestra in the hotel restaurant.

She consulted the clock-face which was always in that mind's eye by which she lived, by which she moved, always aiming to fit the social events and the sightseeing in so that there would be no awful gaps in which she might be left to reflect upon herself.

"Well, look, I could just spare half an hour—no more. We should have to come away right after that."

Frederic smiled. "Thanks, Mom." Half an hour was an enormously long time—easily long enough to reach the golden apple. For by now he was almost sure that it was an apple.

It was a long time but Skeleton-face, as Frederic silently named the lank guide, wasted it. When he had taken the little party around the various chapels and the choir and shown them the Grinling Gibbons carvings and the altar, Frederic hoped that now they would go up to the golden ball.

But the quiet cold sibilant voice said, "Now, if you will just come this way . . ."

And it lured them downstairs among the vast piers of the crypt and it seemed reluctant to leave this place. It kept them staring at the huge and horrible iron funeral carriage that had brought Wellington's body here, while it gave them endless precise details about the manufacture of this ugly thing. It hissed over the tomb of Nelson, and of Wren himself, and over the resting places of the silent multitude of bishops, and artists, and military and naval men.

This cold gloom was the natural habitat of the voice and Frederic felt that it wanted none of them to leave, it wanted them all to stay here. It would talk smoothly and quietly until they were lulled to sleep and then, somehow, it would get them lying stiff and dead with the others under the hard heavy stone floor.

So just as the voice was saying, "This is the sepulchre of Archdeacon—" Frederic cut in with a wail.

"I wanna go upstairs!"

That was where the voice began to hate him.

"Now, if you will just come this way . . ."

They went upstairs, past a notice saying *To the Golden Gallery and Ball* and up some more stairs, up and up and up.

As they mounted behind the steady-paced guide all the party began to lose their breath and make little sighs and smiling grimaces at each other. Except Frederic, who was tense with excitement and anticipation.

Maybe this guide wouldn't *give* him the ball—(which, of course, was really an apple)—but if Mom saw how much he wanted it she would buy it for him. It didn't matter how much it cost—Mom was the richest lady in the world. She could buy him the whole Cathedral if she wanted to. But he only wanted the apple.

The richest lady in the world gasped, "Oh dear! I didn't know it was going to take as long as this."

They got to the top of the winding staircase and with his heart throbbing in his breast Frederic followed the guide through the only doorway there.

"*Ooh!*" they all said as they found they were all in sects perched precariously on a narrow rim immediately beneath the arching interior of the great dome, that only an iron railing stood between them and the spreading gulf beneath. Far, far below other insects crawled over the black-and-white checkerboard of the floor. They were in a vast but bounded universe.

Frederic peered up to where the browning murals curved together and met around a spider's gallery and realized that although he was very high up the golden apple was at least as high again above him still. There must be another staircase somewhere that led up through the dome. Perhaps a hidden secret staircase.

He hesitated and tried to go back but the heavy grown-ups pressed all about him and carried him forward. And then they stopped, because the guide had stopped.

Skeleton-face said, "This is the famous Whispering Gallery. It has peculiar acoustic properties which I shall now demonstrate to you. If you would kindly move around to the opposite side of the Gallery and stand listening against the wall . . ."

"I don't want—" began Frederic. But Mrs. Stagg grabbed his hand and said in a low irritated whisper, "Oh, come *on!*"

The group moved slowly along the curving ledge with the fearful drop on its right-hand side, at which some of them dared not look and others only vouchsafed fleeting sidelong glances. There was a hush over everything.

Frederic was impatient and wanted to run. But this was a place where you neither ran nor shouted. The great Cathedral stood impassive and suffered these insects to crawl over it so long as they moved slowly and reverentially. Frederic felt that if he shouted the Cathedral would start angrily and shake all these invading creatures out of its crevices.

At last they reached the side of the Gallery opposite the doorway, beside which the guide had remained standing, dwarfed by distance. They arranged themselves in a line, kneeling with one knee on the seat, putting one ear close to the wall.

Frederic did not put his ear very close. He had no wish to hear that voice again. Nevertheless he heard it, distinct and loud, as if the guide were standing beside him—yet he could see him, a thin little shape a long way off, with all the width of the dome between them.

"I am speaking only in a whisper, yet you hear me clearly. The inward diameter of this dome is one hundred eight feet and the outer diameter one hundred forty-five feet. The eight murals which you see on the inner surface of the dome were painted by Sir James Thornhill and represent episodes in the life of St. Paul . . ."

The voice went on about St. Paul and Frederic sensed that its owner had no great liking for the saint—there was a new sneering undertone. The voice wanted to have done. So did Frederic. On an impulse, Frederic put his mouth close to the wall and said shrilly, "We don't want to stay here. We want to go up to the golden apple."

"Frederic!" exclaimed his mother, shocked and alarmed. Her voice became amplified to that of an angry giantess and boomed hollowly all about them.

The guide's voice had stopped. There was a moment's awful silence, which Mrs. Stagg spent with a guilty flush spreading over her cheeks.

Then—"Now if you will just come this way . . ."

The voice was sibilant and insinuating. It hinted at wonders which could make all you had seen so far become thin and flat.

But Frederic was five years old and therefore he knew that the voice really said, "I hate you all, especially the boy, and this is the way out and I shall be glad to see the last of you."

The voice had no intention after all of leading the way up the secret staircase to the golden ball.

The party shuffled round the great semi-circle back to the door—and Skeleton-face, who stood awaiting him like Charon. Frederic kept his eyes on his own feet and would not look up. For he knew that deep in those dark eye-sockets somewhere above his head animosity burned like a flame and if the other people hadn't been there . . . He was glad now that he was in the middle of a bunch of grownups. They were his unconscious protectors.

Huddling close he watched his feet and his mother's feet descending the stairs. And presently they were crossing the black-and-white floor, then the dirty black steps outside the Cathedral, and then—hurriedly—the sidewalk.

Then he saw the running-board of the car and looked up and there was Jim grinning at him and the fear in him unfroze.

"Get in, Frederic, don't just stand there," said his mother, pushing him. "Go as fast as you dare, Bates—we're ten minutes late now. What *will* Lady Cornford think?"

Frederic had not shone before the Lady. He had been silent and, when pressed, sulky. And, when pressed again, rude—very rude.

When they got back to the hotel Mrs. Stagg decided on disciplinary measures. "You will go straight to bed now, Frederic. And you are *not* to look at your picture-books in bed. I've had more than enough of you today."

The boy who had caused his mother to shout in a cathedral and look small, who had been rude to an English Lady and again made his mother look small, was left alone in the bedroom with his guilt.

He felt no remorse, only an intense aching regret that tomorrow they would be leaving London and the golden apple behind. Forever, probably. Someone else would come along and take the golden apple away while he was on the silly ship or back at silly school in Boston.

He got out of bed and went to the window. The buses swung dizzily in and out of Park Lane and for awhile he watched them and the little people down there who dodged them and took sanctuary in green Hyde Park. It was summer and there was still an hour or two of daylight left.

He decided nothing. It was as if someone else had taken over his body suddenly and made it act with purpose. He found himself putting on his street clothes, buttoning them up.

Then he was opening the door quietly, surveying the passage, and then he was at the open window at the rear of the building, scrambling through it, and then he was watching his feet descending the webby iron steps of the fire-escape just as they had descended the staircase in St. Paul's.

The feet seemed to know the way though it was easy enough. It was almost a straight road back to St. Paul's. But it was a very long road and the feet were very tired when they got there and climbed the dirty steps in the pale rose light coming up the hill from the sinking sun.

He entered to the sound of far-off singing. There, down at the end of the great nave, candles burned on the altar and before them two lines of people in white surplices sang sweetly together and the organ made quiet thunder over their heads. There were other people too, watching them, in the dim pink light reflected from the windows below the dome.

In fact they were so intent on their watching and the choir was so intent on its song that no one noticed him stealing down a side aisle, between the chairs and up the stairs which led to the Whispering Gallery.

The old verger who took the entrance money was no longer there and this gave Frederic heart. All the guides would have gone home by now, Skeleton-face among them. Now all he had to do was to find a place to hide for just a little while until the choir and the congregation had gone home too, leaving St. Paul's—and the golden apple—to him alone.

Up the stairs there was a corridor leading to the library and in that corridor he had noticed a certain secluded alcove. He hoped he could reach it soon for his legs were aching and very tired . . .

When he awakened, his shoulders and legs were painful with cramp for the alcove was small even for him. Rubbing them he went exploring in the dark. Soon he had other places to rub, for there seemed to be a lot of things to bump into and they were all hard. What chance had he of finding the secret staircase to the apple? It must be well hidden and hard to detect even in the daytime. He wished he had thought to bring his torch. But then he hadn't intended to fall asleep and stay here until after dark.

He was not afraid for the ball shining in the sunlight shone still in his memory and he felt that it was even now shining there in actuality somewhere above him. When he reached it and unscrewed it—(but it was an apple, really, and he would just pick it)—it would continue to glow and light his way back down the stairs and along the streets to the hotel. He bumped and blundered

along the wall like a blow-fly on a windowpane and all at once fell
through a doorway. As he lay there his foot, extended behind him,
discovered the top of a stairway.

And then, quite distinctly, he heard slow steady footsteps coming up that dark stairway.

He caught his breath and picked himself up. He must not be
discovered now. He went on through the doorway and so emerged
into a very dim yellow light. He was in the Whispering Gallery,
uncertainly lit by a moon striving first to pierce a veil of nimbus
cloud and then the dusty windowpanes of the Cathedral.

He hesitated. There was only this one door, which was the sole
entrance and exit to the Gallery. The footsteps were louder now
and began to echo. He fled from them, keeping close to the seat
along the curving wall in a stumbling yet stealthy sort of run, trying to make no noise in a place which he knew magnified sound in
a terrifying way.

Yet he was still not really frightened—only excited.

It was a long way around to the place diametrically opposite
the door, the place where they had all stood listening in the afternoon, but it did not seem quite so far this time because he could
run. There he sat on the seat, hunched up against the wall, trying to
make himself so small as to be invisible and holding his breath lest
the same treacherous wall caught the small sound of his presence
and flung it around in revealment.

A threadbare patch in the flat cloud passed under the moon
and the spacious murals on the dome overhead suddenly stood out
distinctly with an odd stereoscopic effect. And the dark little ob-
long of the doorway on the far side of the Gallery became visible.

Below, in the immense well of the Cathedral, he saw now that
here and there an electric candelabra glowed, each casting its little
circle of light, frayed and thin at the edges—a few tiny wide-
scattered oases in a black desert.

But now he watched the distant doorway opposite—and
waited.

His vision became a little blurred with the intensity of his
gaze. Presently it seemed that a small vertical strip of the dark rec-
tangle had detached itself and floated away from the main body.
And then this little black stroke became still. He rubbed his watering eyes and looked again. There was no doubt about it. The thin
black shadow was quite separate from the frame of the doorway.

Then the cloud thickened under the moon again, the murals
became blurs, the doorway and the shadow merged into common

blackness and only the small glints of electric light far below retained their clarity and shape.

He hoped the shadow would go back through the doorway. He sat, still hunched, gripping the edge of the seat. He was trembling a little but was not really afraid.

Then his heart leapt into his throat as a voice spoke right beside him. A sibilant chill voice, cloaking malice with a surface politeness—*"Now, if you will just come this way . . ."*

He shrank and cowered. His trembling became a violent shaking as fear passed through him like a series of electric shocks. A pain gripped his stomach and he pressed both hands against the place, doubled up. He could not control his breathing now—it came in loud rapid gasps, as if he had just been plunged into cold water.

For ages, it seemed, he sat tied in a knot of pain, gazing terror-struck through the railing at the points of light below—remote as stars—dreading to look up at Skeleton-face standing over him, unable to face the cavernous eye-sockets and the white fixed grin, shrinking from the imagined touch of a thin hand.

But no hand touched him.

Then the smothered moon broke free to throw a wealth of silvery light about him and it was apparent that there was no one standing over him. He peeped under his eyelids—over there. The shadow remained small and distant by the door. It was so perfectly still that a hope suddenly struck him it was not a man at all but just the shadow of some ordinary thing he had not noticed before. Yet it had seemed to move . . .

He watched it, relaxing gradually as the thin shadow remained stiff and stationary as a gatepost.

He told himself, not in so many words but with the rough apprehension of the imperfectly articulate, that he had been frightening himself with an imagined bogeyman.

But he had not imagined that voice. That had been real enough. Still, there was probably an explanation any grownup could make clear to him. He supposed that everything you said in a Whispering Gallery went echoing around the Gallery for ever and ever because there was no way for the sound to get out—it was like a fly caught under an upturned bowl. He expected that the echoes became rarer and rarer as time went on until you hardly heard them at all.

All he had heard was a belated echo of the words Skeleton-face had kept using in the afternoon.

Then he jumped again, as the same freezing voice said right alongside him, *"If you will just come this way . . ."*

The palms of his hands became sticky with sweat, and his scalp prickled. But he told himself that it was all right. The shadow hadn't moved. It was only that old echo again.

He noticed it had dropped a word this time. How could the sound of that word, *"Now,"* have escaped? Why, of course, it would have slipped out through the doorway as the echo went past on its travels. That was how echoes died, losing a piece every time they went slowly round. It would have to be something like that, otherwise everything everybody ever said would have gone on sounding forever and it would be like a great crowd shouting all the time.

Well, it wasn't any good just sitting there. He'd have to start looking for the staircase to the golden apple. His mother might already have discovered he had left the hotel and she would guess where he had gone and come after him.

He stood up slowly, not taking his eyes off the shadow by the door. It remained still. If he went to the left he would approach the doorway from the side away from the shadow and wouldn't have to go past it at all. *Well,* he thought, *I must go now.* He took a deep breath.

And then the clouds made a sudden rush at the moon and all but extinguished it. The silvery light ceased abruptly as if it had been switched off. It was darker than ever.

He paused, irresolute, his courage evaporating. He could not go around the Gallery in this darkness. He might not be able to distinguish the doorway when he came to it and he might go past it to where the shadow was. But that was silly—if there was no light there could be no shadow.

Nevertheless fear was stronger than reason. He stood there, clutching the iron railing and looking down at the little lights below. Suddenly he wished he were down there in the safe steady light that did not go out and leave you trapped on a high shelf and at the mercy of unseen shadows.

But if he were down there, he would be further away from the shining golden apple. If he were to attain that prize he must be courageous and bear the nervous ordeals that lay on the path to it. To deserve the apple you must be brave.

His fingers tightened on the railing as the mouthless voice said near at hand in the dark, *"You will just come this way . . ."*

This time it sounded less like a request than a command. *"You will come this way . . ."* It was as if the voice knew that it was losing some of the words it could use and was trying to counterbalance the loss with greater persuasion.

Frederic thought, *It's quite all right, really. If I stay here long enough the echo will have no more words left, it will die out altogether. Perhaps the shadow will go with it. Perhaps the shadow has nothing to do with it.*

However he was glad when the bright moonlight suddenly flooded the dome again. At least he was glad until—

He screamed as he saw that the shadow had moved in the darkness, had advanced nearly halfway towards him around the Gallery and was still coming on steadily.

He turned and fled in the opposite direction. As he blundered along the curving path, sometimes banging a knee against the endless seat, sometimes slipping and grabbing the railing for support, he cast a terrified glance across the moonlit spaces to see where the shadow had got to.

It had ceased to pursue its original course around the Gallery. It had turned back, was moving swiftly the other way to head him off before he could reach the door. And it was moving faster than he could.

He spun around, choking with terror, little thin screams coming from him as he ran. This time he did not blunder or slip. Self-preservation told him that he could afford no mistakes and the sheer desperate will to live made his feet fly with speed and precision.

For now he knew—he did not know how he knew but he knew—that the shadow was the shadow of Death. And Death wanted to take him and put him with the other dead people under the cold floor of the crypt.

He was back to where he had been, diametrically opposite to the doorway. And the shadow too was back to where it had been, by that doorway. He collapsed on the seat, whooping for breath but keeping his staring eyes on the shadow. It seemed to have returned to complete immobility.

Then the voice came again, quietly this time, almost coaxingly, *"Just come this way . . ."*

It seemed to imply that if he were just to go along to it everything would be all right and there would be nothing to worry about.

But he knew it was a trap. He would not go. He would hang onto life as long as he could because there was still hope. The voice had lost two of its words this time. Perhaps it had called after him as he ran from it and haste and terror had deafened him to it.

The great dome overhead was almost radiant now with light from the unshielded moon and the human figures crowded in the arches of the murals were a tense silent audience looking down on the narrow circular track where Frederic had to run for his life.

He believed they were watching him and he wondered whether they were on his side. St. Paul seemed to be. He stood up there, one hand pointing upwards towards the spider's gallery at the apex of the dome, towards the golden apple. "That's the way you want to go, Frederic," said his expression.

"I know, I know," whispered the boy. "But how do I get up there?"

And the voice of Death spoke again, calling, *"Come this way . . ."*

"No!" cried Frederic, starting to his feet and going a few paces. The shadow glided in the same direction too, coming around to meet him. He ran back and the shadow stopped as if it were watching him, weighing his intention, then moved back to cover the doorway.

And so Frederic stopped again. It was plain that he could never reach the doorway safely whichever way he went, for the shadow had the advantages of position and speed of movement and could always get there first. Was there to be no end to this horrible game?

Yes, he thought desperately, *there must be an end when the echo dies. And that must be soon now.*

He pressed his hot brow against the cool iron railing. There were, he noticed now, mosaics just under the Gallery itself, between the arches which fell away from beneath them into bottomless gloom, and they all pictured angels flying confidently. What mattered it to them that they were at a fearful height. They were borne by their trusted wings.

He thought, *If only I had wings! I could escape Death. More than that—I could fly up there and pick the golden apple.*

His forehead burned and droplets of sweat trickled slowly down the iron bars. His head ached as though a fever had come upon him and the angels seemed to advance and recede before his blurring gaze as if they had come quite away from the wall and were indeed flying over the back wall.

He watched them for some time, feeling dull and heavy-headed, and they seemed to be aware of him and smile at him and indicate by their slow weaving motions that it was quite easy to fly. Anyone could do it. *He* could do it if he only tried.

Then suddenly he remembered the shadow and looked up at the opposite side of the Gallery. And it was gone!

Then he caught a movement away to the right and there was the shadow, much taller, well past the crucial halfway mark on its way to him. It had taken advantage of his preoccupation with the angels to chance leaving the doorway to come around after him.

It had won the awful game. Even if Frederic ran his hardest for the door the shadow had gained enough ground to overtake him easily before he reached it.

It was too near. It was Skeleton-face, all right. He could see the dark eye-cavities turned steadfastly upon him, the gleam of teeth, as the tall thin figure approached.

He scrambled up onto the rim of the railing before him, which was not easy for the rim was turned back inwards. But he mounted to the top of it and balanced there like a wire-walker. He looked up. Somewhere up there, beyond the dome, was the glittering prize he would never now reach.

But St. Paul still pointed upwards like an inspiration. "Have faith!" he seemed to say. "Have faith!"

And the angels seemed to be calling in chorus, "Have faith, Frederic, and you can fly like us. Have faith and you can fly up to the apple."

Frederic teetered, arms outstretched, on the edge of cavernous space below and above. He took a quick peep sideways. Skeleton-face was almost upon him, lipless mouth open to speak.

"*This way . . .*"

"You can fly. You can fly. Have faith," called the angels together.

"I have faith. I'm coming," said Frederic with a new strength and began to extend a foot quite steadily and calmly.

"*Frederic!*" It was his mother's voice, loud with alarm. A warm relief flooded right over him. Mom had found him, had got here just in time. She would save him from Skeleton-face—she would pay him to go away. She could pay anything, she was so rich.

He looked eagerly around but he couldn't see her. There was only Skeleton-face reaching for him.

And then he realized with a sudden horrible sinking of all his energies that the cry was only the echo of his mother's exclamation of the afternoon. It must have been slowly circling the Gallery ever since. He was sick with disappointment.

And then bony hands reached for his ankles and he leapt outwards into space.

It wasn't a leap of faith. It was merely a leap to avoid Death.

In confusion and wretchedness he fell past the angels, fell into darkness. The lights of the candelabras grew bigger as he fell and they illumined something that lay below them.

A golden disk.

He was turning as he fell and couldn't obtain more than fleeting glimpses of it but he could see that he was heading straight for it.

Could it be that somehow, in a way he couldn't understand, he was succeeding after all? That he was to reach—

The golden disk flashed up hugely now and dazzled his eyes.

The verger on the night watch had happened just by chance to glance up and catch what looked like a tiny figure balanced on the rail of the Whispering Gallery. He tried to shield his eyes from the immediate light of the candelabra over his head and see past it more clearly up into the moonlit dome.

It *was* a figure and even as he watched it jumped out into space.

"M*y God!*" he said, and rushed forward.

A thin shout came from above—*"Way . . .!"*

He stopped, uncertain.

The figure fell down past the mosaics, past the golden organ pipes, past the red canopy over the high pulpit, arching ever outwards to the center of the floor as it came.

He saw it hit the large circular brass plate set into the floor, immediately over Nelson's tomb, immediately under the ball and cross 365 feet above. And he hid his eyes.

When he looked again a delta of red rivulets was spreading from the crumpled little shape that lay on the brass plate in the center of the star with the long black and faded pink points— bright red trickles which matched the scarlet of the altar screen.

It was a small child, a boy. Dead—naturally.

He sought his fellow verger on the watch and brought him to the scene. Only it wasn't quite the same. The brass ring shone clean and bright—and clear. There was no body. There was no blood.

The second verger put his arm about the other, who had suddenly begun to shake, and led him to the chairs by the lectern.

"Sit down and rest, Alex," he said. "Don't worry. It's all right. It once happened to me."

Alex looked at him in slow surprise, his lower lip quivering, his hands shaking like those of a very old man.

"Nor are we the only ones," said the second verger. "It happens—every so often."

"When did it first—*really*—happen? Don't tell me it didn't."

"Over twenty years ago. It was a boy named Stagg—an American boy. He had strayed from his hotel, somehow found his way here and got up—there. His mother was distracted when she found him gone. But he had been here in the afternoon and for some reason wanted very much to return. And he was due to go home the next day. So she guessed he might have come here. But she got here just too late—he was already on the rail, just as you and I saw him. She shouted his name. But he fell."

"Do you think she startled him? He was performing some idiotic balancing trick and—"

"Did it look like that to you?"

Alex looked unseeingly at the golden lectern with the big golden eagle bearing the Bible on its back and wings outstretched and eyes staring keenly up at the dome.

"He jumped," he said in a low voice.

"Nobody knows why."

"But he saw me," Alex said. "He must have seen me and thought he was going to hit me. He shouted *'Way!'* "

"*Someone* shouted 'Way!' I heard it too when the thing happened to me. But it didn't sound like a boy's voice. He was only five, you know."

"If it wasn't he who was it?"

The second verger shrugged his shoulders and became absorbed in removing a few hairs that clung to his black cassock.

Without looking up he said, "There have been many temples on this site. Before this was Old St. Paul's and before that a Saxon church stood on this spot for nearly five hundred years, and long before that the Romans had a temple here—a Roman altar of stone was uncovered here in eighteen-thirty.

"I remember reading about that in the chronicles. There was a carved representation of Diana on it, was there not?"

"Yes. Diana, Goddess of the Hunt."

Alex looked at the other sharply. "Was it a—a sacrificial temple?"

The second verger pursed his lips, picked up a long brown hair carefully by the ends, held it up to the light of the candelabra and regarded it without answering.

"What did you say the name of the boy was?" pursued Alex.

"Stagg," said the other, letting the hair drift gently down—it floated away under a chair. Then he looked straight at Alex and said firmly, "Which may be a coincidence or it may not. We shall never know. The one thought that really terrifies me about this affair, the thought I don't want to face, is this—does that poor child have to suffer his frightful experience over and over again, every time it happens? Is he caught in some vicious circle of time and unable to escape?"

"I don't think so," said Alex. "What's past is past. We have merely, by some trick of time, been given a glimpse of that past. Like looking at an old film in which the characters go through the motions but are only unfeeling shadows."

"For our souls' ease," said the other, soberly, "we must believe that."

They sat brooding, two tiny figures side by side under the great dome in the little pool of light from the candelabra. Each was grateful for the other's company. For all around them black shadows filled the enormous arches and the silent chapels and the long, empty passages. Under their feet, spreading beneath the thick walls into the ancient churchyard besieging them in the night and into the burial grounds below that, were the bones of the innumerable dead. The great and the small. The famous and the forgotten. The human and the—possibly nonhuman.

Before them the golden eagle of the lectern, rising on its claws with excitement, gazed eagerly and unwaveringly up at the Whispering Gallery as if it were absorbed in watching a tense and perpetual drama . . .

"Now, if you will just come this way . . ."

The voice was sibilant and insinuating. It hinted at wonders which would make all you had seen so far become thin and flat and forgotten. Marvels unmatched lay just around the corner and the voice knew the way . . .

DOUBLE TROUBLE

ON MONDAY MORNING George Gray stepped out of the bathtub. It was a large bathroom and the cake of wet soap on the floor was very small, but George's instep alighted unerringly on the soap. He performed a complicated acrobatic trick of the sort which is usually preceded by a hush and a roll of drums, and followed by terrific applause. There was no applause this time. George sat naked on the cold floor and decided that his neck was not broken, but that all his ribs undoubtedly were.

At the breakfast table his newspaper tore as he opened it, right across his favourite comic strip. He tried to hold the two pieces together with one hand while he reached with the other for his toast. But he'd forgotten to switch the electric toaster off. As he jerked his burnt fingers back, his elbow caught his coffee cup and emptied it into his lap. In the process the newspaper tore again; he screwed it into a ball and used it for mopping-up operations.

He had to change his pants, and so he was late for work—and at Boulter & Schwartz Inc., Radio and Television Engineers, the shop manager told him so, at some length.

This was all just the beginning.

When he started to get down to work, things really got into their stride. He blew two 15-inch cathode ray tubes in the first half-hour. His electric soldering iron short-circuited and blew half the fuses in the factory. He hit a nail with his hammer, only it was his thumb nail, and not the 3-inch nail he was holding. It went on like that—all day.

In the late afternoon, when he was called to the boss's office for the fourth time, Mr. Schwartz said: "Now, look here, Gray, if I have you on the carpet many more times you'll wear a hole in it. What's the matter—are you taking a course in sabotage?"

"If I am, I'm doing a pretty good job on myself," said George grimly. "I have twenty-three broken ribs, by my count, two burnt fingers, a smashed thumb, three cuts from broken glass, and a headache."

"Well, Gray, I think you'd better go home before I have a mutilated corpse on my hands, to say nothing of a demolished factory. It's not your lucky day, nor mine, either, I'm beginning to
think."

"I've had it happen before," said George. "Never quite so bad
as this, but days when every darned thing goes wrong. I know the
signs—I've got a big fat jinx on my tail."

"Well, get him out of here. And don't come back until you've
shaken him off."

"Very good, Mr. Schwartz."

So George took off his overalls, and had a wash (only scalding
himself slightly) and went straight across the street to a bar. It was
a close, stifling day, and he helped himself liberally to the ice. He
wasn't backward with the beer, either.

There was only one other customer in the bar, a small, thin,
and very worried-looking old man. He was wearing a heavy,
black, double-breasted jacket and the sweat was rolling down his
shrunken cheeks. Continually, he removed his spectacles and
wiped the moisture of humidity from the lenses. When he wasn't
doing that, he was taking out what appeared to be a large, turnip
pocket-watch and studying it anxiously. In between times he managed to sip at his tall glass of lager.

The bartender was one of those taciturn people who looked
upon customers merely as interruptions in his study of the sports
columns, and so George, who felt he had to speak to someone, as
he'd made himself so unpopular during the day at the factory that
no one would address him kindly, caught the old man's eye and
remarked "Hot," reflecting that this remark wasn't so.

"Yes, it certainly is, Mr. Gray," said the old man, mildly.

"Oh, you know me? I'm afraid I can't quite place you. Are
you connected with Boulter & Schwartz?"

"Oh no. I work for Nuisances Xenogenous."

"Come again?"

"Nuisances Xenogenous. 'Xenogenous' means 'produced by
external agency'."

"You mean, you're an agent?"

"In a sense, yes."

"For 'Nuisances'? What's that: itching powder, rubber spiders,
squeaking cushions, and so forth?"

"We—ell, something like that. Here's my card."

George took it and read:

JONAH HOODOO
Junior in Nuisances Xenogenous

He frowned, and turned it over, and on the back was written, in a shaky hand:

When you—Have 'flu—You're blue.

"Oh, ignore that," said Mr. Hoodoo, hastily. "It's not one of my better efforts."

"Your own composition?"

"Yes, but—"

"I think it's swell," said George. "May I keep it?" It would be something to show his friends at Boulter & Schwartz for a laugh, when he had friends there again and when they felt like laughing.

"Sure. I realise, of course, that I've a long way to go yet before I'm as good as—say, Keats. I have to admit that at the moment he's the better man. But I keep trying, though, and one day—just a moment."

He produced another card, laid it face downward on the bar, and wrote something on the back with a leaky fountain pen. He showed the result, modestly, to George.

John Keats—Always beats—My feats.

There was a blot after "feats."

"An admirable impromptu performance," said George. "It's quite as good as the other. It merits a drink. Another lager?"

"Thanks. You know, I was really cut out to be a poet. My head's full of rhymes. I find it hard to concentrate on anything else. I guess that's why I've never really got on in this Nuisances Xenogenous line. Do you know, I'm the oldest Junior in the business?"

"Really?"

"Sometimes I think I'll never become a Senior Technician. I'm not getting any younger. And my eyesight's getting bad, real bad. And my PK isn't what it used to be. I never used to worry, but now I find I'm doing it all the time. It's playing the devil with my genius—er, my little versifying talent, that is."

He took out his pocket-watch, on its chain, and regarded it anxiously.

George had reached to pour another lager for the old man, and as he brought his arm back he knocked over his own glass. Beer ran all over the counter.

"Tut-tut," said the old man, without looking up.

"Don't worry," said George. "I've been doing that sort of thing all day. There's a jinx on me or a hoodoo—hey!"

He stopped, and pulled out Mr. Hoodoo's card and stared at it.

"Then I did see right," he said, slowly. "Jonah Hoodoo. Junior In Nuisances Xenogenous. J.I.N.X. You're the jinx!"

Mr. Hoodoo was still peering at his watch. "That's right," he said, vaguely, and continued to peer.

"What do you keep taking that thing out for?" asked George, irritably. "Have you got to catch a train?"

"No, Mr. Gray, there's something wrong with it, I think. Or it may be my eyes. Or—" He looked up suddenly at George. "This is what I've been waiting here to ask you. Are you twins?"

"Eh?" George was startled.

"Have you a twin brother?"

"No. Why? Do I look like him?"

"Yes. That is, if you *had* a twin brother, which you say you haven't . . . Mr. Gray, what you just said doesn't make sense." The old man's voice became querulous.

George said: "Well, that's news. You haven't said anything that made sense from the moment I first clapped eyes on you."

"It's quite simple. I'm a professional jinx. I've been working on your behalf all day."

"On my behalf!" echoed George, but throwing in a little yelp. "Barkeep—two beers. Both for me."

"In return," said Jonah Hoodoo, "I want to ask you for a small favour."

"Sure, anything. I'll break my neck for you—I've nearly done it once to-day already."

"You're a television engineer. I'd like you to check up on my set—the reception seems most unsatisfactory. Or it might be my wretched sight—I don't know. Here, look."

He held out his pocket-watch. Only it wasn't a pocket-watch. The bulbous glass of it was a small, bright television screen, with the black and white image faintly flickering.

George's technical interest submerged his grievances. "My, that's cute. A miniature portable. I've never seen one of those." He reached for it.

"You can't take it off the chain," the old man warned. "The current comes along that. It's hooked up on to a circuit in the lining of my jacket."

George peered at the bright disc. "H'm—something wrong. It's developed a double image."

"Oh, it *is* the set, after all. I'm glad. I was afraid my eyes were petering out altogether and I was getting double vision."

"What programme is this?" asked George. "No sound—only vision? All I can see is a guy sitting on a stool looking at something in his hand. There's, another guy beside him, but he's cut off. The set seems to be a bar—it's *me!*"

The last word came out as a squeak of surprise.

"Naturally," said Mr. Hoodoo. "You're my charge to-day, and I've had to keep you under observation so that I could see where to help you. It's the normal jinx procedure—all jinxes have these sets. Only because you came out double I've been thinking you were twins. So I've had to work twice as hard to keep you both amused. Actually, of course, there's only one of you, so you've had two helpings."

"Yeah," said George. "It dawned on me that I'd run into double trouble. Now, before I ram this little gadget down your gullet, just tell me this. Why pick on me? What had I ever done to you?"

Mr. Hoodoo looked injured. When he spoke, he also sounded injured. "You misunderstand the function of jinxes altogether. It's a high and noble calling. Our job is to keep you interested in life, to save you from appalling boredom. We have the same high intention as fleas on a dog. The dog would degenerate into a lazy, lifeless and aimless creature without his fleas: they supply the *quo animo,* they give the dog *purpose.* With them he is never at a loss for an occupation. In the same way, we are the necessary irritant, the spice in your life—"

"You're the cream in my coffee, eh?" grunted George. "Well, I'd be a sight happier without you."

"Oh no you wouldn't. That's a delusion. In a perfect world, where everything went right, just as you'd planned it, you'd be bored sick. You'd long for something to go wrong for a change. Perfection is something to be avoided—the old Greek sculptors knew that. That's why, if they produced what they thought was a perfect piece of sculpture, they'd deliberately make a flaw in it, mar it, just a little. They knew that once they'd achieved perfection they'd be at the end of their tether: there would be nothing left to try for in life."

Mr. Hoodoo was really in earnest. He mopped his brow, and wiped his glasses again, and peered at George to see if he had mollified him. But George was still fascinated by the little TV set. He asked: "How is it powered?"

"I have a battery in each jacket pocket. There's an antenna in my hat. The circuit, as I've said, is in my coat lining."

"I wondered why you were keeping your coat on, on a sweltering day like this. I get it now."

Mr. Hoodoo sighed. "Yes, it's one of the burdens of our profession. You can always spot a jinx by that occupational sign, I'm afraid. Any time you see a poor guy sweating in a heavy coat in midsummer, he's almost sure to be a jinx."

"How many jinxes are there around?"

"I'm not allowed to say. But quite a lot, I can tell you that."

"Where's the TV camera? How does it keep focused on me wherever I am?"

"Mr. Gray, you're approaching forbidden territory. In the articles I signed as an apprentice, it expressly stated that no trade secrets must be divulged."

"Forbidden territory—I like that!" exploded George, and then lowered his voice as the bartender looked up from his newspaper. "My bathroom's forbidden territory too—how dare you spy on my private life like that! It *was* you who made me take that tumble this morning?"

"Yes, Mr. Gray."

"What I want to know is, how could you make me tread plumb on that soap?"

"Soap?" echoed Mr. Hoodoo, vaguely, and stared into space.

"Yeah—"

"Shush," said the old man, raising a finger. "Don't interrupt—I'm inspired." His hand dived suddenly for his fountain pen, while the other hand fumbled for a card.

Carefully, he wrote down:

Why grope—For soap,—You dope?

"There," he said, self-approval spreading over his face, "I do believe that's my masterpiece. Like it?"

George began deliberately, "I think it—"

"If you say you like it," said Mr. Hoodoo hurriedly, "I'll tell you about the soap."

"I was going to say I think it is perfect," said George, which wasn't what he was going to say at all. "Let's have some more beer." He ordered.

"Not *quite* perfect," said Mr. Hoodoo, looking gratified just the same. "I *could* make it perfect, with a little polishing. But, there, that's just the thing we have to avoid." He studied his masterpiece.

"The soap," reminded George.

"Oh, yes. Well, there's nothing to it, really. Merely psychokinesis—the PK effect, as Dr. Rhine prefers to call it. Mind over matter. All jinxes have very highly developed PK centres: it's a necessary qualification for the job. I just have to look at the television screen and concentrate, and I can move any object I see in it. Distance makes no difference, as Dr. Rhine has shown. Of course, it takes a lot of mental energy. I can cause only small effects, like moving the soap to the spot just under your foot, or sliding a cup of coffee along a few inches so that your elbow will encounter it—"

"I ought to charge you for the dry-cleaning of my pants," said George. "I suppose you made me knock over that glass of beer here, too?"

"Yes, but I'm afraid my PK isn't what it was. I didn't move the beer to quite the right place: it should have gone all over you instead of over the counter."

"If you've got any more ideas like that, you'd better forget 'em."

The old man took a pull at his lager.

"Let us say," he said, wiping his mouth, "That I shan't worry you any more if you'll promise to repair my TV set."

George considered. "O.K., in that event I'll promise to try to repair it. I don't know if I can until I've examined it properly. And I'd have to work on it in my private workshop at home."

"Let's go," said Mr. Hoodoo, getting off his stool.

"Not yet. I've not finished my little jag. I planned to get steamed up somewhat, and I'm going to. Now, let's get down to some quiet, steady drinking."

Some time later George looked blearily along the line of empty bottles between him and Mr. Hoodoo, and saw that his companion had fallen asleep on his stool, his glasses pushed up on his forehead. There was a half-full glass of lager in front of him. George reached out, very carefully, and tipped it over.

Mr. Hoodoo awoke with a start: "Ooh!" Dazedly, he felt the wet bottoms of his pants. He put one foot on the floor—it squelched in his shoe.

"Dear me. I musht have trodden in a puddle. How long's it been raining?"

"Hours," said George, turning his glassy gaze back to the bottles. He counted slowly and with difficulty up to ten. "That's ten dead men. Not bad. That's 'nough. Let's go now."

"Jus' minute. Inshpiration."

Mr. Hoodoo struggled with his pen and a card. He handed the result to George. "Howzzat?"

It was almost illegibly written. George stared at it, but his eyes wouldn't focus properly, and it was doubtful whether he could have read it even if it had been printed in letters a foot high.

"S'fine," he said, handing it back. "You're geniush."

"But you didn't read it out," protested Jonah. He did:

"That'sh ten—Dead men.—Little hen."

"Better'n Shakespeare, Jonah—don't mind if I call you Jonah?" George, laughed foolishly, slid from his stool, and flung his arm about Jonah's shoulders. They staggered out of the bar into the suffocating evening.

"Y'know" said George, "one thing's been worrying me. Shpying on me in b-bathroom. T'ain't right . . . Are there any—any lady jinxes?"

"Lotsh. Oh, lotsh," said Jonah, solemnly.

George said again: "T'ain't right, y'know."

"S'all right—no need to worry. Lady jinxes only have charge—ladies. Men jinxes only have charge—gen'l'men."

"But I don't wanna be *anybody's* charge," expostulated George. "T'ain't right. Who's your bosh? I wanna have a talk with your bosh—have thish sort of thing shtopped. Who's the bosh of all the jinxes?"

Jonah leant confidentially towards him, hanging on him, so that they both stopped in the middle of the pavement, swaying. He put a finger to his lips and whispered: "It's the High Jinx. Don't tell anyone. He's a very shpiteful old man, and he doesn't like me. He's shtopped my promotion all these years. Says I'm not good enough to be a Junior, let alone anything better. And I sho want to be—to be a Shtinx."

"A what?" said George, as they began lurching on again.

"A Shenior Technician In Nuisances Xenogenoush. A full-blown Shtinx."

"And he's shtopped you? He's a dirty—"

"Shush," said Jonah. "Don't shay it. He might be watching ush right now. He's alwaysh checking up on how we jinxes go about our job. Dear me, I'd *never* get to be a Shtinx if he knew we were calling him names. I'm shupposed to be looking after you."

George looked slowly back over his shoulder. He gripped Jonah's arm.

"Look! I think shomebody's following ush."

Jonah peered round, swaying.

"I can't shee anybody," he said, turning. He tripped over George's foot, which wasn't where it should be, and went full length into the gutter. It was a very dirty gutter, at that point. George helped him up. There was garbage smeared all down the front of him.

"Where's my glashes?" said Jonah, feeling his forehead, where they were not. "I musht have my glashes—I can't shee without them."

"Here they are," said George, treading on them. "Oh, look, you've trodden on them! They're broken."

"Oh dear," moaned Jonah. "I feel ill." Abruptly, he *was* ill—in the gutter.

"Oh dear," he said again, afterwards. "What's happened to me?"

"It'sh all right, Jonah, my apartment's only just over the way. Come on, I'll shee you there."

George helped Jonah along.

"Everything'sh going wrong," grumbled the old man. "My TV shet won't work, I tread in a puddle and shoak my shock—"

"Huh?" grunted George.

"Shoak my shock. Then I fall in a gutter and shpoil my coat, and break my glashes, and then I'm shick all over the place . . ."

"It'sh shimple enough," said George. "You've got a jinx on your tail. A big, fat jinx. You're a jinx with a jinx."

He began to chuckle. It seemed immensely funny that he was the jinx's jinx now. He was still chuckling when they stumbled into his apartment. After that, he didn't remember anything much.

He awoke long after breakfast time. He was lying on the divan, fully clothed, but very crumpled. A thin little old man in his shirt-sleeves was brushing away at a black coat on a hanger. George frowned. Then he recollected Jonah Hoodoo.

He said: "How now, brown cow? Had chow?"

Jonah looked across at him. "Say, that's pretty good. Mind if I make a note of that one?"

"Help yourself," said George, and the old man wrote it down.

It turned out that Jonah hadn't eaten, so George cooked up something between breakfast and lunch. "I'm really late for work to-day," he said, as he served it.

Jonah regarded his face anxiously. "You're not going to work to-day? You were going to fix my video—remember? I must have it in going order as soon as possible."

"That's right," said George. "And you were going to leave me alone. That was the deal, wasn't it?"

Jonah nodded.

"Okay, I'll phone the works and tell 'em I won't be in to-day. After what happened there yesterday, they'll probably be relieved."

He phoned, and they were relieved. The shop manager said they were still clearing up the debris. George wasn't to come near the place until he had shaken off his jinx.

"It's all under control," George assured him. "I'm working on that right now."

Jonah said: "My poor head! Have you got any more aspirins?"

George found him some, and then the old man began grumbling about his broken spectacles and then about the condition of his coat, and then he borrowed some petrol to remove some of the stains which the brushing hadn't. As he dabbed and rubbed, with his nose almost touching the cloth as he peered short-sightedly at it, he mumbled: "I must be in bad with the High Jinx, or he wouldn't have set another jinx on me like that. Wonder what I've done wrong? Guess it must be dereliction of duty. I shouldn't have let you off for the rest of the day. I'll have to work twice as hard to-day to make up for it."

"Huh?" said George. "What's that? You said you wouldn't worry me any more if I promised to repair your set."

"I meant I wouldn't worry you any more *to-day*—which was yesterday, of course," said Jonah, glibly. "I couldn't do more than that—why, I've been assigned to you for the rest of this week. And it's obvious that the High Jinx doesn't approve of my non-attention to duty yesterday evening. I must get into his good graces again, or I'll never become a Stinx."

"I can think of six rude answers to that one," said George, bitterly, "but I shan't waste the time. Get out of here. Come on—get."

"Mr. Gray—your promise!" said Jonah, shocked. "I must have my video fixed, or I can't work again."

"Exactly. Get."

"Mr. Gray, you must understand that my work is for your own good. It is to protect you from your sinful pride. Over-riding pride leads always to disaster. Remember Niobe—she was too proud of her children, and they were all slain because of that pride. You wouldn't want that to happen to you? A little humility is good for the soul. I am thinking of your soul, Mr. Gray."

"That wasn't your story yesterday," said George, grimly. "Do you have a different spiel for each day of the week? As I see it, you're a paid hireling of a half-wit who gets a kick out of making a monkey out of decent folk."

"Half-wit?" repeated Jonah, distressed. "Oh, my dear Mr. Gray, do be careful of what you're saying. The High Jinx will—"

"The High Jinx," said George, briefly, "is a ———." It was something much less respectable than a half-wit. Jonah collapsed into a jelly of quivering apprehension.

"Oh, Mr. Gray—"

"For the last time—get going!"

Jonah held out his TV set. "Your promise," he said, pathetically. "It's unlucky to break a promise."

George glared at him speechlessly. Then an idea percolated into his angry mind. With an effort he sat on the volcano which was trying to erupt within him, and said, very nearly calmly: "All right, give it to me. I'll fix it. We don't want to be unlucky, do we?"

He took the set into his workshop, and shut the door on Jonah.

He emerged half an hour later, with the little set in his hand, and without a word fastened it back on to Jonah's watch-chain. Jonah peered at the screen showing the small bright image of George's living room and the man in it.

"Wish I had my glasses," he muttered. "It's going to be very difficult until I can get a new pair. Still, I can see you've rectified the double image fault. Thank you very much. I hope you will have no hard feelings about my work in future."

"I wish you luck," said George, elliptically.

"Thank you, indeed. You're a nice fellow, really. It'll be a pleasure to work for you. Now, just one last small request before I go. Could you give me the address of a good optician? I must order some new spectacles."

George gave him an address. It was the address of a mortician on the far side of the town.

"Thank you," said Jonah. "I shall tell him you advised me to go to him as a customer. Well, good-bye now. I can't wish you good luck, being what I am,"—he laughed nervously—"but remember it's all for the best in the long run. I shall be thinking of you."

"And I shall be thinking of you," George assured him. "Good-bye."

Jonah couldn't see the stairs very well, and when he stepped off the bottom one he found it wasn't the bottom one. He picked himself up, gingerly felt the tooth-marks in his tongue, and blundered out of the door. He turned right and put his foot down a drain.

"Dear me," he muttered, extricating it, and peering covertly up and down the street. There were a number of people about, and as it was a damp morning they were all wearing raincoats. Anyone of them might have been the jinx that was still, obviously, persecuting him on the orders of the High Jinx. He felt like a sheep that had strayed being nipped back into the flock by the sheepdog.

He went along the block and around the corner, out of sight from George's apartment. It was plain that he must get back on duty at once.

He pulled out his video and studied it. The image was still single—he could make that out—but the detail was blurred: that was his bad sight, of course.

Odd, he thought—Mr. Gray must have left the apartment directly after him, for he was now standing in a street. He was holding something in his hand and looking at it: an object that gleamed—probably his cigarette case. Here was a chance—Jonah visualised George having to pick up all his cigarettes from the damp ground, for the good of his soul. He summoned his PK reserves and willed the object to slip out of the victim's hand and fall to the sidewalk.

At which moment his TV set slipped from his own fingers, slipped right off the hook of the chain, and smashed into pieces on the wet sidewalk. Little springs and screws, pivots and wheels, coils and microscopic tubes danced a brief ballet, and then lay still around the bright splinters of the small convex mirror George had fitted in place of the screen.

Jonah regarded the debris in dismay. No good asking Mr. Gray to repair *that!*

Fancy a jinx doing a thing like this to him! It was outrageous. It must be a renegade jinx, someone outside the union.

But he knew, really, that there were no renegade jinxes. What had been done to him must have been done at the direction of the inscrutable High Jinx. So drastic an act could symbolise only one thing: he was washed up, finished. So far from the High Jinx endorsing his promotion to a Stinx, he had underlined his oft-expressed opinion that Jonah Hoodoo wasn't even good enough to be a Junior.

But inspiration calls upon geniuses even in the midst of their greatest tragedies. Perhaps it is at such times that the call sounds clearest. Jonah Hoodoo heard the call and pulled out his pen and pinned down inspiration in mid-flight.

That sphinx,—High Jinx,—Sure thinks—This gink's—No Stinx.

He regarded the crowded hack of the card with great satisfaction. He had been cramping his genius in the confines of the triplet form. It needed five lines, at least, to express itself. Perhaps, one day, he might even write an ode!

It had to be admitted: he was a poet, and nothing else. To think of the years he had wasted as a jinx!

"I resign," he said aloud, and felt the burden fall from him.

He was old, but it was never too late. Titian painted *The Battle of Lepanto* when he was ninety-eight. Goethe was over eighty when he wrote the second part of *Faust*. There was plenty of time. Jonah Hoodoo marched down the street triumphantly towards his new life.

On the way he fell over an ashcan. But that sort of thing didn't matter any more—not to a genius. Indeed, it was ennobling.

THE TWO SHADOWS

"O, BLESSED NECESSITY!" cried Leonardo da Vinci, in his day, knowing that it was the prime incentive. Man had to be driven to work his best miracles. Creditors at one's heels were a sharper spur to the artist than his own inspiration.

The first voyage from Earth to Mars was certainly not the fruit of a hunger for knowledge—or of technicians in love with their work—or even of pride seeking power upon which to fatten.

It sprang from the starkest of all necessities—preservation of the species.

A divided Earth, struggling with a divided mind to preserve itself, had fallen into the desperate error of preventive war. The disease germs, as thick as clouds in the atmosphere, were proving to be the conquerors of both sides. Earth, quivering under the impacts of countless atomic missiles, many darted into its side by its own satellite and human colony, flung out a seed.

The seed was styled the *Nuova Vita*—as a sign that the Earth really knew better than it had behaved—and it was a rocket-ship five times the size of the Lunar vessels. It had both atomic and chemical drives. It had come straight off the drawing board. Its size and power were unprecedented. There was no time for real tests. In effect it was a tissue of theory, launched naked into cold space, carrying twenty-six souls and the hope of the human race—at least the Anglo-American part of that race.

The gamble, it seemed, had come off. The seed missed the stony places—it was landing on the comparatively fertile soil of Mars. It was a thousand feet above that soil, sitting on its tail of braking chemical jets, descending with beautifully slow deliberation.

The pilot said happily, "We've done it!"

Fate never likes to be anticipated. A second later came a great light and a great heat. The habitually almost motionless atmosphere of mars was scorched and stung into agitation. The heated air expanded almost like an explosion, tearing the concentrated gas-jets of the ship into long tenuous streamers.

The *Nuova Vita* tilted irrevocably off balance. It became a bone of contention between gravity and the upstreaming air. Its majesty had departed. It was a straw tossed by forces it had lately controlled.

They tossed it into a grassy area two Earth-miles from an ice-blue channel. But the soil was thin. There was hard rock beneath it and the rock broke the back of the *Nuova Vita*. It broke the backs of many of the little humans within and others died through the sheer concussion.

The wind howled over the wreck, under the sun—and under the small newborn companion to the sun.

Thomas Jefferson Johns ran for his life among the firs. Luckily, the snow hadn't come yet but the bitter wind, driving against his face, was the herald of it. There was plenty of snow on the saw-edged peaks of the Rockies distant behind him.

Unhappily, not so far behind him, came the grizzly bear.

He looked back fearfully over his shoulder to see who was gaining. He never saw because he ran his head against a branch and was knocked off his feet. Flat on his back he went and the ground seemed to be rocking like a boat beneath him. One side of his head felt as though it were bursting open. Much more of this and he would be sick.

The great head of the grizzly, with its small eyes and licking red tongue, loomed over him. He felt too ill to care now. The beast put its paws on his shoulders, began to shake him.

"Don't, don't—you're hurting my head!" John cried foolishly.

The bear seemed to go misty at the edges, become a mere dark form that was shaking him. Then it stopped and was still and he lay back, his eyes gradually refocusing it.

It wasn't a bear now. It was a big dark man with an olive skin and contemptuous brown eyes—John Malatesta.

Malatesta! The real world returned to him now. Malatesta, Schultz, Martin, Haywood, Liza, Pinky, Kilpatrick, Danby, Foster . . .

There had been twenty-six of them including himself. The big business man, the chemist, the engineer, the agriculturist, the physician, the geologist, the cook, the bacteriologist, the artist—and the rest. All hand-picked, albeit hastily, by a harassed Government for their qualifications to start a new growth of mankind and yet preserve some of the knowledge and culture from the main stem which was dying.

He, Johns, had been picked, not merely because of his fame as a poet or because he was a Nobel Prize winner for literature but because also he had once been a teacher and a noteworthy educationalist.

How far Malatesta had been picked and how far he had pulled strings to force his election into the chosen few was not known to anyone on the ship but Malatesta himself. He had qualifications, of course. He was the chief of a huge organization in the States. With his organizing ability went toughness of mind and body and immense drive. He was the man to get things done. The only drawback was—the things had to be done his way.

Still, he was in a minority and could be curbed. There were other tough people on the ship, particularly Judge Hackman.

Johns struggled to sit up. There was a thin cold wind blowing.

"That's better," said Malatesta. "But take it easy. There's no hurry. We've got all the time there is."

Johns held his aching head—very lightly because it was painful to touch.

"What hit me?"

"Mars. Want to hit it back?"

Johns shook his head and wished he hadn't. More carefully he turned it to look around. Again he wished he hadn't.

This crazy tangle of broken alloy, with sharp swords of steel bristling from it, had been the main cabin. Once, he had seen a car wreck in which the two vehicles had met head on at the aggregate speed of a hundred and twenty miles an hour. This was worse, and bigger and there were a lot more bodies—and parts of bodies.

"Oh," he said and suddenly the nausea he had dreamed of returned and was made actual.

Gasping for breath afterwards, he turned red wet eyes on Malatesta.

"Tender stomach, eh?" said Malatesta with cynical amusement. "I'll break it to you gently, son. You and me are the only two left alive. And I'm not too sure about you."

Johns could only stare at him. Schultz, Martin, Haywood, Liza, Pinky, Kilpatrick, Danby, Foster . . . All those who had become his friends, sharing this unparalleled adventure—carrying the torch for humanity together—full of a sense of nobility and responsibility—kindly and tolerant, indeed loving toward one another because they had a common aim in life, a great aim, and were there to help each other toward it.

All killed on the march by one senseless blow? Their aspirations mocked by fate and thrown on this ghastly scrapheap?

All—except himself and Malatesta, the one man he had regarded with antipathy and avoided?

He laid his head on his arm and cried, like a child who has suddenly discovered that the entire family has gone out and left him alone in the house—except for the big rough dog he dislikes and fears.

"Good," said Malatesta. "Keep it up. We're short of water. The tank got busted and it's all gone into the ground."

Presently Johns looked up and found he was alone except for—He got dizzily to his feet and scrambled out of that horrible place and away from the broken ship. It was surprisingly easy. He seemed to flutter in long jumps like a goose. Of course, the lesser gravitation . . .

This was Mars—just a lot of thin sick-looking grass, spreading in all directions. The sky was a very dark blue, almost black overhead, where faint stars twinkled. There was a singing in his ears which he had noticed at high altitudes in the Rockies. It came from the low air density.

Then he noticed that springing at thirty degrees from each other, from his feet across the grass, were two shadows, one fainter than the other. And despite the chill breeze there was warmth on the back of his neck.

He turned. There were two suns hanging in the sky, bright and white. Both were considerably smaller than the Sun he had known on Earth and one of them was appreciably smaller than the other.

He was no astronomer but he realized there was something definitely out of order here. However, before he could think about it much, Malatesta came up in long floating strides from somewhere along the great length of wreckage.

"Since you're up," he said, "you can give me a hand with things. Well, what do you think of Mars?"

Johns gestured toward the two suns. "I don't get that."

Malatesta said, "Perhaps you're not quite awake yet. It's obvious enough. I told you—you and me are the only two left alive—*anywhere.*"

Johns grappled with his incredulity.

"You mean?"

"I mean that smaller sun up there is the Earth we left three months ago. I don't know who threw the bomb that started the chain reaction or whether it was too many bombs at once. I don't even know who won the war. I guess *we* did—we're the only survivors."

Johns gave a long sigh. The immense tragedy of it seemed to come pressing down from the sky onto his shoulders. He felt like Dante gazing into the Inferno—abandoned by Virgil, left utterly alone, not knowing the way out. He was the last of his kind. Malatesta didn't count. Malatesta was an insensitive ape.

He felt the tears trying to come again and he fought to keep them back. Malatesta would sneer. Then he thought, "What the hell do I care what *he* thinks? Why should I accept *his* judgment on what is right behavior? He's no more than a half-educated hoodlum."

Nevertheless he turned his face away and bowed his head, lest Malatesta should see.

"What are you doing—composing an epic poem about it?" said Malatesta sarcastically. "You're wasting your time. There's no one left to read it—except me. And I'm tone-deaf. Snap out of it. We're going to live, so we'll have to have a place to live in. Come back to the wreck and help me."

Malatesta's idea of being helped meant that when he said, "Carry that outside" or "Bring that here" Johns was to do it immediately and alone. Whenever Johns found a thing too heavy to lift Malatesta would, grumbling and impatient, take one end of it with a vigor which made it plain that he could have carried the whole thing himself without effort.

But it was mainly by Johns' labor that the rough shack, with its table, chairs and couches, was built from suitable portions of the wreckage.

"Right," said Malatesta, surveying it. "That's good enough for now. It'll keep this damned wind off anyway. Now for a meal. It's lucky the cook's galley wasn't too badly burnt—even though the atomic heaters are no good. The whole system is smashed.

"But the food-store and the refrigerator vault stood up to it. There's plenty of grub in them. Go get a couple of loaves, a can of beef, some butter and cheese and crackers—we'll find ways of cooking some other time. Here are the keys."

"What about doing a bit of work yourself?" Johns broke in angrily. "Do you think I'm the maid-of-all-work here? I've done enough—far more than my share. *You* go and get the food."

Malatesta looked at him searchingly. He tossed the little bunch of keys in the air, caught it on its slow descent.

"Right," he said again. "If that's the way you want it."

"It's only fair—" began Johns in a high protesting voice but Malatesta turned on his heel and went.

He returned presently with the food and made a pile of sandwiches on the table. He drew up the couch alongside, lay back on it comfortably and reached for the top sandwich. Johns watched him eat two, then put his hand out tentatively for the third.

"Hands off!" snapped Malatesta. "No work, no eat. That's how it is. That's how it's going to be. That's how it always was—I didn't run a soup kitchen, you know. My workers had to *work* for their grub."

Johns stared at him. Then he said with quiet acidity, "You're wrong with both your facts and your analogy. Firstly, I *have* worked—hard. Secondly, I'm *not* one of your employees. On that ship we all had equal standing. Half that food is mine."

"No it isn't," said Malatesta with his month full. "You're wrong with *your* facts. We all had equal standing on the ship—yes. There were twenty-six of us. That makes your share of the food one twenty-sixth, not a half. The second thing to understand is—we're not on the ship now."

"That's a childish kind of sophistry. The others are dead. They have no use for food."

"How do you know? Did you ask them? No—you just want to take it because they're helpless to stop you. That's all right. I agree with your philosophy and I'll underwrite it. I take the food, not only because they're helpless to stop me but because you are also."

"I see, Malatesta," said Johns, deliberately. "Might is right with you, eh?"

"You've got it, son." Malatesta helped himself to another sandwich. "That's what I believe because it's the truth."

"It isn't," flashed Johns. "You know it isn't. That's what you believe but only because it suits you to."

"Everybody believes what they'd like to believe. You only believe in a system of equal shares for all because you're weak—too weak to fight for your share. So you invent this thing you call social justice to get your share for you, so that you don't starve. You believe in social justice because it suits you to. I'll take the survival of the fittest—that suits me."

"Then I take it that you intend to starve me to death?"

"Mr. Johns, you take a very pessimistic view of things. The food is your—all of it—if you can take it from me. Of course, I could break your neck with one hand—that's a risk you'd have to take. Or you could kill me if you could think of a method. Again you'd be at a slight disadvantage. I have this, you see—and you haven't."

He pulled an old-fashioned automatic pistol from his pocket and held it balanced on his palm.

"A curio," he said, "but lethal. It was my grandfather's. He was an Italian who went over to the States to set up business—in nineteen twenty-four, it was. He ran a gang of bootleggers and made a pile. When Prohibition was repealed he went into legitimate business. It became the family business. I owe much to him."

"Including your ideas on morality, no doubt, you filthy hoodlum."

Malatesta was off the couch in a bound. The pistol butt caught Johns on the bridge of his nose. He went over backward with a yelp of surprise and pain. The blood ran thickly from his nostrils. He blew and spluttered.

"Oh, stop squawking," said Malatesta. "That was only a love tap. I doubt if it's even broken your nose-bone. Regard it as a warning. I don't resent your insult as such—they're just words. What I don't like and won't have is your acting as though you're superior to me. You're not in any way.

"People learn from life, my friend, not from books. Experience is the only teacher—maybe you think *you* are. You've taught a lot of kids a lot of nonsense in your time. But you've nothing to teach me. You don't know anything. You don't even know that your college education and Nobel Prize don't qualify you as a superman—or even as a man."

Johns was holding a bloody handkerchief to his nose. His head still hurt from the landing crash and now it hurt in another place. But the worse hurt was to his sense of dignity. He had been caught by surprise and yelped like—

He had yelped like one of his own pupils many years ago. Somehow, he always remembered coming up silently that day behind young Perkins, who was absorbed in a comic when he should have been absorbed in Euclid. He remembered the joyous little

spasm of power-feeling as he twisted the boy's ear and pulled his
head around—to face his master.

He had been the master then.

It wasn't nearly so good being the pupil. He resented it
fiercely. He hated Malatesta. If there *was* a way to kill him he
would—

No, he mustn't think that. That was giving way to blind passion. He was above that now. One could never be a master if one
couldn't control his own passions. *He that ruleth his spirit is better
than he that taketh a city.*

Detachedly he wondered if young Perkins had felt like killing
him on that far-off day.

He must control himself with this roughneck. He must feel
himself superior but not make a parade of it. But he must never,
never allow himself to feel inferior, certainly never act as one.

"You want to earn a cup of coffee?" asked Malatesta suddenly.

Johns, still holding his handkerchief to his nose, nodded. He
would not trust himself to say anything. He might be too sarcastic.

"Right. Take that bucket. There's a water channel about two
miles off in that direction. I saw it just before the smash. Bring
back the bucket full and you can have your coffee and—I'll be
generous—a couple of sandwiches."

Johns picked up the bucket and went slowly over the long thin
grass, his two shadows moving ahead of him.

This first sally into unexplored Mars should have been a great
moment. Instead it presented itself as a wearisome task. It was
Malatesta's fault, of course—his brutal materialism was death to
all poetry and wonder and beauty. He poisoned romance. He belit-
tled the really big things of life and magnified the pin-pricks. He'd
have to be careful not to adopt his stunted values.

Damn his nose—would it never stop bleeding? His handkerchief was like a red flag. His face seemed to be little but a throbbing proboscis. He had never been struck before in his life. It
seemed to have knocked his sense of values spinning.

It was all wrong. He should be overwhelmed by the tragedy of
the sudden end of homo sapiens. But he had seen that coming for
too long. It had happened at last, that was all.

He felt a certain sense of loss but it was for the Acropolis, for
the Uffizi Galleries, the Louvre, the Sistine Chapel, the Taj Ma-
hal—not for the lately living people of Earth. The hills that Shake-

speare had walked on around Stratford-on-Avon, the City of London, redolent with history . . .

He had had no living relatives. As for the rest of his fellows, he had known few, respected fewer, loved none. None except his traveling companions on the *Nuova Vita*. That had been his real world. That was where he belonged, where he had found himself at last, among the elite. The loss of those people was a far greater tragedy than the loss of Earth.

The voice of one of the élite bellowed after him. "What are you trying to do—walk backwards? I want that coffee today. Get a move on."

Johns made a noise between a groan and a growl. "Shut up, you slimy thug!" he hissed in sick hatred. But he knew that Malatesta was too far away to hear him. Nevertheless he quickened his pace.

His handkerchief had become a sodden useless ball. Irritably he threw it to the ground. It alit on what had seemed to be a small gray stone half-hidden in the grass. The stone came alive with a leap and bounded off like a rabbit, giving a back kick with its rear legs. It was like an earless rabbit with the smooth gray skin of a mouse.

He watched it until it had vanished in the distance. So there was animal life on Mars after all. An irrational hope sprang within him. Were there somewhere intelligent Martians who could paint and sculpt and build, make music and write, think and discuss?

The great telescopes on the Moon, their magnification unhampered by any blurring atmosphere, had raked the planet for signs of intelligent life and seen none. Empty deserts of red dust, yes, and vast green plains. But not a town anywhere.

Most of the mapped canals were there but it seemed that the regularity of them had been an optical illusion. They were no straighter than any river. There was no more plan to them than to the Grand Canyon. So people had dropped the description "canals" and called them what Schiaparelli had really called them—channels.

Ahead of him now he could see the line across the broad strip of green that was one of these channels. Despite the lift given by the lesser gravity it seemed an age before he reached it.

There wasn't much to it then. The grass was longer and greener at its banks and that was about all. Compared with some of the other channels it was but a thread —fifty feet across. The water was pale blue, clear and cold. He could see where the soil ended and the rock-bed began. There was moss on the rocks at the bottom and he could have sworn that he saw one green rock move—a crustacean, surely.

The banks were just earth and rock—without trace of any Martian engineering. The water seemed to have worn its own channel. He tried to put the silly hope out of his head.

He drank, then washed the blood from his face. His nose had stopped giving but not hurting. He filled the bucket and took a last look around. The channel went waveringly from horizon to horizon. The other bank looked the same as the one he was standing on.

The long grass waved silently in the wind. There was nothing else to see. He turned his back on it and set out for the great ragged shape of the wreck under the two small bright suns. It was the only prominent feature in the flat landscape.

Presently he trod on something that rolled beneath his foot. He stumbled and spilt about a third of the water. Then he picked up the object. It was a knob of rock, twice the size of a man's fist.

As he inspected it his heart began to quicken. That irrational hope returned. Surely, surely, it had been consciously shaped? There were deep eye-sockets, a jutting nose, the suggestion of a mouth and chin. A primitive attempt at a human head or a badly weather-worn but comparatively modern one? Or—was it just his own wishful thinking?

Perhaps—there could have been very little erosion in this climate. But it looked as good as many museum pieces he had seen. He put it in his pocket and resumed his journey.

When he got back all the sandwiches were gone and Malatesta said, "Why the hell didn't you *fill* the bucket?"

However, Malatesta had got some utensils from the ship and started a fire with splintered bookshelves. Johns went and got some more bread from the foodstore.

After they had finished the coffee they lay back and smoked. Johns got out the stone head and looked it over closely.

"What's that?" said Malatesta lazily.

Johns told him what he thought it might be. Malatesta was merely amused. He gave the thing a rough examination and tossed it back.

"Meteorite," he said. "You can see where it's pitted by the friction."

"But the shape?"

"Have you ever been to the Garden of the Gods, near Colorado Springs? The place is—was—lousy with chunks of rock that looked like heads. You're just superimposing a pattern subjectively, like Lowell peering at this planet from Flagstaff a century ago and making neat little maps of the canals. Or like a patient of Rorschach's—the gink who started the psychiatrists playing the ink-blot game."

Johns looked at him with surprise. Malatesta then was not wholly a throwback to his gangster grandfather despite his brutality and his deliberately coarse and ungrammatical speech. Sometime, somewhere, he had read books and some of it had stuck.

"I prefer to think it's the work of an intelligence," said Johns, shortly.

"Naturally. You believe what you want to believe like I said. You hope somewhere you'll find intelligent companionship—not like mine. Me, I don't go for poetry or anything else that ain't any good to me."

"Your disapproval doesn't destroy the value of poetry," said Johns. "It's an eternal and indestructible value, far above your or my criticism. The same goes for any of the art forms—and Truth and Beauty and Goodness."

He breathed the last words so that the capitals were almost visibly apparent.

Malatesta, on the couch, regarded the glowing end of his cigarette. Then he said, slowly, thinking it out, "The sonnet form was a human invention—and it died with humanity. So did any standards of art form whatsoever. They were pretty unstable even when they existed—yesterday's art is today's laugh.

"Most of the naked Venuses of the so-called Old Masters are fat, unsightly lumps by the Two Thousand and Three A.D. standards of feminine beauty. Beauty is a matter of fashion, nothing more. If Mona Lisa had tried to get a job in the New York TV studios as an actress she'd have been told to go home and find her eyebrows."

"And how do you dispose of Goodness?"

"Just another matter of custom. Cannibalism was evil in America. In Polynesia not so long ago your grandmother's shade would have felt horribly slighted if you hadn't eaten her corpse and so absorbed her good qualities.

"I could give you a thousand examples of the same act being thought good in one place and evil in another. And you can kill people with kindness, you know. As for truth—no one's answered Pilate yet."

Johns stared at him. "I'm darned if I can make you out," he said. "One minute you talk like a thick-eared mugg and the next like a university graduate."

Malatesta laughed a fat laugh of self-satisfaction. "I've been both. And I'm schizophrenic."

"You're all wrong anyway. We try to superimpose patterns on material, certainly. But these patterns are eternal standards which we glimpse through our imagination and try to record so that others may see them more clearly."

"If the patterns are eternal why do they change so often?"

"They don't. It's our imperfect vision, bad guesses and fumbling execution. Truth is outside of us and eternal."

Malatesta said, "The pragmatists don't think so and I'm a pragmatist. All thought is personal and purposive. Abstracts are figments. A judgment which is not prompted by motives is impossible. The only test of a truth is—does it work? If it doesn't it's meaningless."

"The opinion of the majority is against you."

"What majority? Listen, son—wake up! There's just you and me and no one else. There ain't a majority. My belief is just as good as yours."

Johns was shocked into consideration. He looked at his feet, thinking—if there are only two people in the world and one is a paranoiac and the other a manic depressive, what are the tests of sanity? Where are the standards of rational behavior?

Then he said, "I don't mean to be offensive. I have had more training in these things. My greater experience can be regarded as the majority."

Malatesta gave him the Bronx cheer, for old tradition.

"Can be regarded—by whom?" he jeered. "Only you, of course. I'm two hundred pounds—or was on Earth—to your hundred and forty. I'll choose to regard that extra sixty pounds of me as the majority."

"On the other hand I'm taller than you," snapped Johns spitefully. He knew he was talking foolishness.

"But I'm the better pool player," said Malatesta suavely, completing the reduction ad absurdum.

"This is nonsense!" cried Johns, angrily. "You can't just ignore history and pretend that this is the beginning of the world. What about Buddha and Aristotle and Lao-Tsze and—"

Malatesta swung around and pointed violently upward, over the wreck, at the sky. "What about them?" he flung back. "See that star? It's just a star among a billion other stars. There may have been saints and sinners on the others too—and where is their wisdom now? That's finished, written off.

"I'm not pretending this is the beginning of the world—it *is* the beginning of the world as far as I'm concerned—*my* world!"

And in that moment, as Malatesta sat rigid with his arm up-flung, a form emerged slowly from the wreck. Both men stared at it. "A Martian!" thought Johns, suddenly flushing with a new excitement. *"A Martian!"*

Malatesta let his arm fall. He swore under his breath. "This certainly *is* the beginning of the world," he said. "And *how!* Johns, here comes our majority."

She was dazed and her white dress was barred with black dirt and her fingers were bleeding. She was small, brunette, rather plump and they didn't recognize her at first.

"It's the nurse," said Johns, suddenly, recalling the face when it wasn't smudged and tear-stained. She had been a quite little thing, keeping well in the background, and her services had not been required during the voyage. He hadn't heard her exchange a word with anyone and he wasn't sure of her name though he had heard it.

While he stood there, remembering her, Malatesta walked out to meet her. Johns cursed himself for his slowness. Malatesta picked her up, carried her over the wreckage-strewn grass and laid her on the couch.

"Get her a drink of water, beautiful dreamer," he said.

Presently they got her story in a faint Nebraskan accent. It was short. She had been in the women's lavatory when the crash came. She didn't remember anything after that except awakening in darkness under a load of wreckage and fighting for hours, pulling and pushing at the stuff, to get out.

She recalled scarcely more of what happened before that. She had only the sketchiest memory of the ship and the voyage. She remembered there were people. Just people—no names to them. She didn't remember Malatesta and Johns.

"I thought I'd gone right through what's left of the ship," said Malatesta. "Didn't think of the ladies' room. Maybe I've got loss of memory too. What's your name?"

She didn't remember. She knew she came from Ogallala on the south fork of Platte River and had been a nurse.

Malatesta said, "We'll have to call you something."

"What about just 'Nurse'?" suggested Johns.

Malatesta rubbed his dark bristly jowls. "Nope. We'll call her Madge."

"Madge?" echoed Johns.

"Short for Majority, wideawake. Do I have to explain everything?"

The next morning, Johns was awakened by the clang of the bucket dropping beside him.

"More water," said Malatesta, standing over him. "I want breakfast."

Johns got up. "And a shave, too, no doubt," he murmured.

"Hell, no. I'm never shaving again. From now on I make my own social conventions."

"I'll come with you, Tom," said Madge.

As they walked side by side over the grass she said quietly, "He doesn't like you, does he?"

"The feeling is mutual. We haven't a thing in common. By the way, do you like poetry?"

"I—I think so. I don't know much about it."

"I could teach you if you're willing to learn. *He* isn't. You know, whether Art lives or dies depends wholly on you."

"Huh?"

"Art is the communication of feelings, ideas, standards. I am an artist in a vacuum—with no one to communicate to. Actually an artist can't exit without an audience. No one ever writes or paints for himself alone. Those that pretend to were thinking of posterity. It's possible that we'll have no posterity. Will you be my audience, Madge?"

She smiled for the first time. She had nice teeth. "Sure, I'll try to be appreciative."

"Thanks a lot."

All the way to the channel and back he expressed himself to her—his moods, his ideas, his fancies. He didn't give her much chance to talk.

As he was explaining to her his own theory of what Picasso had been getting at she exclaimed suddenly, *"Ooh!* What's that?" She pointed to a moving object in the grass.

He broke off, rather irritated by her branching attention; he'd thought she was absorbing the whole of it.

"Oh, that," he said. "There's plenty of 'em about. I call 'em Martian rabbits."

"Wonder if they're good to eat?"

"One day we'll have to find out. That food-store isn't going to last forever. Perhaps we'll finish up eating grass, like Nebuchadnezzar."

"Neb—who's he?"

A bit wearily he explained.

Three more days passed and nothing much happened except that the wind died down and became almost imperceptible, and the heat of the two suns could be more strongly felt. Malatesta seemed content to lounge, sleep, smoke and be sarcastic at Johns' expense. His one other diversion was Madge. What irked Johns was that Madge didn't seem to mind. In fact it was becoming plain that she preferred Malatesta's company to his.

On the fourth morning the split became apparent.

"Get the water," said Malatesta, so tersely and contemptuously that Johns grabbed the bucket with the wild idea of swinging it at that bristling contemptuous face. But an anticipatory pain in the nose caused him to throttle the intention.

Instead he gripped the bucket firmly and said, "Isn't it about time we moved to the channel-side? Then we'd have water on tap. Anyway this is an unhealthy spot. That ship's beginning to smell."

"I don't mind the smell," said Malatesta, "and all the water I need is brought to me. I like it here. There's a convenient larder with a lock on the door. There's nothing like that along by the channel."

"There may be all sorts of things better than that if we look around. We've never tried to explore any of this planet. We've scarcely moved from the ship."

"I'll think about it when I have to," said Malatesta. "Not before."

"You're some organizer," said Johns bitterly. "You haven't done a thing."

"You're some writer. You haven't written a line."

"What's the use?" cried Johns. "There's no one left to appreciate it."

"Exactly. Why bother? We all do it to cut a figure, don't we? And if there's no one to applaud us . . ." Malatesta shrugged.

"You don't claim *you* were an artist?"

Malatesta regarded Johns with a queer look that combined derision and defense.

"In a way, yes. A better way than yours at that. Art is only expression. You express yourself merely in words. I in action. Try my way. You may get to like it. Begin now—go and get that water."

"To hell with the water!" exploded Johns and flung the bucket away violently. It landed, bounced slowly and rolled across the grass to where Madge sat. She got up and walked across to the two men.

"Don't hit him, Jack," she said.

"I'm not going to," said Malatesta. "It's impossible to teach this guy. He thinks he knows it all. I could see it would come to this. Here's your marching orders, Mr. Know-All. Clear off. Fend for yourself. I'm tired of keeping you. You don't belong in my world. You contribute nothing but belly-aching. Scram out of here and don't come back."

Johns went a little pale and compressed his lips. "I was going anyway. I can't stomach this emperor and slave routine any more. You're mad and you're best left alone. Come on, Madge, we'll go start our own world."

Madge said, "I'm staying with Jack."

"What?" said Johns and looked appalled. "Why, for heaven's sake? He'll only make a slave out of you. He's impossible to live with. Is it because he's got the food? You don't have to worry about that. There's plenty of rabbits for us and shellfish and water. We might find edible vegetation somewhere."

"It isn't that," cut in Madge, irritably. "I'm staying with Jack because I prefer to. He's got the right ideas. And he's a *man.*"

Malatesta grinned suddenly and put his arm about her waist. Johns felt a queer sharp pain. It was loneliness stabbing at him. It was as if he had been shut out of life, alone, unwanted.

"But—" he said weakly. "But I thought, Madge, you understood."

"You bore me sick," she said. "Yatter-yatter-yatter all the time about things that don't matter any more. Your feet don't touch the ground anywhere. I want a family. I want kids and a man who knows how to bring 'em up. Can you imagine what it'd be like for me with you, doing things your way?

"I'd be doing all the man's work, while you'd be sitting with the kids, pumping 'em full of poetry and high-falutin" useless stuff, teaching 'em everything but how to look after themselves. That's the only important thing in *this* world—how to look after yourself. There's no college here to feed you just for lecturing."

"The majority, you see, Johns, is on my side," said Malatesta, his grin broadening.

All at once Johns hated them both with impotent fury. He turned away and walked toward the bucket.

Malatesta's grin vanished. "Leave the bucket!" he snapped. "That's my property. Leave everything except yourself."

Johns bent and picked up the stone shaped like a head.

"I trust you will allow me to take this?" he said with gritty mock-politeness.

"Sure. Start a museum with it. Now git!"

Without a backward glance Johns went. The world was against him. It seemed idiotic to think of one man and one woman as "The world" but factually it was very nearly true.

He had a mad impulse to smash things and there was nothing to smash except the weak bending grass-stalks. Then a "rabbit" crossed his path and instantly he smashed the stone down on top of it and broke the creature's back.

With that killing, the violence ebbed from his system, left him feeling weak and empty. He stared down at the broken mouse-skinned body. It looked pitifully small and lonely.

Unconsciously he identified it with himself and regretted his unplanned action. He might have caught the creature, tamed it, made a friend of it. If anyone ever needed a friend he did.

He picked up the stone thoughtfully and walked on. Presently he stopped, went back and picked up the rabbit. Perhaps a fellow couldn't help relapsing to childhood sometimes and feeling a need for pets and dolls to confide his troubles to. All the same he had to eat. He was on his own now. He must learn to be self-reliant.

He strode on, frowning, the stone in one hand and the rabbit in the other. What was it Emerson had said about self-reliance?

After a time he forgot Emerson, and by practise became expert in using the head as a throwing stone. He could hit a rabbit on the run at ten paces.

A fortnight later Johns floated on his back in the channel, gazing up into the dark blue sky at the two small suns and the faint stars. The air was still, the blue water placid. It was quiet and nothing disturbed the peace or threatened to.

And he felt like screaming.

Sometime in the turmoil of Earth he had dreamed of life on a desert island. Once he had seriously thought of going into a monastery.

"Utter fool!" he said aloud. One thing he had learned—he was not by temperament a hermit. But then, Robinson Crusoe had had his Man Friday, his parrot, his goat. And the monks had fellow monks—and books.

How he longed for books! Even so they were only a substitute for the spoken word. Oh, for someone to speak to—even Malatesta! The man was not unintelligent although he was a brute. If he, Johns, had kept his temper they might have got along after a fashion.

Madge he still thought of with bitterness. She had not even troubled to argue with him. She had listened to him in silence, thinking only of him as a fool. It still hurt. But why should he consider her opinion worth anything? She was the fool, not he.

If only she had not at first seemed so pleasant. And if only she weren't so pretty . . .

Why should she keep drifting into his mind's eye? Why should he bother to waste another thought on her? She was perfectly matched with Malatesta. A pair of pragmatists. They could, no doubt, raise a family of pragmatists, all of them unaware of the eternal truths because there was no poet to instruct them. A tribe without poetry.

He floated, with the water dulling his ears, quoting aloud the Caliph in *Hassan.* " 'Ah, if there shall ever arise a nation whose people have forgotten poetry . . . though their city be greater than Babylon of old, though they mine a league into earth or mount to the stars on wings—what of them?' "

What had Hassan answered? " 'They will be a dark patch upon the world.' "

He tried to recall more of it and was impatient because he could not. He stared up at Earth, thinking of all the literature that had perished.

Pater had advised the world to "burn with a hard, gemlike flame." Now it was doing it—literally. In Earth's dark history there had been many a "burning of the books." This, the last, could never be surpassed. It was a funeral pyre and no Phoenix would arise from the ashes.

Not unless *he* did something about it.

The gloom that sat heavily upon him seemed to form itself into as heavy a cloak of responsibility, a garment he had tried to ignore, had tried to pretend was something else.

There had been a good library in the *Nuova Vita.* Much technical stuff but also a fine selection of literature intended for preservation. How much of it had been destroyed in the smash? It was his duty to preserve what was left.

Probably it was the last remnant of culture in the Solar System. So far as he could judge from a fortnight's trudging up and down the channel-side, peering at the distances, there was no sign of any Martian civilization, old or new. Perhaps there had never been one.

He had spent hours examining the stone head and was still undecided about it. Perhaps Malatesta had been right—perhaps he was reading a pattern into the chance work of nature merely because he wanted to see that pattern. On the other hand he might be just as right himself.

Surely, here on Mars, the eternal values reigned and had been glimpsed by some sentient indigenous creatures? This carven head was a sign, a symbol, a reassurance of that. Sometimes he was sure of it and glowed with excitement. At those times life would flood with meaning again.

And then at others the stone became a lifeless lump in his hands, drained of significance, just a gray-black meteorite. Then everything, including himself, was purposeless and of no more account than the dead stone.

No, the only chance was the books. He must get them.

Spurred by the resolution, he swam to the bank.

Everything looked much as before around the wreck except that at a little distance from the shack a large bright fire burned, sending up a wavering column of black smoke. As he neared it he could see Malatesta sitting on his couch by the fire. There was a heap on the ground at his side and occasionally Malatesta reached out, took something from the heap, threw it into the dire.

Johns looked around hopefully for the small plump figure of Madge. She was nowhere in sight.

When he was close enough to see just what Malatesta was doing he gave something between a shriek and a shout and ran toward the fire.

"*Stop that!*" he yelled. "*Stop it,* I say!"

Malatesta looked up at him calmly. "Thought I told you to stay away from here."

"Don't put any more of those books on the fire. I warn you," said Johns, breathlessly.

"You're a bit late. We've had the fire going for over a week."

"You vandal!" Johns dropped his throwing stone and knelt by the fire. It was all burning books, a tangle of charring gilt edges, leather bindings, printed rice paper.

He raked out one that had not properly caught and burned his fingers slapping at the smoldering spine. He raked out one that had not properly caught and burned his fingers slapping at the smoldering spine. He dropped the book. It fell open at a page than began complacently, *We can, I believe, take it for granted that in the world of 2200, which we are trying to foresee with our imagination, the present ideological conflicts will have resolved themselves and mankind will have united under a common liberal education . . .*

In a spasm of bitter disgust he thrust the book back into the flames.

"Make up your mind," said Malatesta, sarcastically.

Johns glared at him. "There is no need for this sort of thing. The grass provides endless fuel. You've only got to pull it up and let it dry. As I've done."

"Ah, but you didn't have any books. They burn longer than grass and give more heat. I prefer warmth to idealism."

"You'll have to make do with grass in future. I want those books."

Malatesta looked him up and down appraisingly.

"Your fortnight in the wilderness seems to have toughened you up. Nevertheless I could still beat you up with one hand. So quit talking that way."

"It won't always be like this," said Johns between his teeth. "You're too fond of that couch. You're running to fat and self-indulgence. I'm getting stronger."

"Come back when you think you're strong enough," said Malatesta with steel in his voice. "I'll be ready for you. So will my sons—there'll be a lot of 'em and they'll be tough—because I know how to bring 'em up."

"Brought up on your philosophy they'll be a generation of vipers."

Malatesta clenched his fist hard. In the same instant Johns grabbed his throwing stone and stood up. They regarded each other, frozen, tense. Then, slowly, Malatesta let his hand open.

"You still don't like my ideas, huh?"

"They're the quintessence of evil. You could build nothing from them but a soulless hell."

Malatesta gave a short, hard laugh. "That's funny. I've always regarded *you* as the serpent in this particular Garden of Eden."

"Your mistake. You're the serpent in these parts."

"As I recall it," said Malatesta, "The serpent made Eve eat of the forbidden Tree of Knowledge of Good and Evil. That's exactly what you tried to do with Madge. Haven't you discovered yet that knowledge and happiness are incompatible? I thought you knew your Greek philosophy. I'd rather be a happy pig than an unhappy Socrates. If we're ignorant, Madge and me, we're happy in our ignorance. You and your Truth!"

He spat and there was a confirmatory hiss from the fire.

He went on, "Why must your sort always interfere, always preach, thinking you know it all and that everyone else has got to think the same as you? It was fanatics like you who brought our world to destruction. We're satisfied with making our won little truths to suit ourselves—no factory stuff.

"Each man to his own belief and let the other guy alone. But that's not good enough for you. You've got to pretend that yours is the *only* truth and try to stuff it down our throats. Intolerant fool! What a hell *you* would make here if you had your way—as you made a hell upon Earth."

"You idiot!" said Johns, fiercely. "Earth went up in flames simply because of millions of people like you making themselves a law unto themselves. You undermined the belief in morals which was our only hope. When that code fell Earth fell."

Malatesta seemed not to have heard him. He had picked up a book from the heap and was regarding its title.

"The Works of John Keats," he said. "Well, well. 'Beauty is truth, truth beauty—that is all ye know on earth and all ye need to know.' On Earth. But this is Mars."

He tossed the book casually into the fire. An instant later the throwing stone crashed against his skull and killed him.

Johns stood over the body, fallen from its couch, not seeing it, not seeing anything but a red mist. When it cleared he was sick and the works of Keats had gone forever.

There came a cry, the thud of a dropped bucket, the wash of water over the grass. Then Madge came running and flung herself on the body, sobbing and crying, *"Jack! Jack!"*

Johns watched her dully for a moment. Then he went off a little way and lay on the grass, face downward, making a pillow of his arms. His head was whirling and he could get nothing straight.

Presently, she came and stood over him.

"You murderer!"

He half-turned his head, and mumbled, "He—" He stopped. What was the use of trying to explain to her the loss of Keats or the chain of clashes which had led up to that last act of vandalism being the immediate pull on a hair-trigger? There must have been half-a-dozen mixed motives, which he had neither the ability nor the will to sort out.

"He went for his gun," he said. "It was self-defense."

"That's a lie," said Madge, coldly. "He never had his gun. Because I had it. I've still got it and I'm going to use it. Turn around. Do you want to be shot in the back?"

Slowly he turned over and sat up. Madge's face was pale and tear-stained, but determined, and the automatic that pointed down at him was steady. Over her left shoulder burned the Earth—over her right the Sun.

"Every time I went to get the water, he would give me the gun—in case I met you and you tried anything. He didn't care about himself. He could have killed you with one hand."

"I guess he told you that himself," murmured Johns, wearily. "Okay, go ahead if you believe you ought to. I give up. Whatever you believe you're as right as I am. When I am gone you will always be wholly and absolutely right—until you die."

The gun began to tremble a little.

"I loved him," she said. "He was rough but—I loved that man. Now you've killed him. I'm going to kill you. That's justice."

"If you think so. But that's an abstract he didn't believe in, of course. If you kill me, thinking that, I win. But is your motive really justice? It might be revenge—or anger at being deprived of his attentions—and his children. Don't give it a name. Just act how you feel—that was his philosophy and yours. I'm not afraid. What have I to live for?"

"You killed him because you wanted me, didn't you?" she said.

"If you think so. What does it matter now? Shoot—get it over with."

"Oh!" she said, suddenly, and threw the gun away and burst into tears. "I don't want to be alone!" she sobbed.

"And I want so to have children."

He stared at her in amazement. Then he got up and took hold of her, swinging her half-around. He kissed her and she clung to him.

"Don't leave me alone!" she cried. "Don't ever leave me alone!"

He held her, tightening his grip. "It's all right, Madge. We'll keep together. We're all that are left—anywhere."

Over her shoulder he saw their united shadows slanting across the grass in a long V. Only two of them left but between them they had four shadows.

It was odd but it was Malatesta's materialistic philosophy, adopted by Madge that had now saved his life. Madge had let him live only because she needed him, because of the practical outcome. If he had succeeded in imbuing her with his abstract ideals he would be as dead as Malatesta.

Had he been wrong? Would he ever really know?

Was there something symbolic in the double shadows or was he reading patterns into things again? Here a man cast one shadow by the light of the sinful suicidal Earth, another by the light of the life-giving Sun. Wherever you stood you could not escape the duality.

So long as there were the two sources you were bound to be affected by them both. You could not choose to stand only in the light of one.

"We are what we are according to our lights," he said, under his breath. Madge pressed herself even closer to him.

It was some time later that he discovered that, though Malatesta's skull had been split open, it had been sufficiently hard to do the same to the missile which had struck it. The stone head was gaping apart, showing its own brain.

The cells of the brain were tight-packed in the cavity—thousands of rolls of incredibly thin but tough metal tape, scarcely an eighth of an inch wide. He could just make out some of the little colored pictures on them. To those who had made them they must have been great banners, blazoning forth the history and knowledge of their race.

"Think of it, Madge!" he said, excitedly. "Of all the incredible luck! To stumble like this on the records they preserved for posterity. It *was* a head—humanoid, too. I wonder where the body is? We must look for it."

"There may be lots of 'em around," she said. "Our people were always doing that sort of thing, weren't they?"

"Who'd have thought the Martians were such tiny folk!" he said. "There was I, carrying this in my hand, scanning the horizons

for man-sized relics. There must be plenty of traces but we'll have
to look under the grass, not over it."

"Uh-huh," she said, more concerned with the fire, which was
dying down just as the rabbit-stew was nearing the boil. She
reached for a book and gave it to him to censor.

He glanced at it absently:

"Lord, no, not that one! We'll need it when we get down to
work, making our instruments."

He laid *Microscopy and Optical systems* on the grass beside
him.

She handed him another. He looked at it, and smiled. "We'll
need that, too." He laid *Obstetrics* on top of the other book.

Patiently she held up another for his inspection.

"Brrr!" he said. "Burn that."

She poked *Income Tax Accountancy* carefully under the pot
and the flames gathered life. She peeped into the pot and was satisfied with what she saw. The stew was thickening nicely and they
would have a rich supper. It seemed just about the most important
thing in life to her at that moment.

PAWN IN REVOLT

AS HAD ALWAYS BEEN HIS HABIT, the old man had doodled on a writing pad all the time they had talked. The same old wolves' heads, full face, left profile, right profile. They were rather fuzzy wolves now, because Luben's hand trembled with age. His voice quavered a little, too, but there was no wavering in his mind: that was fixed in the pattern of Corporism, and it was not set by senility: it had grown rigid in his youth. For he had realised then that Corporism was the final answer to everything. Only the fools, the ignorant, and the misled could not see that, and they were unimportant anyway.

"You must return within a month," he said.

"A month?" echoed Parleck. "I was thinking of at least a year. If I come and go too frequently, it may arouse suspision—"

"If you leave it as long as a year, you won't be able to return at all."

Parleck stared at the old man, his eyes widening.

"You're not—?" he said, and found he could add no more.

"*I* am not," said Luben. "*We* are. The council decided this morning. Do you not agree with them?"

"Well—I—"

"I know. You're half Albish, and you're sentimental about the island. But it's become much more than just an island. When you wander along its lanes and through its orchards you must remember this: you are not strolling through a garden—you are walking the deck of a great aircraft carrier, moored off our coast and in the service of our most powerful enemies."

"That I realise," said Parleck, slowly.

"And that you are not walking that deck in the role of a casual visitor among friends, but as a spy among those who have repeatedly proven themselves to be our bitterest enemies."

"That also, I realise."

"Do you—fully? I wonder. I'm not satisfied with your recent reports, Parleck. I don't think you're doing all that your duty to your fatherland demands of you."

"I thought there were no more fatherlands or motherlands—only Corporism."

The point of Luben's pencil stopped on the ear of a wolf which had got out of hand in drawing.

"True," said the old man, quietly. "But Negovia is the fountain head of Corporism, and we owe it to the world to keep the fountain head uninjured and freely flowing."

"I have reported what I have observed in Albion. And I have observed no signs of any intention to attack the fountain head."

Luben abandoned the misshapen wolf and rolled the pencil gently between his fingers.

"If you were to observe Negovia you would see no signs of any intention to attack Albion. Nevertheless, the intention is there. Intentions are made to be concealed. The Albish and their allies intend to attack us. We need no confirmation of that intention: we know it exists, because its existence arises logically out of the immutable laws of Corporism. All situations grow out of other situations, and each stage is predictable if you know your Corporism. What isn't always predictable is the exact time when each stage is to be reached. This is what is wrong with your reports, Parleck—they give no indication of the time. If it is to be more than a year hence, we're not worried—and our enemies will by then be in no position to worry. But if it's to be before we are ready . . . that's why I want you to go to Albion at once and glean from Sanders some idea of the date. We must know."

"And if it *is* before we are ready?"

"We must stall them by making a show of renouncing Corporism and seeing the error of our ways. We must give them the hope that Corporism will collapse of itself without their having to do anything about it. The Albish have a natural inclination to take the line of least resistance—we must play on that inclination. At least, until our hydrogen bombs are ready: the piles are working night and day."

"I see that you have thought it all out."

Luben smiled faintly. He said: "This sort of thing is no effort for me, any more than it was for Machiavelli or Hitler. In the mass, men are children: they have no character, and one just plays on their hopes and fears. It is too easy. I often wish I—the Council—had a more worthy opponent. But our enemies are democracies, headless animals, confused with a thousand dissonant desires and beliefs which cancel out. They have no binding philosophy such as we have. They have no direction, no common impulse—except that of blind self-preservation, which will lead them to a so-called preventive war."

"But are *we* not heading for a so-called preventive war?"

There had been little life in Luben's smile, and now it expired altogether.

"There will be nothing 'so-called' about it. As a nation Albion will cease to exist in a matter of minutes. Half a dozen H-bombs could do it, strategically placed—one of them on its capital, of course. And there's no comparison about our intentions. Their war is designed merely to maintain the status quo. Ours—to extend Corporism and peace to the whole world and end wars forever!"

His rheumy eyes could still summon a spark from the revolutionary fire of his youth. His quavering voice could still recall an echo from old, stirring addresses. And age and dignity underwrote them with authority.

"I shall expect useful information within the month," he said, abruptly. "This audience is ended."

Parleck saluted, and left.

The door had scarcely closed behind him before Luben pressed the bell-push under his desk.

Novik, coming in answer from his office below, passed Parleck on the stairs. They smiled and nodded at each other perfunctorily, but said nothing. Each distrusted the other because they had nothing whatever in common, and if Parleck understood Novik, it was certain that Novik did not understand Parleck.

Novik was pleasant-faced, perfectly mannered, always agreeable to those in authority above him. He was also agreeable to his subordinates and expected them to be agreeable to him, which they were. It was a little odd that they were, because not so long ago they were in authority over him. They had, on their various levels, never quite fathomed how Novik, while agreeing with all they said should somehow have taken over a role in which they found themselves agreeing with all he said. His quiet suggestions had imperceptibly changed into quiet directions, without arousing resentment or jealousy, in a manner which seemed just in the natural course of things.

His gentle infiltration had brought him into the orbit of Luben's notice, and Luben had for some time watched his progress with a secret amusement which became a secret admiration.

He had himself fought his way up with violent haranguing, intimidation, maneuvring with cliques, even conspiracy, and—once—murder. Only as old age began to cool his blood and sap his strength did he begin to appreciate—and practise—the power which lay in subtlety.

When he thought he had mastered it, he became aware of the real master approaching him from below. Had he been younger, he would have fought off and maimed the insidious usurper, for his philosophy was that of the wolf pack: kill or be killed.

He had been leader long enough to recognise a challenge, in whatever form it came. But he knew that soon he would have to relinquish the reins through sheer feebleness, and he would rather hand them over with dignity to a chosen successor than have them taken from him. So for some time he had been keeping his eyes open for such a worthy successor.

At first, before changing his mind and choosing Novik, he had considered Parleck. Parleck was the right age, he was a man of character and intelligence, he had always been a diligent Corporist, a courageous good organiser, energetic.

He was only half-Negovian. That shouldn't make any difference, because Corporism was supra-national, and even full-blooded Negroes filled offices of trust in the Council. The trouble was that he was also half Albish—his father had been Negovian ambassador in the Albish capital and married an Albish woman. The ambassador had held his post for many years, and so Parleck's formative years had been half Albish too.

How far could Parleck be trusted?

Luben put the question to Novik as soon as he came in.

Novik answered, standing there at a sort of relaxed attention: "I have often wondered."

Luben waved him to a chair. (Parleck would seat himself without giving it a thought, but Novik always waited politely for permission).

"Any conclusions?"

"We can trust him quite a long way, if we are to judge solely by his service to our country as a diplomat and—an agent."

"Say spy, if you mean spy," said Luben, testily.

"A spy, then," said Novik, easily. "His information, even on top secret level, has never been found inaccurate in a single particular, so far as I know."

"Agreed. But lately there hasn't been much of it, and what there is, is relatively unimportant. Of what use to the Council is gossip about Cabinet intrigue when what they desire to know is the size of the atomic bomb stockpile, the amount of heavy hydrogen being produced (and we know Albion *is* producing a lot), and, above all, the contemplated date of attack."

"He may be keeping something back."

"That's what I'm afraid of. The Albish are a reserved, insular, silent people, and there are some of those characteristics in Parleck—you can never be wholly sure of what he's being silent and reserved about."

"That's so. And I've noticed a tendency of his of late to cast doubt on the moral fitness of actions, as though morality were something more than just a temporary convention for convenience's sake. He seems to have lost sight of the eternal principle of Corporism that progress can only be made by breaking conventions—*any* sort of conventions."

" 'But are not *we* heading for a so-called preventive war?' " echoed Luben, from his memory, and mused a while. "It's true, of course, but—"

"But the rightness of an action depends upon who performs it," said the other, anticipating the quotation from the Corporist Handbook.

Luben nodded.

"Therefore," continued Novik, "judging by the fact that we do not fully know his inner beliefs, we cannot trust him at all. He is a dangerous man."

"Dangerous men can be used—like any other men," said Luben, sliding open a drawer and taking out a chessboard and a box of pieces. "For myself, I trust Parleck—at the moment."

He began setting up the pieces.

Presently, the pair were immersed in their daily game of chess.

The Negovians were great chess players. Indeed, they saw life largely in terms of the game. They could not conceive that any move of any sort by anyone was likely to be anything but a calculated move towards capturing their king. The diehard Corporists believed that there were no generous, disinterested, or altruistic actions, that nobody gave away anything that wasn't a premeditated sacrifice for a later and greater gain, that nothing was straight-forward and all was camouflage for ulterior motives.

Of course, there were a lot of pawns in the game, too, whose names were John Smith, Joe Doakes, and Ivan Ivanovitch—silly little things, almost useless, with their heads full of idiotic misapprehensions about the meaning of life, gaping oaf-like at sunsets, pottering in their gardens and growing inutile flowers, pretending to help their neighbours (but really out for their own ends, naturally), pawing their fat wives, rearing ugly little juniors, slapping paint on canvas and scribbling rubbish on paper, building the equivalent of sand castles.

But they weren't wholly useless. You couldn't very well play chess without pawns.

The two men crouched over the ivory figures.

So far Luben hadn't lost a game. When he did, he knew it would be time to hand over to Novik. He felt it would be soon. This past week Novik had extended him to his utmost and left him an exhausted victor.

"You know," said Novik, presently, "I understand your mind better than I do Parleck's. He's the one man I can't figure out. I think I shall have trouble with him."

"He's not *your* trouble yet," reminded Luben, pointedly. "However, you needn't be afraid of him. He's a poor chess player."

~ ~ ~ ~ ~

"You're a queer bird, Parleck," said Sanders, with a quizzical smile. "I don't think I've ever really understood you, not even when we were at school together."

Parleck lay back on the green bank, chewing a piece of grass. Dog-roses climbed over the hedge above him. A blackbird sang in a chestnut tree, against the blue sky. Scents drifted in the air: new-mown hay, wild flowers, distant wood-smoke.

Parleck said dreamily: "This is a beautiful country. I could live here for ever, if only I weren't a man without a country . . . that's why you've never understood me, Sanders—I've always been without a home-land. I've never really—belonged."

"I think I see what you mean. Mixed blood, mixed upbringing. It must have been the very devil."

"You don't know how I envied you. Here, with your so-very-Albish family, your school and its traditions, your field games and sportsmanship, your friendships, deep and enduring because they've been dug hardly out of a protective seam of reserve . . . in Negovia there are no real friendships: there is surface bonhomie and there are alliances of convenience. That's all. Because the only faith is in Corporism, not in people. Nobody trusts anyone there in the way in which I trust you."

"Thank you," said Sanders.

"But you can't trust me in the same way—because I am not Albish."

Sanders bit his lip. He said, awkwardly: "I trust you as a friend, in personal matters. You may have anything of mine. But you know my position as Defence Minister forbids my entrusting you with what is not mine. The secrets of State are not my secrets. I wouldn't divulge them even to my closest Albish friend."

"Let alone a Negovian Corporist playing a double game," said Parleck, removing the chewed grass stem and smiling at it.

Sanders flushed. "Don't be a fool," he said shortly. "I never implied—"

"No, you're too much of a gentleman to imply such a thing. You're polite, and pretend such things aren't done, and yet you know they are done. You have given me information in the past, and had information from me. Correct information on both sides. Give and take. I've often given you more than the Corporist Council has thought. I've just as often given the Corporist Council less than you suspected. My bias is towards your side, but—and this is the thing people don't understand about me—*I am on neither side.*"

"Then why play this dangerous game?"

"Because it seems to me that it is what destiny intended me for. All my early life I cursed that destiny which denied me happiness. For happiness is a sense of fitting naturally into an environment. My environments were changed and interchanged too rapidly: I was never wholly at ease on Albish playing fields or on Negovian parade grounds, beneath the oaks in the rain or under the firs in the snow, talking light banter or discussing weighty Corporist promulgations. I was torn between two ways of life, belonged to neither. Then one day I grew up and realized I belonged to something greater than either—humanity."

"So you became an umpire?"

Parleck laughed. "The Albish and their way of seeing life as a field game! Healthier than Negovians, though, who see it in terms of an indoor game—chess. No, I became more of a universal father, quietly interfering now and then in the rather too rough games children play sometimes, trying to save them from hurting themselves. Negovia and Albion would have been at war long ago if it hadn't been for my good offices."

"What sort of offices?"

"Contrary to the respected principles of Corporism, wars are bred from ignorance, misunderstanding, and fear rather than from deliberate intention. I've kept each side in as little ignorance about the other side as possible, and thus each side felt more secure than if it had to rely only on imagination and suspicion: the Negovians, at least, always tend to imagine the worst, perhaps because they expect, and have often had, the worst from everyone. Unfortunately, while I have palliated the Corporist disease, I've not been able to cure it. And now it's broken out beyond my control and looks like reaching a crisis. Which is why I am here, to see what can be done."

"An unofficial diplomat, eh?"

"The plain stark truth is the only good diplomat. I am going to give you all of the truth I know. It would no doubt help humanity if you were to be as frank. But if you put Albion before humanity, and leave me in ignorance—well, it can't be helped. I can't make you grow up by anything other than example."

Sanders plucked a wide blade of grass and split it slowly down the middle. He was as intent on it as if it was a major operation.

He remained silent.

"Negovia intends to bomb Albion flat, in a lightning raid, within a year," said Parleck, with brutal suddenness.

Sanders' fingers froze, and then slowly resumed pulling the shreds of grass apart. He had gone a little pale.

"H-bombs?" he said, colourlessly.

"Yes."

Sanders separated the shreds, and then flung them down with an abrupt motion.

"Maniacs!" he said, briefly, bitterly.

"They think they will make the world safe for Corporism."

"Maniacs!" repeated Sanders. "How many converts do they expect to get by such methods?"

Parleck shrugged. "They think the truths of Corporism are self-evident, that everyone except a few villains is converted already and only waiting to be liberated. They imagine that if they don't strike first, your Government will."

Sanders was very angry now. "They pride themselves that they are realists above all else. Heaven help us, they live in a crazy fantasy of their own creation!"

Parleck had a brief vision of Luben and Novik brooding over their chess-board.

"They certainly do," he said. And then, more as a statement than a question: "You weren't, of course, intending to strike first?"

"Of course not," said Sanders, shortly. "We—" And then he checked himself. When one was angry, one was liable to say too much. It was quite possible that what he said now would go back to those who had chosen themselves to be Albion's enemies. "Of course, we have made every preparation for defence," he went on, giving Parleck a sidelong glance.

"What defence is there against H-bombs? The Negovians will use at least six of them."

"Surely you can't expect me to reveal—"

"There's nothing to reveal," said Parleck smoothly. "The only defence is to attack first. That you won't do, because there's nothing to go on except my say-so—and even if you accepted it, the Prime Minister wouldn't. Nor would the nation. Look here, Sanders, I'm not fencing and probing and playing at 'Let's Pretend.' As I told you, I've grown out of all that infantile, nationalistic mummery. Try to be adult for a moment, and face the truth. It may be worth it."

Sanders was irresolute. Then he said, almost defiantly: "Very well. We have a passive sort of defence: deep shelters. But I realise they're not likely to be very effective. One penetration bomb will crush them by earthquake. All right, we have no real defence."

"That's better," said Parleck, and for the moment Sanders felt as though he were being addressed by a stern, but just parent. This Parleck, who'd once been under his captaincy in the school football team, this fellow whom (in his heart) he'd always looked down on a little because he was only fifty per cent. Albish—no, he would never get to the bottom of him. But it was queer, the way the man inspired trust.

"Now," said Parleck, "I felt pretty low about it myself when Luben dropped the bombshell on me. But in the 'plane coming over I reviewed the situation detachedly, and then, you know, I saw there *was* a defence against the H-bomb. A very effective defence."

"Go on."

"You have in this country, I know, many atomic piles producing heavy hydrogen—"

"Purely in respect of possible retaliatory measures, I assure you," said Sanders, quietly. "Not in view of making any attack."

"I believe you, where Luben wouldn't—and doesn't. Now, this is my idea . . ."

~ ~ ~ ~ ~

"Well?" said Luben, and Novik looked up expectantly too.

"I shall send in my report," said Parleck, looking down at the chess-board without expression.

"Good, but let's have a verbal resumé now," said Luben. "First things first—did you get the date?"

"I had it confirmed from Sanders' own mouth that Albion does not propose to attack."

Luben stared at him bleakly. He said: "Then it is plain that Sanders has begun to suspect you. The old school tie link has worn thin. I'm afraid your usefulness as a spy is ended, Parleck."

"I am quite sure that Sanders wasn't bluffing," said Parleck, and Novik gave a little smothered chuckle.

Luben smote his forehead in a despair that was half genuine.

"Will you never grow up, Parleck. All statesmen bluff all the time. It's the game—it can't be played any other way. If everyone put their cards on the table, how could any game be possible?"

"It couldn't," said Parleck. He didn't express his contempt for the game, query its necessity, nor enlarge upon the evils arising from it. People believed what they wanted to believe, and conversion by reason was highly unlikely—in the case of Luben and Novik, quite impossible. They loved the game of power politics for the same reason that they loved chess, and that love was ineradicable.

"Very well, then. So the upshot of your report is that you have nothing to report?"

"Not quite. I have returned with some useful and, as usual, reliable information."

"Well?"

"The Albish have prepared a perfect defence against hydrogen bomb attacks. I don't know what form it takes—I couldn't find out. But I can assure you that they have one. And the Council had better reconsider its decision about the war."

Luben toyed with a captured bishop. He glanced across at Novik, who was grinning. "More bluff!" said Novik's expression. "What a fool!"

Luben said quietly: "I have a feeling, Parleck, that you don't approve of our preventive war, that you would like to stop it. I can't make up my mind whether you've been fooled or whether you seek to fool the Council. Until I can, you will be kept under open arrest."

"I have done my duty. I have given you correct information," said Parleck stiffly. "If I may be permitted an observation: it is possible to doubt too much. There are people who tell the truth."

"And you are one of them, eh?" murmured Luben. "We shall see."

~ ~ ~ ~ ~

Some weeks later, Luben sent for Parleck, which he had not done since the arrest.

Luben tugged some sheets of typescript from under the Roman paper-weight fashioned in the likeness of the wolf-mother of Romulus and Remus, He spun the thin sheaf across the desk to Parleck, who picked it up curiously and sank into a chair with it.

It read:

RADIO ANNOUNCEMENT (NEWS) ALBION (2nd PROG,) August 9th. 12,00 hrs.

"Mr. Sanders, the Defence Minister, this morning in Parliament read a statement which is to receive world-wide publicity.

"He said: 'In view of the fact that it seems to be the accepted thing is these serious times that wars should start without declaration or warning of any kind, so that the aggressor may virtually win the war outright through the surprise element, the Albish Government has felt it its duty to take measures to protect the country against the likelihood of such unprovoked attacks, especially as it is aware that just one H-bomb could wipe out all our capital and a much greater area beyond it.

" 'To put the matter bluntly, it has been the opinion of the Government that the only effective deterrent against H-bomb attacks is the threat of instant reprisal in kind. It still is our opinion. But we have never lost sight of the possibility that the aggressor's initial attack may be so overwhelming as to destroy the victim's ability to mount an attack in reprisal. Indeed, that is certain to be the aim of the aggressor. To defeat

*this aim, we have taken precautions to see that a reprisal at-
tack IS made, instantly and AUTOMATICALLY.*

" 'The more deadly weapons are, the more likely they are
to become boomerangs. It was tacitly recognised that gas was
a dangerous weapon of this kind, and therefore no one dared
use it in the last war. In our view, the H-Bomb can also be
made an unusable weapon for the same reason.*

" 'In the nerve centres of this country, we now have a pattern of containers of heavy hydrogen liquefied under a pressure of over 100,000 lbs. These containers are scientifically
placed, so that the explosion of one would start an instant
chain reaction in the others. The material of which they are
composed is an excellent conductor of heat. They are also
carefully camouflaged. In themselves they present no danger:
to set them off it would take the heat and pressure from an H-
bomb exploding in the vicinity of just one of them.*

" 'Now, our technicians have calculated that the energy
produced by the hydrogen-to-helium change in respect merely
of the containers situated in this city would be sufficient to
cause utter devastation within a radius of 1,500 miles. At the
moment we have to fear attack only from countries whose
capitals, and a large part of the countries themselves lie
within this radius.*

" 'Thus any attempt to destroy Albion by hydrogen bomb
attacks will automatically ensure the destruction of the greater
part of the aggressor's own country. It goes without saying
that our own country would be totally destroyed, but in the
event of an unprovoked attack that would have happened anyway. As Albishmen, we are gratified to know that should we be
attacked we can be sure of bringing our enemy down with us,
and that we can still claim that we shall never be beaten,
whatever happens.*

" 'However, I do not visualise such a spectacular end to
our destinies. We are safer now than we have ever been since
atomic weapons were invented, for, knowing these facts, it
would be suicide for anyone to attack us. We shall add to our
heavy hydrogen store so that there is no safe distance from
which any aggressor might launch an attack. If any independent country feels that our defence measures place it in danger,
we make these points:—*

" '1. Any atomic war which starts would in any case
spread into a world war: in the nature of things, there can be
no neutrals these days.

" '2. We have, naturally, no intention ourselves of ever
starting a war, and so no danger threatens from us, but only
from demonstrable lunacy on the part of other powers.

" '3. If other countries copied our defence measures,
atomic war would become impossible forever, for any outbreak of it would destroy the planet at once.

" '4. We feel that in these times independent countries,
playing at power politics and respecting no common law, are
themselves a greater danger to the world than our defence
measures. It is only because independent countries put nation-
alism and self-interest before World Law, giving the latter no
more than lip service, that we have been driven to our own
stern measures to maintain peace. We hear too much about
their rights and too little about their greater duty.

" 'We give these facts solemnly to the world. Let those
who anticipate aggression reflect upon them. It may occur to
them that the love of power beyond a certain mark leads to
disaster. We have indicated that mark. They pass it only to
lose all power for all time. This is a warning effective from
now.' "

Novik had come quietly into the room while Parleck had been
reading, but when Parleck replaced the document on Luben's desk
neither of the other men was looking at him. Novik, it seemed,
was having trouble with an obdurate cigarette lighter, while Luben
doodled on a writing pad—more wolves.

The silence continued.

Parleck was too familiar with the technique of creating nervous tension to be affected by it. Easily, he lit a cigarette and settled
back in his chair to await what might come. He was not going to
initiate any move.

And so it was Luben who presently felt he must break the silence.

He slipped the pad into a desk drawer suddenly, looked up as
though he had forgotten Parleck was there, and then said in a high
peremptory voice: "Is there any reason why you should not be
executed summarily?"

Parleck exhaled a thin stream of pale blue smoke.

"Is there any reason why I should be?" he countered, undisturbed.

"Yes—this Albish announcement."

"I have an idea that I warned you that some time ago that the Albish had prepared a perfect defence against H-bomb attacks. This announcement merely corroborates the accuracy of my information. Should I be executed for doing my job efficiently?"

"You are not speaking to a fool," said Luben. "I don't believe in coincidences. There's always a connection between events which follow upon another's heels too quickly. In this case, you're the connection, because there can be no other. The Albish Government would not have gone to these drastic lengths to protect their country from H-bomb attacks unless they had definite information that someone was preparing to attack them very soon. You gave them that information."

"Have you any evidence to back such an accusation?"

"I don't need evidence," said Luben. "I know."

"In that case, there's no use arguing about it. I know the quality of your intellectual conceit: once you get an idea in your head which you want to believe, you're right, you're infallible—as infallible as Corporism itself. You'll keep on torturing me until I make the confession you want to hear—whether the confession is only a lie to end the torture or not. Well, I'll save you the time. For once you are right. I told Sanders about the Council's plan—which means *your* plan, of course. More than that, I told him how to counter it—the containers were my idea."

Novik started. Luben's scrawny old hands began trembling so violently that he put them out of sight, below the edge of the desk.

"You miserable traitor!" said Novik, in an icily cold voice.

Parleck regarded him calmly. "From where I stand, you are the traitors—both of you, traitors to humanity. I do not serve you, nor Corporism, nor Negovia, nor Albion—I am a pawn in revolt. I serve only humanity. And humanity calls for world peace. I have answered that call. Now you can bring on the firing party."

Luben recovered control of himself.

He said: "Idealists always sound slightly ridiculous, especially when playing the martyr. There will be no firing party, and no brave last words. I don't want you to come to such a quick, neat ending thinking your perfidy has triumphed. I'll just tell you this: you have been under suspicion for a long time. I gave you the information about our plan of attack solely that you might pass it on to the Albish. I'm glad they're concentrating on H-bomb defence.

It takes their minds off the possibilities of bacteriological warfare. Their containers will be of little value against the bacteriological bombs which will rain down on them within a month, and kill them within the hour. Novik, arrange for Parleck to have a holiday so I that he can think these things over. The Manoberian salt mines are an ideal place for quiet thinking—send him there. A nice long vacation, say for a period roughly equal to the rest of his life. Though, of course, it may not be a very long holiday, after all— those salt mines don't agree with everyone. I complained before, Parleck, that you are slow in growing up. You are incredibly naive—humanity surely deserves better servants . . . Take him away, Novik."

~ ~ ~ ~ ~

"Mate!"

It was just a month later.

Novik tried to keep the triumph from his voice, but his first victory after over a year of endeavour meant everything to him¬— and he had a shrewd idea that it meant as much to Luben.

The old man sat there, drooped, exhausted. There was a film of sweat on his forehead: he had been driven to putting forth more mental effort than ever before. And it had been in vain.

"Another?" said Novik, with a smile which was malicious because Luben was not looking at him. Nevertheless, Luben knew the malice was there. He shook his head wearily.

Novik started putting the pieces away, with fastidious tidiness, in their box.

"Are the bacteriological bombs ready yet?" he asked conversationally.

The old man shook his head again.

"I was speaking to Tanenburg, and he said he doubted if they ever would be ready," said Novik, fitting the white knight in with care.

Luben raised his head and contemplated Novik gravely before speaking. "Tanenburg was under my orders to discuss the matter with no one. This will cost him his post . . . you have an insidious way of getting round people, Novik."

Novik slid the lid over the chess pieces. He rested his fists on the box and met Luben's regard squarely.

"I call your bluff," he said steadily. "You never intended, before Parleck's treachery, to use bacteriological bombs. You knew—and you still know at heart—that there's no way of counteracting their boomerang effect. We could wipe out Albion in a day, sure enough, but just as surely the disease would be rampant here within a week. That sort of victory isn't worth the price—in fact, it's no sort of victory. True?"

"Go on," said Luben, not committing himself.

"You have been driving Tanenburg and his department to make it a one-way weapon, although you knew and he knew that it was impossible. But you didn't like to face up to the fact that you'd failed, that it was time to hand over to me. You just went on, bluffing, hoping irrationally, hanging on, fooling yourself but no one else. I'm sure you didn't fool Parleck."

"I'd failed?"

"Yes, you failed in your judgment of Parleck. I told you he was a dangerous man. But you trusted him—you trusted him too far."

Luben dropped his gaze.

"You are still trusting him—and the Albish—too far," pursued Novik. "You've allowed yourself to become hypnotized by an empty threat: the threat of automatic reprisal. Don't you realise it's merely psychological warfare—defence by suggestion? Our agents have so far discovered no trace of heavy hydrogen containers in Albion. Even if there *are* containers, you may bet your life they don't contain heavy hydrogen. The Albish are too cunning for that. They realise that the mere belief that it's there is sufficient to deter raiders, without its actually needing to be there. And if there *is* one raider bold enough to attack, they'll be finished anyway, and reprisals won't raise them from the dead."

"Because our agents haven't located the containers, it doesn't mean they're not there," said Luben defensively. "The Albish themselves said they are camouflaged so as to avoid sabotage, A container doesn't have to be a plain metal tank. Almost anything could be used as a container: a water tower, gasometer, the boiler of a locomotive lying idle in the railway yards, a petrol truck. There are two million private houses in their Capital alone, anyone of which may conceal a container. A container doesn't have to be anything even resembling a tank—almost any normal feature in an urban area could be hollowed out to make a receiver for heavy hydrogen."

"No it couldn't—not for heavy hydrogen under enormously high pressure. You're frightening yourself with bogeys you're raising in your own imagination. The Albish haven't been playing fool tricks like that with their heavy hydrogen. They've stored it, all right—in the form of bombs to be used on us when they're quite sure we've been duped into not expecting it."

"I've wondered whether they were bluffing, but I was never sure and dared not take the risk," said Luben.

"I'm quite sure they *are* bluffing, and the greater risk is to sit back and do nothing."

Luben passed his fingers through his hair several times, slowly. He was tired and torn with indecision.

"I don't know what to think. I guess I'm getting too old for this sort of thing."

"This sort of thing is only chess on a greater scale," said Novik, and implication was thick in his voice. "That gambit of yours with the queen . . . I realised it was a bluff from the start, and I saw where the real danger lay. But I pretended to be hoodwinked, and led you on . . . into the trap. I have your measure, I know all your tricks, I can never be bluffed again. I'm the master now."

Luben sighed.

"That's right. You are the master now. I was going to hand over the reins to you—you don't have to grab. You seem to know what you're doing better . . . than I know what I'm doing . . ."

Luben's voice trailed away. For a time he stared into space. He'd had a long run. Power had been life itself while he had held it. But one doesn't live forever.

He focussed his eyes on the black and white illustration on the wall from his favourite novel, Jack London's *White Fang*: the fight between the elder leader of the wolf pack and the young leader. He found himself tensing, unconsciously pulling his shoulders back. He stood up. He said firmly, the quaver gone from his voice: "I shall resign from the Chairmanship of the Council to-morrow, and propose your election. But to-day I am still Chairman. Send Tanenburg to me—I'm going to rip his hide off."

~ ~ ~ ~ ~

Two days after Novik became the Chairman, a blast of sun heat smote Albion from the sky. And Albion leaped up to smite back with forty times the power, light, and thunder.

The whole island cracked and split asunder and somewhere beneath the atmospherical fury sank quietly from view. The sea rolled hugely over the spot and then boiled upwards in a scalding cloud of steam that transformed day to a red night of death.

Lethal pressure waves leaped out in all directions, lethal heat waves on their heels with no task to perform but an innocent and hygienic cremation of the dead. Toiling slowly after them came the great tidal waves of steaming water to clean the crumbling land and the traces of death away. They rolled, ever smaller, across the blasted industrial areas to a place within sight of the ruins of the capital of Negovia, where Luben and Novik and the entire Council lay mingled with each other and with the ashes of million of their pawns, all for the first time on a common level. And then they flattened to a hissing stop, as if they had found the sight distasteful, and began to retreat.

Far away on the bleak north-east coast of the continent, Parleck, in the salt mine bored into the mountain-side, heard that a gale of very warm air had sprung up suddenly outside and was beginning melt the snow.

When, in the meal-time break, he went to see, there was nothing to see but a veil of water pouring down over the entrance to the mine, too thick to penetrate. The snows high above were liquefying and coming down the mountain-side in a thousand channels.

He knew what had happened. He knew the Council were no more, that progressively worse ruin and desolation lay all the way from here to the western coastline, and that most probably that coastline now was not the one he had learned from the school map.

No one could get in or out of the mine, and no more work was done that day. They all sat around watching, waiting, listening, speculating. Above the sound of crashing water they could hear the high wail of the sirocco blowing outside.

At evening, the rushing waterfall over the tunnel mouth thinned and became ragged, splitting into several smaller falls, which they could see between. The valley below had become a broad river flowing into the near-by sea, and the gale had eased to a warm breeze. The concentration camp, its inhabitants, commandant, lieutenants, and all the military guard had been washed into the sea.

In this isolated corner of Manoberia the only live souls left were six hundred political prisoners in the mine and a dozen overseers.

"It's not hard to see how the situation here is going to work out," thought Parleck, "and I'm going to help it along. When the survivors elsewhere learn that the ruling clique has obligingly expunged itself, it'll be every man for himself. But here, with this nucleus of responsible and freedom-loving men, we can start to set up law again. Only this time it'll be law based on a moral code, not on expediency, a law for humanity. A law under which a man can have faith."

The only law in which Luben and Novik had believed was wolf pack law. They thought it was a basic and therefore irreplaceable law.

"Poor old Luben and his *White Fang*! He could never have been made to see that things had moved on since man was three parts animal, and rough and ready animal laws had to be superseded. Hydrogen bombs were somewhat more powerful than teeth and claws—and far more indiscriminant.

"The Lubens and Noviks of this world had believed in the survival of the fittest, but they would never have understood how inexorably they themselves would be effaced by that law. Because the test for survival these days was not physical fitness, nor even mental fitness—but only moral fitness.

"And to pass that test you had to believe that some of your fellow men could keep faith and speak truth, and that all gestures did not inevitably conceal an ulterior motive.

"If Luben and Novik had only believed that the Albish meant what they said!"

And then Parleck gave himself a mental shake and returned to the immediate present. There was no time to waste on the "ifs" of the past. It was the "ifs" of the future that mattered now, and it was time to act.

THE UNDISCOVERED COUNTRY

IT SEEMED TO ME I was taking part in some futuristic ballet, slow and symbolic, paradoxically based on a lightning incident of the legendary past: a Scottish border raid.

The chieftain's young daughter stood with her back to us, alone, unsuspecting, half a mile from her village. Phillips and I converged gradually on her from behind, silent as the near-opaque mist which surrounded us all.

We weren't moving in slow motion because we feared her detecting us: there was no chance of that. In fact, we were making all possible speed, but our alloy space-suits were heavy even under the lesser gravity of Pluto. The alloy had to be really thick, for the dense atmosphere encompassing us was more than half composed of an acid gas which ate away metal as fast as sulphuric acid dissolves zinc.

Moreover, we had to be thoroughly insulated against the intense cold of this sunless place.

It was one of those mad miracles of Nature that the girl needed no protection at all against either the cold or the corrosive atmosphere. Stark naked, she was at ease in her own element.

It was another miracle that, however different her internal structure, and with the certainty that her body cells were of a type beyond the knowledge, almost beyond the credence, of modern biochemistry, her shape was humanoid. And very feminine. Her skin was smooth and white. She might have been a marble Greek goddess.

We reached her together and lifted her gently, trying not to hurt her with our metallic fingers. She was hard and rigid and it was indeed as though we were carrying a marble statue back to the ship.

We followed the narrowing beam of the searchlight to its source on the hull of the *Icarus*, and waited at the door of Lock Two. There was a disturbance in the chemical-thick atmosphere around the ship. In the dim reflected light, it was streaming like inhaled smoke through an orifice in the hull: the pump's sucking mouth.

We examined our captive. This unknown Plutonian girl, whom we'd playfully styled "The chieftain's daughter, Pocahontas", had slightly changed her position. Her elbows, which had been pressed against her sides, were now a couple of inches from them.

Her hair was long and black, and she certainly had two human-seeming eyes, a nose and a mouth, but it was hard to discern details out of the direct shaft of light.

Then the pump ceased, its orifice closed like an iris lens, the atmosphere slowed in its swirling. The glass-lined storage tank was full to capacity with compressed Plutonian atmosphere.

In the ship, Captain Shervington pulled a lever, and the circular, safe-like door of Lock Two swung open. Like the rest of the hull, it was already deeply scarred with erosion. Whole patches were blistering and bubbling like paint under a blow-torch. We slid the stiff body through into the receptacle behind. It was like loading a frozen carcass into the refrigerator of a meat van.

The door closed on it and we made our entry through the other lock, into our own atmosphere. The air-lock door had scarce shut behind us when the *Icarus* began to take off, the Captain having left the pump and lock controls for the pilot's seat.

We had come some 3,600 million miles to Pluto to spend ten minutes there, get what we'd come for—and get out.

Two ships had been here before us. They had lingered too long. Neither returned.

The first reported the startling news that bleak Pluto was inhabited. It had landed on the outskirts of a community of some kind. The ship's searchlights, enfeebled by the dark mist, just revealed the rough shapes of a group of smallish houses but nothing of their structure. They could have been the primitive huts of savages—or the ultra-modern dwellings of a highly-civilised race.

The natives, humanoid and naked, did not come running. They seemed either unperturbed or petrified. They stood around almost like statues. But not quite. The statues *were* moving, with infinitesimal speed, towards the ship.

So reported the captain after watching them for half an hour. It was his last report. His radio went dead. In the light of later knowledge it was presumed that the acid atmosphere had eaten through the antenna and probably also fatally holed the hull.

The second ship didn't wait around so long. It sampled the atmosphere, got a rough idea of its nature and what it was doing to the ship, and took off again in a hurry. The skipper's last interference-distorted words were: "Main jets erratic, ship difficult to control. That terrible atmosphere seems to have eaten chunks out of the vents. Side squirts pushing us off balance. I'm afraid——"

The rest was silence.

Plainly the skipper's fears were realised and the ship crashed.

We, the crew of the third ship, *Icarus*, were at least fore-warned. We knew we'd have no time to stop and exchange pleasantries with the Plutonians, especially as it was apparent that the tempo of a Plutonian's life compared with a human's was like a snail's compared with a fruit-fly's.

The only way for humans to contact Plutonian life was to capture a specimen of it and take it home to study at leisure . . . if it could be kept alive long enough. And that was our mission.

We stewed in our suits as the *Icarus* fought to climb out of the Plutonian gravity pit, trying not to wonder too much about the condition of *our* vents. But they held out. We reached the required speed and began the long coast home. It was a relief to shed both weight and the suits.

Phillips, biologist, biochemist, and medico, was now the most responsible man of the trio, as he had always been the most accomplished. The bigwigs of the Institute of Planetary Biology, in the faraway Cromwell Road, wanted to examine a living, functioning Plutonian, not merely to dissect a corpse.

Captain Shervington, his own highest hurdle successfully jumped, could afford indulgence when he saw anxiety creasing Phillips' sweaty brow.

"Don't panic, Phillips, we'll all muck in and keep her in good shape . . . It *is* a woman?"

Phillips nodded so nearly imperceptibly that I felt confirmation necessary. I said: "It's a woman, all right, skipper, and she's certainly in good shape."

"So I thought," said Shervington. "I've got an eye for that sort of thing, even at forty paces on a dark Plutonian night. Let's have a closer peep."

He moved, but the conscience-taut Phillips anticipated him, hauling himself down the rungs, hand under hand, to the lower deck where the girl floated weightlessly in the clearplast container, Lock Two. Her outline was faintly blurred by the misty atmosphere which had entered with her.

Phillips glanced at her, then busied himself with the pumps regulating the flow of fresh atmosphere from the supply stored under pressure in the big tank. Considering her extremely slow rate of respiration, there should be more than a sufficient supply to keep her alive during the six weeks voyage home. The big problem was that nobody knew what Plutonians ate or drank—or even if they did.

The Captain and I looked Pocahontas over carefully. With her long hair afloat, her eyes staring wide, she looked like Ophelia drowning.

Now that we could see her features properly, there was nothing really unhuman about them. The pupils of her eyes were unusually large, as though dilated by digitalis, but that was necessary for light gathering on darksome Pluto.

After long seconds, the skipper said quietly: "She's beautiful."

"I wonder if she has a sister?" I said.

Captain Shervington mused: "I wonder what's in her mind and whether we'll ever contact it."

There was no more time for wondering: we had our immediate jobs to do. I, navigator and signaller, had to report to Earth via the moon-base link and take our bearings. Shervington had to check the ship's space-worthiness after its acid bath. Phillips had to study his charge.

The cosmic interference was bad, and Earth sounded like an ancient Edison phonograph. But I managed to get the report over, and later the faint cracked voice of Shepherd, boss of the project, filtered through: "Well done, *Icarus*!"

I looked through a porthole at the dusky receding bulk of Pluto. At about this distance, on the approach, we had regarded it apprehensively, and the Captain had quoted wryly: "The undiscovered country from whose bourne no traveler returns."

But now we were returning and the fear which had accumulated through long anticipation was fast dissolving. My spirit felt almost as airy as my body, and Shervington's report that the ship had escaped with negligible damage made relief complete.

Fame and a knighthood were the prospects now.

We returned to Pocahontas. Phillips was having a field-day with the various remotely controlled clinical gadgets with which the clearplast container had been fitted by long-sighted scientists. He'd successfully clamped the pulse meter on her wrist and its indicator was registering a full swing every half-minute.

"That appears to mean she's living about forty times slower than we are," said Phillips. "At least, organically. It doesn't necessarily mean her thought processes are correspondingly slower, although, of course, they must be slower than ours."

Men had long known that in sub-zero temperatures life processes were incredibly sluggish. How the Plutonians and ourselves were ever to get mentally in step was another problem, but obviously the initiative rested with us, the quicker-witted. If only a Plutonian could be kept alive under laboratory conditions on Earth, a way could surely be found.

Plutonian speech must be so slow as to be unintelligible to a human ear, each syllable perhaps minutes long. But if it were tape-recorded, and the playback speeded up to suit the comprehension of our lingual experts, and if their efforts at response were accordingly slowed down . . . there remained possibilities.

Phillips was currently fiddling with the blood-sampler. It was like an outsize hypodermic syringe swivelling freely on a bearing set in the clearplast. He was directing the needle-sharp point at Pocahontas' upper arm. An inch from where he was probing, on the white flesh, was a yellowish blob, like pus.

I indicated it. "What's that?"

Phillips replied irritably: "A pinprick—I missed the main vein. It doesn't follow because her pulse is in the normal place her whole artery system corresponds to ours. Damn it, give me a chance—I haven't even located her heart yet."

"Her blood is yellow?" asked the Captain, eyebrows raised.

"What colour did you expect it to be—blue?" snapped Phillips, still having trouble manipulating the sampler.

Tactfully, the skipper let it pass. In silence Phillips found his mark, and drew off a tubeful of amber fluid—apparently it turned bright yellow only after congealment. He set it aside, then hauled himself across to the atmospheric tank, carrying a flask with a screw top. Just where the pipe left the tank for the container, there was a manually-controlled valve with an open outlet. Phillips screwed the flask into the outlet and turned the valve's handwheel.

The flask filled with the foggy atmosphere of Pluto. Phillips shut off the valve, stoppering the flask adroitly, and said: "These two samples will keep me busy for a bit. I'll see you later. Keep an eye on Pocahontas."

"Right," said Shervington. Phillips retired to his "stinks corner" up above. If he could successfully analyse the atmosphere, I would radio the formula to the Institute and they'd synthesize vol-

umes of it in readiness for Pocahontas's arrival. He didn't expect
to get far with the blood, working alone under no-gravity conditions, but he hoped at least to make a start in understanding Plutonian metabolism. A team could carry on from there, much faster,
on Earth.

Six weeks without sustenance could kill a human. But that was
the equivalent of only one day for a Plutonian. Perhaps in less than
another Plutonian day, some satisfactory food could be prepared.

"Nevertheless," said Captain Shervington, after voicing this,
"kidnapping a girl and starving her for two days is a bit rough. I
hope we learn enough Plutonian to say we're sorry. Just her bad
luck she happened to be out for a walk on her own when we
landed."

"Good luck for us," I said. "The Institute wanted a female
preferably, to get a fuller idea of the reproductive system."

"Maybe she just lays eggs, Graham."

"Maybe. You know, until I saw that yellow blood . . ." I
trailed off.

The skipper looked at me quizzically. "You thought she
wasn't so very different from us? You fancied, perhaps, some kind
of Edgar Rice Burroughs romantic affair with her if she could be
stepped up to our tempo?"

I grinned, and veered away. "I'd better test the radio link
again."

He grinned after me. The link was all right: the usual mixture
of words, crackles, and repeat requests. I came back later, and we
spent some time just watching the figure in the container. Pocahontas gradually changed her position to a more reposeful one,
though her hands were beginning to clench. Her eyes became half
closed and she seemed nearly asleep.

"Her old man's going to wonder what the devil's happened to
her," commented Shervington, and yawned. I yawned, too. I was
beginning to feel pretty tired and surmised it was the unwinding
after the peak of nervous tension. I rubbed my eyes: they were
smarting a bit.

"I think—" began Shervington, relaxedly, then broke suddenly
into a fit of coughing.

"Got a silly tickle in my throat," he said, hoarsely, afterwards.

I felt a similar irritation, began to cough, and my eyes
streamed tears.

"Something's got into the atmosphere here," said the skipper,
looking around. Then: "Look at that valve! The damn fool!"

I looked at the valve on the tank of Plutonian atmosphere. It looked vaguely swimmy and it wasn't just because of my watering eyes: there was a faint mist hovering round the thing. The skipper cursed and dived at it, holding his nose. He spun the handwheel a turn or two and blundered back.

I felt a sort of heat prickle on my face, which might have been the sweat of fright or the touch of the escaped acid gas.

Phillips drifted down the ladder, carrying a notebook. "I've got this far, anyway. Shove it through the ether, Graham . . . What's that queer smell in here?"

The skipper controlled his anger. "You didn't shut that valve properly. Some of the poisonous stuff leaked out."

Phillips stared at the valve. "I *did* shut it—tight."

Shervington shrugged and said nothing. I said: "Is that the atmospheric formula, Phil—you analysed it all right?"

"Eh? Oh, yes. It's deadly stuff. Can't understand how Pocahontas can flourish in it. A real lungful of it would kill any man—unpleasantly. Just this page, Graham—get it right."

I took the notebook to my signals niche on the upper deck. I looked at the page of chemical symbols and knew it would be a headache to "get it right" via the current ion-blasted reception. I felt even more tired.

However, I was spared that particular headache. The moment I pressed the mike button, the set went dead. No transmission, no reception. Obviously no power. I examined the leads from the power unit: they were in order. I removed the top of the set, peered into the ordered multitude of transistors. Down below them, in a near-inaccessible corner, a screw terminal had somehow worked loose and the end of the relevant power lead had become disconnected and drifted away.

I said something violent and idiotic, and hunted out a long, thin screwdriver. It had the tough razor edge necessary to deal with that slotted terminal. I fished again in the tool-chest, and then: "Graham!" A double-voiced shout, urgent with alarm, came from below. I dropped everything and thrust myself down the rungs, clumsily, because my muscles seemed to have lost strength. The tang of the acid gas hit me like smelling salts. Shervington and Phillips were both fiercely gripping the handwheel of the valve which was obviously leaking again.

"Get the big wrench," panted the skipper, red-faced with strain.

I got it. He and Phillips thrust it between the handwheel spokes and jammed the head under a wall bracket.

"That'll hold it," said Shervington, jerkily.

"What on earth's going on?" I asked.

The skipper mopped his forehead. "We've caught a Tartar. Pocahontas is trying to kill us, that's all."

"What?" I stared at him, then at Pocahontas. Her eyes were quite closed now; so also were her hands, clenched into little fists.

Phillips said strainedly but with eyes alive with interest: "It must be psycho-kinesis—what else? The handwheel can't be turning itself—there's no reason why it should: no vibration or anything. It undoes itself slowly but with tremendous power. It took two of us all our time to shut the valve again and keep it that way."

"It's taken a lot out of me," said the skipper. "I feel as weak as hell."

"So do I," said Phillips.

"And I," I said. "And I haven't been exerting myself. Do you think she could be tapping our strength in some peculiar way?"

The skipper shrugged and said: "Frankly, I don't know what to think."

Phillips said: "I believe you're right, Graham. In some mediumistic way she's drawing off some of our energy and using it against us. Judging from her physique, unaided she wouldn't be able to turn that wheel against the resistance of anyone of us."

"I've been in some peculiar situations in my time," said the skipper, "but nothing to match this. Seems we've to fight ourselves in order to stop ourselves from killing ourselves. Put the know-alls at the Institute in the picture, Graham—perhaps they can come up with a few helpful suggestions: they talk as if they know all the answers."

"The radio is out of order, pro tem." I told Shervington why.

"Bad maintenance," he grunted.

"Or psycho-kinesis," I joked, with a feeble grin, which became feebler when I and the others suddenly realised it might be no joke, at that.

"Get it fixed, anyhow," said Captain Shervington.

I started to go, then impelled myself to the handwheel and hammered with my fist at the wrench. I'd spotted that it was being slowly withdrawn by an invisible hand. The other two had to help me before we could force it back in place.

Breathing heavily, the skipper said: "This is becoming impossible. This damn valve's got to be watched every minute. How the devil are we ever going to get any sleep? How can anyone go to sleep, anyway, knowing that someone's trying to flood the ship with poison gas? Phillips, can't you do something to make her unconscious? Drug her or something?"

Phillips scratched his head. "From the look of her she might be unconscious right now—maybe only asleep, maybe in a state of trance. Psycho-kinesis is subconscious force. She mightn't even be aware of what her mind is doing. It may be just the natural sense of self-preservation functioning automatically."

"Nonsense!" said Shervington, emphatically. "She's not merely trying to save herself—she's deliberately trying to murder us."

"Let's be fair," I said. "She didn't ask to be snatched away from her home, her people, her planet, never to see them again, condemned probably to die—for I think the odds are against our being able to keep her alive for very long."

Nobody had an opportunity to comment on that view. For, at that moment, the side jets of the ship began firing, swinging her round so that the sudden radial force pressed us tightly against one wall. Then the balancing jets steadied her and we were coasting along tail-first.

"Who the—" began the skipper, and then the main drive jets began blasting, decelerating *Icarus*, making the ceiling our floor and pinning us to it under several g's. The ship gradually lost impetus. Presently, we were able to crawl, painfully and with swimming senses, towards the upper deck—which seemed like the lower deck at first, but became lesseningly so—and towards the control console.

Before we could reach it, the deceleration was completed and acceleration in the reverse direction had begun. The upper deck was again "above" us, and the ship was hurtling nose-foremost back towards Pluto.

When we got to the console, we could do nothing effective to change the situation. We had six hands between us, and still couldn't regain control of the ship. Admittedly, we had been weakened and were slow and our brains were spinning, and only the captain was an expert on the console. But even if we had been properly fit, defeat would have been difficult to avoid when switches, levers, and stud buttons wouldn't retain their position for more than two seconds after we'd taken our fingers off them.

A mind employing many streamers of force, the captain's own technical know-how, and our stolen strength, brushed our combined residual effort aside.

The tables had been turned. We were now the kidnapped, Pluto-bound.

We gave up and looked at each other's white faces.

"I'll pump her full of morphia," said Phillips, unsteadily.

"It's too late for experiments," said Shervington, rather shrill with nerve-strain. "This P.K. effect seems to be working at the speed of thought, and thought works a hell of a sight faster than organic processes. The morphia may take days to do its job—that's if it affects her at all. By then we'll all be dead. We must kill her first."

"No!" I exclaimed, shocked.

"By heaven, no!" exclaimed Phillips. "The Institute—"

"Blast the Institute! Their skins are safe."

"She's *my* responsibility," said Phillips, excitedly. "I want a living specimen—"

"Face the facts, you fool!" shouted the skipper. "We're not taking her back now—she's taking *us* back. To our deaths. It's her life or ours."

Phillips was leaning with his back against my signals desk. His knees were bent slightly under the steady acceleration. He clasped his head and muttered distractedly; "Give me time."

But his fate allowed him no time. Concurrently with the skipper's gasp of exasperation, Phillips also gasped. And with mouth and eyes wide open, he pitched forward, face down on the deck. The handle of my long thin screwdriver protruded from under his left shoulder-blade. The rest of the tool had skewered his heart.

As we gazed in horror, the screwdriver slowly began to pull itself from the wound. Shervington and I scrambled madly to the lower deck. As we reached it, the main drive cut out and free fall returned to confuse us further.

I saw the wrench disengage itself from the handwheel and float loosely around. The handwheel resumed its slow, inexorable unwinding. I fought my way to it and clung to it, but my feet failed to find purchase and the wheel began to turn me with it.

The skipper had made for the lever operating the door of Lock Two. Surprisingly meeting no opposition, he yanked it over. The circular door at the end of the container swung open and the Plutonian atmosphere, under pressure, squirted out into the vacuum of space, carrying the drifting, weightless alien girl with it. Feet first, the beautiful body passed from our sight, and Shervington closed the door behind it.

The hand wheel began to slow in its turning until at last I could stop it. No part of Phillips' strength could be used against me, and the girl must be using her own strength to fight asphyxiation.

Shervington hung on to his lever, afraid that she might try to force the door of Lock Two open again. But she made no measureable attempt. Possibly she knew, drifting and dying in space, that even if the door were re-opened, there could be no way back for her.

My grip on the handwheel was like having my finger on her pulse. I could feel the opposition gradually weakening. It must have taken her over ten minutes to die, for it was that long before I forced the wheel to a complete standstill.

The last few minutes were pure terror, for the bloodstained screwdriver came floating slowly down from the upper deck. It hung before my eyes like Lady Macbeth's vision of the dagger. Then it levelled itself and came at me, point foremost.

Luckily, it came so slowly that I was able to grasp the sticky and horrible thing and hold it off till Shervington came to my aid.

If the Plutonian girl hadn't divided her ebbing strength, I might easily have shared the fate of Phillips. I still have nightmares about that little predicament.

I said, shakily: "Thanks, skipper ... Objection withdrawn. You were perfectly right to kill her."

He made no reply, and directly it was clear that Pocahontas was dead he went to the upper deck. I followed reluctantly.

Poor Phillips was drifting a few inches above the floor. Between us we strapped his body to his bunk. Later he would have to leave us via Lock Two: there was no option.

Then Shervington stared expressionlessly through a port at the shadowy bulk of Pluto, to which we were still coasting.

I heard him mutter: "The undiscovered country ... So it will remain. Perhaps for ever."

He turned *Icarus* about, and we defied augury and returned.

FORGET-ME-NOT

If a man could pass through Paradise in a dream, and have a flower presented to him as a pledge that his soul had really been there, and if he found that flower in his hand when he awoke—Aye! and what then?

Samuel Taylor Coleridge

SINCE THE COMING OF LIGHT THAT DAY, nervous restlessness had increasingly possessed Direk. All of a sudden he jumped up with an exclamation of impatience.

"Where are you going?" queried Lock, the ancient, one-eyed philosopher.

"Round the world," said Direk, shortly.

"Again? Well, I shall still be here when you come back."

"I don't doubt it."

Direk walked away, stepping over the recumbent bodies of his sleeping and dozing fellow creatures. He circumvented the little groups of those who were up and busy with their social intercourse of gossip or were playing the eternal games of marbles, beetle racing, or wrestling.

The world was certainly round. The wall seemed straight as he looked along its length—or as far along it as he could see in the dim light—and it seemed straight as he walked along parallel to it. But Direk knew from experience that he had only to walk far enough and he would come upon Lock again, reclining there in his area by the wall, just as he had left him. Only, of course, he would come upon him from the other side.

There were too many people in the world. When walking, one was always bumping into them, jostling against them, or treading on them. There were no lonely places where a man might go and think, but so few of the people ever seemed to feel the need to think. For the most part, they were content to sleep and gossip, play and gamble, breed children, and fight viciously and purposefully for the largest possible share of the food which fell from the sky.

The sky! It was a dark mystery. Even in the daytime, all that could be made out were the circles of glowing golden light set regularly over the sky.

Those lights illuminated only the world below them, and showed nothing of what might be above. The spaces between them were but empty shadows, which merged into a common black obscurity as the eye sought to penetrate them. The flat, hard, grey cakes of food fell silently from those spaces, at irregular intervals, in varying quantities, in unexpected places, but they always fell.

It fell mostly in the day, but sometimes it fell in the night. Then the food hunt, the snatching and grabbing scramble in pitch blackness, was exciting.

Sometimes, one came upon a whole cake when crawling in the dark, intact. Then the trick was to drag it back to one's personal area, concealing the possession from the other seekers by adroit movement and a loud pretense of having been an unsuccessful seeker yourself.

Direk strode on.

Presently he came to the broad stream which ran swiftly in its deep, straight stone gully in a line right across the center of the world. Its source was in a metal grating in the wall on one side; its mouth was in a similar grating on the opposite side. The stream slaked the thirst of the people, bathed them, and carried away their waste matter. It was the gift of Dree.

Direk leaped easily across it, and in so doing he dropped into a little episode of pain among all of this human play. On the far side of the stream, a dozen or so people were gathered around one who lay on his back groaning and bleeding. A couple of women were bathing his wounds and the rest looked on.

A dark-visaged spectator whispered to Direk: "This has long been due to him. He stole his own children's food. It is right that Dree should punish him severely."

Direk nodded in agreement, and inspected the victim, who was a middle-aged man. There were blue, swelling welts on his chest, and his left ear which was half torn off was still bleeding steadily.

Direk caught the muttering of another gossip, gleeful of his momentary capture of attention: "His hands are covered with burns, too!"

Direk went on thoughtfully. He was mentally surveying his past history, and wondering whether there was anything he had done that might merit such punishment, but he felt no sense of guilt.

He did not want to do anything that might bring upon him that swift horror that came in the night. Once he had slept right beside a man destined to be chastised by Dree. Sometime during the night the man vanished mysteriously. Next morning he was found lying on the far side of the world with his tongue rooted out, so he was unable to tell of his experiences. Nobody ever was! The victim was always unconscious when found, and remembered nothing but having gone to sleep.

At length Direk came back to the stream, crossed it again, and soon saw Lock sitting just where he had left him. Only now the philosopher was attending to a still figure that lay beside him.

When Direk got nearer he saw that it was a feminine back that Lock was tenderly bathing, and the soft smooth skin of that back was torn and rent by long straight gashes, from which the blood welled slowly and persistently.

Direk stood over them. He felt slightly sick, and disgusted with he knew not what.

"Another sinner?" he said. "It seems that Dree was busy last night."

The female, whose face he could not see, gave a little sob. Lock did not look up, but frowned as he bent to his task.

"It's Sondra," he said quietly.

Sondra! In this one young girl was concentrated all that made life tolerable for Direk—beauty, grace, unselfish sympathy, and love. For a moment he grappled with sheer unbelief. Then with a choked exclamation he sank on his knees beside the girl, and gently turned her head that he might see her face. A poor, tear wet face it was, with the eyelids puffed from crying.

"Why? *Why?*" he said, in a low angry growl.

"Never mind," said Lock sternly. "Go, change this water—bring fresh."

In a daze Direk took the hollowed stone, which served for carrying water from the stream, and refilled it. He had grown up with Sondra, and knew her to be incapable of any evil action or thought. She was a unique personification of unspoiled innocence. Even Lock, old and wise as he was, had his moments of selfishness and spite.

All the time he was getting the fresh water, this "Why?" hammered through his brain, and when he returned he again asked it aloud of Lock.

"It is not for us to question the ways of the Almighty," said Lock. "No one would know why but Sondra herself."

All Sondra could say, in a little moaning voice, was: "I don't know. I don't know."

"Then," said Direk, "Dree is evil, and if I could get my hands on Him I should strangle Him."

"That is childish nonsense," said Lock. "For one thing, Dree is a spirit, and you could no more strangle Him than you could strangle water. For another thing, He is a benevolent spirit, and all that He does is for our ultimate good, though it may not seem so if you take only the short view."

"What good came of your eye being knocked out?" demanded Direk.

"Your life—and Sondra's," said Lock. "For I learned not to keep all my food for myself. Until then, I did. I watched orphaned children starve, because they were not strong enough to fight, while I gorged myself. Then one night I lost my eye. That made me look into my heart and discover my evil. I went seeking abandoned children and found you and Sondra. Thus, through me, Dree saw to it that you did not starve to death."

"That came from the goodness of your own heart, and from nowhere outside it," said Direk.

"Still you are speaking without observation and without thought," answered Lock. "Now, look at this."

He reached out and plucked a mushroom from the little bed he had cultivated in one of the rare patches of thin soil.

"Did that come from me?" he demanded. "It is fine food, and Dree grows it, obviously for no other purpose than our pleasure and sustenance. Observe the stream—again it is plainly meant for our convenience. And what about the food that falls from above without our even asking? Yet for all this, man is still thoughtless and ungrateful."

"That's all chance, like the results of marble games," said Direk, surlily. "The conditions just happen to be so."

"If the nature of these be chance, then it follows that these punishments must also be accepted as chance, and it is reasonless to rile against them," said Lock neatly.

"Words only," growled Direk, making Sondra comfortable by pillowing her head on his shoulder. They had done all they could for her back now, and she lay with her eyes almost closed, clinging to her lover.

"Let us see," said Lock, gathering together a handful of broken pieces of rock. Then he threw them on the ground again. They scattered every which way.

"That is chance," said Lock, regarding them. "This is design."

He arranged the eight pieces in the form of a square within a square.

"Well?"

"You still observe nothing? Why, with my one eye I can see ten times as much as you who have two. Now look up at the lights in the sky."

Direk did so. He saw that they followed Lock's pattern.

"Design," commented Lock. "Therefore it follows that there must be a Designer. When you remember, in addition, that those lights regularly disappear that we may sleep and regularly come again that we may see to go about our business, then it is plain that the Designer is a benevolent one."

"Possibly," conceded Direk with reluctance, "but I think he is a poor one. I'm certain I could design better conditions for life than these."

"You are not satisfied with life?"

"No," said Direk shortly.

"Well, you'll leave it in time. We all do. That's part of the design."

"Yes, we leave it—dead—finished," said Direk, with bitterness, thinking of the appearance of the stiff unfeeling corpses before they vanished, as always, in the mysterious shadow of the night.

"Finished only with this life, here. Then we go to a world of light and beauty, where there is no more pain or hunger. A place to which I have given the name 'Heaven'."

"A place which exists in your dreams only," said Direk, gently stroking Sondra's hair. Her eyes were quite closed now, and she was beginning the deep-drawn breaths of sleep.

"You are wrong again. I have seen a wondrous picture of it, and if you would only use your eyes instead of going about grumbling, you could see it too."

"Where? How?" demanded Direk.

"I did not want to tell you about this until you were spiritually ready for it. You are still rather childish and impatient, but it seems that—unlike the others—you sometimes have thoughts above food. So perhaps this vision will give you peace, as it did me."

He paused, then went on: "You know the area of the Mullen family; that alcove in the wall, twice the width of a man, which seems to be topless—?"

"I know the thing," interrupted Direk. "Why, it runs right up into the sky!"

"It goes above the lights, certainly, but it does not reach the sky."

"How do you know?"

"I have been to the top."

"What?" Direk stared at the old man incredulously. "That doesn't make sense. The lights are immensely far above us. Why, they say that each of them alone is much bigger than the whole world, and they only look so small because they are so distant."

"They say," nodded Lock. "That means nothing. Actually, the lights are relatively small and quite near. I repeat, I have climbed higher than they. I have no witnesses, because food was falling at the time and that took the people's attention. Anyway, the light is not very bright in that area."

"And the picture is at the top?"

"Yes. There is a small slit from which a very bright light comes in a flat, narrow beam. It is the light of Heaven. It takes courage to face it, but if you nerve yourself to put your eyes to the hole, you can do it. You have to keep your eyes shut at first, and then open them only the smallest fraction and look between your lashes—you will conquer your pain, and see Heaven."

"But how do you climb? There is not a crack in which one might get a finger."

"Set your back against one side of the alcove and press your feet against the other side," said Lock. "Then you may work your way up by lifting your back and feet alternately, a little distance at a time. It is arduous and dangerous work. I myself made the journey only once. I was a young man, but even then I almost fell from exhaustion several times. I have not attempted it since, but I have not needed to. I have seen the 'vision,' and I shall never forget it. It is fast in my memory, and every night ere I sleep I see it glowing yet."

"If I would climb before dark, I must go soon," said Direk. He looked down at Sondra tenderly. She was fast asleep. The wounds on her back had ceased bleeding at last.

"I was afraid of your eagerness," said Lock, troubled. "Now if you go and fall, Sandra will die of anguish. I should have kept my silence longer. I ask you to wait, until Sondra is better, at least."

"I have waited in this dreary world long enough," returned Direk. "Here, old one, take my place as a pillow."

Gently he disengaged Sondra, without waking her, and passed her to Lock. When the old man was supporting her comfortably, Direk kissed her softly on the cheek and stood up.

"I shall be back," he said.

"And I shall still be here," said Lock.

"I don't doubt it," said Direk, again.

The Mullen children were playing in the alcove when he got there. If he attempted to clear them out, it would have meant an argument and possibly a fight with the Mullens, for they were a clannish, stupid, and aggressive family. There was a distant shout of "Food!" and everyone in the neighborhood dashed madly in the direction of the cry, so, like Lock, Direk made his ascent without an audience.

After an age of effort, he paused and thought he would have to give it up. He was high above the ground now, and the people below looked curiously small and fore-shortened. He was trembling, not only with muscular strain, but also with fear of this dimension with which he was quite unfamiliar—the height made him feel sick. His back had been skinned by the friction of his laboring climb, and blood and sweat dripped from him. Still he had not reached the level of the lights, but he was nearing it. Those mysterious, opalescent round shapes had become long thin ellipses from this viewpoint.

Another spurt . . .?

He put his last bit of strength into it, mounted into shadow, and all at once became cognizant of the ledge of a recess at his side. He levered himself on to it, and sat and stretched his cramped leg and back muscles. The relief was enormous.

Presently he explored his new surroundings, groping his way into the recess. It became a narrow passage that burrowed and twisted its way into the wall. Negotiating a sharp curve, he came abruptly upon a thin but intensely bright beam of light, shoulder high, cutting across his path like a bar of some refulgent stone wedged by its ends between the opposing walls.

It was sometime before he could bring himself to apply his eyes, in the manner described by Lock, to the slit in the left-hand

wall, which was the source of the light. Although he was squinting, with his eyes almost shut, the pain of its stabbing brightness
was like sharp splinters being pressed into his pupils. But he persisted, bearing it, seeking the "vision."

Gradually, as if he had to teach his eyes to see (and, indeed,
they had to be adjusted to receive the impressions of colors of a
kind and intensity hitherto unencountered) he made out the form
of the incredible picture.

There was a green, green land stretching far and wide, to a
wall of brightest blue on which were set curving white shapes. In
the foreground a sparkling stream ran—not dead straight, like the
one he knew, but wound in a fascinating way. Beside it stood
strange brown erections, that forked into a multitude of fingers
which bent back and down and overhung the stream. These fingers
seemed to hold hundreds of green patches, which every now and
then swayed gently in concord. At the further border of the
world—somewhere near the base of the blue wall, he judged—was
a line of jagged and irregular objects, mostly grey and green and
white-topped. He could make nothing of them.

For a long time he peered, reluctant to drag himself from this
sight of wonderland, but the knowledge that night must soon come
nagged him, as he could not make that descent in the dark.

He tore himself away, and stumbled uncertainly back along
the passage, his eyes watering from the strain of resisting that
overpowering light, the effect of it still blinding him. But the picture he had seen was in his mind's sight as clearly as if he were
still looking at it.

"I observe that you have seen Heaven," was Lock's dry comment on his return, "and are still seeing it," he added, regarding
the young man's expression of half-dazed rapture.

Direk did not answer, but like a sleep-walker took the stone
cup to get fresh water.

Sondra stirred in her sleep as he applied the cold liquid, and
awoke. Seeing Direk bending over her, she put an arm round his
neck and slowly drew his head down to kiss him on the lips. They
murmured together awhile, and Lock made a fine show of being
inattentive.

When Sondra had dozed off again, Direk said suddenly:
"Lock, when was it you saw Heaven? How long ago?"

"Oh, it was in my youth . . . I was scarcely older than you are
now."

"But it was after you had lost your eye?"

"Yes."

"H'm," said Direk, and reflected a moment. "And you think—"

"Food!" interrupted Lock urgently.

Direk glanced up and saw the square cakes falling, black against the lights. They were landing quite near.

"I'm not hungry," he said. "Now, look here—"

"Never mind about you," said Lock, rather harshly. "Sondra has not eaten all day. She will be hungry in the night. I could get a little, perhaps, but not enough. I am too old to fight well."

"I'm sorry," said Direk. "Here, take her from me."

The old man relieved him of the sleeping Sondra, and Direk leaped up and dived into the wild mass of people scrambling and struggling for the food. By the time he got there it had all been gathered up, but he saw a fellow staggering away with both arms supporting a pile of six or seven of the cakes. Direk snatched two off the top, and turned back.

The man snarled at his retreating back like a beast, put the remainder down and rushed after him. Direk was expecting it. He spun round and extended his free arm like a straight iron bar, standing with legs astride and braced. The man, unable to check his speed, ran his mouth full tilt into the bunched knuckles at the end of the strong, stiff arm. It snapped his head back, his feet went flying up and he landed on his back on the floor with a frightful jar. There he lay, nothing moving about him save the thick stream of blood from his burst mouth. And even before he had hit the ground, the pile of cakes he had left behind him had disappeared.

Direk returned with his prize.

"As I was saying," he said, squatting down, "you thought that was a picture you saw of Heaven?"

"Naturally it was a picture. You can't expect to see Heaven itself in this life."

"Nevertheless, you have seen it," said Direk, slowly. "It looked flat, like a picture, to you, because you have only one eye. You can't detect perspective, but I had two eyes, and I saw."

Lock looked at him with his mouth open.

"Another thing," pursued Direk. "Did you not perceive things *moving?*"

Lock shook his head dumbly.

"Well, I did, so don't tell me I don't observe things."

"I—I thought perhaps the water in the stream seemed to move," stammered Lock, "but the sight of my eye isn't very good. I couldn't rely on it. I thought it a trick of the light." He recovered some part of his poise. "All the same," he pronounced, "even if it did appear to move, it may still be only a picture, marvellously constructed by Dree to give us some inkling of our destination."

"It isn't a picture: it has depth and distance . . . So you think you're going to walk in that green land after you're dead?"

"I do."

"If you could somehow make that slit larger, I believe you could walk there now," said Direk deliberately.

"If I did not judge what you say to be only a mad dream of youth, I should call it blasphemy," said Lock sadly.

Direk felt a little surge of annoyance.

"Look, old fellow, you're wise and aged, and you see much that I miss, but your mind is as narrow as my finger. Have you never thought upon the nature of the 'Not-Here'?"

"This world is all there is, my son. The wall is the edge of a substance which stretches to infinity. This hole in it was hollowed out by the hand of Dree that we may have space in which to live and move."

"You exasperate me, Lock. You are bound in 'Here' by the circle of your own closed mind, even more than by the circle of the wall. Honestly, I believe you *like* it here!"

"We must be here for a purpose, and I am content to let that purpose remain Dree's business."

As Lock spoke, the golden lights above dimmed and quickly went out. Night had come. "Goodnight," added the old man, settling himself to sleep and trying not to disturb Sondra, who was still half reclining upon him.

"Good-night," responded Direk, not very graciously. He could not sleep for a long while.

It must have been near dawn when he awoke with a wild sense of falling. Indeed, he was falling, for he had gone to sleep sitting with his back to the wall, and suddenly that support had been removed. He found himself lying stretched out in a daze, with his head singing from the collision with the floor.

The floor? Did it, then, somehow extend into the wall? He maneuvered himself onto his hands and knees, and felt about in the darkness. It became apparent that the wall had opened immediately at his back in the shape of a rectangular hole, and through it lay a mounting series of hard levels. It was his first experience of a staircase. A great excitement seized him. There was a way out of "Here!" This staircase itself lay in the "Not-Here!"

In a fever of exploration he began to climb it, clumsily, feeling the way ahead of him. Up and up, seemingly endless, it went . . .

At last he perceived light above him, not the dim golden glow he was accustomed to, but a strange and strong pearly light. Presently he found it emanated from another rectangular opening. He crawled up to it and peered through, shading his eyes.

He looked out on the world he had seen through the slit, but it was not bathed in dazzling light as he had seen it then. Instead, there was a misty sort of gray light, which he found he could bear without squinting.

The green land looked quite shadowy, a sort of dark gray-green. The distant wall, which had been an intense blue, was a dirty white, with grey blurs on it, and it towered up so high that he could not see any top to it: it seemed to curve towards and above him, until it was cut by the straight upper edge of the hole.

He stepped out through the frame into this strange world, peering up, seeking to see that top—and recoiled with a little gasp. He had trodden on something soft. In his world there was nothing soft save human flesh.

—And so he discovered loamy earth and thick grass.

He braced himself to move forward into a land of wonders . . .

A little later, he sat on the bank of the stream in a state of trembling ecstasy trying to take stock of all the staggering discoveries he had made. He had to piece them together and deduce what he could from that wonderful mosaic.

First, what Lock and all the others thought was the whole world was but a small cavern beneath the great cylindrical tower which reached up towards the roof of the far greater outer world, He could not guess how far above him this roof was, but it and the circular wall about were joined imperceptibly in one huge curving expanse. He had walked all around the tower but found no aperture in it other than the one he had come from.

Second, this outer world was made of a far greater range of materials than his, which was almost wholly stone. He had examined the trees by the brook, and made nothing of them. There seemed to be no purpose to them, but in the distance there were other similar objects, both singly and in groups. They were all, somehow, very pleasing to look at. He had investigated plants and bushes, seeds, berries, and flowers.

The flowers engrossed his attention most of all. Their delicacy, coloring, sweet scents, and fragile loveliness combined to

shape his opinion that they were the greatest treasures in this
world. He had come upon a clump of very small ones of a shade of
blue so rich that it thrilled him to look at it. He could not bring
himself to leave them, so, greatly daring, he had plucked one of
them, and now carried it with infinite gentleness in his palm.

Again, there were new kinds of life. He could see silvery
things darting about in the clear waters of the stream. He had already marvelled at the flying birds and their coloring, and once or
twice he had seen a little brown and white thing running swiftly in
the distance with a queer hopping motion.

And the air—it was like a drink of water after a long thirst—
fresh, cool, invigorating. It made him feel so much more *alive* than
he had ever felt.

The sky-wall had perceptibly brightened. It was becoming difficult to look at squarely. The smudges upon it in one direction
had become creamy-white shapes. In the opposite direction they
were still darkly grey, but somehow marvellously lit from beneath
so that they had edges of undreamed-of brilliance. The whole wall
over that way was becoming stained with a red brighter than
blood, and growing brighter still.

He had the feeling that this world was waiting in awe for the
coming of something of infinite majesty. He waited, too, cowering
a little on his bank in uneasy anticipation of the unknown.

A few long moments later, there came a great light moving up
the red-stained side of the sky-wall. He beheld an overpowering
vision of a disc of pulsing red-white light in the center of a crowd
of flags and banners of living color, for such had those grey
smudges become. Then he dropped his head, and shielded his
blinded, aching eyes. He could not look at it directly again.

But he had seen the sun.

When he dared to raise his head at last, the world had been transformed into the landscape he had seen from the slit—A verdant
carpet stretching away to the brightest blue. The smudges were
now everywhere curving white shapes, and they had changed their
positions. As he watched, they were still changing, infinitely slow.

The mist was gone, and at the distant border of the green land
there stood, clear to view now, the line of jagged and irregular objects, grey-green and white-topped. They spurred his curiosity. He
decided to walk to them and investigate their nature.

He had to walk with lowered head and half-shut eyes: the
brightness of everything about him hurt him like fire.

Some hours later he was forced to rest. He had walked a distance equivalent to many times round his own world, and his legs cried out for respite. So he sat under a tree, seeking in its slight shade some relief from the incandescent light which had in some mysterious way moved up the wall until it was somewhere above his head.

The great tower was far behind him now—looking no taller than a man seen at five paces, but the objects ahead of him along the skyline seemed only slightly larger. They must still be an immense distance away.

He concluded that they were great risings of the land, reaching far upward, higher than the tower. Even so, they were low and small against the immense arc of the blue wall, which therefore must lay an unthinkable distance beyond them.

Upon the side of one of those rises was a tiny group of white marks. It was at the very limit of his vision—his eyes watered as he tried to make out the form of it—but he could swear that the marks were regular. It was inexplicable, but he felt drawn towards those marks.

Just then, something landed with a plomp at his feet. It was a shining ball. It had, apparently, dropped from the sky. Was this the food, then, of this strange land? He nibbled at it cautiously. It was succulent—and delicious! The food of the gods, indeed. For the first time it occurred to him that eating could be a pleasure in itself, and not merely an antidote to hunger.

The ball was soon gone, and then he noticed others hanging from the tree-branches above him. He did not think of trying to reach them. No doubt they dropped from time to time as Dree saw fit to release them for food.

Wouldn't Sondra enjoy one of those!

With a little pang of dismay, he realized that he had given no one but himself a thought in this long rapture of exploration. He was being utterly selfish. He had discovered a way into a wonderful new world, and had rushed greedily into it, leaving Sondra and Lock and all the others shut up in their gloomy cave.

He must go back and set them all free.

But—the mystery of those distant land-risings and the marks? He gazed at them ardently again, and felt a quick pain in his heart and a strange yearning. Again that sense of being drawn towards distances.

There was an inner battle, but the issue was clear. The goal of his desire was evidently too far to reach this day. Sondra would be worrying about his long absence—no doubt was already worrying—apart from which, she and Lock would be needing food again. They were not strong enough to get it themselves. Love brought duty as its companion. Sondra's back needed further attention, too . . . He wished he were two people: one who could go on happily exploring, and one who could go back and fulfill what conscience expected of him.

But Sondra and Lock were bound up with him. He must go back . . .

On that reluctant journey, the white curved things on the sky moved up over his head and became grey again, and then from above came pouring water in a heavy shower of drops all over the land. It was cold and fresh, and soon he was streaming wet as if he had bathed in the stream. He had been hot and dusty from travel. Dree had seen his need again, and sent this refreshing bath.

In the midst of it there came without warning a terrific flash of light that sent him, blinded and in awful fear, grovelling face-downwards in the wet grass, while a mighty rumbling passed along the sky above him. He judged that he had been given a glimpse of the presence of Dree Himself . . .

When at last he reached the opening in the tower, he had seen the glory of a sunset, and the world was fading into darkness. He entered the aperture and set foot on the stairs, and then was compelled to take a last look back at Heaven.

The sky was as black now as the sky of his own world, but its mystery was even greater. For truly scattered over it were thousands of tiny twinkling lights that he had not perceived there in the day. He saw the veiny silhouette of a tree against them, and the beauty of it suddenly caught him by the throat.

Some wild voice within him urged him not to forsake that world, not even for a moment, but against that was the gnawing sense of the long separation from Sondra. He was aware of a growing ache to see her again. With sudden resolve he turned his back on Heaven and began to feel his way down the dark staircase. He would find Sondra and bring her out to see this wondrous night.

They would have this one night together under the twinkling lights, just the two of them with all that wide world to themselves.

Tomorrow they would let everyone else come.

He reached the bottom of the stairs and found himself on a level stretch of stone which he did not recall. He walked gingerly across it, his arms extended forward and feeling with his fingers, he encountered a wall barring his way. At that moment of surprise, a queer sensation that he was growing heavier came over him. His feet were pressing against the floor, his knees giving. Then the sensation ceased suddenly, with a strange sickening little upheaval in the stomach.

As he stood, bewildered, the wall rolled aside with a rumble, and he found himself staring into a queer-shaped little world flooded with golden light.

"Come forward," commanded a deep slow voice.

He advanced, blinking, adjusting his eyes to the light.

"Stop," said the voice, and now he could see that it came from someone seated on a raised platform before him. He had not seen a throne before, but there was one, and its occupant was an old but huge and powerful man with a luxuriant white beard. He looked benevolent, if not formidable, and his white-lashed blue eyes twinkled as he gazed down at Direk.

"So you came back, Direk," he said.

"Who are you? How do you know my name?" asked Direk uncertainly and in some awe.

"I am Dree. I know everything."

"You are Dree of the world outside?"

"There is no Dree of the world outside. I am Dree of this world."

He pointed an enormous wrinkled forefinger at a large screen which was set upon one wall. On it Direk saw a downward view of a part of his old world, showing a portion of the straight stream which ran in its gully across the center. It was a living picture, taken apparently from a place high up on the curved wall. Although most of the people lay stretched on the floor in slumber, some still moved around, and the flowing water of the stream could be seen distinctly.

Direk did not think to inquire how such a picture could be: it was one of Dree's miracles, to be accepted as such. One thing, however, caused him to wonder.

"But—isn't it night there now?" he asked. "How can we see them?"

"The lights do not really go out at night: they change their emission frequency to the infra-red band. Unlike the human eye, the television camera is sensitive to infra-red rays. Oh yes, I watch my people night and day. The good shepherd, as one might say."

Hardly a word of this meant anything to Direk.

"From 843 different angles," added Dree. "Now look at this— Angle 547."

There was a row of dials and pointers along the inner side of one arm of the throne. Dree turned his attention to it and began manipulating things.

While he was so engaged, Direk darted swift glances at his surroundings. All one wall was a window, and through it could be seen the black sky of the outer world, with its thousands of points of light. The landscape beneath was the faintest possible outline: scarcely more than a slight difference of shade.

Directed through the window to some point out on that land-scape was a long cylinder, on a tripod, a good many paces from Direk. At the near end of it was a small square screen. It was an instrument for magnifying distant things, Direk guessed. He gave a glance at the image on the screen. With a thrill of recognition, he saw the pattern of white marks he had been striving to reach. They seemed to be things like white boxes with regularly spaced lights on their sides, and around their bases he was sure he could see tiny moving things. He yearned to go over and examine the image close at hand.

But at that moment Dree said: "Behold!"

Direk turned to see that on the other and larger screen had ap-peared a close up view of Sondra and Lock lying side by side. They were both awake. Lock looked worried, and Sondra tearfully distressed.

Direk started as their voices came from the screen.

"He'll never come back," sobbed Sondra. "No one has ever been away as long as this."

Her accents went right to Direk's heart. He felt sick with shame.

"Try to sleep now, Sondra," said Lock, soothingly. "We'll have another look around in the morning."

"They've been walking about looking for you all day," said Dree, with what seemed to be an air of satisfaction. He put a finger on a switch. The screen went dark and silent. "Microphones eve-rywhere," he added inconsequently.

"I must get back to her," exclaimed Direk. Please let me go now, Dree."

"Presently, presently," murmured Dree. "So you didn't think much of the outer world, eh?"

Direk stared. "It was marvelous beyond belief," he said slowly.

"Then why did you come back?"

"To fetch Sondra, of course, and all the others."

"As I thought," said Dree. "You want your woman. You want company. You're not big enough to stand out there alone—as I stand alone. That's the difference between Dree and a man."

"But," began Direk, astonished and dubious, "I love Sondra."

"The word 'love,' as you use it, is merely a covering for a multitude of personal needs and desires," said Dree. He did not look benevolent now: his blue eyes were hard. "You desire Sondra physically, you desire her reassurance of your own existence, you desire her praise and admiration and service. That's all. Only Dree is entirely unselfish. I bestow all my attention on you people, tirelessly, unceasingly, while you sleep and play and fight. I give you strength and purpose in life—you develop your muscles and will and alertness in the struggle for the sustenance I drop calculatingly among you, so that you will not be bored or listless. I give you your days and nights, your food and drink and shelter, chastise and correct you when necessary, and watch over you always—for you are all my children."

"You . . . chastise us?" repeated Direk, haltingly.

Dree picked up a heavy whip and weighed it in his right hand. His eyes were gleaming strangely.

"Certainly I do," he said softly. "You must be taught right from wrong."

"Why did you beat Sondra?" burst out Direk. 'she has never done anything wrong!"

"I can't always make personal distinctions," said Dree, throwing the whip down carelessly. "Sometimes I do, as in the case of that philosopher friend of yours, Lock, for instance. His eyes saw too much for his own good. He was always peeping and prying into things, a habit that had to be corrected in time. Usually I just pick on anyone as a representative for the general sins. The one suffers for the many. It's the example that counts, you see. The others learn to behave themselves just as much as the one who is chastised."

A vision of Sondra's torn back rose before Direk's eyes. A burning anger gripped him, however, he restrained himself and spoke carefully.

"Supposing the victim is really quite innocent?"

"Nobody is quite innocent, except for me," said Dree. "Punish anyone at random, and he himself will begin to seek and find reasons for his own punishment. For, like all of you, his heart is full of guilt, and he realizes he can blame no one but himself. Just as you feel guilty for leaving your kind."

"*You* opened the way for me to do that," Direk pointed out.

"Correct. The wall of your world is full of concealed doors, passages, elevators, all controllable from here. There are a hundred ways in. That is how I take my victims in the night. First I make sure everyone in the vicinity is asleep, of course. My chosen ones soon wake up when they feel my lash and tongs and burning brands! How they squirm!" His eyes were glowing now, and his tongue licked his lips. Direk was appalled.

"After their punishment, I obliterate the memory of it by hypnosis," Dree went on with something like a chuckle. "I don't want them comparing their stories and getting to know too much about me. The fear of the unknown is a most powerful deterrent."

Direk felt that Dree was shrinking rapidly in his view, while he himself was becoming larger and of more importance.

He said: "Then why let me know so much? Why let me discover that outer world?"

Dree smiled a twisted smile.

"You were only the guinea-pig in an experiment. You were just a sample I took out in a test-tube and held up to the light to see how my people were shaping. You reacted just as I thought you would. You were not strong enough for the outside world and had to fly back to the shelter of *my* world. For there is no Dree out there, and no one to look after you. I thought perhaps some of you might develop aspirations and am always watching for the first signs of that. That is why I left a peep-hole for the stronger ones to find. Oh yes, I watched your climb, and heard what you had to say about it. Very perceptive, your theory of the 'Not-Here,' but brain without character is useless. You are the strongest of the people down there, but you still can't do without me, you see. You had to come crawling back."

Direk kept his thoughts on that to himself.

"And what now?" he asked.

"I shall chastise you, and put you back where you belong— among the other worms called 'Men'."

"Are you not afraid that I shall tell of what I have seen?"

"I am Dree. I am not afraid of anything. From your kind down there it is plain that there is nothing to fear nor ever will be. Worms! I know them too well, much better than you do, for I have studied them for generations. Tell them all you like, and see where it will get you!"

"I shall!" declared Direk, and took a purposeful pace towards the platform. That was as far as he got. Dree touched a button; a sort of ripple seemed to pass from the throne and through the air, and then an invisible force held Direk firmly in his tracks.

"You *dare* to think of attacking me!" said Dree in a low grating voice, as though he were straining to suppress white-hot fury.

He descended from the throne, deliberately, trailing his lash, and advanced with his eyes almost bolting from his head. Tiny bubbles of foam were clinging to the hairs at the corners of his lips . . .

Sondra and Lock found Direk the next morning quite near their area. He was unconscious. Never before had a man been flogged so fearfully by Dree. There was scarcely a square inch of his skin untouched.

For two days he was in delirium. Sondra, despite her own condition, nursed him constantly. Lock fought like a fiend to get them all food.

When at last he came to his senses, and told them the whole story, they thought he was still delirious.

"But I tell you, Lock, I know what I am saying!" he said, with force.

"Yes, of course," said Lock, soothingly—and maddeningly.

"I can't help wondering about Dree," said Direk, presently. "It is certain that he is a sadist, and mentally and morally unbalanced. There are dark and tortuous corridors in his mind. He is living in a world of myth. I believe that deep within himself he is tortured by some awful sense of inferiority, which he won't admit, and this lordship over us is an attempt to justify himself to himself. I wonder how he originally got this hold over us?"

He pondered a while.

"Now, those white markings on the far away slopes. From what I saw I judge them to be the dwelling places of other men—some superior kind of men. They were huge and wonderful places, lighted under the night sky. I'm sure that's where the people of Heaven live, Lock. Perhaps he lived there once, and was cast out for some sin against the community. Thus he came to live in this solitary tower, quite alone, brooding over being spurned by his fellows. A mind like that would seek revenge, of course . . ."

He mused further.

"Suppose he stole the infant children of his judges, brought them here before they could even talk or have any clear idea of their environment, and kept them in this place? A race would grow up under his domination, thinking of him as Dree and knowing of no other place than Here. Thus, in his twisted view, he would turn the tables and become judge of the species who had judged him. But some of us may have inherited the dim childish memories of our ancestors, and so feel intuitively that there is a place other than Here, as I did."

"You don't know what you're saying," muttered Lock, glancing around almost apprehensively, as though he expected the wrath of Dree to strike them then and there.

"But you think Dree may know what I'm saying?" asked Direk, with a quizzical smile. "I have little doubt that he's listening and watching at this moment. Dree won't assault me again—Not yet, anyway. To do so would be to admit that he fears me, and he won't admit that to himself. He has a fierce pride, so will choose to ignore me. He's rather pathetic, in a way, but I think underneath it all, he has a burning desire to be loved and wanted, but doesn't know the right way to go about it. Dree was quite incapable of understanding what brought me back voluntarily to Here. Sometimes he deludes himself that we all do love and need him. Your sort of talk, Lock, about suffering being necessary to make us appreciate what we get, must be music in his ears—and strengthening to his attitude."

"This is all—remarkable fantasy. Remarkable fantasy," muttered Lock, half to himself.

Direk suddenly felt dejected. All the eager spirit of his exposition ebbed from him. How did he know that this grand erection of supposition and guesses, based on the memories of his experiences, was not, after all, more than "remarkable fantasy"? He did not, and could not know. Even those memories—might they not be only further illusions—dream-stuff thought up by his anguished mind during his period of delirium?

He turned over with a groan, and would say no more. Was it his imagination that sensed Dree laughing at him?

It was later that same day, as he lay there brooding, that his gaze fell upon a little brown wisp of a thing lying among Lock's mushrooms. He picked it up, wonderingly. There was something oddly familiar about the shape of it.

"What is this?" he besought Lock.

"That? It was a little plant-like thing we discovered clenched in your hand when we found you. I planted it in my patch of soil, but it withered and died. I don't think it had a proper root."

Strength flowed triumphantly back into Direk.

"This was the little, lovely flower of marvelous blue that I plucked and carried with me in Heaven—just as I told you in my story. You see, it *was* true!"

"It is true that you went to Heaven, as others have been, for you were flogged by Dree, and He dwells there. But you cannot really remember how you came by that flower, for not one of us remembers the actual experience of our punishment in Heaven."

"No, Lock, that will not do. I *know* now. Call the people around. I would tell them of Heaven, and give them hope that it can be attained in our life-time."

Shaking his head doubtfully, Lock obeyed. Presently Direk, with Sondra by his side, described his journey in the outer world to a curious and wondering crowd. When he had finished, he waited for their comments.

"A place where you have to walk about with half-shut eyes or be blinded? That wouldn't suit me," said one.

"Only one little piece of food all day? Not enough," said another.

"Water pouring all over you from the sky? Most uncomfortable," said another.

"You walked half the day and never reached the wall? We'd lose our friends, our children, and ourselves in a place as big as that," said another.

"Queer beasts running and *flying* about? They might kill you as you slept," said another.

"It must have been wrong to go there—look how severely you were punished," said another.

They made these remarks with only a mock seriousness.

"Is there not one man among you who really believes there is such a place as I have described?" demanded Direk.

No one spoke. There was a titter.

Direk remembered Dree's words: *"From your own kind down there it is plain that there is nothing to fear nor ever will be . . . Tell them all you like, and see where it will get you!"*

No doubt Dree was watching this meeting with ironic amusement at Direk's discomfiture.

Direk fought down his despair.

"Any of you men has only to climb up that recess in the Mullen's area to see it for himself," he said.

"And how do you climb it?" asked one.

Direk explained.

"A mad thing to do at the behest of a visionary," answered the man. "Who wants to break his neck for a dreamer?"

There were murmurs of approving laughter.

"No volunteers, you see," said the man turning away.

For a moment, the bitter despair of this further disappointment got on top of Direk. "What *is* the use?" he thought to himself. "Worms! He was right in that. He has nothing to fear from them."

Then determination not to be beaten surged up again, indestructible. Tight-lipped and white, he rose unsteadily to his feet. The movement burst open some of his scarce-closed wounds.

"Darling! What are you doing? You mustn't stand!" whispered Sondra in tense anxiety, and Lock tried gently to force him down again.

"Follow me, all of you," said Direk, staggering forward and throwing off the restraining hands of Sondra and Lock.

He led them, with uncertain steps, to the Mullen's area.

"There is one volunteer," he said, grimly, and prepared himself to climb. That silenced the crowd.

Lock said "No!" urgently, and stepped towards Direk. "You are too weak. Let me show them how. I have done it once—I can do it again."

"Not at your time of life, old one," said Direk. "Look after Sondra. That's your task. As for me, you have no idea of the strength that moves me now!"

He began to climb, while the crowd watched, and Sondra hid her face on Lock's shoulder. He climbed very slowly and painfully, but even so, he soon tore open all the wounds on his back. Still he persevered, and at long last passed up into the shadow.

When he disappeared from view, the crowd lost much of its interest. Some began to drift away, while others collected in little groups and started playing gambling games. One of the groups was spattered with drops of blood falling from the unseen and straining climber above. They swore, and moved their position.

At length, Direk could be seen descending. Sondra and Lock watched breathlessly every inch of his downward progress. From his dazed expression, he was plainly at the limit of his physical endurance, and only blind will kept him moving mechanically.

When he was almost down, Dree produced one of his masterstrokes of irony.

Food began to fall in quantity some little way off. With a whoop, the whole remaining audience, except Sondra and Lock, rushed away to scramble and grab and fight. And Direk, in a dead faint, fell the last ten feet like a rag doll. Sondra and Lock managed to break his fall to some extent.

He was in a terrible condition, like a man flayed alive—but he was alive.

They eased his position as much as they could, and Sondra ran to get water. He was just managing to partially sit up and sip it, when a couple of the sons of the Mullen's family came sauntering back munching lumps of their newly acquired food.

"Well?" said one of them, with his mouth full. "Did you see Heaven again?"

"The slit is closed from without," answered Direk, in a painracked voice. "The view is blocked now."

They looked at each other and winked, then burst into raucous laughter.

"As good a tale as any," said the spokesman. "Meanwhile, this is our area. Clear off!"

Sandra and Lock half carried, half dragged Direk back to his own area, where they gently laid him down. He looked as if he would never move again. Lock went to get water to bathe the maltreated wounds.

"Dearest," said Sondra, softly. "I believe in Heaven and all you have said about it, but you don't ever have to worry about taking me there. Wherever I am with you, so long as I am with you, that is Heaven for me."

Direk hid a wry smile, and thought to himself, "There are longings in a man's heart no woman will ever understand."

"And don't be discouraged because the slit is closed," she said.

"Far from that, I am vastly encouraged," he said, in a voice so firm that it surprised her. "You see man is being paid a compliment. Despite the present appearance of laxness, the seeking of easy pleasures, the selfishness, the seeming lack of imagination, there *is* something in these 'worms' which Dree fears, whatever he boasted. The closing of that slit is an act of fear. He dare not allow man any further glimpses of Heaven. Dree is uneasy on his throne."

To himself he said something it would not be politic to say aloud: "He said there are a hundred ways into Here. To me that means there are a hundred ways out!"

His eyes fell again upon the poor little brown stalk of the flower among the mushrooms. It was brittle now, had already broken in two and soon would be dust. He remembered the one-time wondrous blue of it.

"You may fade and vanish," he thought, "but the memory of you, and where you came from is a lasting one which I shall not forget!"

CONDITIONED REFLEX

ARTHUR HAD BOUGHT THE RECORD of Mossolov's *Steel Foundry* and insisted on playing it over and over again, while he lay back in the armchair with his eyes shut and bliss on his face. The room rocked to the sound of great pistons that needed oiling and the efforts of the clumsy giant who kept dropping bags of assorted scrap-iron.

Seth Barnard could stand it no more. Gingerly, he got up and tried to tiptoe out. His sleeve-buttons brushed against a steel ash-tray and produced a faint metallic *ping!*

Arthur bounced up in his chair and tore his hair. He registered anguish, pain, disappointment, shock, high blood pressure, animal rage, and a few other things it was difficult to put a finger on in the short time the show was on.

He roared, "You ungainly oaf! You've ruined it."

"The sound—" began Seth, but he had no chance against Mossolov. He waited until the steel foundry had closed down, and said: "The sound I made is at least known to musical notation, which is more than any of that din is."

"Din?" repeated Arthur, now putting in some pretty good facial work on astonishment. "Din? Are you *quite* mad?"

"Sometimes I wonder. I must be. Else why should I stay here enduring your performances as a jitterbug on the high wire, and your infernal records of street noises, and this dead-and-alive hole known—to nobody except its inhabitants—as Peterville?"

"So we're back to that, huh? This was where I came in, about a year ago. You were belly-aching then that nothing ever happened in Peterville. Then those atom creatures came and made this place a miracle town, poured gold on you, gave you a newspaper and a fine swimming pool—"

"There's only two inches of water in the pool now, and I'm not a flatfish," snapped Seth. "The atom things ought to have remembered that it never rains here. Anyway, that was all of a year ago. I've had nothing since to put in the newspaper except Births,

Deaths, and Marriages, and I've had to invent most of those just to give people something to talk about."

He went to the window and stared gloomily out.

"I'm not asking much," he said. "An earthquake or two, a few murders, a suicide or so, just to show someone's *living* around here."

"Living?" echoed Arthur. "By the sound of it, if you had your way you'd slay us all for your—"

"Hey, what was that?" interrupted Seth, on his toes, trying to put his face through the glass.

"For once you ought to know what you're talking about: you're there, not me."

"Something flashed down across the sky—a red, glowing thing. Seemed to land out there in the desert. Look, you can see a faint trail in the sky."

Arthur jumped up, bounded to a closet, and then bounded to the window. A kangaroo couldn't have done it better.

"Lemme see . . . Ha, a meteorite, as I thought! You can see where it hit—there, where the trail ends. Must be all of twenty miles off. Let me get a bearing on it."

He shoved Seth aside and juggled with the compass he'd picked out of the closet.

"In a few moments," he said, "we should hear the sound of it landing."

Almost immediately there came a noise like a door slamming far off. They wouldn't have noticed it if they hadn't been listening for it. Peterville at large ignored it.

"Here's something for your rag," said Arthur. "Come on."

"It might have been if it had landed twenty miles nearer," said Seth, gloomily. "It's just wasted itself out there in the desert—hasn't killed a soul." He followed Arthur to the garage.

The area Arthur had calculated to contain the impact point was miles off the road. They bumped as near to it as they could in the car, weaving across the sand and through the cacti, and then they walked for another couple of miles or so. There were so many ridges looking so much alike in these parts that you had to keep track of your position by taking compass bearings continually, otherwise you were likely to wander in vast circles until you died.

They topped a ridge, and there below them, half buried in the sandy floor of the shallow valley, was what they were looking for.

"Seems to be a misguided missile," said Arthur, staring at the slim, fifty-foot rocket.

"The next war will probably start through the Army blowing up its own launching ground with a boomerang rocket and thinking it's being attacked," said Seth. "Darn it, that's killed my headline: A VISITOR FROM OUTER SPACE. I can't blow this up into anything much."

They went down the slope towards the thing.

A thin man with a frowning yellow face stepped out suddenly from behind the rocket. He wore a leather suit like the unheated one of the old-fashioned aviator. He pointed a tubular instrument, about a foot long, at them, and pressed a trigger on it. It went *click-click,* but nothing else happened. With an indistinct oath, the man started fiddling with dials set in its butt.

"Lordy!" said Seth. "And no place to hide."

It didn't appear safe to try to scramble back up the slope.

"There's only one sensible thing to do," said Arthur, and put up his hands.

"Perhaps you're right." Seth did the same.

The man, having re-set the dials, again pointed the instrument at them and pulled the trigger. *Click-click.* Nothing else.

"Hey!" said Arthur, loudly. "Don't you know the rules? Can't you see we've got our hands up? What more do you want us to do—sing to you?"

"Spare me that," said the man, with a heavy but unplaceable accent. "And take your hands down—you look ridiculous. Is either of you mechanically-minded? This thing won't work."

"We'd love to repair your gun so that you could shoot us," said Arthur. "Or would you prefer us to jump off a cliff?"

"It's not a gun. It's a robot-control. I landed the ship badly and broke a few things, including this, it seems."

"You—You were in that rocket?" said Seth, incredulously.

"Certainly. You don't think I walked from Mars?"

"Mars?" Seth and Arthur made a chorus of it.

"That's what you call it, isn't it?"

Seth just gulped. Arthur walked up to the man and looked at him keenly. He looked perhaps sixty, with white hair straying from under the helmet.

"You certainly did land with a bump, didn't you?" said Arthur. "How does your head feel?"

"I'm quite all right. I didn't land on my head."

"How long have you had jaundice?"

The man sighed. "It's the natural complexion on Mars. I am a Martian. I was born there. This is my first trip to Earth, although, of course, I know all about it. I'm *not* a deranged Earth-robot with delusions. Darn this thing! If I could only get it to work, I shouldn't have to stand here arguing with you."

"Why not?" asked Seth, coming up.

"Because it's a robot-control, and you are robots."

Seth and Arthur looked at each other, and shrugged slightly.

Arthur said: "What's your name, Martian?"

"Burp," said the man.

Arthur waited politely. There was a silence.

Arthur tried again. "I said, what's your name?"

"Burp," said the man.

"His name's Burp," said Seth, gleefully.

"Indeed?" said Arthur. "I was beginning to think it was Karel Capek. Oh, well, it was bound to happen. Edgar Rice Burroughs used up all the polite names. Even he touched the funny-bone sometimes. Well, Burp, I think you'd better come home with us. Unless you prefer to travel by rocket?"

"The ship's all right," said Burp, "but I never use it for journeys of less than a million miles. Anyway, I doubt whether I shall ever want to use it again."

"Why, aren't you going back to Mars to tell them all about us?"

"They know it all. That's why I left the place. You can't tell them anything. Any time you start to speak to anyone, they say "I know just what you're going to say, and you're wrong." I just had to get away from them so that I could go and live among some simple, ignorant people."

"That's why you came here?" asked Seth.

"Naturally."

"You've made a ghastly mistake, brother. Arthur here is the one man in the world who knows everything about everything. He'll soon have you on the lam again."

"He's exaggerating," said Arthur. "Actually, there are one or two things I'm ignorant about—but they're things just not worth knowing. By the way, where and how did you learn English?"

"Your radio broadcasts, of course. I speak all your Earthly languages, except Scotch, which I can't manage because I've only got one tongue. Talking of Scotch, I hope you have some at your home?"

"If I had my way, alcohol would be used only for rocket fuel and for pickling bodies," said Arthur, loftily.

"Come on, Burp," said Seth. "Let's go pickle our bodies."

They were a long time getting back to the car because the compass needle developed a fault and kept thinking that the North Magnetic Pole was in Jamaica. After which, it discovered its mistake and pointed to the Azores. Then it went in for ballet, and did some pretty pirouettes.

"You must have over wound it," accused Seth, but Arthur stuck the thing in his pocket and said: "I don't need it. The car's over in that direction."

"How do you know?" asked Seth.

"Because I can see it."

Seth drove, and in the back of the car an argument developed between Arthur and Burp.

"I am *not* a robot—I can show you my birth certificate," Arthur was saying indignantly.

"You are. All you Earth people are. You're merely machines run to seed. Your earliest ancestors were the slave-machines we Martians brought here to do our fetching and carrying when we first explored this planet, a million or more years ago. We left the things behind—they weren't worth taking back."

"That's lunatic talk!" stormed Arthur. "Worse—it's—it's science-fiction!"

That was the nastiest insult in Arthur's extensive collection: he was an earnest student of science. The employment of it meant that he was really getting het up.

It became a dogfight. Seth caught only bits of it, as the car rattled noisily along the dusty road toward Peterville.

"Your own behaviorists will tell you . . . Touch the cornea and you blink . . . Pavlov . . . dog . . . All habits . . . chains of conditioned responses . . . completely predictable from known stimuli . . ."

"Nonsense!" Arthur was shouting. "You're trying to prove through behaviorism that reasoning doesn't exist and at the same time you're trying to prove by reasoning that behaviorism doesn't exist you can't have it both ways."

"I can!" cried Burp. "*I* can reason about behaviorism because I'm not subject to its laws. I'm free to reason, think, and act for myself. You can't reason at all—only pull out chains of ideas linked together: you're like a phonograph and half-a-dozen records."

Arthur made vague screaming noises, indicative of, disgust, contempt, anger, refutation, accusation, and general disagreement.

"Control yourself, Arthur, or you'll overheat your bearings," Seth shouted back over his shoulder, maliciously.

They were entering Peterville. Seth slowed down. The car overtook old man Smith ambling along the wayside.

" 'Morning, Smithy," called Seth.

"Howdy, Seth. What you got in the back—coupla coyotes?"

"Only Arthur and a Martian," said Seth.

"Yeah? Where did he buy it?"

"I believe it bought him," Seth called back.

When they reached the bungalow, Arthur shot out of the car as if he'd been catapulted. His gangling figure vanished through the doorway, shouting over its shoulder: "Come on, I'll show you in black and white!"

As Burp started to, get out, Seth said: "Hold it a moment—let him go. I'm the editor of the newspaper here—I want a story for tomorrow's edition. Give me the lowdown on Mars and the Martians. Do they favor pajamas or the old-fashioned nightie? How many wives are you allowed? Have you killed off your politicians yet? Do you have racketeers? Do——"

"I'm a journalist myself," said Burp, coldly, "and my price for contributions of that sort is a dollar a word."

"Oh, so you *do* have racketeers," said Seth, equally coldly. "Okay, go in and drink my Scotch. My price is five bucks a finger. Never mind about the article—I'll make it up."

"I'm sure you would have done so in any case," said Burp, and turned and walked into the bungalow.

Seth went round to the composing room and set up a double column about Mars, the Martians, and Burp in particular. Half of it came out of *Popular Astronomy,* there was a steal from Wells, and the rest of it, dealing with Burp in particular, came out of Seth's own head. It appeared that Mars had become too hot to hold Burp . . .

When he entered the lounge, there was a cold war on.

They were on to cybernetics now.

"Just a matter of negative feedback," Burp was saying. "Excessive feedback in a steering gear is exactly the same as purpose tremor caused by an injury to the cerebellum. A neurosis is merely wild oscillation of the mechanism—'hunting'—before it breaks down completely."

"I'll grant you that the brain cells are simple relays—" began Arthur.

"Do you also grant me that your nervous system includes devices for integrating, differentiating, frequency modulations, wave synthesis, storage, scanning, and group transformations from one co-ordinate system to another?"

"Being *my* nervous system, those are just its simplest devices," snapped Arthur. "However, I know what you're going to say—"

Burp groaned. "Don't say that. You sound like a Martian."

"All right, I'll admit it—our technicians have reproduced all of those devices electrically, both separately and combined. But none of their contrivances has produced any poetry yet."

"Poetry is basically only emotion. Your elementary machines have produced emotion. Look, in this issue of *Electronic Engineering*—"

"I know what you're going to say," said Arthur.

Burp shrieked. "Don't say that! It makes me mad!"

"The homeostat," said Arthur.

Burp threw his leather helmet across the room. He tore at his springing white hair. Seth thought: Why, he looks just like Arthur! Except for the jaundice.

Burp said fiercely: "I insist on instancing this case."

"Then tell him," said Arthur, boredly, indicating Seth, and sat down and put his feet up.

"Yes, tell me," said Seth. "Nobody ever tells *me* anything."

Books and journals were lying strewn all over the chairs, the bureau, the occasional table, and the phonograph. They were ankle-deep on the floor, and Burp came plowing through them at Seth.

"All right," he said, "listen to Barnard. This is the sort of thing you should put in your newspaper instead of idle chitchat. The homeostat is a machine designed by Dr. W.R. Ashby, and demonstrated by the Electroencephalographic Society at the Burden Neurological Institute, in Bristol, England, on May 1st, 1948."

"How d'you spell it?" said Seth, taking notes.

"What?"

"Bristol."

"Never mind. The homeostat is a group of four electromagnets, supplying a self-feedback, and with 390,625 combinations of feedback patterns to choose from. The four magnets are free to swing and seek a stable, balanced point, just as an animal seeks its optimal condition. So it is goal-seeking, just as you robots are goal-seeking, using negative feedback to swing you on the line to your goal."

"My goal at the moment is a Scotch," said Seth, getting it. He drank it at a gulp.

Burp stared at him.

"Go on," said Seth. "I don't understand a word of it, but maybe my readers might. Maybe."

"My price for further information is a snifter."

Seth gave him one.

"Ah!" said Burp afterward, looking a little less jaundiced. He continued: "I'll put it simply, as you're simple-minded. Negative feedback is the resultant of impulses received from yourself and your goal so that you are guided to make the distance between them zero, as in a radar-controlled anti-aircraft gun, receiving impulses from the target plane and its own shells. Without feedback, it would aim anywhere; with positive feedback, it would try to miss the plane by the greatest distance—a neurotic procedure, defeating the *raison d'etre* of the machine."

"Like the way you're missing the point," interjected Arthur.

Burp ignored him, and went on: "Animals, as you style yourselves, work on basically the same principle, though you have fashioned many different feedback combinations and have learned to use them. A cat, for instance, with its goal of self-preservation, learns to go *toward* red meat (negative feedback) and *away* from red fire (positive feedback). As a kitten, its behavior is merely chaotic—"

"So are your facts," yawned Arthur. "Cats are color-blind."

Burp quivered with silent rage.

"What's that?" said Seth, watching him interestedly. "Oscillation setting in?"

Burp took hold of himself with an effort. "Another Scotch," he muttered.

Seth poured him a stiff one, emptying the bottle.

"I'm beginning to see how you got your name," he said. "Come on, give."

"Ah!" Burp sighed as he put down the glass. "Well, a mammalian brain, you see, is just a machine that has learned how to approach its goal by a flexible route, its aim remaining unchanging. If one path is blocked, it works out another. It works out essential parts of its own wiring. So does the homeostat. Its inventor did everything he could think of to stop the magnets from reaching their stable arrangement. But between them they always worked out a new circuit so that they got there."

"What did he do?" asked Seth.

"He reversed the polarity, even the magnets themselves. He put physical obstructions in the way of a free swing of the magnets. He tied two of them together with glass fibre, so that they had to move together. Whatever conditions he imposed, they beat him."

"That's a point you'd better consider," said Arthur, lazily. "The homeostat developed to play chess, for instance, could eventually play with subtlety and strategy beyond that of the inventor himself. Now—"

"I know what you're going to say!" said Burp, furiously. "Don't flatter yourself. Your model is known to us Martians as Mark B. VII—a primitive and very inferior one. There's no comparing you and me—I'm not a machine, but a natural product, of beauty, delicacy, wonder and infinite complexity. Whereas you and your materialistic, miserable little ten billion thermionic tubes, a mere *machina ratiocinatrix—*"

His voice was drowned by a flood of music.

"Brahms' First Symphony!" shouted Arthur, shutting the lid of the phonograph. "No machine created that!"

"Emotional stuff, and emotional reasoning!" bawled Burp. "The homeostat produces any amount of emotion. Put obstructions in its way and it will exhibit all the signs of frustration and disappointment. It sulks inactively, then shows hysterical over-action and frantic over-compensation, and if you—"

"For crying out loud!" exclaimed Seth, going to the phonograph and turning it off. "Let's have a truce. This nerve war is getting me down. What about some lunch?"

"I'm not hungry," growled Burp. "But I'm still thirsty."

"Okay, then let's all go over to Ted's Bar and get to be pals—"

"Count me out," said Arthur, nastily. "I'm not one of those natural products of beauty and delicacy which need constant pick-me-ups. I'm only a poor old robot with a weakness for primitive noises. I guess there must be a short in my circuit somewhere."

It was very quiet in Ted's Bar, because Ted was the only person there and he was not given to speaking to himself—or much to anyone else.

"Two double Scotches, Ted," said Seth. "Meet my friend, Burp—he's just come from Mars."

"Pleased to meet you," said Ted, setting out the glasses. "Have a nice trip?"

"So-so," said Burp.

Seth took the drinks and Burp over into a corner, out of ear-shot of Ted.

"I have to apologize for Arthur's behavior, Burp," he said, quietly. "I'm always having to do it. He's a good guy, quite bright in his way, but too tense. He doesn't know how to relax. If he'd only behave like a human being, have a smoke and a drink now and again, see things in their proper perspective instead of bursting blood vessels over mole-hills—"

"He can't behave like a human being because he's a robot," said Burp, reflectively. "But he's gone off the beam—his mechanism is "hunting." Most unstable. But don't worry about me—I can handle him."

Seth sipped his Scotch, watching Burp over the glass.

"You're really on the up-and-up about our being robots, aren't you?" he said, presently.

"Yes, of course. If only I could get this robot-control to work . . ."

He was still carrying the instrument, and he frowned at it and played with it.

"I must get me a banner-line: MARTIAN SAYS ALL EARTHMEN MECHANICAL TOYS. No, that won't do. What about—*Jumping Jehosophat!*"

"That won't do either," said Burp. "There's no point to it."

But Seth was gaping over Burp's shoulder at a quite unprecedented spectacle, one which put Martians and their utterances in the shade.

Arthur had entered the bar. It was as though an archbishop had entered the lowest dive on the San Francisco waterfront.

He was obviously ill at ease and uncomfortable, and equally obviously doing his best to conceal it and look amused, detached, and tolerant about it, as though he were being shown over the place against his real inclinations and didn't like to offend the guide. But he couldn't quite control his puritanical nostrils, which every now and then twitched and said: "How sordid!"

With him was Doc Benson, the surgeon at the hospital.

"Hello, Arthur," said Seth. "Slumming?"

But Arthur had gone deaf. He looked around with a faint, fixed smile, and hummed tunelessly to show that he was quite unperturbed.

"Hiya, Seth," said Doc. "What'll you and your friend have?"

"Hi, Doc. Scotch, thanks—that okay for you, Burp?"

Burp nodded.

The Doc went to the bar, and ordered. "What's for you, Arthur?" he called.

"Coco-cola, thanks."

"Straight?"

"Er—yes."

The Doc brought the drinks on a tray into the corner, and tried to maneuver everyone into a chummy little circle. But Arthur kept slipping out of his hands like a bit of wet soap and remained hovering uncertainly on the fringe. It was as if he were expecting the cops to raid the joint at any moment and didn't want to be identified with the group of debauchees.

"What's the matter, Arthur?" asked Seth. "Delirium tremens isn't infectious."

"If it were, I'd have caught it long ago," snapped Arthur, but the old fire was lacking. Seth grinned and enjoyed himself. Arthur was so habitually the master of his environment that it made a welcome change to see him in the rare role of a fish out of water. But it was all very odd: why had Arthur cast himself for such a totally unsuitable role?

Another odd thing soon became noticeable. Doc Benson kept up a running fire of small talk and wisecracks that mostly misfired, and never once referred to Burp as a Martian or evinced any curiosity about where he'd come from and why. It was odd because curiosity about other people's business was the salient characteristic of the Doc.

Doc became boastful about the new Peterville Hospital, its furnishings, grounds, apparatus, and so forth.

"All going to waste," he said, "because we haven't had a single darned patient since the place opened. I just haven't anything to do except sit in Ted's bar here and try to work up an appetite. We have the best darned cook you ever saw—why not come along to lunch, Seth, and bring your friend? We've steaks today—the way Joe does 'em they'll be as sweet as a nut."

"No, thanks, Doc, I've got a heavy date with the linotype."

"How 'bout you, friend?"

"I'm not hungry," said Burp.

Arthur whispered something in the Doc's ear.

"That so?" said Doc. "H'm. Well, I guess we'll be getting along."

"We?" said Seth.

"Arthur's accepted my lunch invitation."

"I've left some cold ham for you, Seth," said Arthur. "But there's—er—only one pickled onion left."

"Wish you'd keep your fingers out of that jar," grumbled Seth.

"Oh," said the Doc, as if he'd just remembered it. "I've got to replenish the cellar."

He brought two bottles of Scotch from Ted, while Burp looked on with thirsty eyes.

"Sure you're not coming along?" said the Doc, with a sidelong glance.

"Sure," said Seth.

"I think I shall, after all," said Burp, hurriedly, "if you don't mind."

"Sure, come along," said the Doc, and Seth saw a look of triumph flick over Arthur's face as the three of them went out.

"Well, what do you know, Ted?" Seth said. "Never thought I'd live to see the day that Arthur came in here."

"You can never tell about people," said Ted, sententiously.

"Arthur isn't people. The Martian's right—he's just a calculating machine. But I wish I knew what he's calculating at this moment."

Seth cut half of the *Popular Astronomy,* gave the late Mr. Wells back his property, and reworded the Burp section to give a much more sympathetic picture of him and his statements and behavior. It might have been because of the whiskey's mellowing effect. It might have been because Seth regarded Burp more warmly now he had shared a friendly drink with him—which one could never do with Arthur. It made Burp appear much the more human of the two.

Or perhaps it was because he felt a little afraid for Burp. To one ignorant of Arthur's nature, the war paint was invisible, no smoke signals stained the sky, and the drums were silent. But Seth knew that Arthur was on the war-path, and his goal was Burp's scalp. And if he had to use double negative feedback to reach that goal, he would. Seth wished now that he had been quick enough to have warned Burp.

He spent a long time over the story, and when he went around to the lounge Arthur and his intended victim had returned and were at it again.

Burp was saying loudly: "The work of Watson and Rayner and Lecky has shown that nothing else so far observed will produce the fear response in early infancy but a loud sound or a sudden loss of support. They are the fundamental unconditioned stimuli calling out a fear reaction. Every baby, except one, of a batch of a thousand examined by them was found to catch its breath or cry when a loud sound was made behind its head or when the blanket was jerked away from under it."

"I *was* that thousandth baby," said Arthur, grimly. "I'm the exception which proves the rule."

There was a loud bang on the door-knocker, and Arthur jumped a foot.

Seth laughed. "I'll go." No one heard him. The argument gathered fury, became a storm. They were both shouting at once, now—it was like a mildly dramatic moment in an Orson Welles film.

The caller was a pretty young nurse from the Peterville Hospital. She pushed a large buff envelope into Seth's hand and said: "For Arthur, with Doc Benson's compliments. I believe Arthur is waiting for it."

"Thanks, Hilda. Why not come on in?"

"No, thanks. It sounds too noisy in there. I prefer peace and quiet."

"So do I," said Seth. "What about tomorrow evening, around six, back of the swimming pool? That's a quiet spot."

"Okay," said Hilda. "Bring a friend—but not Arthur this time. I want to keep my friends."

Seth grinned and saw her off. Then he examined what was in the envelope and stopped grinning. When he was able to, he started thinking. Then he parked the envelope just outside the door of the lounge and once again braved the field of battle.

"You only get the backwash of it in back areas like Mars," Arthur was stating, not so very far from the top of his voice. "I'm in the forefront of scientific research here, and I'm telling you that the latest work had shown that fear and rage can be evoked in totally *new* situations, in which learning by conditioning has not been involved."

"Is this one of them?" asked Seth, but he might as well have been in the wilderness.

Arthur went braying on: "Hebb has demonstrated *spontaneous* fear in chimpanzees by suddenly showing them mutilated and dismembered bodies and other such unusual stimuli. The point is, being laboratory bred chimpanzees, they had had no previous experience of that sort. It's quite obvious that merely a shock to one's sense of fitness of things—"

"All this is a shock to *my* sense of fitness of things!" bawled Seth. "I'm fed up on all this brawling. This happens to be *my* home too. Shut up, both of you, and let me say something, will you?"

They both stopped and looked at him.

"Now with this guy, Barnard, here, I can prove my point," said Burp suddenly, before Seth could open his mouth again. "In your case, your mind being slightly more complex, prediction is difficult, I admit. But Barnard is so simpleminded that in relation to him prediction is as easy as foretelling that a train will reach a depot which is on the lines ahead of it. For instance—"

He grabbed a pencil and a pad from the bureau, scribbled rapidly, and passed the pad to Arthur.

Seth watched him irately, then turned abruptly toward the door.

"Where are you going, Seth?" said Arthur.

"To the composing room. I'll say what I have to say in print."

Arthur read out from the pad: "As you read this, Barnard will be on his way to the composing room to insert some unflattering remarks about me in his article, because that will be his response to my (a) frustrating his desire to speak (b) describing him as simple-minded in the extreme."

Seth glowered, and sat down on the nearest chair and folded his arms.

"You're wrong, you see. I'm not going."

"Read on," said Burp.

Arthur read: "When you've read the first sentence of this to him, his response will be not to budge after all, to show that he is not a robot but has an independent will."

"Now I *am* going," said Seth, grimly, and went.

When he returned after about an hour's work, the storm had abated. All was quiet in the lounge. Burp was sitting in an armchair reading a book at a great pace—turning a page every four or five seconds—and Arthur was standing moodily looking out of the window, drumming with his fingers on the ledge.

"What's the matter, Arthur—expecting someone?" said Seth.

"I was," grunted Arthur.

"Perhaps now you'll allow me to say my little piece," said Seth. "I should like—"

"Hah!" shouted Burp, suddenly sitting bolt upright and slamming the book down. "Revolts! Utterly *revolts!*" he yelled, with his eyes popping out of his primrose face. *"Revolts!"* he screamed, and burst into wild, hysterical sobs, clutching his head.

"What the—" said Arthur.

"He seems to have struck a stimulus," said Seth. "I'd better get him another sort of stimulant."

He popped across the street to Ted's Bar, and returned with a bottle of Scotch. Burp was huddled in the armchair crying quietly to himself.

Arthur was examining a page of the open book. "I don't get it," he said, looking at the title on the spine, and returning to study the page. *"The Murder of Edgar Allen Poe* by J.A.T. Lloyd. Page two-hundred-and-ten . . . Ah, this is it."

Seth set a full tumbler on the arm of the chair beside Burp, and went over to see what Arthur meant. Arthur pointed to the passage where Poe exclaimed, with a look of "scornful pride": "My whole nature utterly *revolts* at the idea that there is any Being in the Universe superior to *myself!"*

"That's funny, Arthur," said Seth. "That's what you're always saying."

"Rubbish!" said Arthur. "Why, I shouldn't even consider such a crazy idea for a moment, let alone allow myself to be revolted by it. I just *know* there isn't—"

"I must say that Earth produces remarkably fine alcohol," said the calm, appreciative voice of Burp. He was sitting up, sipping, and looking as if he were enjoying life.

"Well, well," said Seth. "And I must say that you produce some remarkably quick change, Burp,"

"I expect the workings of a free mind *must* seem remarkable to robots with fixed chains of ideas," said Burp, complacently. "You see, *you* can't select *your* ideas: they're all bound to one another by chains of association. You can't think of a hamburger, for example, without also thinking of a perspiring canine, which in turn is associated with a cold cat, and so on. You cannot separate and isolate your ideas, because your minds produce chains of ideas as a sausage-machine produces chains of sausages, linked together. In fact, a sausage-machine is a very good analogy of your type of brain, because it *is* only a machine. Whereas mine is not, and can deal with thoughts totally distinct from, and unconnected with, one another. Thus, I can change my moods at will, unlike you, who are slaves to—"

"I can't stand any more of it!" Seth shrieked suddenly, marched to the door, and returned bearing the big buff envelope.

He gave the envelope to Arthur. "I deliver him into your hands, Arthur. Don't spare him."

Arthur peeped inside the envelope.

Burp watched him curiously. "What's all this?"

Arthur said: "Burp, why didn't you eat those steaks at lunch today?"

"I wasn't hungry."

"You never are," said Arthur. "And you never will be, with an inside like this."

And he whipped out the big X-ray negative from the envelope and held it up. It showed an intricate mesh of cog-wheels, coils, containers, springs, pipes, and apparatus for which there was no name.

Burp's lower lip drooped. He looked like a baby from under which Messrs. Watson, Lecky and Company had whipped the blanket.

"Oh! You know!" he wailed, thinly and petulantly. He collapsed back in his chair, sniffing miserably.

"I was suspicious from the first," said Arthur. "When my compass needle started playing tricks, and I noticed it was being affected by your movements. It was trying to follow you. Not merely because of the mass of steel in you, but also because of the amount of electricity being generated in you. You're fuelled by alcohol, aren't you—hence the continual injections of whiskey. How is the energy extracted from the alcohol and transformed into electrical energy?"

"Only a human could be so indelicate at a time like this," moaned Burp.

"It doesn't matter. I'll probably work it out from this— diagram. It's strange, Burp, that you're a mechanical man and yet not a bit mechanical-minded. You're full of theoretical knowledge, but practically you know nothing. That was quite an inspiration of mine when I saw the Doc going to the Bar, and caught him, and told him about you, and conspired with him to inveigle you to the Hospital."

"Only a human could be so treacherous," sniffed Burp.

Arthur went on: "It was quite plain when we were showing you the clinical apparatus that you couldn't tell one thing from another. You didn't even know that when you were standing between the two screens, and we were kidding you that it was a thing for sunray treatment, that we were actually taking an X-ray photograph of you."

"Even on Mars there is no one quite so low and deceitful as you," mumbled Burp.

"Oh, you wonderful Martians, who know everything! You're all just robots, aren't you?"

Burp was silent.

"Aren't you?" Arthur's voice was like a whip-crack. He was playing attorney for the prosecution, and enjoying every second of it.

"Yes," blurted Burp.

"That's a lie," said Arthur, quietly, toying with his victim. "You're a robot, certainly, but you're not a Martian. You're merely a mechanical servant of the real Martians."

Burp seemed to wither and shrink even more, and Seth began to feel sorry for him.

"Model Mark B.VII" Burp muttered, despairingly.

"And," continued Arthur, "you've developed a mechanical fault, causing instability—'hunting,' as you like to call it—which has produced an effect akin to paranoia. If you were human, we'd call you a cyclo-thyme, too."

"Hey, how do you know all this?" asked Seth.

"Inference," said Arthur, shortly. "The way he kept desperately trying to prove that we were only machines, while he was something superior. There was something obviously pathological in his over anxiety to make that point. The way he went off the handle each time I spoke to him in a way that reminded him of a Martian addressing him—"

"I hate them! I hate them!" cried Burp. "They would never treat me as if I were a man too. I am! I am! I have feelings, too. I have ideas of my own—grand ideas! They would never let me try to explain them. They always said: 'I know just what you're going to say, so keep quiet, keep your place. You're only a machine. We know all your ideas, because we put them into you. You don't have to bore us with all that old stuff.' And they would point their robot-control tubes at me and make me dumb."

Seth was going to say " 'Dumb's' the word," but the words stuck in his throat, and instead he said: "Leave him alone, Arthur, he's had a pretty raw deal."

"And he's got a pretty raw inferiority complex from it, for which he over-compensates to the point of mania. Did you notice how it got touched off when he stumbled on that sentence of Poe's? Poe, of course, was another—"

"All right, Arthur, let up," said Seth. "He's had enough."

"I want only one more admission from him, and that I'm determined to have," said Arthur grimly. "Burp, that story you told about our being robots left here on Earth by the Martians a million years ago was another load of hooey, wasn't it?"

"Yes," whispered Burp. "I made it up. I . . . ran away from Mars to find someplace where *I* could be the boss and give the orders. I thought, in a small hick-town like this, there wouldn't be any opposition."

Arthur gave a bark of triumphant, Mephistophelian laughter, and said: "You picked the wrong place. No one tells me what to do."

"It's strange," Seth mused, "but the victim of a bully always seems to get a yen to act just like the bully."

"Not strange at all," said Arthur. "Just the normal psychological reaction."

Burp got up slowly, picking up the bottle of Scotch by its neck, and went toward the door. He looked like a bent, old man.

"Where are you going?" asked Seth.

Burp paused. He said, in a defeated tone: "I'm going to look for some other place to live. Somewhere where perhaps there are nice people who will treat me with respect. I couldn't stay in Peterville—after all this."

He slouched out. Through the window, they watched him take the dusty road heading out of the town. Impulsively, Seth opened the window and shouted after him: "Want a lift?"

Burp turned, shaking his head. "No. I don't want to see either of you again . . . Goodbye. Thanks for the Scotch."

He turned again and plodded on, presently becoming a small speck in the distance.

But Burp must have got a lift somewhere on the road, for it was only an hour later when there was a distant roar and they rushed to the window to see the tiny splinter which was the rocket mounting the sky on a pillar of white gas. It went up and up, leaving only a twisted, darkening trail.

"Bon voyage!" said Seth. "As he said he only uses the rocket to travel distances of more than a million miles, I guess he won't be looking for any more suckers on this planet. Arthur, you shouldn't have frightened him off. We might have learned something of scientific value from him."

Arthur snorted. "Not him! I always knew exactly what he was going to say . . . H'm. I see he's left his little gadget behind."

He picked up the robot-control tube, which had fallen down behind the bureau, and began fiddling with it.

"Oh, well, that's something to remember him by," said Seth. "I suppose it's no use my waiting any longer for you to start tidying up all this assorted literature you and he have decorated the room with?"

Arthur didn't answer, and with a sigh, Seth went around picking up and piling the books. As he picked up Norbert Wiener's *Cybernetics,* he heard *click-click* and then he had a queer impulse to place the volume on his head and mince around the room like a pupil practicing deportment. He obeyed the impulse.

"Hah!" said Arthur. "Then it *does* work."

He was pointing the tube at Seth.

Seth wanted to yell "switch it off!" but his jaws seemed to be held in an unseen vise. He continued, against his will, to parade up and down absurdly, balancing the book on his crown. Then *click-click* sounded again, and he was released.

"Very interesting," said Arthur, dodging as *Cybernetics* flew past his ear. He waited patiently until Seth had exhausted his breath, his rage, and his Army vocabulary. "A wire had come off a terminal, that was all. Nothing to it. Yet that robot fiddled with it for hours and couldn't see it. Can you imagine such a hopelessly unpractical creature?"

"My imagination's working on other things right now," said Seth, breathlessly. "If you ever do that again—!"

Then something occurred to him. "Holy Pete, do you realize what it means? I'm a robot!"

"I've always thought so," said Arthur.

"And you are, too."

"Nonsense!" said Arthur, loudly. "I've disproved all that."

"Just think of the power this gives us! We could run Peterville completely. I could make Judge Aldley eat out of my hand—literally. Why, we could run the world!"

"Exactly," said Arthur. "But this thing wants one more slight adjustment first."

He picked up a lead paperweight from the bureau and hit the robot-control a smashing blow with it. The tube had been made of something as brittle as plastic and far more friable. It fell into small, powdery pieces.

"Oh," said Seth, shocked. "What did you do that for?"

"We've had enough paranoia around here for one day. I like Peterville as it is. I won't have it turned into a marionette town. I like people to act the way they want to, even if I agree with none of them. If everybody agrees with me, and does exactly what I tell them to, who am I going to fight with? Do you want to make this *really* a dead town?"

"Sorry, Arthur," said Seth. "And thank you."

Arthur said: "That's all right. I'm like that. The dopes who live here don't think I care about them or anyone else but myself. That's all right. They're entitled to think, even though they're wrong."

"And all the time, underneath, you have a heart of gold."

"I don't boast about it," said Arthur.

"Of course not . . . By the way, supposing someone else had got hold of that thing and used it on *you?*"

"It wouldn't have worked," said Arthur. "No one can tell *me* what to do."

"You didn't smash it to keep anyone from trying?" asked Seth, innocently.

"Don't be a complete idiot, man!" said Arthur, very loudly indeed. "Don't talk such utter nonsense."

"Sorry," said Seth, gently. "I can't help myself. I'm only a robot."

TESTIMONY

MY FIRST WEEK IN HOSPITAL—and the nights seemed endless.

Maybe that was because then I was still acting as though life itself were endless. The doctors were vague in their manner to me. Hopefully, I assumed they *were* vague and unsure about their diagnosis. But they didn't seem at all worried.

Why should I worry if they didn't?

Few of us are realists. Take a hard look at the world around us—all of it that you can see. Keep looking. Before long, if you're at least halfway human, you'll have to look away. The sheer amount of visible pain and unhappiness becomes more than you can bear to watch. So we kid ourselves and allow ourselves to be kidded.

Then one day it hits you right between your averted eyes.

As it did me in my second week in hospital.

The doubtful science of economics is shot through with fantasy. Yet underlying the gaseous theory is bedrock fact. Juggle with the figures all you like but in the end you can't buck them. Figures determine your life—and can terminate it.

Seven thousand is a nice round sum, a multiple of a lucky number. It's not so luck for you, though, if it refers to pounds sterling when all you have in your bank account is a small fraction of that.

At that time £7,000 was the price of a haemodialysis unit, more loosely called a kidney machine. That nailed it as the price of life for people like me. Correction: plus running costs of around £1,000 per annum.

Thirty-five is also a multiple of lucky seven. Applied to years it may not seem so lucky to a left-on-the-shelf spinster. Hope must be running a bit low by then. It should be better for a man. Halfway through his three-score-and-ten, he should be on the point of emerging from self-centred and therefore unhappy adolescence, which runs later than you think. Some of the spontaneity of youth still remains, his prime lies ahead, his best is yet to be.

Unless he were me.

Thirty-five years are just a few too many. Age bars you from a free gift of one of those rare and precious kidney machines. Unless, maybe, you had a family to support. I hadn't. I'd left it too late.

Still, there are always tougher cases than one's own. I shouldn't grumble, although, being me, I did.

I had lost a kidney early in life but its mate had taken on double duty and stood the strain well through decades. This year, though, it seemed to be getting tired. I'd been sent to hospital, I thought, so that it could have some kind of special rest treatment. It would recover. It was when they started probing my financial status instead of my body that the truth hit me.

My kidney was packing up altogether and me with it. My nights and days were numbered and the total wouldn't reach three figures.

As I say, I shouldn't grumble. I could have been 14 years old, like the lad two beds from me. Only twice seven years looked like being the total of Bob's lifespan. He shared my troubles— medically, financially, and numerically. Age barred him too. He wasn't old enough to be a useful citizen or the head of a family. Nor was he rich. So, like myself, he wasn't quite important enough to save.

The difference between us was that I had had a run for my money, what money there had been. I had seen flying fishes play in the blue southern oceans, sunset reddening the Valley of Kings, Everest from Darjeeling, the towers of Manhattan, the misty glories of the Western Isles . . .

And, ironically, Naples.

Young Bob had never been further from London than Bognor Regis.

I had had more women that I had fingers and toes. I'd kept the fingers and toes but none of the women, which was just as well, as it had turned out now. Bob was not precocious. I doubted that he'd had even as much as a kiss and a cuddle from anyone but his mother.

I had learned to treasure Shakespeare. Bob hadn't overcome the schoolboy's inoculation against him. Great music had sustained my soul. Bob hadn't progressed beyond tribal chants and the rattle of sticks and drums.

He didn't know what he was losing. Maybe he never would have gone on to discover much of it, anyway. But I knew what I was saying goodbye to. You don't appreciate the full value of things until you start losing them—and the future is sans eyes, sans ears, sans teeth, sans every damn thing.

I tried to look my last on all things lovely every hour. Not too easy in this particular ward which, I had come to realize, was the last caravanserai for incurables. All the same, there were some lovely characters there, especially among the nurses. It seemed wrong that they should be spending their working lives on the banks of the Styx. Yet I never heard them complain. They buttressed one's belief in human beings, as their inadequate wages soured one's belief in social justice.

For the rest of us except the devout, the crazy, and the past caring. Death cast his shadow over all things. Colours look pretty dim in shadow.

Everybody brought us flowers to cheer us up. To a healthy eye, which could well see Sloane Square again, the ward sometimes looked like a marquee at the Chelsea Flower Show. My unhealthy eye saw them as floral tributes come before their time—or saw beyond them to the crematoria from which some of them may have come *after* their time.

I preferred to regard the bowl of bananas on my bedside cabinet. The associations seemed warmer. They were a cheerful yellow bespeckled with black sin—bent, assymetrical, shaped by the haphazard pressures of their own bunch. You could hardly imagine them growing in God's perfect garden.

Not that I had anything against heaven. I liked what I could see of it from my bed. The windows were tall and the slices of sky therefore generous.

I saw more of the night sky than of the day. My day was a series of increasingly frequent dozes beginning to merge on the way to a diabetic coma. In the waking intervals I watched the clouds on the sky-blue ocean slowly changing their coast-lines: all those bays and capes and river deltas in a state of continuous recreation. But I saw them more often illumined from behind by the moon.

Some nights the sky was cloudless and moonless. Then, and only then, came occasionally the feeling that possibly life was more than a pointless happening. Lying there staring at the circling planets and the so-called fixed constellations, the prodigious gem-scatter of the Milky Way and the tiny, hazy glows of galaxies mind-shaking distances away, I lost all sense of self and with it my damning self-pity. I was an integral part of all that and inseparable from it. I wasn't destined to be cut off in my prime. I wasn't going to be cut off at all.

Queens have died young and fair but the tragedy was illusory. Millions of young soldiers died in the war that has always been going on somewhere, but their souls went marching on—in another form, on another level, somewhere in this space-time continuum.

Disillusionment, if that's what it was, would come with the dawn, though. Against a nearing clatter of breakfast crockery, real and hard, the dream-dozes would enshroud me again. Everything was dream-stuff, anyway, though there were too many nightmares for comfort, and total oblivion might be preferable to the bumpy wheel of life. There was no strain in oblivion.

There were no stars and no ethereality the night the Healer came. The clouds weren't making any fanciful maps. Indeed, there was only one cloud: an amorphous mass had fallen from that heaven, sagging over the roof of this old hospital and weeping its remorse straight on to the slate tiles. It, anyway, was changing its form and level, and the gutters overflowed trying to cope with it.

The windows were no more than streaming black oblongs. No view, no promise.

I felt definitely out of tune with the Infinite.

But the Infinite came in out of that wet darkness, into this dim-lit place where all the lights were dying, to us, to me.

Past the night-nurse, writing in her window-walled cubicle by the door. To pause for a moment beside the first bed, in the far corner from me, and touch the sleeping occupant. I never knew the name of the occupant nor what he suffered from apart from senile decay. To me he was just the Old Man Who Fell Out of Bed. He fell out at least once a night, never seemed to hurt himself, and was always apologetic to the nurse who helped him back.

The Infinite, just a shadow in the shadows at that distance, passed to the next bed.

I raised myself on to one elbow, trying to make out what was going on. The other insomniac in this ward, Peters, had made it that bit more difficult. Night illumination here was supplied by low-wattage lamps under frosted glass panels in the floor, so that no light shone directly into our eyes. But Peters complained that it kept him awake. He covered the panels with single sheets of newspaper, further diffusing the glow. The matron asked if anyone objected. No one thought it worth making an issue about. So Peters was tolerated. It was a tolerantly run hospital and they were particularly tolerant to us in this ward. They didn't plague us with fussy rules, they recognized our humanity, maybe the more so because it was ebbing.

The Infinite, moving quickly but quietly from bed to bed, was halfway down the ward before I could discern that it was in the shape of a hatless man in a dripping raincoat which was rain-darkened from grey nearly to black.

Clearly an intruder, not a doctor.

I called out: "Who's that? What are you doing there?"

The Infinite replied in a low but angry voice: "Shut up and mind your own bloody business."

And moved on to the next bed.

He hadn't awakened anyone he'd touched, so far as I could see. But then, he might have cut their throats, so little could I see.

His anger sparked mine. I felt more anger than fear, and it was directed more at the staff than at him. Their tolerance had become slackness and let a lunatic loose among us.

I opened my mouth to call the night nurse, then shut it. She had heard my challenge to the lunatic and was on her way with trained briskness. Nurse Doyle, a petite *colleen bawn.*

The stranger was at Dave Young's bed, opposite mine, when she caught up with him, so I heard her whisper quite clearly.

"Don't disturb the patients, please, sir. Come along to my office and tell me what 'tis you're wanting."

The stranger answered, also in a whisper but a fierce one.

"Leave me alone. I know what I'm doing."

"And what, pray, are you doing?"

"Snatching their unbelieving and therefore damned souls from hellfire, in your particular view, no doubt." More than sarcasm, it was nearer to hatred. "Go back and finish your love letter to Paddy, my girl, if you want to help your patients. I'm not harming them. I'm healing them."

"What? Now that will be quite enough of that, who ever you are. If you don't leave at once, I'll fetch the doctor on duty. And the porters."

"Oh, go to hell, woman."

He pushed her aside impatiently and bent over Dave, who had been awakened by these exchanges and was just raising his head.

The stranger put the heel of his palm against Dave's forehead and, not ungently, pressed him back on to the pillow.

Dave lay very still. Still as death? His heart was in a condition where almost any kind of shock could stop it.

Nurse Doyle seized the stranger's arm and tried to pull him away. Deliberately, sadistically, he bent her fingers back until I heard the joints crack. Her slight, small body went taut with agony but she made no sound.

That was when I, weak as I was, forced myself out of bed.

The stranger released her fingers. She turned to escape. I had never seen a nurse run but I expected to do so now. I was wrong. She saw me, hesitated, than came across to me unsteadily. Her feet scuffed the paper away from a floor light and suddenly her pretty face was lit from below. I caught the fear in her eyes. I had the measure of Nurse Doyle and knew it wasn't fear for herself but for her charges.

Disciplined habits resumed control. She became impersonal again.

"Back into bed, Mr. Hall, please. You're not to get up yet."

The professional white-lie code: make them think there's always hope, that one day they'll be up and around again. Meanwhile, rest and be a patient patient.

"But—"

"No buts." She helped me back, tucked me in, trying not to hurry. But her wrenched fingers were shaking. Then she went off up the ward, still trying not to hurry. But the click-click-click of her heels on the parquet floor was faster than brisk.

The stranger stared after her. Suddenly I was afraid he might follow and attack her. To pull his attention away, I said loudly: "Can you really heal people?"

He looked my way, silently. Then all at once he came striding across. The upflung light momentarily revealed the face of a devil. I was reminded of a performance of *Faust* in which Mephistopheles was lit only by a low-level spotlight, a theatrical trick which makes even unexceptional faces appear sinister.

And this was no ordinary face. The devil in it was no mere surface illusion of light and shade.

He stood over me, tall, gaunt, majestic in his strange wrath. His hair was black, sleek, wet as that of a drowned man. His frown was beaded with rain-water. His chin jutted, square and sharp as a chisel's edge. His nose was high-bridged, almost a beak. Disappointment lines ran from it to the corners of his mouth, which was contemptuous, snarling. Yet it was a sensitive, full-lipped mouth.

He had been around for quite a while but I couldn't be sure of guessing his age within a decade.

He stared at the number above my bed. Then he regarded me with, I thought, increased fury.

"What are you doing in *that* bed?"

"Dying—that's if you have no objection."

"None at all. Get on with it," he snapped. He turned as if to go, then abruptly wheeled back. "You're privileged, my friend—do you know that? You die in a hallowed place."

"Well . . . that's nice to know."

"My son died in that bed. He was only a boy."

"Oh. I'm sorry."

"How could you be sorry?" he challenged. "You didn't know him."

"I'm sorry, anyway. Just as I'm sorry for Bob there. That boy . . . two beds along. He's only fourteen and he's dying too."

The stranger looked sharply across at the small still shape under the bedclothes.

"I couldn't save my son. Why should I save that boy? He's nothing to me, any more than you are."

Suddenly I was weary of his unprovoked aggressiveness. What a way to squander energy—that precious life-energy! I was truly sorry about the loss of his son, but—

"What the hell's eating you?" I asked, irritably. "What's your grudge against people?"

"Simply that they exist, damn them, they exist. Do you want to go on existing?"

"Yes—but hardly like this."

"I can change that. I can make you as hale a man as ever you were."

"I doubt it."

"Doubt won't save you. I condemn you to life." He bent towards me, extending a hand. His face, at close quarters, quite awed me. I seemed to look beyond his eyes into a riven soul. There was despair behind the hate, agony behind the contempt. His psyche was blasted by an emotional storm fierce enough to drive him out of his mind.

I could feel the electrical disturbance, the stress and distress, affecting my own mind.

Emotion at such extreme pitch can break through to some other plane where the body's laws—and, indeed, some natural laws—are irrelevant. The berserk warrior feels no wounds. The martyr glories in the fire. The visionary sees God in His firmament. The prophet pierces the veil hiding the future. The medium demonstrates psycho-kinesis. And the spiritual healer performs miracles.

I knew with sudden certainty that the force possessing this man could heal me.

I knocked his arm aside. "Not me. The boy. Go to the boy."

My mind was whirling in confusion but I held on to that thought.

The stranger glowered at me.

"Who the devil do you think you are—Sir Philip Sidney? His need is greater than thine and all that balls?"

"Go to Bob," I said, faintly.

"Damn you for a fool. You and that silly little nurse. Your sort defeat your own ends. You drain the spirit from me . . . It's going. Here, before it's too late."

He clapped his hand to my forehead. Sudden intense heat and blinding light. It was like having an exploding atom bomb all to myself. Maybe a man struck by lightning experiences much the same.

After that—nothing. No light, no sound, no stranger, no hospital, no Rodney Hall.

But they all—except the stranger—returned, as the sunlight returned, in the morning. All clear and sharp, unclouded by poisonous waste residues in my brain and bloodstream.

It was as though I had been born again.

Dave Young, complying with hospital regulations, had included a bathrobe among the necessities he brought with him. But it was never a true necessity. His valvular condition was too serious for him to be allowed to set a foot out of bed.

It was a new bathrobe, a shining light blue. He was wearing it now, for the first time. His eyes shone as brightly as it did. He was on the visitor's chair at my bedside watching my face eagerly.

I focused on him.

"Rod, wake up, blast you," he said. "You *would* be almost the last, wouldn't you? How are you feeling? You look fine."

I sat up without the usual struggle to do so. I felt energetic, enterprising, and hungry. Lord, that forgotten feeling: a'raring to go!

"I feel fine. I feel bloody wonderful. What's happened? And you, Dave—they've let you get up? What goes on?

The ward was alive and buzzing. Excited people were moving around or standing in small groups, talking, talking. It was like a cocktail party except that tea was the only drink going; and that, despite their excitement, most of the people were keeping their voices down. They couldn't believe their own luck. They felt almost guilty about it. For many of the mortally sick were still with us, their unhappiness accentuated by the realization that they were the unchosen, the still doomed.

Dave said: "It's unbelievable, Rod. Some of us have been cured overnight. Restored—completely restored, I mean. A miracle's happened here, man, a bloody miracle."

Then I remembered.

"Someone came in the night," Dave went on. "Nobody knows who he was. He slipped past the reception office without being seen. But Nurse Doyle saw him. She spoke to him. So did you, she says."

"Yes, that's right. My God, it's true: he *was* a healer."

"Who was he? Did he say?"

"No, Dave, he didn't. I've never seen his face before but I'll never forget it."

Some of the others noticed that I was awake now. They came crowding round my bed, watching, waiting for me to speak again. Among them was the Old Man Who Fell Out of Bed. He still looked old but nothing like so decrepit. He was erect, his eyes were alert, his body had lost its tremors. He must have suffered something worse than just senility, else he would have been in the geriatric ward. But now, clearly, nothing ailed him.

He addressed me in the calm, round-vowelled accents of Eton and Cambridge. "In whatever guise He appeared, He was our Lord, I'm sure of that. I envy you, sir. You were privileged to witness the Second Coming."

I said, wryly: "I'm sorry but I can't really credit that. He wasn't remotely like the Christ of the Testaments—apart from one thing: he was a man who had suffered a great deal. But not meekly and patiently, as the Lord did. He was far from gentle and his language was far from mild. I don't think he loved anyone, let alone everyone."

"That may well have been your personal impression of him," said the Old Man. "Perhaps mine, too, had I encountered him. But don't forget that you—and I—were ill then, and confused. Sick-

ness does so cloud the mind. Speaking for myself, at least, I've
had some difficulty of late communicating with my fellow men
with any clarity. I just couldn't make out what they were saying.
But the Lord has restored me. I am whole again. Blessed be the
name of the Lord."

"Amen," said Peters. His voice was quiet and sincere, lacking
its usual querulous note. He was relaxed and at peace. I realized
that the cross-grainedness had been a symptom of his illness.

"How about Bob?" I asked suddenly. "Did he do anything for
young Bob?"

"We're not sure yet," said Dave. "The pair of you just went on
sleeping. Bob's still asleep. Nurse Doyle's with him."

I swung my legs out of bed and dug in my locker for my
dressing gown. It was crumpled under books and papers, sugarless
chocolate and other accumulated litter. I had had shrinking hopes
of ever wearing it again.

The others began to drift to Bob's bed. I joined them. Bob lay
on his back, eyes closed, arms resting on the counterpane. He was
so still that I feared he was in a coma. Nurse Doyle was taking his
pulse, eyes on her wristwatch. Dr. Payne stood at the other side of
the bed, watching. He was trying to maintain his persona of a
completely inscrutable man but the bafflement showed through.

"Still normal," said Nurse Doyle. "And strong."

Dr. Payne nodded curtly, as though this were exactly what he
had expected to hear.

I saw Bob's eyelashes move. There was a touch of colour in
his cheeks which I had never seen there before. I knew then that it
was going to be all right. The healer's hand had not lost its power
before it reached him.

Bob opened his eyes.

To me it was like the sudden swinging open of great gates
which we had seen shutting in our faces. It was a renewal of the
broken promise of life. I was overcome. There was a strange aural
delusion of heralding trumpets and men's deep, rich voices singing
a psalm of thanksgiving.

I wanted to speak to Bob. I wanted to ask Nurse Doyle what
had become of the healer. I could say nothing at all. I turned away
as the weak and embarrassing tears came.

After that, the inquisitive, matter-of-fact people: the newspaper
reporters and the TV interviewers. Then the check-ups, the X-ray

sessions, the visits by leading specialists. And then, at last, release into the living world beyond the hospital walls.

The Miracle of Ramsden Hospital is remembered particularly because it was the first of its kind. Also because of the mystery surrounding the Healer (the capital was bestowed by the popular press) in those early days. He had vanished back into that midnight rainstorm as anonymously as he had emerged from it.

By the time Nurse Doyle had located a porter and returned with him, the Healer had gone. She hadn't been absent all that long: they had missed him only narrowly. She wondered why they hadn't encountered him leaving through those long corridors. She seemed half inclined to believe that he had dematerialized, like a spirit. On the other hand, she jibbed at accepting the existence of a spirit so disrespectful to her Church. The Healer, from that aspect, was altogether too earthy.

Like all the others, she asked me for my impression of him.

I said: "Well, what struck me most was his obvious unhappiness. He seemed divided against himself: in the throes of some wild mental or spiritual conflict. I'd say he was on the verge of a complete nervous breakdown. He was consumed by hatred and resentment. Something must have hurt him really badly. And yet, despite that, he did what he did. He helped, he cured—as far as he was able to. Something possessed him—I don't understand what."

"Oh, dear, what a pity," she said. "That poor man was in need of treatment himself. Oh, it's a shame, it is, that I tried to have him thrown out. I didn't realize what he was doing. If only I hadn't interfered. 'Tis possible the other poor souls in the ward might have been healed too. It was God's work I tried to stop."

"You can't blame yourself for that, Nurse. It was the way he went about it. He behaved so strangely that I thought he was crazy, too—and in a sense he was, of course."

"I wonder if they'll ever trace him."

"Small chance if last night was just an isolated incident. They've so little to go on. No one but you and I, Nurse, properly saw him. But if he goes on behaving like that, he's bound to be caught in the end. In a way, I hope he will be discovered. I'd like a chance to see him again and thank him for saving my life."

But I never did see the Healer again—not in the flesh, that is. So I've chosen to express my thanks in writing, in this form. I'm only one of so many, of course, who have similar cause to thank him. Only those who have actually entered the Valley of the Shadow of Death, all hope gone, can know what it means to feel a rescuing hand pluck them back into the sunlight. I've tried to convey something of what it was like for me, though my inadequate talent fails to bridge the gap between experience and description. But at least I've made this effort.

Many have blessed the Healer. Some have hated him. Some have vilified him cynically. Some have even called him a fake, which, in the face of the indisputable evidence labels them as fools.

Some feared him superstitiously, believing he was in league with the Devil. In one sense, they weren't so far wrong.

My own belief is that the Healer, like the rest of us, was neither wholly good nor wholly bad, not superhuman but all too human. His only significant failing was his inability to accept that. He set his standards impossibly high, for himself and for all of us. Thus he created his own agony.

But let it be remembered that through his suffering the pain of multitudes was eased. And somewhere deep in that distorted nature he must have felt that this was a good thing.

For I hold and testify that basically he was a man of good will. Had there been more of that breed in this power-greedy world, especially on the influential levels where they are particularly scarce, he would never have been driven into his lonely personal hell.

And I should not have lived to write this.

Forget Him Not—
The Best of William F. Temple

Unless you're of that sort who picks up a new book and immediately reads the afterword or story notes first, you've just had the pleasure of reading through a truly remarkable collection, one that has been some ten years or more in the making. That a retrospective volume (or volumes) comprising the best short fiction of William F. Temple hasn't already appeared is somewhat of a puzzle. Whereas I didn't have the pleasure of knowing the man as Mike did, everything I've seen or heard indicates that not only was Bill Temple a hell of a writer, but also a hell of a nice guy who remained very accessible to his readers throughout his life, and his writing maintained a high level of quality from the very beginning. In short, except for having committed the literary sin of never authoring the Big Novel, (although the omni-presence in various forms of *Four-sided Triangle* ought to count for *something*) he would seem to fit the mold of being exactly the type of author who is recognized by the mainstream publishers with a door-stop volume containing his best work. Sadly, such a volume never came about.

Mike Ashley and Bill had discussed such a project, and while it didn't materialize, Mike had a file full of stories close at hand when I mentioned that I'd like to do a "best of" collection for the (at the time) newly revived Darkside Press (2001). I was delighted to discover that not only had this project been discussed, but that Bill's daughter and her husband were long-time fans and very much in favor of the idea. Agreements were made, Mike presented me with an excellent collection (a little longer than what we usually did, but with William F. Temple, I was okay with going over budget just a bit.)

This wasn't going to be just another Darkside Press book, this was an *event*! Putting my marketing hat on, I began to think of some additional ways to ensure that the book would have the sort of impact in the marketplace that would be commensurate with the collection's importance . . . Perhaps a guest introduction from Bill

Temple's former roommate and fellow writer, Sir Arthur C. Clarke?

A crazy idea on my part? No, as it turned out, the friendship of Sir Arthur and Bill and his family had continued over the years and Bill's daughter was pretty confident that Sir Arthur would contribute some sort of remembrance, even if just a page or so. For that matter, he might even be wiling to sign a few copies of the book for our life-time subscribers. It looked like everything was in the stars for *A Niche in Time* to be one of our most noteworthy releases . . .

Then things began to happen . . . Bad things . . . First, Sir Arthur passed away, then my job disappeared, and then the real cataclysm hit, my wife and long time heart and soul of Midnight House and Darkside Press was stabbed in an attempted mugging and spent over a month in the hospital, a stay that completely wiped us out financially. Then just as she was recovering I went down with emphysema and we were forced to leave the Pacific Northwest for the high desert of New Mexico where I can breathe (more or less). Midnight House/Darkside Press managed to put out one more book and then went on hiatus . . . It's been a few years, and we're slowly climbing back out of the hole. My new imprint under the Ramble House umbrella has been a success . . . In the last two years we've released over twenty books under the Dancing Tuatara Press label focusing on the horror genre. The success has been such that it seemed reasonable to expand and go back to my first love, the science fiction and fantasy of an earlier generation.

We launched the series with a collection by master pulpster Malcolm Jameson and followed up with selections by Richard Wilson, Evelyn E. Smith, and Robert F. Young. It seemed that reviving the William F. Temple project would be a natural.

Fortunately, all parties were still up for the idea, but this isn't quite the book that Mike intended it to be. For one, we did have to trim out several very fine stories due to the restrictions imposed by financial realties. We decided that at the very least, two volumes would be required. I foolishly began thinking of them as "Mike's selections" and "John's selections" until I saw Mike's proposed contents . . . There was a very heavy overlap and if there had been no restrictions due to length, it's likely that all the stories on both lists would have made it in as neither of us found anything to object to on the other's list. However, a 600-page book wasn't going to happen, so we're left with two collections of similar size. Three stories from Mike's initial selections have been moved to *Magic Ingredient,* our May release, which will include all of my favorites that weren't already picked for this volume.

All told, the reader is definitely the winner as two good-size books allows us to use more stories than one big book. However, as I'm looking over the contents of this volume and *Magic Ingredient* and peeking at my Temple bibliography (with scores of notes written all over it), it seems that two volumes aren't going to quite get the job done. . . I don't suppose that there are any objections to a *third* collection coming out next year or the year after?

Cheers,

John Pelan
Midnight House
Gallup, NM

Coming in January 2012 — *The Two Suns of Mercali*
by Evelyn E. Smith, #5 in John Pelan's
Classics of Science Fiction & Fantasy

RAMBLE HOUSE's

HARRY STEPHEN KEELER WEBWORK MYSTERIES

(RH) indicates the title is available ONLY in the RAMBLE HOUSE edition

The Ace of Spades Murder
The Affair of the Bottled Deuce (RH)
The Amazing Web
The Barking Clock
Behind That Mask
The Book with the Orange Leaves
The Bottle with the Green Wax Seal
The Box from Japan
The Case of the Canny Killer
The Case of the Crazy Corpse (RH)
The Case of the Flying Hands (RH)
The Case of the Ivory Arrow
The Case of the Jeweled Ragpicker
The Case of the Lavender Gripsack
The Case of the Mysterious Moll
The Case of the 16 Beans
The Case of the Transparent Nude (RH)
The Case of the Transposed Legs
The Case of the Two-Headed Idiot (RH)
The Case of the Two Strange Ladies
The Circus Stealers (RH)
Cleopatra's Tears
A Copy of Beowulf (RH)
The Crimson Cube (RH)
The Face of the Man From Saturn
Find the Clock
The Five Silver Buddhas
The 4th King
The Gallows Waits, My Lord! (RH)
The Green Jade Hand
Finger! Finger!
Hangman's Nights (RH)
I, Chameleon (RH)
I Killed Lincoln at 10:13! (RH)
The Iron Ring
The Man Who Changed His Skin (RH)
The Man with the Crimson Box
The Man with the Magic Eardrums
The Man with the Wooden Spectacles
The Marceau Case
The Matilda Hunter Murder
The Monocled Monster

The Murder of London Lew
The Murdered Mathematician
The Mysterious Card (RH)
The Mysterious Ivory Ball of Wong Shing Li (RH)
The Mystery of the Fiddling Cracksman
The Peacock Fan
The Photo of Lady X (RH)
The Portrait of Jirjohn Cobb
Report on Vanessa Hewstone (RH)
Riddle of the Travelling Skull
Riddle of the Wooden Parrakeet (RH)
The Scarlet Mummy (RH)
The Search for X-Y-Z
The Sharkskin Book
Sing Sing Nights
The Six From Nowhere (RH)
The Skull of the Waltzing Clown
The Spectacles of Mr. Cagliostro
Stand By—London Calling!
The Steeltown Strangler
The Stolen Gravestone (RH)
Strange Journey (RH)
The Strange Will
The Straw Hat Murders (RH)
The Street of 1000 Eyes (RH)
Thieves' Nights
Three Novellos (RH)
The Tiger Snake
The Trap (RH)
Vagabond Nights (Defrauded Yeggman)
Vagabond Nights 2 (10 Hours)
The Vanishing Gold Truck
The Voice of the Seven Sparrows
The Washington Square Enigma
When Thief Meets Thief
The White Circle (RH)
The Wonderful Scheme of Mr. Christopher Thorne
X. Jones—of Scotland Yard
Y. Cheung, Business Detective

Keeler-Related Works

A To Izzard: A Harry Stephen Keeler Companion by Fender Tucker — Articles and stories about Harry, by Harry, and in his style. Included is a compleat bibliography.

Wild About Harry: Reviews of Keeler Novels — Edited by Richard Polt & Fender Tucker — 22 reviews of works by Harry Stephen Keeler from *Keeler News*. A perfect introduction to the author.

The Keeler Keyhole Collection: Annotated newsletter rants from Harry Stephen Keeler, edited by Francis M. Nevins. Over 400 pages of incredibly personal Keeleriana.

Fakealoo — Pastiches of the style of Harry Stephen Keeler by selected demented members of the HSK Society. Updated every year with the new winner.

Strands of the Web: Short Stories of Harry Stephen Keeler — 29 stories, just about all that Keeler wrote, are edited and introduced by Fred Cleaver.

RAMBLE HOUSE's LOON SANCTUARY

52 Pickup — Two thrillers from 1952 by Aylwin Lee Martin: *The Crimson Frame* and *Fear Comes Calling*

A Clear Path to Cross — Sharon Knowles short mystery stories by Ed Lynskey.

A Jimmy Starr Omnibus — Three 40s novels by Jimmy Starr.

A Roland Daniel Double: The Signal and The Return of Wu Fang — Classic thrillers from the 30s.

A Shot Rang Out — Three decades of reviews and articles by today's Anthony Boucher, Jon Breen. An essential book for any mystery lover's library.

A Smell of Smoke — A 1951 English countryside thriller by Miles Burton.

A Snark Selection — Lewis Carroll's *The Hunting of the Snark* with two Snarkian chapters by Harry Stephen Keeler — Illustrated by Gavin L. O'Keefe.

A Young Man's Heart — A forgotten early classic by Cornell Woolrich.

Alexander Laing Novels — *The Motives of Nicholas Holtz* and *Dr. Scarlett*, stories of medical mayhem and intrigue from the 30s.

An Angel in the Street — Modern hardboiled noir by Peter Genovese.

Automaton — Brilliant treatise on robotics: 1928-style! By H. Stafford Hatfield.

Away from the Here and Now — A collection of SF short stories by Clare Winger Harris.

Beast or Man? — A 1930 novel of racism and horror by Sean M'Guire. Introduced by John Pelan.

Black Hogan Strikes Again — Australia's Peter Renwick pens a tale of the 30s outback.

Black River Falls — Suspense from the master, Ed Gorman.

Blondy's Boy Friend — A snappy 1930 story by Philip Wylie, writing as Leatrice Homesley.

Blood in a Snap — The *Finnegan's Wake* of the 21st century, by Jim Weiler.

Blood Moon — The first of the Robert Payne series by Ed Gorman.

Calling Lou Largo — Two hardboiled classics from William Ard: *All Can Get* (1959) and *Like Ice She Was* (1960)

Chariots of San Fernando and Other Stories — Malcolm Jameson's SF from the pulps are featured in the first book of the John Pelan SF series.

Chelsea Quinn Yarbro Novels featuring Charlie Moon — *Ogilvie, Tallant and Moon, Music When the Sweet Voice Dies, Poisonous Fruit* and *Dead Mice*. An Ojibwa detective in SF.

Cornucopia of Crime — Francis M. Nevins assembled this huge collection of his writings about crime literature and the people who write it. Essential for any serious mystery library.

Crimson Clown Novels — By Johnston McCulley, author of the Zorro novels, *The Crimson Clown* and *The Crimson Clown Again.*

Dago Red — 22 tales of dark suspense by Bill Pronzini.

David Hume Novels — *Corpses Never Argue, Cemetery First Stop, Make Way for the Mourners, Eternity Here I Come.* 1930s British hardboiled fiction with an attitude.

Dead Man Talks Too Much — Hollywood boozer by Weed Dickenson.

Death Leaves No Card — One of the most unusual murdered-in-the-tub mysteries you'll ever read. By Miles Burton.

Death March of the Dancing Dolls and Other Stories — Volume Three in the Day Keene in the Detective Pulps series. Introduced by Bill Crider.

Deep Space and other Stories — A collection of SF gems by Richard A. Lupoff.

Detective Duff Unravels It — Episodic mysteries by Harvey O'Higgins.

Dime Novels: Ramble House's 10-Cent Books — *Knife in the Dark* by Robert Leslie Bellem, *Hot Lead* and *Song of Death* by Ed Earl Repp, *A Hashish House in New York* by H.H. Kane, and five more.

Don Diablo: Book of a Lost Film — Two-volume treatment of a western by Paul Landres, with diagrams. Intro by Francis M. Nevins.

Dope and Swastikas — Two strange novels from 1922 by Edmund Snell

Dope Tales #1 — Two dope-riddled classics; *Dope Runners* by Gerald Grantham and *Death Takes the Joystick* by Phillip Condé.

Dope Tales #2 — Two more narco-classics; *The Invisible Hand* by Rex Dark and *The Smokers of Hashish* by Norman Berrow.

Dope Tales #3 — Two enchanting novels of opium by the master, Sax Rohmer. *Dope* and *The Yellow Claw.*

Double Hot — Two 60s softcore sex novels by Morris Hershman.

Dr. Odin — Douglas Newton's 1933 racial potboiler comes back to life.

Evangelical Cockroach — Subversive fare from Jack Woodford

Evidence in Blue — 1938 mystery by E. Charles Vivian.

Fatal Accident — Murder by automobile, a 1936 mystery by Cecil M. Wills.

Ferris Wheel Hussy — Two from Aylwin Lee Martin: *Death on a Ferris Wheel* (1951) and *Death for a Hussy* (1952)

Finger-prints Never Lie — A 1939 classic detective novel by John G. Brandon.

Freaks and Fantasies — Eerie tales by Tod Robbins, collaborator of Tod Browning on the film FREAKS.

Gadsby — A lipogram (a novel without the letter E). Ernest Vincent Wright's last work, published in 1939 right before his death.

Gelett Burgess Novels — *The Master of Mysteries, The White Cat, Two O'Clock Courage, Ladies in Boxes, Find the Woman, The Heart Line, The Picaroons* and *Lady Mechante*. All are introduced by Richard A. Lupoff who is singlehandedly bringing Burgess back to life.

Geronimo — S. M. Barrett's 1905 autobiography of a noble American.

Hake Talbot Novels — *Rim of the Pit, The Hangman's Handyman.* Classic locked room mysteries, with mapback covers by Gavin O'Keefe.

Hollywood Dreams — A novel of Tinsel Town and the Depression by Richard O'Brien.

Hostesses in Hell and Other Stories — Russell Gray's violent tales from the pulps. #16 in the Dancing Tuatara Press horror series.

I Stole $16,000,000 — A true story by cracksman Herbert E. Wilson.

Inclination to Murder — 1966 thriller by New Zealand's Harriet Hunter.

Invaders from the Dark — Classic werewolf tale from Greye La Spina.

J. Poindexter, Colored — Classic satirical black novel by Irvin S. Cobb.

Jack Mann Novels — Strange murder in the English countryside. *Gees' First Case, Nightmare Farm, Grey Shapes, The Ninth Life, The Glass Too Many, The Kleinert Case* and *Maker of Shadows.*

Jake Hardy — A lusty western tale from Wesley Tallant.

Jim Harmon Double Novels — *Vixen Hollow/Celluloid Scandal, The Man Who Made Maniacs/Silent Siren, Ape Rape/Wanton Witch, Sex Burns Like Fire/Twist Session, Sudden Lust/Passion Strip, Sin Unlimited/Harlot Master, Twilight Girls/Sex Institution.* Written in the early 60s and never reprinted until now.

Joel Townsley Rogers Novels and Short Stories — By the author of *The Red Right Hand: Once In a Red Moon, Lady With the Dice, The Stopped Clock, Never Leave My Bed.* Also two short story collections: *Night of Horror* and *Killing Time.*

Joseph Shallit Novels — *The Case of the Billion Dollar Body, Lady Don't Die on My Doorstep, Kiss the Killer, Yell Bloody Murder, Take Your Last Look.* One of America's best 50's authors and a favorite of author Bill Pronzini.

Keller Memento — 45 short stories of the amazing and weird by Dr. David Keller.

Killer's Caress — Cary Moran's 1936 hardboiled thriller.

Lady of the Yellow Death and Other Stories — Tales from the pulps by Wyatt Blassingame. #14 in the Dancing Tuatara Press series.

League of the Grateful Dead and Other Stories — Volume One in the Day Keene in the Detective Pulps series. In the introduction John Pelan outlines his plans for re-publishing all of Day Keene's short stories from the pulps.

Man Out of Hell and Other Stories — Volume II of the John H. Knox pulps collection.

Marblehead: A Novel of H.P. Lovecraft — A long-lost masterpiece from Richard A. Lupoff. The "director's cut", the long version that has never been published before.

Master of Souls — Mark Hansom's 1937 shocker, introduced by weirdologist John Pelan.

Max Afford Novels — *Owl of Darkness, Death's Mannikins, Blood on His Hands, The Dead Are Blind, The Sheep and the Wolves, Sinners in Paradise* and *Two Locked Room Mysteries and a Ripping Yarn* by one of Australia's finest mystery novelists.

More Secret Adventures of Sherlock Holmes — Gary Lovisi's second collection of tales about the unknown sides of the great detective.

Muddled Mind: Complete Works of Ed Wood, Jr. — David Hayes and Hayden Davis deconstruct the life and works of the mad, but canny, genius.

Murder among the Nudists — A mystery from 1934 by Peter Hunt, featuring a naked Detective-Inspector going undercover in a nudist colony.

Murder in Black and White — 1931 classic tennis whodunit by Evelyn Elder.

Murder in Shawnee — Two novels of the Alleghenies by John Douglas: *Shawnee Alley Fire* and *Haunts.*

Murder in Silk — A 1937 Yellow Peril novel of the silk trade by Ralph Trevor.

My Deadly Angel — 1955 Cold War drama by John Chelton.

My First Time: The One Experience You Never Forget — Michael Birchwood — 64 true first-person narratives of how they lost it.

Mysterious Martin, the Master of Murder — Two versions of a strange 1912 novel by Tod Robbins about a man who writes books that can kill.

Norman Berrow Novels — *The Bishop's Sword, Ghost House, Don't Go Out After Dark, Claws of the Cougar, The Smokers of Hashish, The Secret Dancer, Don't Jump Mr. Boland!, The Footprints of Satan, Fingers for Ransom, The Three Tiers of Fantasy, The Spaniard's Thumb, The Eleventh Plague, Words Have Wings, One Thrilling Night, The Lady's in Danger, It Howls at Night, The Terror in the Fog, Oil Under the Window, Murder in the Melody, The Singing Room.* The complete Norman Berrow library of classic locked-room mysteries, several of which are masterpieces.

Old Times' Sake — Short stories by James Reasoner from Mike Shayne Magazine.

One Dreadful Night — 1940s suspense and terror from Ronald S. L. Harding

Pair o' Jacks — Two works by Jack Woodford: *Find the Motive* and *The Loud Literary Lamas of New York.*

Perfect .38 — Two early Timothy Dane novels by William Ard. More to come.

Prose Bowl — Futuristic satire of a world where hack writing has replaced football as our national obsession, by Bill Pronzini and Barry N. Malzberg.

Red Light — The history of legal prostitution in Shreveport Louisiana by Eric Brock. Includes wonderful photos of the houses and the ladies.

Researching American-Made Toy Soldiers — A 276-page collection of a lifetime of articles by toy soldier expert Richard O'Brien.

Reunion in Hell — Volume One of the John H. Knox series of weird stories from the pulps. Introduced by horror expert John Pelan.

Ripped from the Headlines! — The Jack the Ripper story as told in the newspaper articles in the *New York* and *London Times.*

Robert Randisi Novels — *No Exit to Brooklyn* and *The Dead of Brooklyn.* The first two Nick Delvecchio novels.

Rough Cut & New, Improved Murder — Ed Gorman's first two novels.

Ruled By Radio — 1925 futuristic novel by Robert L. Hadfield & Frank E. Farncombe.

Rupert Penny Novels — *Policeman's Holiday, Policeman's Evidence, Lucky Policeman, Policeman in Armour, Sealed Room Murder, Sweet Poison, The Talkative Policeman, She had to Have Gas* and *Cut and Run* (by Martin Tanner.) Rupert Penny is the pseudonym of Australian Charles Thornett, a master of the locked room, impossible crime plot.

Sand's Game — Spectacular hard-boiled noir from Ennis Willie, edited by Lynn Myers and Stephen Mertz, with contributions from Max Allan Collins, Bill Crider, Wayne Dundee, Bill Pronzini, Gary Lovisi and James Reasoner.

Sand's War — The second Ennis Willie collection

Satan's Den Exposed — True crime in Truth or Consequences New Mexico — Award-winning journalism by the *Desert Journal.*

Satan's Sin House and Other Stories — Dancing Tuatara Press #15 by Wayne Rogers – Gore and mayhem from the shudder pulps.

Gelett Burgess Novels — *The Master of Mysteries, The White Cat, Two O'Clock Courage, Ladies in Boxes, Find the Woman, The Heart Line, The Picaroons* and *Lady Mechante.* All are edited and introduced by Richard A. Lupoff.

Sam McCain Novels — Ed Gorman's terrific series includes *The Day the Music Died, Wake Up Little Susie* and *Will You Still Love Me Tomorrow?*

Sex Slave — Potboiler of lust in the days of Cleopatra by Dion Leclerq, 1966.

Shadows' Edge — Two early novels by Wade Wright: *Shadows Don't Bleed* and *The Sharp Edge.*

Sideslip — 1968 SF masterpiece by Ted White and Dave Van Arnam.

Slammer Days — Two full-length prison memoirs: *Men into Beasts* (1952) by George Sylvester Viereck and *Home Away From Home* (1962) by Jack Woodford.

Sorcerer's Chessmen — John Pelan introduces this 1939 classic by Mark Hansom.

Star Griffin — Michael Kurland's 1987 masterpiece of SF drollery is back.

Stakeout on Millennium Drive — Award-winning Indianapolis Noir by Ian Woollen.

Star Griffin — 1987 SF classic from Michael Kurland gets the Ramble House treatment.

Strands of the Web: Short Stories of Harry Stephen Keeler — Edited and Introduced by Fred Cleaver.

Suzy — A collection of comic strips by Richard O'Brien and Bob Vojtko from 1970.

Tales of the Macabre and Ordinary — Modern twisted horror by Chris Mikul, author of the *Bizarrism* series.

Tenebrae — Ernest G. Henham's 1898 horror tale brought back.

The Amorous Intrigues & Adventures of Aaron Burr — by Anonymous. Hot historical action about the man who almost became Emperor of Mexico.

The Anthony Boucher Chronicles — edited by Francis M. Nevins. Book reviews by Anthony Boucher written for the *San Francisco Chronicle,* 1942 – 1947. Essential and fascinating reading by the best book reviewer there ever was.

The Best of 10-Story Book — edited by Chris Mikul, over 35 stories from the literary magazine Harry Stephen Keeler edited.

The Black Dark Murders — Vintage 50s college murder yarn by Milt Ozaki, writing as Robert O. Saber.

The Book of Time — Classic novel by H.G. Wells is joined by sequels by Wells himself and three timely stories by Richard Lupoff. Lavishly illustrated by Gavin L. O'Keefe.

The Case of the Little Green Men — Mack Reynolds wrote this love song to sci-fi fans back in 1951 and it's now back in print.

The Case of the Withered Hand — 1936 potboiler by John G. Brandon.

The Charlie Chaplin Murder Mystery — A 2004 tribute by scholar, Wes D. Gehring.

The Chinese Jar Mystery — Murder in the manor by John Stephen Strange, 1934.

The Compleat Calhoon — All of Fender Tucker's works: Includes *Totah Six-Pack, Weed, Women and Song* and *Tales from the Tower,* plus a CD of all of his songs.

The Compleat Ova Hamlet — Parodies of SF authors by Richard A. Lupoff. This is a brand new edition with more stories and more illustrations by Trina Robbins.

The Contested Earth and Other SF Stories — A never-before published space opera and seven short stories by Jim Harmon.

The Crimson Query — A 1929 thriller from Arlton Eadie. Perfect way to get introduced.

The Curse of Cantire — Classic 1939 novel of a family curse by Walter S. Masterman.

The Devil Drives — Odd prison and lost treasure novel from 1932 by Virgil Markham.

The Devil's Mistress — A 1915 Scottish gothic tale by J. W. Brodie-Innes, a member of Aleister Crowley's Golden Dawn.

The Dumpling — Political murder from 1907 by Coulson Kernahan.

The End of It All and Other Stories — Ed Gorman selected his favorite short stories for this huge collection.

The Fangs of Suet Pudding — A 1944 novel of the German invasion by Adams Farr

The Ghost of Gaston Revere — From 1935, a novel of life and beyond by Mark Hansom, introduced by John Pelan.

The Gold Star Line — Seaboard adventure from L.T. Reade and Robert Eustace.

The Golden Dagger — 1951 Scotland Yard yarn by E. R. Punshon.

The Hairbreadth Escapes of Major Mendax — Francis Blake Crofton's 1889 boys' book.

The House of the Vampire — 1907 poetic thriller by George S. Viereck.

The Incredible Adventures of Rowland Hern — Intriguing 1928 impossible crimes by Nicholas Olde.

The Julius Caesar Murder Case — A classic 1935 re-telling of the assassination by Wallace Irwin that's much more fun than the Shakespeare version.

The Koky Comics — A collection of all of the 1978-1981 Sunday and daily comic strips by Richard O'Brien and Mort Gerberg, in two volumes.

The Lady of the Terraces — 1925 missing race adventure by E. Charles Vivian.

The Library of Death — By Ronald S. L. Harding, Dancing Tuatara Press #20.

The Lord of Terror — 1925 mystery with master-criminal, Fantômas.

The N. R. De Mexico Novels — Robert Bragg, the real N.R. de Mexico, presents *Marijuana Girl, Madman on a Drum, Private Chauffeur* in one volume.

The Night Remembers — A 1991 Jack Walsh mystery from Ed Gorman.

The One After Snelling — Kickass modern noir from Richard O'Brien.

The Organ Reader — A huge compilation of just about everything published in the 1971-1972 radical bay-area newspaper, *THE ORGAN*. A coffee table book that points out the shallowness of the coffee table mindset.

The Poker Club — Three in one! Ed Gorman's ground-breaking novel, the short story it was based upon, and the screenplay of the film made from it.

The Private Journal & Diary of John H. Surratt — The memoirs of the man who conspired to assassinate President Lincoln.

The Secret Adventures of Sherlock Holmes — Three Sherlockian pastiches by the Brooklyn author/publisher, Gary Lovisi.

The Shadow on the House — Mark Hansom's 1934 masterpiece of horror is introduced by John Pelan.

The Sign of the Scorpion — A 1935 Edmund Snell tale of oriental evil.

The Singular Problem of the Stygian House-Boat — Two classic tales by John Kendrick Bangs about the denizens of Hades.

The Smiling Corpse — Philip Wylie and Bernard Bergman's odd 1935 novel.

The Stench of Death: An Odoriferous Omnibus by Jack Moskovitz — Two complete novels and two novellas from 60's sleaze author, Jack Moskovitz.

The Story Writer and Other Stories — Richard Wilson, #2 in John Pelan's SF series

The Technique of the Mystery Story — Carolyn Wells' 1913 book on mystery writing.

The Time Armada — Fox B. Holden's 1953 SF gem.

The Tongueless Horror and Other Stories — Volume One of the series of short stories from the weird pulps by Wyatt Blassingame.

The Tracer of Lost Persons — From 1906, an episodic novel that became a hit radio series in the 30s. Introduced by Richard A. Lupoff.

The Trail of the Cloven Hoof — Diabolical horror from 1935 by Arlton Eadie. Introduced by John Pelan.

The Triune Man — Mindscrambling science fiction from Richard A. Lupoff.

The Universal Holmes — Richard A. Lupoff's 2007 collection of five Holmesian pastiches and a recipe for giant rat stew.

The Werewolf vs the Vampire Woman — Hard to believe ultraviolence by either Arthur M. Scarm or Arthur M. Scram.

The Whistling Ancestors — A 1936 classic of weirdness by Richard E. Goddard and introduced by John Pelan.

The White Peril in the Far East — Sidney Lewis Gulick's 1905 indictment of the West and assurance that Japan would never attack the U.S.

The Wizard of Berner's Abbey — A 1935 horror gem written by Mark Hansom and introduced by John Pelan.

Two Kinds of Bad — Two 50s novels from William Ard: *As Bad As I Am* and *When She Was Bad*, featuring Danny Fontaine

Wade Wright Novels — *Echo of Fear, Death At Nostalgia Street, It Leads to Murder* and *Shadows' Edge*, a double book with *Shadows Don't Bleed* and *The Sharp Edge*.

Welsh Rarebit Tales — Charming stories from 1902 by Harle Oren Cummins

Through the Looking Glass — Lewis Carroll wrote it; Gavin L. O'Keefe illustrated it.

Time Line — Ramble House artist Gavin O'Keefe selects his most evocative art inspired by the twisted literature he reads and designs.

Tiresias — Psychotic modern horror novel by Jonathan M. Sweet.

Totah Six-Pack — Fender Tucker's six tales about Farmington NM in one sleek volume.

Trail of the Spirit Warrior — Roger Haley's historical saga of life in the Indian Territories.

Ultra-Boiled — 23 gut-wrenching tales by our Man in Brooklyn, Gary Lovisi.

Up Front From Behind — A 2011 satire of Wall Street by James B. Kobak.

Victims & Villains — Intriguing Sherlockiana from Derham Groves.

Walter S. Masterman Novels — *The Green Toad, The Flying Beast, The Yellow Mistletoe, The Wrong Verdict, The Perjured Alibi, The Border Line* and *The Curse of Cantire*. Masterman wrote horror and mystery, some introduced by John Pelan.

We Are the Dead and Other Stories — Volume Two in the Day Keene in the Detective Pulps series, introduced by Ed Gorman. When done, there may be as many as 11 in the series.

West Texas War and Other Western Stories — by Gary Lovisi.

Whip Dodge: Man Hunter — Wesley Tallant's saga of a bounty hunter of the old West.

You'll Die Laughing — Bruce Elliott's 1945 novel of murder at a practical joker's English countryside manor.

RAMBLE HOUSE

Fender Tucker, Prop.   Gavin L. O'Keefe, Graphics
www.ramblehouse.com   fender@ramblehouse.com
228-826-1783   10329 Sheephead Drive, Vancleave MS 39565

Lightning Source UK Ltd.
Milton Keynes UK
UKOW042354140313

207650UK00002B/28/P

Questions

Each spread covers the key objectives for each area of the curriculum. There is a clear explanation of the topic. The questions are designed to encourage your child to investigate the topic outlined on the page. The activities provide an opportunity for your child to consolidate their learning in a fun way.

Parent's Guides

The Parent's guide offers further explanations of the key objectives and the vocabulary introduced, as well as advice on how to help your child to approach these tasks.

Head Teacher's Award

On each spread you will notice the Head Teacher's Award symbol. This award has been designed to provide motivation and acknowledge success. Your child will need your help to establish whether or not they have sucessfully answered the question, which will help you to gauge their level of understanding and how you might be able to support their learning in the future.

Practice Papers

When your child has confidently covered the revision section at the beginning of this book, there is a series of practice reading tests for them to work through that are similar to those that they will face in the real test. More details on these can be found on pages 38 and 39.

What You Can Do to Help

It is important that your child does not feel pressurised by these activities, as they are designed to be interesting, fun and enjoyable. Remember, this is not new learning, but a series of activities that consolidate established learning. You can support your child by giving plenty of support and encouragement when working on the questions and activities.

Motivate your child to succeed. Reward your child for every Head Teacher's Award they get – discuss this with your child to agree a suitable reward.

Keep the tests in perspective. Remember that SATs are as much a test of the school's success as of your child's ability, so do not cause your child anxiety by over-stressing the importance of the exams. Nor are SATs an end in themselves: they are part of a whole process designed to ensure that your child has a solid foundation for later learning and success.

Phonics

A B C D E F G H I J K L M N O P Q R S T U V W X Y Z

All the words below are phonically regular**. This means that you can sound out every letter and there are no tricks in the word.**

jam   nuts   tins

cup   pan   rug

sink   bin   steps

In these words the second letter or vowel does not make its sound, but its letter name instead, for example in plane **the a makes a long sound or** aay**. This is because the e on the end has changed the vowel sound from** short **to long. This is known as a** split digraph **or** magic e**.**

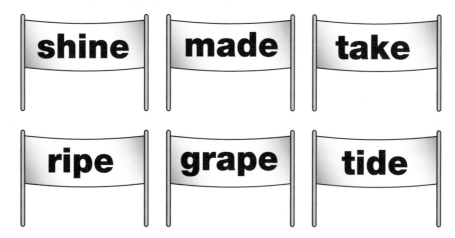

shine   made   take

ripe   grape   tide

Questions

1. Do you know all the sounds that the letters of the alphabet make?
2. Can you say their names as well as their sounds?
3. Can you sound out all the letters in the phonically regular words in the pictures?

Activity

Read all the split digraph words and then try to find more in books, comics and magazines. You could make a list to record all your finds.

6

Vowel Phonemes

oo	good	look	took	book	rook	hook
ar	jar	cart	part	smart	apart	start
oy	boy	joy	toy	coyote	royal	annoy
ow	cow	brown	crown	town	down	how
air	chair	pair	fair	repair	stairs	hair
or	short	sport	sort	thorn	morning	born
er	her	were	supper	under	jumper	thunder
ear	fear	hear	dear	spear	tear	earring
ea	bread	head	dead	tread	thread	spread

The groups of coloured letters above are known as vowel phonemes. Sometimes the phonemes can make more than one sound, for example, oo can make a short sound as in good. In good it sounds almost like a u sound. It can also make a longer sound as in moon. In moon it sounds a bit like a cow mooing!

Question
Can you read all the words with the vowel phonemes making the correct sound?

Activity
Choose one of the vowel phonemes and add more words to the ones that are already there. Some are easier than others, so choose carefully.

Parent's Guide
Phonics play a very important role in reading and spelling. Your child should be able to say all the letter sounds and names before they go on to learning about vowel phonemes. Understanding about split digraphs helps with spelling and you can help by pointing it out and explaining the changes it makes in words when you are reading.

High-frequency Words

These are some of the words you will see most often when you are reading. They are called high-frequency words. Learning to read them on sight will make your reading more fluent.

can	in	ran	two
dad	did	next	be
a	from	not	has
at	is	man	new
yes	jump	us	saw
and	am	help	now
sister	next	bed	too
or	cat	off	as
on	put	but	your
it	get	got	to
mum	him	had	with
big	an	his	do
after	must		out
up	very		that
went	if		she
dog	dig		they

Parent's Guide

The words have been organised so that the regular words (ones that can be phonically sounded out) are in the first three ladders. The irregular words are more difficult and have to be sight learnt.

8

Questions
1. Can you read these words?
2. How long does it take you to read them all?

Activity
Time yourself for two minutes and see how many you can read. Try again and see if you can improve your time.

HEADTEACHER'S AWARD

go	my	can't	little	because
come	see	about	old	seen
you	away	over	some	first
day	play	once	than	down
was	no	then	were	school
look	for	who	by	good
are	he	take	made	been
the	all	way	our	girl
of	said	half	when	back
we	here	one	came	last
this	more	much	don't	your
me	love	so		house
like	many	want		home
going	live	boy		time
one	after			them
their				where

9

Spoken and Written Language

There is a difference between spoken and written language. When recalling events, written language is used, but spoken language can be added if you wish to use the exact words that would be said.

So that the reader knows this, the writing is set out using speech marks and a new line is used each time someone speaks.

NOW READ THIS:

1. The fairy godmother asked Cinderella if she wanted to go to the ball. Cinderella sadly looked down at her old and dirty dress and said that she couldn't go dressed in rags.

2. 'Do you want to go to the ball Cinderella?'
   asked her fairy godmother.
   'I can't go dressed in rags,' said
   Cinderella, looking sadly down
   at the old and dirty dress.

Parent's Guide
Some children have difficulty in moving from spoken language to the written form. It will help your child to make this transition if you encourage them to look carefully at how the spoken word is treated in writing. An awareness of punctuation is crucial to reading with expression.

Questions

1. Which of the two accounts on page 10 uses spoken language?
2. How do you know?
3. Which writing uses only the past tense?

Activity

Read these sentences and see if you can say the words each person or animal is speaking. The first one is done for you.

The wolf asked Red Riding Hood what she had in her basket.

What have you got in your basket?

Red Riding Hood said that it was full of lovely cakes.

The little man told the young girl that she would never guess his name.

Mrs Mouse warned Maxi not to go anywhere near the woods.

Time and Sequential Words

You need to understand that if stories are to make sense, they need to be written in a special order. Using link words such as 'at first', 'next', 'after that', 'in the end', ensures that ideas are linked throughout a story.

READ THIS STORY:

After breakfast, as it was a lovely day, Jim and Alice decided to go swimming.

First they took off their clothes and put them together on the sand with their towels on top. Then they ran into the water and had a lovely time swimming, playing and splashing around.

Later, when they got a bit tired, they decided they would go back to the beach and lie in the sun. Suddenly Jim shouted 'Our clothes are in the water. The tide must have started to come in.'

In the end they managed to get everything together but had to go home in very wet clothes.

Questions
1. Can you say the words that are used to link the sentences?
2. Which words show that the action in the story is just beginning?
3. Which words show that the story is about to finish?

12

Fact or Fiction?

Can you tell the difference between fact and fiction? Fiction books are books where the story has been made up. Factual books, or non-fiction books are books that tell you about something that is true.

TALES OF THE MOUSE

Goldilocks and the Three Mice

THE LONELY BUTTERFLY

Cheeses From Around the World

DOGS!

THE TIGER'S TEETH

Cats – What They Are Really Like?

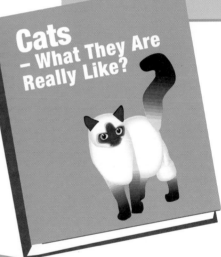

HEADTEACHER'S AWARD

Question

Look at the front covers of some of Major Mortimer Mouse's books.
1. Which of his books do you think are fiction?
2. Which books do you think are factual?

Activity

Look at your own books, or the books in the library. Can you decide which are fiction and which are non-fiction?

A GREAT ADVENTURE

Comparing Books

Sleeping Beauty

Once upon a time there was a beautiful princess. At her christening an evil fairy cast a spell and said that when she was sixteen, she would prick her finger on a spinning wheel and fall asleep for a hundred years. The King and Queen tried to make sure that all of the spinning wheels were destroyed. But, on her sixteenth birthday the Princess met an old woman who had a spinning wheel. The Princess asked if she could have a turn, pricked her finger and fell asleep. Everyone in the whole kingdom fell asleep and a forest grew all around the castle.

One day a woodcutter was riding by. He chopped his way through the forest and found the Princess. He kissed her hand and she woke up. Everyone else woke up too. The Princess and the woodcutter fell in love and got married. Everyone lived happily ever after.

Goldilocks

One day a little girl called Goldilocks was walking through the forest. She saw a little house and decided to go in. On the table she saw three bowls of porridge, one small, one medium and one large. The small bowl of porridge was delicious and she ate it up. Then she saw three chairs, one small, one medium, and one large. Goldilocks broke the small chair when she sat on it. Goldilocks felt tired so she went upstairs and found three beds, one small, one medium, and one large. The small bed was just right for Goldilocks and she lay down and went to sleep.

While she was asleep Baby Bear, Mummy Bear and Daddy Bear came back to their house for their breakfast. They were very cross when they saw that their porridge had been eaten. They were furious when they saw that Baby Bear's chair had been broken. They growled very loudly when they found Goldilocks asleep in Baby Bear's bed. Goldilocks woke up in fright and ran away. Goldilocks will never go into anyone's house on her own again.

Parent's Guide

Your child needs to be able to compare books by different authors that have been written on a similar theme. Encourage your child to think and talk about the different settings and characters in the stories. Help your child to evaluate the books, forming their preferences for certain stories and giving reasons for what they do and do not like.

Little Red Riding Hood

Little Red Riding Hood went to take some flowers to her Grandma who was ill in bed. Her Grandma lived at the other side of the forest. On the way a Wolf saw Little Red Riding Hood and decided to trick her. The Wolf rushed ahead to Grandma's house, shut Grandma in a cupboard and got into bed instead.

When Little Red Riding Hood arrived she thought that Grandma looked different.

'What big eyes you've got,' said Little Red Riding Hood.
'All the better to see you with,' growled the Wolf.
'What big ears you've got,' said Little Red Riding Hood.
'All the better to hear you with,' muttered the Wolf.
'What big teeth you've got,' cried Little Red Riding Hood.
'All the better to eat you with!' roared the Wolf, as he jumped out of bed.

Just at that moment a woodcutter was passing by Grandma's cottage. He heard the Wolf roar and burst into the room. When the Wolf saw the woodcutter's axe he ran out of Grandma's house, deep into the forest. The woodcutter helped Grandma out of the cupboard and made everyone a cup of tea to recover from the shock. Little Red Riding Hood will never walk through the Forest on her own again.

Mouse has started to compare the books:
• **Goldilocks and Little Red Riding Hood are set in a forest from the start of the story. In Sleeping Beauty, a forest grows all around.**
• **The main character is a girl.**
• **There is a woodcutter in Red Riding Hood and Sleeping Beauty.**
• **In Goldilocks and Red Riding Hood the little girl is in the forest on her own.**
• **I like the story of Little Red Riding Hood the best because it is exciting when the woodcutter bursts into the room.**

Question

Read the three stories carefully. Mouse has started to compare the books – he has been thinking about all the things that are similar. Can you think of some ways in which the stories are different?

Activity

Think carefully about the stories, the different characters and the different events. Write a sentence explaining which is your favourite story, and why.

Can you think of two or three of your favourite books that have been written by different people and compare them?

Learning and Categorising Poetry

Mouse has been gathering his favourite poems together. He has started to put his poems into categories. These poems all rhyme and are all about mice!

GINGER CAT

Sandy and whiskered, the ginger cat
Sniffs round the corners for mouse or for rat;
Creeping right under the cupboard he sees
A little mouse having a nibble of cheese.

On velvety paws with hardly a sound
The ginger cat watches, and paddling around
He finds a good hiding-place under a chair
And sits like a statue not moving a hair.

Then baring his claws from their velvety sheath
He pounces, meowing through threatening teeth.
But puss is too late, for sensible mouse
Was eating the cheese at the door of his house.

Mary Dawson

Question
1. Can you see that the rhyming pattern in this poem is different to the first one?

Activity
Learn a poem by heart. Choose a very simple one and see if you can recite it for a parent or friend.

Diagrams are another way of finding out information and learning new facts.

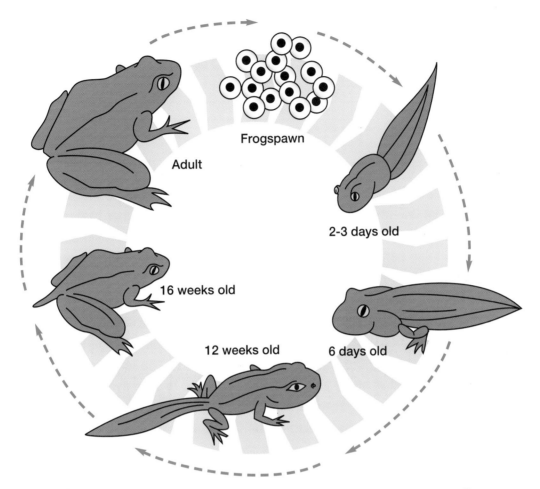

Frogspawn

Adult

2-3 days old

16 weeks old

12 weeks old

6 days old

This diagram is called a cyclical diagram as the whole process can keep being repeated.

HEADTEACHER'S AWARD

Question
Can you 'read' the diagram and explain what is happening at each stage, even though there aren't many words to help you?

Activity
Draw your own chart to show something that you are familiar with or are interested in.

Parent's Guide
Your child needs to be able to decide if a non-fiction text or book is suitable for their purpose. This is an important skill to learn as it saves time when working independently. You can help your child to develop these skills by talking and making decisions together about non-fiction texts.

Introduction to the Practice Papers

The National Tests

The national testing of chidren at the end of Key Stage 1 (Year 2) takes place during May. Many of the children will also do a reading task with the class teacher that can be carried out any time from the beginning of the spring term. In practice, most teachers leave them until nearer the testing period to allow children to make as much progress as possible before being assessed. The reading task is usually an enjoyable one for both teacher and pupils, as considerable time is spent sharing books on an individual basis. The task takes place as part of a normal classroom activity; the child is invited to select a book from several options, a mixture of fiction and non fiction. The books on the list change from year to year, but they will all be of roughly the same standard of difficulty. The teacher will read the beginning of the book and at some point the child is asked to take over and read a passage of about one hundred words. The teacher will then ask questions to determine understanding and response. From this, assessments can be made about which level the child is reading at.

Content of the Test

In May the children go on to take the reading comprehension test as part of the English SAT. In order to ensure that this test is administered fairly, changes to the usual classroom layout may be necessary so that children can work undisturbed, individually and without being allowed to discuss questions or copy answers. This test is in a booklet with numbered spaces. The children read a small amount of text and answer questions relating to it before moving on to the next section. Some questions are multiple choices, where the child has to tick a box, and some require a written sentence. There is no time limit for the test, however it usually takes place on one day, with a break after about thirty minutes. The children will then be given time at the end of the test to check their work. If a child does particularly well in the task and test they are entered for the next level.

If the teacher knows that a child both reads and comprehends at a high level then it is not necessary to carry out the task described. These children will go straight on to take the level 3 reading comprehension test. This is slightly different in format – all the reading is in one booklet and the questions are usually in a separate one. The level of reading is more advanced and some of the questions are more inferred than literal comprehension.

How are the National Tests marked?

At Key Stage 1, the class teacher marks the tests and tasks. The reading task and test results are reported to you as a level with a grade. The expected level for seven-year-olds is level 2. This is broken down into A, B and C. Children achieving 2A are working at the top end of the expected level, 2B in the middle and 2C in the early stages of the level. Some more able children go on to achieve level 3, which is not graded. Less able children are awarded level 1 or a W (working towards level 1). The child's chronological age is not taken into account when awarding levels and it should be remembered that some children are still six when they take the tests.

How Should I Use the Practice Papers?

The reading comprehension practice papers provided are similar to the ones your child will take in the actual test. When your child is working on the comprehension test, you should remember that this should be unaided work and encourage them to have a go at reading any words that they are unsure of. This should be done in a supportive way, perhaps by reminding the child of how well they are doing when working independently. Remember, the idea is to develop confidence and not to cause unnecessary worry. It is recommended that all children attempt the level 2 practice paper to build confidence. If your child struggled with level 2 then do not suggest going on to level 3 as they are not yet ready.

On completion of the practice paper, it would be helpful to mark it together so that you are able to identify any problem areas and work on them. Answers to the practice questions are provided at the back of the book and from the number of marks gained you will have a rough idea of your child's level.

If your child continues to struggle with a subject you should discuss this with their teacher, who may be able to suggest an alternative way of helping your child.

Test 1: Reading and Comprehension 1

Little Mouse's Adventure

Read the story here and then answer the questions about it. There are two practice questions for you to try first.

Practice Questions

One day Little Mouse decided to go for a walk as he was very bored with living in his hole with his brothers and sisters. They were all growing bigger each day and there was no room to play.

A. Why did Little Mouse go for a walk?

....

....

B. Who did Little Mouse live with?
Tick the correct box.

His aunt and uncle ☐

His brothers and sisters ☐

His cousins ☐

His friends ☐

He told his brothers and sisters that he was going to explore the big, wide world.
'Don't go!' they all cried together.

12. Why did Little Mouse stop running?
Tick the correct box.

1 MARK

He was tired ☐

He heard a noise ☐

He couldn't see ☐

He saw a snake ☐

It was as black as night inside the cave. Little Mouse stopped to listen. All was quiet except for a sound like the wind blowing gently in the trees. Slowly he crept forward, putting his paws out in front of him until he felt and smelt hot air blowing towards him. It was a lion!

13. How did Little Mouse creep into the cave?
Tick the correct box.

1 MARK

Slowly ☐

Quietly ☐

Quickly ☐

Noisily ☐

14. How did he know there was another animal in the cave?

1 MARK

....

....

45

'Oh no! I'm in the lion's den,' squeaked Little Mouse to himself.
Just then a great big roaring voice shouted 'Who's there?'
Little Mouse turned and ran as fast as his legs could carry him.

15. What did the lion's voice sound like?

1 MARK

....

16. What did Little Mouse do next?
   Tick the correct box.

1 MARK

He stood still	☐
He cried	☐
He sat down	☐
He ran away	☐

He did not stop. Over the sharp rocks, around the long grass, through the short grass, until he came to his own hole. Little Mouse was too tired to talk and fell straight to sleep. Tomorrow he would tell everyone about his adventure – when he felt braver.

17. Why did Little Mouse go around the long grass?

1 MARK

....

....

18. What did Little Mouse do when he got home? Tick the correct box.

1 MARK

Fell asleep ☐

Ate some food ☐

Told everyone about his adventure ☐

Played with his brothers and sisters ☐

Test 1: Reading and Comprehension 2

Information on Explorers and Survival

Read the story here and then answer the questions about it. There are two practice questions for you to try first.

Practice Questions

This part of the book is about explorers and how to survive in the wild. Here are some dictionary explanations to help you.

Explorers . . . . .people who travel to find new places.
Survive . . . . .to stay alive.
Shelter . . . . .a place to keep you dry, warm and safe.

A   What is this part of the book about? Tick the correct box.

Children and playing

Animals and zoos

Explorers and survival

Writers and books

B.   Why do we need a shelter?

. . . .

. . . .

The Vikings came from the North, to look for new lands, over 1000 years ago. They used long boats, which they rowed, or sailed, across the sea. They came to England and may have even gone to America.

19. Why did the Vikings leave the North?

1 MARK

....

....

20. How did the Vikings cross the sea?
Tick the correct box.

1 MARK

By ship ☐

By long boat ☐

By plane ☐

By train ☐

In 1868 an Englishman called David Livingstone walked all the way across Africa. No one heard from him for three years. He walked through the jungle and found many new places. He discovered a huge waterfall that he named Victoria Falls after the Queen of England.

1 MARK

21. How long was Livingstone in the jungle? Tick the correct box.

Three months ☐

Three years ☐

Three days ☐

Thirty years ☐

1 MARK

22. What was the name of the Queen of England?

....

Today there are very few places in the world left to find. Explorers are now looking into space. In 1969 an American called Neil Armstrong became the first person to walk on the Moon.

23. Where are explorers today looking to find new places?

1 MARK

....

24. Finish this sentence. Tick the correct box.

1 MARK

Neil Armstrong was the first man to walk on...

The Moon ☐

Mars ☐

The Sun ☐

The stars ☐

THIS NEXT PART IS ON HOW TO SURVIVE.

HOW TO KEEP SAFE IN THE DESERT:

Carry plenty of water. You won't live long without it. Do not walk during the day when it is very hot. It gets cold at night, so you will need to have something warm to put on.

25. What do you really need to take with you in the desert. Tick the correct box.

....
1 MARK

Sweets ☐

Apples ☐

Water ☐

Crisps ☐

26. Why do you need something warm at night?

....
1 MARK

....

....

Suddenly, someone was reaching for him. He was carried gently through the garden, past a window and

through a door. He was too weak to struggle. At first he crept to a dark, low place and wouldn't come out.

But sweet, rich smells were drifting towards him. He sniffed the air, remembering. Then slowly, nervously, he moved towards the smells and began to eat.

He had learnt to be brave.

As the warm air slipped back into the days, the cat grew strong and healthy. Sometimes he lay in the garden, lazily watching insects. Sometimes he caught the muddled smells of people and scraps and places with a hundred lights. But he never slunk through the shadows to find them.

He was quiet enough to be petted.

Patient enough to be cuddled.

Brave enough to be stroked.

He had learnt to be loved.

62

Big Cat Facts

CATS AROUND THE WORLD

All cats are mammals and they are native to every part of the world except Antarctica and Australia. Cats are adapted to live in deserts, forests, mountain-sides and grasslands.

TYPES OF CAT

There are 38 kinds of cat. Pet cats are the smallest and the tiger is the biggest cat. Although they vary in size, they all belong to the same family.

HUNTING

Big cats kill other animals for food but are not hunted themselves, except by man. Their bodies are designed to help them hunt. Big cats like to kill their prey quickly before it can fight back. Many cats are nocturnal and hunt at night when it is cooler and they won't be seen.

LIFESTYLE

Big cats stay in their own territory. Most live alone, only coming together when they mate. They live alone because there is not usually enough food in one area for a large group of cats. The exceptions are lions. They live in a group called a pride.

Cat's Bodies

EYES

Cats can see at night just as well as they can in the day. Their eyes are close together at the front of their heads so that they can guess distances well.

EARS

A cat's ears are rounded in shape so that they can pick up sound from many directions. They are set high on a cat's head to give them the best chance of hearing the sounds around them.

NOSE

Cats have a very good sense of smell and can pick up scents in the air. Many big cats use their nose and mouths to 'taste' the air to see if any other animals have passed by.

TONGUE

A cat has a rough tongue that is covered in tiny spikes. These help when the cat washes its fur and when it scrapes meat away from skin.

1 MARK

1. What had kitten learnt to be? (page 56) Tick the correct box.

Kind ☐

Watchful ☐

Helpful ☐

Sleepy ☐

1 MARK

2. What do you think the word 'stray' means? (page 56)

....

....

1 MARK

3. What could kitten smell down the dusty evening streets? (page 57) Tick the correct box.

Dusty, dirty smells ☐

Sweet, rich smells ☐

Exciting, spicy smells ☐

Greasy, hot smells ☐

1 MARK

4. Why did the kitten keep to the shadows? (page 57)

....

....

1 MARK

5. What did the place of rich, sweet smells have a hundred of? (page 58) Tick the correct box.

People ☐

Children ☐

Lights ☐

Tables ☐

1 MARK

6. Why did the rich, sweet smells drive the kitten crazy? (page 58)

....

....

1 MARK

7. What colour were the kitten's eyes? (page 58) Tick the correct box.

Green ☐

Brown ☐

Blue ☐

Black ☐

1 MARK

8. What did the cats do to each other when they were fighting? (page 59)

....

....

1 MARK

9. What tells you that the kitten was frightened? (page 60)
Tick the correct box.

His fur rose and his eyes were wild. ☐

He ran away to find a place to hide. ☐

He went back to sleep. ☐

He ate his breakfast. ☐

1 MARK

10. What made the kitten come out from the dark, low place after he had been rescued? (page 61)

....

....

1 MARK

11. What season do you think it is at the end of the story?

....

1 MARK

12. What was the very last thing that the kitten learnt?
(page 62) Tick the correct box.

To be careful ☐

To be frightened ☐

To be loved ☐

To be quick ☐

These questions are about the **Big Cat Facts** information you have just read. There are two practice questions for you to try first.

Big Cat Facts

Practice Questions

A. **Where are the only places that cats are not native to? Tick the correct box.**

Antarctica and Australia ☐

India and America ☐

Africa and China ☐

Asia and Europe ☐

B. **Name one of the types of places that big cats live.**

....

Information on Explorers and Survival

A. Explorers and survival.

B. Keep us dry/warm/safe.

19. To find new lands/places.

20. By long boat.

21. Three years.

22 Queen Victoria.

23. They are looking in space.

24. The Moon.

25. Water.

26. The desert gets cold.

27. To keep you safe from snake bites (or any answer which identifies protection).

28. To keep you safe.

29. What to take with you.

30. In case you get lost/to show you the way.

31. First-aid kit, torch, map.

Number of marks	0–8	9–18	19–24	25–31
Level	(inclusive) Level 2 not achieved	(inclusive) Level 2C achieved	(inclusive) Level 2B achieved	(inclusive) Level 2A

Answers: Reading and Comprehension (Test 2)

Award one mark for each correct answer.

The Stray Kitten

A. At the edge of a road.

B. Any references to insects or small creatures. Bits of food is also acceptable.

1. Watchful.

2. Any reference to the fact that the kitten does not have anyone looking after him.

3. Sweet, rich smells.

4. Any answer that refers to the dogs, cars, noise.

5. Lights.

6. He was hungry.

7. Green.

8. Any answer that mentions one or more of the words used in the text: they arched, hissed, spat, clawed.

9. His fur rose and his eyes were wild.

10. He was very hungry and could smell the sweet, rich smells again.

11. Late spring, summer.

12. To be loved.

Big Cat Facts

A. Antarctica and Australia.

B. Any one of deserts, forests, mountainsides or grasslands.

13. 38.

14. The tiger is the biggest cat.

15. Any reference to the fact that it is cooler at night or that their prey won't see them.

16. A pride.

17. They are nocturnal. They hunt at night. Their prey comes out at night.

18. They 'taste' the air.

19. To wash itself or to scrape meat away from skin/bones (accept either).

20. It washes itself with its tongue.

21. Any reference to blending into the background of where it lives.

22. They are padded.

23. The cheetah.

24. They are being hunted or poached for their skin or body parts. They are also shot when they go too near to where man is living. Some people hunt them for fun. People make medicines from them. (Reference to any of these).

Number of marks	0–13	14–26
Level	Level 3	Level 3 achieved

Answers: Revision Section Questions

Page 11
1. The second passage.
2. It uses speech marks.
3. The first passage.

Page 12
2. First.
3. In the end.

Page 15
1. Yes.
2. The references to night time, the wind blowing, animal noises etc.
3. When he heard another noise that came from inside his room.
4. His heart beat faster and he spoke in a shaky voice.

Page 20
1. 1902.
2. 100.
3. Mouse Tales.
4. Ninety Nine Ways of Avoiding Cats.

Page 21
1. Tales of the Mouse, A Great Adventure, Goldilocks and the Three Mice, The Lonely Butterfly.

2. Cats – What they are Really Like, Cheeses from Around the World, The Tiger's Teeth, Dogs.

Page 24
3. Examples of pairs of rhyming words would be cat and rat, sees and cheese (the last words in each sentence pair).

Pages 27
1. Examples of rhyming words would be string and sing, caper and paper; the last words in each sentence pair.
2. No.
3. Yes. It makes you want to say the words in the style of the rain it is describing – loudly, etc.

Page 29
They all have question marks at the end.